MARKED TO DIE

A TRIBUTE TO

MARK SAMUELS

EDITED BY

JUSTIN ISIS

Welcome to *Marked to Die: A Tribute to Mark Samuels*. This book consists of a foreword, eighteen (mostly) fictional stories and a coda, all inspired by the life and work of Mark Samuels. At this point there are four options:

A) You're familiar with Mark Samuels and his work and want to get on to the stories without time-wasting introductions. In this case, turn the page and get started.

B) You picked this book up at random and have never heard of Samuels, or have heard of him but don't really know who he is and have never read anything by him. In this case, turn to the "About the Authors" section at the back, where a brief biography is contained. It's probably best to read about the contributors while you're at it, to get a sense of their shared history with him.

C) You're unfamiliar with Samuels but just want to get to the stories anyway. No worries, turn the page.

D) You've already lost interest in the book and are about to close it DON'T FUCKING CLO . . . you closed it, didn't you? Wanker. Have fun with that Julian Barnes book or whatever.

CONTENTS

CONTENTS

The Shadowy Companion

A Foreword by Mark Valentine

We were sitting outside a tavern in Abergavenny, in that lull of the afternoon when the lunchers have all gone and the teatime drinkers are not yet in. We had been to the one bookshop in the town, of course, and had seen the alabaster effigies in the great church, and been shown the town tapestry, occupying all one long wall of the old tithe barn, and proudly and eagerly displayed to any chance visitor who happened to stray inside. Indeed, we half-wondered whether, if we stayed too long, future visitors might see *our* faces stitched into the tableau, mutely imploring.

We had been out, also, to the little museum, through the wrought iron gates and up the gravel drive, and seen there on loan Arthur Machen's tobacco bowl in old worn wood, looking for all the world like one of those holy healing cups or dishes kept in a solemn aumbry in some remote Welsh farmhouse, and shown only to those of 'the line,' or in sore need of its sovereign remedy.

And I looked across at my companion and said to him, for the serpent was in my tongue for a moment:

"As to Machen now. Certainly he had the art of the incantation in him, there's no denying that. But what do you think to the words said of him by a poet once, just in passing, as if he wasn't quite worth more attention than that?"

Here I paused, to remember the scornful phrase as exactly as I could.

"'A smell of stale incense about him', wasn't that it? What is the right response to that? For you must admit it has enough of the truth to smart."

And here the man across the table blinked at me and stubbed out in an ashtray a cigarette of rank fumes, and exhaled a great grey sigh.

"Better stale incense than fresh brimstone," he said. I laughed: but he was looking at me gravely.

"Sometimes, though," he said, "our severest critics get at the essence of us in a way we might not otherwise quite see. 'Stale incense,' he says. I wonder. Machen, you know, had the art of sensing incense where none should be. He tells how the odours of paradise came to him in the high street of Holborn: and the scent of Persian roses was sent to him among the drab backstreets of unknown London. It was as if the rarest perfumes of an extravagant realm beyond ours were sometimes escaping to lure him with these fragrant clues of its real existence. This 'stale incense': surely that is simply the condition of the world we are in, where we see only the faded, lost semblance of the supernal and Real? But if we could once know the true incense, the attar newly risen from the altar. . . ."

"And the 'therefore' of his experiences?" he continued. "Well, Machen's 'very tentative hypothesis' for such curiosities, given in *The London Adventure*, is a model of cautious inference."

He paused, and closed his eyes in concentration. The wan light gathered around his pale forehead, and he counted out the old Welsh writer's maxims on his white fingers.

"'That a human being is a world and cosmos of forces that reach out to other worlds wholly, or almost wholly, unknown and unconjectured; that, in most cases and probably, as things are, for the best, these forces and powers are dormant and unsuspected; that occasionally and by accident they assert themselves and produce results which prove—nothing.'"

"Nothing," he repeated, opening his eyes again and gazing over the scrubby little pub garden, with its bay trees in boxes and rusted cypresses, as if he were looking with new eyes at a changed scene. Then he sighed.

"And why do we smell only stale incense and rarely have the odours of paradise about us? Because we have fallen into language. Words. What if words were not after all a great blessing but an obstacle? An interference with direct experience? If we had not developed language, would we have developed instead a finely tuned apprehension of each other's moods and feelings, quite close to telepathy? Might we also see, hear, smell and feel everything around us more intently, more intensely? Could we have become closer to the immediate, the immanent world, 'things as they are'? Instead of living in the moment, it's as if we have to convert that moment into a scrambled code of itself, its signifier in words. Like looking at the shapes 's e a' instead of at the sea itself."

The silver haze of his extinguished cigarette still drifted in the air, which had the last bite of winter about it.

"Imagine a society," he resumed, "in which there are no words and all communication has to be by expression, or by action, or at most gesture. How carefully and attentively we would look at each other's faces, hands, posture. And then someone, perhaps not adept at either the signalling or the reading, makes a shape using stones or leaves, a shape that is trying to say the same as the face or the hands, but isn't as quick or flowing or free as those, as alive: and so for the first time the made sign takes the place of the passing moment. Soon human beings are surrounded by a cloak of falling letters, while beyond the wind blows, and the world we ought to know instinctively speaks to us only in whispers."

"Yes," I objected, "but what about communication across distance? You can't see the face of a friend if they live in Khatmandu while you are in Caerleon. Or, rather, now, of course you can, but only artificially. You won't have the sense of their presence,"

But he shook his head.

"You are not remembering your Machen well. 'All the wonders lie within a stone's throw of Kings Cross.' Meaning, of course, not that there is anything special about that particular railway terminus, but simply that we should be able to find all we need for our spirit in any place close at hand, however humdrum it may be. The study of a few paving stones could be the work of a lifetime, you see. Why do we need to concern ourselves with things at a great distance when we should cultivate our own garden? And, similarly, when friends want to send messages to each other across distances, why use words rather than pictures? Why is it better to write the word 'm o o n' than to paint a moon?"

Just then, a pale sunlight faltering through blown clouds illuminated in flickering gusts the glasses in front of us, laced with the last lingering dregs of our beer, so that they shone for brief moments like precious vessels. And the same weak rays caught in glints the scarlet and brass of the ashtray. Even as I watched, I wanted to write the moment down: and in that wanting it was already ebbing away.

"Yes," I replied, "I have observed visitors to places who, instead of experiencing the place, photograph it. They are so intent upon capturing an image of it (which is the place more than once removed, with lost dimensions) that they do not in any sense feel or know the place itself. I remember sitting in a pew at St David's Cathedral once while the visitors roamed around attached to their cameras and guidebooks instead of simply looking, or being in the place. The camera is another filter, like language."

"We have abstracted the world," my companion said, "but can we abstract the word?"

He gazed thoughtfully at the empty glasses in front of us. I got up and fetched some more beer. He nodded on my return and began rolling pensively another cigarette, fashioning it with intent deliberation like an ancient worshipper making an idol. Then he put the pale taper to his lips, struck a match and sucked in the narcotic fumes of the rank tobacco he used.

"So that," he resumed, behind the veil of the smoke, "it is no longer a sign for something, or a way of conveying information, but instead is a thing in itself. Instead of being a grey replica of things in the world (or in our heads?) it itself becomes a thing in the world. Can this be done? Music does. Whatever programmatic or descriptive qualities a piece of music may be intended to have (and much has none), it still exists as a thing in itself, experienced by the listener as a primary contact, not as a code."

"I have seen some experiments," I said, "where poets have tried to re-imagine words and letters in that way."

"Yes, and I know the sort of thing you mean. Ingenious in its way, and sly. Certainly, these might make the reader think, and even perhaps think about why we need the text. But though the king has abdicated, he has not left the palace. He is not out in the streets or among the trees: he is merely hiding behind the curtains.

"No, no, we must think of our Machen again," he continued. "Remember those signs chalked upon walls, those shapes made by worked flints? How they startled his savants wandering in the streets of the city or out in the wilds of the country? Here were things which clearly had some meaning, but not a meaning we could know in this our world. They were outlandish. And so, the texts that are sometimes experienced as a thing in themselves are not in fact the books we hold in our hands but those words we encounter in a strange or unusual context."

We both stared out into the street as if looking for inspiration. A lorry drove by slowly in the traffic. Some regulatory notice painted on its rear had been partially obscured by a sticker, so that it now read only: "This vehicle is not." We noticed it at the same time and laughed together.

"Not quite like that, though," said my friend. "A painted sign, say, a piece of grafitti, or words chalked on the path. If in a wood I came across a notice reading "xaxaxar", for example, that would be to me a thing in itself, since it is not (in any language I know) the sign for another thing. I might then begin to speculate upon what it "means", which would involve wondering about who put it there, and what they "meant". I should probably try to work out if some of the letters are missing, have fallen off or faded, to try to convert the shapes to a word, a code, that I do know. Already, of course, the original curiosity, surprise, puzzlement—a primary experience—has become a little distanced. But still in essence the encounter is a primary one, unmediated by the mask of language."

"That is a very hard task for the writer," I said.

"But I believe we have to try," he replied. "We have to use words to undo words, to suggest what lies beyond words. Machen again, of course: *Hieroglyphics*. Literature must be the language of the Shadowy Companion."

The end of his thin cigarette glowed briefly as he drew in its own stale incense. He nodded.

"And our task is harder even than that," he said, "for we also have to invoke the grey fumes without denying the palpitating breath of roses. We have to give glimpses of a world that sometimes seems to work like a machine bent on some inexorable but inscrutable task, with all of us caught in its coils, cogs meshing always with the absurd, frantic pistons pushing away at the futile."

"And yet," he added, his voice now only a murmur which seemed to be a part of the rustling of the withered bushes and the passing noises of the road, "we may also at times suggest a slight faltering in the grinding of the machine, or the brief opening of an unknown vista suggesting that the machine is not all that there is."

Rapture

by Reggie Oliver

It was over a week after they arrived that Alan finally met the new tenants. They occupied the flat next to his on the top floor of a mansion block high above the Archway Road, and though he had not seen them, he had heard their music regularly through the thin wall that separated their apartments. He had also heard their voices when they sang along with the choruses they played. A number that Alan assumed was called "Shine, Jesus, shine!" because they were the only words he could distinguish, was a particular favourite of theirs. When that was being played he not only heard enthusiastic contributions from a male and female voice, but also an occasional fusillade of rhythmical thumps as if they were dancing. He suspected that his flat and that next to it had been one in the past and that an enterprising developer had converted it into two with more consideration for profit than the comfort of future occupants.

But the little flat had been a lovely thing when Inez had been with him, a haven in which the two had thrived on love and little else apart from Alan's intermittent earnings as a website designer. But there had come a time when the earnings were rather too sporadic for comfort and Inez had tired of their intimacy. Within weeks of their parting, a dismally undramatic event, she was, as Alan liked to put it, "shacked up with" a commodity broker who had a flat in the Docklands. During their last phone call Alan had quoted Garrick to her:

"Love and a cottage, eh, Fanny? Ah, give me indifference and a coach-and-six!"

The witticism was unappreciated. It had not been a cottage, Inez had protested quite justly, but a one-bedroom flat in Hampstead, and Nigel was the proud owner of a Porsche, not a coach and six.

Solitude suited Alan in some ways, though not in others. He had time now to think and to go for long walks on Hampstead Heath. The autumn in which he found himself had bronzed the trees among which he walked in the twilight, and not even the rustle caused by the vigorous couplings of gay men in nearby undergrowth, disturbed his serene melancholy. But there came a time when the tenth or eleventh rendering of "Shine, Jesus, shine!" began to prey on his nerves, especially when he was trying to complete a job of work on his PC. So one morning, he knocked on the door of number 16A Archway Mansions. (He was 16B.)

As he was doing this it occurred to him as strange that he had never actually seen its occupants, either putting out the rubbish or going to and from work, which presumably they did. All he knew was that their names were Tim and Marcia Hembry because he had seen their names on mail when he was collecting his from the mansion block's entrance lobby.

Almost as soon as Alan had knocked, the door was opened by a woman in her early thirties.

"Marcia Hembry?"

She nodded.

"Hello, I'm Alan. Alan Marston from next door."

"Oh, yes! Alan Marston. Hi! How nice to meet you at last!"

Alan noted the faint suggestion that he should have made himself known before. Marcia was flaxen-haired, pale with no make-up, but by no means unattractive, and wore a loose-fitting shift dress which hinted at a good figure beneath its folds. Her voice was pleasingly neutral with a suggestion of the north: perhaps Lancashire?

"Won't you come in?"

"Oh, thanks."

She wore such a charming smile that Alan began to feel awkward about his mission which was, in essence, to ask them to turn their music down. She ushered him into the living room. Alan noted that it was a considerably larger flat than his.

"Can I get you a cup of tea? I've just got the kettle on."

"Oh, well. . . . Thanks."

The room was neat and tidy to an almost fanatical extent. The walls had been painted a pale mushroom colour, a hue echoed in the carpet and furniture. Even the books in the one bookshelf had a regimented look about them, their spines, many of them matched in colour and height, in a rank as straight as a row of guardsmen. On the walls a few posters, affixed by Blu-tack with meticulous attention to symmetry, were the only elements of real colour in the room. They depicted scenes of conventional beauty: alpine pastures bathed in sunshine, russet autumn woods, a sun setting (or rising) over the sea. Across these colourful images in large white Italic script were inscribed biblical or devotional texts:

The Lord will come and not be slow

Prepare ye the Way of the Lord

And, across a blood-red sun setting behind foam-flecked waves:

The Day of His wrath is at Hand.

Alan was lost for a moment in contemplation of these items. When he turned round, Marcia was standing before him with a cup of tea which she proffered. She smiled but her look was searching.

Alan said: "Thank you, Marcia. Actually, I came here because . . ." And he explained. Marcia listened to him with an unchanging expression, and a stillness that was calculated to suggest deep concentration. The smile was maintained even when Alan voiced his complaint about the noise quite forcefully.

After a pause she said serenely. "I'm sorry if you've been upset by our music, Alan."

Alan noted the use of the conditional. When people wanted to give the appearance of apologising without actually doing so, they tended to use the word "if". The word "but" often followed, or was implied. He remembered Inez when she left him: "I'm sorry if you feel I've let you down, but . . ."

"It's not the music *per se*," said Alan, "so much as its volume."

Marcia's little frown on the words *per se* suggested that she found this pedantic locution irksome, perhaps because it hinted at intellectual superiority.

"We are very strong believers," she said. "Not everyone is lucky enough to share our faith."

Alan wondered if she was merely obtuse or deliberately missing the point. He thought the latter.

"Perhaps you ought to show more consideration to those less 'lucky' than yourselves."

Marcia was now definitely discomposed by the irony in his tone. He had been right: she was not obtuse. She said: "I was sorry to hear about your fiancée leaving you."

It was now Alan's turn to feel uncomfortable. How did she know? Inez had left several days before the Hembrys had moved in.

"Thank you," he said stiffly.

Marcia smiled warmly and touched his arm. "You know," she said, "nothing happens without a reason."

"As a metaphysical proposition that is open to question." Alan was now deliberately hoping to annoy Marcia, but she merely giggled. Just then the bedroom door opened and a man entered.

"Hi! You must be Alan. I'm Tim." He grinned and shook hands with Alan vigorously. "Marcie got you a cup of tea, I see." Alan was beginning to feel he had walked into a carefully staged event.

Tim was dark and beginning to lose his hair, but the general impression was of youth and enthusiasm.

Marcia said: "Alan was just saying that the wall between our flats is rather thin." This was odd. Alan had said no such thing, though he may have implied it.

"Yes! Right! But look, Alan it's really good to meet you at last. Really glad you dropped in. Marcie and I have a pretty full-on life and we keep incredibly busy. As you may know we're heavily involved in our local church. Hey, look, why don't you come along some time: see what we're up to?"

"Oh, yes! Cool!" said Marcia.

"Nothing heavy. We're not going to lay a big number on you or anything. You know: 'are you washed in the blood of the lamb?' That kind of thing." He laughed and waved his hands in a vague parody of an evangelical gesture. Marcia waved her hands too, joining in the fun. "But you could get to meet some pretty cool people. You'd be surprised. I gather you're living on your own at the moment."

"You seem to be remarkably well informed."

"Right. Well, it's sort of my business. I'm a human resources consultant in a big firm." Alan thought that that could mean just about anything. "I gather you're in computers."

"I design websites, among other things."

"Cool! Terrific! Look, give me your card. I might be able to put something your way."

"Thanks, but I really called because——"

"Alan was a little concerned about the noise," said Marcia.

"*Shine, Jesus, Shine!*" said Alan, determined not to be deprived of his grievance.

"Come again?"

"I am becoming a little overfamiliar with it."

"Oh, right," said Tim, whose capacity for empathy seemed even less marked than Marcia's. "Great praise song, though, isn't it?"

"In moderation perhaps. But not when it's coming through the wall in the early hours of the morning."

"Right. Right," said Tim. "Point taken. But hey, lighten up! Look, Alan, I'm really glad you called. I have a feeling we are going to be great mates. You know something? I hope you don't mind my saying it, but I believe the Lord has given me a real place in my heart for you."

"Yay!" said Marcia, clapping her hands. Both of them beamed friendship at Alan. In the face of this overwhelming *bonhomie*, there was little he could do without seeming very unpleasant. So Alan finished his tea, chatted for a while, and then parted with them on good terms.

In the days following their encounter the evangelical choruses were kept in check, though occasionally he could hear what sounded like dancing at odd hours. It was curious also that after their encounter he began to see one or other of them several times during the day: in the passage outside their flat, in the hall collecting mail, even in the local supermarket; and on each occasion he was greeted by a brilliant smile and a friendly, "Hi, Alan!"

At about five one afternoon Alan had decided to get a takeaway from the local Indian. It was not that he was particularly well-off at that moment, but he had some work on which might relieve his dire financial distress in the near future. He felt he deserved a reward, however meagre. While he was in the hall unchaining his bicycle, he heard a now familiar voice behind him.

"Hi, Alan!"

He turned and saw Marcia. She wore tight jeans and a black sweatshirt, not low cut but embracing her body closely enough to show that she had no brassiere and could get away with it. Her face had that scrubbed, make-upless quality that others, careless of words, might have called "innocent". Alan thought that neither its effect, nor its intent was entirely innocent.

"I was just popping out," said Alan, who was given to imparting redundant information at moments of tension.

"Cool," said Marcia. "Look, we're having some people round for a meal this evening. Just an informal gathering. Why don't you come along? About seven. It would be great to get to know you better."

"Fine. Thank you very much." Alan suspected the worst and would have evaded it if he could, but he had no talent for lying effectively at short notice.

"Cool. Oh, and by the way, don't bother to bring a bottle of wine or anything. It's nothing heavy, but we don't drink."

"Not even water?" was the reply Alan thought he should have given, but he just said: "Right! Thanks!"

Determined at least to show that his life had not been completely turned round by this invitation, Alan decided to go out anyway. He took his bicycle and pedalled up the Archway Road to the Heath. There he wandered a while, as the yellow light faded behind the black branches scribbled across the sky. He watched the men go about their search for instant, passionless sex almost with envy. One caught his eye: he smiled and shook his head in a friendly way.

Shortly after seven and wearing the cleanest shirt he could find, Alan presented himself at the door of 16A. Before he could knock the door was opened by Marcia. She was wearing the same jeans but had changed her sweatshirt for another, similarly figure hugging, but pink this time and with the words *JESUS SAVES!* emblazoned in white across those breasts which were in danger of obsessing Alan.

"Hi, Alan! Come in and meet the gang!"

The "gang" consisted in an elderly hippyish woman with hennaed hair in long corkscrewed curls who went by the name of Vi, a young couple called Dick and Jane who, as their names suggested, looked as if they had stepped out of a children's book about a young couple, and a man introduced to Alan as "Pastor Bill."

"Hi, Alan," he said, grasping Alan's hand with both of his. "Good to meet you at last. I've heard so much about you."

"I'm afraid that comment always makes me incredibly nervous," said Alan, trying to show some spirit in the face of all this bland friendliness. Billed roared with laughter and enfolded him in a bear hug which Alan accepted with reluctance, rather inappropriately calling to mind the men on the Heath.

Bill might have been in his forties: robustly built and inclined to stoutness, gingery, balding and bearded. He wore a brightly checked lumberjack shirt and shiny grey trousers belted across his expanding waist, the silver buckle dazzlingly polished and inscribed with the words *JESUS SAVES!* Everything was immaculately clean and sharply ironed. He gave the impression of someone wearing rather aggressively informal attire.

Alan was given a glass of orange juice and offered a cushion to sit on the floor with Bill who began to interrogate him about his life. Alan had encountered this kind of curiosity before: the kind that mimics real interest, but is really only a means of extracting information that might be used against one at a future date. He was to a certain extent prepared for it, but still found himself giving away more than he would like. He knew that the only way to counter it was to ask questions of his interrogator. Finally he managed it.

Bill said: "I find myself the leader of this amazing church. How the Lord led me to it is just an incredible story of blessing to a hopeless sinner and one day I'll tell it to you, Alan. We began as this little house church, just meeting in people's houses, like here." He gestured round to the smooth pale walls and the assembled company who had now fallen silent and were listening intently to Bill. "Then the Lord blessed us and more and more people began to join and we found ourselves a hall where we could all worship together and it just went from there. Now we're coming up to a thousand followers. We call ourselves *The Church of the Rapture.*" Bill saw the look of puzzlement on Alan's face and burst out laughing. The others also laughed, following Bill's lead.

"Yes, right!" Bill went on, his face now gleaming with mirth. "It's a bit hard to take in. Right, Alan? And don't worry: I'm not going to put a heavy number on you, but I don't mind telling you, we are people who believe in the living power of the Lord Jesus." There were murmurs of assent from the company. "We also have this belief that Jesus is around today and is about to return in glory. I know, Alan, it sounds pretty crazy! But the signs are all there. You've only got to look around you. You've been up to the Heath, my friend. You've seen the face of Sin up there, haven't you? I don't need to go into details."

Despite himself, Alan was impressed. He had been there that evening and though he would not have described what he saw as "the face of Sin", he was conventional enough to recognise that point of view. That was how his parents might have seen it.

The mention of sin was followed by a silence which Tim broke with the words: "Okay, guys, food's up! Come and gather round."

On a table, below the poster which read *The Day of His Wrath is at Hand,* a buffet had been spread out consisting of sandwiches and rolls filled with ham or cheese, anaemic slices of cold quiche and a bowl of salad. With the exception of the odd tomato sliced into quarters it struck Alan that the food looked strangely pale and lacking in colour. The effect was enhanced by the white paper plates, napkins and plastic cutlery that were on offer. Alan held back, not wishing to show any eagerness to partake of this ample but insipid feast. Bill approached the table with the air of a minor member of royalty about to open a new cancer clinic. Alan was glad he had not been too eager: Pastor Bill was about to give a blessing.

"Lord we really do bless these refreshments for our use. May our sinful bodies be strengthened by this mortal bread until we taste of the bread of heaven when you come, O lord, and then we may hunger no more when you take us to your own and the earth perishes in the fire of the flesh. . . ." There was a lot more of this, punctuated by fervent "amens", before the mortal food could be taken and consumed. It was as much an extempore prayer session, even a sermon, as a grace.

There was nothing obvious of which Alan could complain. The food was edible, and the conversation was pleasant, if mild to the point of dullness. Bill told a few jokes of impeccable cleanness, and nobody, to Alan's relief, asked him if he had been saved. He found it slightly disconcerting that anything he said was listened to with exaggerated attentiveness. He only knew he had said something mildly disagreeable to them when it was heard in silence instead of being instantly agreed with. It was no more than a nebulous sense of expectancy in the air that troubled him. These people behaved as if they were passing the time while waiting for something to happen. That in itself might have been tolerable had not Alan had the feeling that he was expected to be a part of that happening. They smiled; they chatted. At one point Marcia put on some music. It was those same religious choruses which had penetrated Alan's walls, but the volume was low and when Dick and Jane joined in the refrains, it was *sotto voce.*

Alan began to feel increasingly restless and alienated. He wondered how soon he could reasonably make his excuses and leave. By way of preliminary he wandered over to the window where the last light of day was streaking the horizon and over London hung a pall of cloud just tinted by the fading light. From their vantage point at the top of a mansion block in the Archway Road, Tim and Marcia had a view down across roofs and trees into the Great Wen that festered below.

"Incredible sight, isn't it?" said Tim, joining Alan. Alan nodded. He felt no need to comment. "You know," Tim went on, "you may think I'm a bit crazy, but I often pray over this view."

"Well, yes. I can understand that," said Alan. And for a moment, he could in a way. Such a view inspired contemplation.

"You can? Right. That's interesting, Alan, really interesting. You know, there's so much sin going on down there and very soon that sin will be consumed by the fires of Hell as they sweep over the world. Only a few will be saved as they are gathered up in the Rapture and will look down in sorrow as our brothers and sisters are laid low and singed by the Lord's Wrath. I have a great pity and compassion laid on me for them by the Lord. I want to save them, every one. But will they be saved? Look! Can you see what's happening?"

Alan looked. For a moment a film passed across his eyes as if someone had sprayed mist in front of them and then they cleared. It was then that the shock occurred, so profound and yet so gradual that he found himself paralysed as he stared out of the window. He hated himself for what he saw; he struggled not to see it, blinking repeatedly so as to rid himself of the spectacle, but he did see it. As he looked he felt the gentle pressure of Tim's hand on his shoulder, as if Tim was pushing a button in his body that had generated the hallucination.

Slowly the clouds that loured like a quilted canopy across the city began to roll and unravel. Some swelled, others retreated until they had formed themselves into shapes moulded and perfected, smooth and shimmering as if they had also gained solidity. Some vast form had been congregated from the miscellaneous vapours, one which moved and pulsed with life. It was at first too vast and unbelievable to see all at once. The impression was further confused by the fact that the form was pitted all over with indentations that looked at first like tears or holes in the skin-like fabric, but which slowly resolved themselves into eyes. A body was stretched across the city, hermaphroditic with pendulous male and female appendages and studded with watching eyes that glinted as they glanced in the fading fire of the sun. Only the head was missing and the extremities of the hands and feet. Its torso rippled and arched like a body in the throes of carnal ecstasy. Alan watched helplessly. Then a bolt of lightning ripped the body apart from chest to groin; there was a murmur of thunder. Alan blinked again and saw nothing but darkness and rain: the vision had gone.

"What do you see?" asked Tim.

"Did you see the lightning?" asked Alan. "Amazing view."

"I have a vision for you," said Tim.

"Look, do you mind? I have the most terrible headache. Thunderstorms often have that effect on me. I just need to lie down. Would you excuse me? It's been a great evening. Thank you so much."

Alan's departure created so many expressions of sympathy and warm farewells that he wondered if it might have been easier just to stay quiet and sit the evening out. Pastor Bill offered to lay hands on his head to cure the pain. Alan hastily said that a couple of paracetamol would "do the trick", rather regretting his choice of words immediately afterwards. Bill seemed oblivious and did not let Alan go until he, with the assistance of others, had uttered a short prayer that the Lord might "in His mercy deliver Alan from this affliction." When Alan had finally left Tim and Marcia's flat and was in the dim corridor outside he gasped for air like a swimmer breaking the ocean's surface after a long dive. In that moment he resolved, even at the cost of appearing rude, to avoid Tim and Marcia thereafter.

The resolution was soon shattered. The very next morning there was a knock on his door. Alan, who was rather expecting this, braced himself for the vivid but unattainable sexuality of Marcia which was already beginning to haunt his half-waking moments, but it was Tim.

"Hi!" said Tim. Alan, who had in him an ineluctable streak of British reserve, was beginning to tire of this ubiquitous greeting. He made a point of never using it, as most people did, in e-mails.

"Hi!" he replied in spite of himself.

"How's the headache?"

"Okay." It was a crystalline morning, washed clean by the torrential rains of the night before.

"Cool. Look, Alan, I was wondering if you could help me out. . . ." Tim said that he had "checked out online" some of the work that Alan had done and was impressed by it. He wished to commission some web design work from him, and mentioned a very favourable hourly rate.

Alan was surprised but wary. The work was for Tim's company, which was called *PanGlobal Systems International* and had, as far as he could gather, something to do with the marketing of software components. Alan understood enough to be able to make a reasonable job of what he had been asked to do, but he wondered why he had been favoured and whether Tima actually had the power to confer such a favour. Nevertheless, there was no way he could turn down this lucrative offer so he signed the contract there and then while Tim stood over him. Tim said it could lead to other work and asked him to "do some real blue-sky invention," "to really think outside the box," and to be, of course, "cutting edge".

Alan was used to this sort of injunction; it invariably came from people who did not know what they wanted. He began almost as soon as he had received the material via e-mail from Tim. It was easy enough, he had done similar work in the past, but he had never experienced quite the degree of vagueness as in the verbiage that Tim's company had produced for him.

PGSI's philosophy is centred on delivering excellence in marketing strategies and holistic systems based on an integrated people-orientated policy that facilitates and empowers through a multi-cultural input. Our motivation is based on the key mission concept of removing non-collaborative barriers through meaningful interactive services that create forward-looking pathways in a caring environment.

There was much more of this nature, and, though Alan tried hard to fathom what it truly signified, it remained just beyond his grasp. At first he relished the challenge and even produced a strapline slogan to add to the mix: PANGLOBAL SOLUTIONS FOR A PANGLOBAL WORLD, but after a while he became disheartened. Nowhere could he find any concrete information on what PanGlobal was doing. He thought of asking Tim but this would be to show weakness and that was the one thing he did not want to do with Tim. Why? He could not be quite sure. He made some progress by mounting a collage of happy young ethnic faces and putting quotations across them: "a one-world system is a system that delivers;" "reaching out pan-globally offers a radical dynamic for the new generation." They came from a "keynote" speech delivered apparently at a "Global Systems Conference" in Dubai by the chairman of PanGlobal, a Mr Stan A. Crithantis. The name was ubiquitous and nearly always featured as the author of PanGlobal's most vapid and nebulous pronouncements, but oddly enough no photograph of Mr Crithantis could be found, even when he searched online. The best he could do was a back view of him shaking hands with the Pope in the Vatican.

Alan managed to rough out some ideas and e-mail them to Tim by the end of the day, then he went for a walk on Hampstead Heath. It was dark by this time and he didn't care where he went. Sentences unbidden plagued his head: "positive entrepreneurship communicated through cutting edge technologies . . ." "Putting excellence first in a global world." It was no use wondering what a non-global world was because it did not exist, least of all in the minds of those who invented such phrases, but they plagued him. The words were like the tunes you hear in hotel lifts, dismal to the ear but hard to shake off. Alan's head was so full and the Heath was now so dark that he barely knew where he was going. Then he emerged from a belt of trees and knew where he was.

He was standing on a rise looking down into a vale innocent of trees. To his left on a ridge stood the severely white classical profile of Kenwood House; to his right and below him was a lake. On the slope in between stood a group of men and women. It was hard to tell their sex because their faces were covered by long dark strands of hair and they wore ragged clothing that fluttered around their pale limbs, but something about their figures hinted at gender. They seemed at first to be doing little, merely wandering in aimless circles around something which stood on a plinth in the dip some yards from the lake.

Alan could not be sure at what he was looking, or why. The figures coalesced into a dark mass and then separated; some crawled, others staggered. A faint murmur of mingled voices was carried up to him through the night air. The darkness increased until he could see them no longer, except as a kind of dark and festering tumour on the landscape. He turned and left the way he had come. It surprised him how he found his way through the dark trees of the heath, how unmolested he was by anything except his own fragmented thoughts.

Almost as soon as he had returned to his flat the telephone rang.

"Hi! Tim here. Thanks for the e-mails and attachments. That's great work you've done for me. I've transferred some money to your account. Like to come next door for a cuppa? You must have been on the Heath."

Alan went, though he would have preferred to be alone. Tim and Marcia greeted him fondly at the door. He was once again disconcerted by the warmth of their reception. Sitting on their immaculate beige sofa was Vi, the hippyish middle-aged woman who had been at their supper party. She smiled at him and waved.

A cup of tea was offered and he was shown a seat next to Vi, who beamed at him.

"I hear you've been hard at work," she said.

"That's right," said Alan guardedly. She beamed again. Were they trying to pair him off with Vi? The idea appalled him. He noticed that another poster had been added to the wall. It was a photograph of flames fiercely burning. In white italics over this violent pattern of red, orange and yellow had been written:

Only the Faithful shall be plucked as Brands from the Burning.

Apart from this and the other messages, all was as bland and beige as a doctor's waiting room. Vi smiled at him, inclining her head encouragingly as if in the hope that he would initiate some sort of conversation. Alan asked her if she lived nearby. She said with a coquettish smile that she was "not far away." Alan suspected that Vi was one of those people who were convinced of their powers to fascinate. It often went, in Alan's experience, with ringletted and hennaed hair.

"I was very impressed by your preliminary work for PGSI," said Tim. "I've transferred your fee to your account. I hope that's all right. By the way, how did you find the work?"

Alan was cautious. "I found some of the wording a little vague."

"That's interesting," said Tim. "That's really interesting."

"I can do the job."

"Of course you can."

Alan thought his tea tasted strange.

"In fact," said Marcia. "We were wondering if you could work on another website for us. Our church."

"I'd be happy to."

"We need to get the message out," said Vi, touching his arm and then withdrawing her hand almost instantly.

"Have you seen the signs?" asked Tim.

"What signs?"

Tim said: "I think you have. Now I'm going to let you into a little secret, Alan. Actually it's hardly a secret at all. I know this sounds fantastic to some people, but the End Times are very near. You have heard of the End Times?"

"The End Times," repeated Vi, smiling and touching Alan again. Alan felt slightly dizzy, and was conscious of a loosening of resistance to his surroundings. He saw smiles surrounding him and they were reassuring in their way.

Tim said: "You have heard of the Antichrist?"

"Well, I suppose so. But what . . . ?"

"You've just been working for him."

"I don't understand."

"PGSI is the Antichrist."

"But *you* work for them."

"On the contrary, Alan. I have been called to work against them from the inside. Look at the signs, Alan. I know you are an unbeliever, but surely you can see the signs. The Bible tells us the Devil comes in a plausible disguise. He works across continents and religions. His systems penetrate all parts of society and technology. He comes in the guise of an Angel of Light. It all fits, you see. Even you have seen the signs. Come to the window."

Alan did as he was told. He felt strangely immune from pressure, but also pliable. He went of his own accord, he told himself.

"Tell me what you see."

The sky had that leprous orange light that you get in London on cloudy nights when a million street lamps send up their illumination to the foggy atmosphere above. Against it some creatures seemed to be swarming, like a flock of starlings settling for the night across a tranquil water meadow. But these were not starlings: they were larger, less compactly shaped with bat-like wings and long, spidery legs. He heard their cries, high and almost inaccessible to the ear, calling in challenge to the senseless air they inhabited.

"Do you see them now?" asked Tim.

"What are they?"

"Do I need to tell you?"

"Demons," said Alan. The word came from him unbidden, one that he had barely spoken in his life.

"Alleluia," he heard Marcia say in the background. And this endorsement gave him a curious feeling of warmth.

"Right, Alan! They *are* demons, my friend," said Tim. "And they are gathering for the last battle. Are you beginning to understand?"

Marcia said: "And are you with us or against us? Remember the word, Alan that 'he who is not with us is against us.' Well, Alan?"

"I'm not quite sure. . . ."

"The End Times are coming when the Great Beast shall rise and all the nations shall war together. Read your newspapers. It's as clear as daylight. We at the Church of the Rapture have seen it coming for ages. But we shall be prepared for we have held ourselves in readiness against this time. And you, Alan, have been chosen to join us—if you so wish."

"But why?"

"Question not the ways of the Lord, Alan. To be absolutely frank, my friend, I don't know myself. But you have been chosen. Consider yourself blessed."

"What is going to happen?"

"On the day appointed we shall put ourselves in readiness and the Lord Jesus shall come in person to take us up into the heavens. That is called the Rapture. There we shall witness from the safety of the bosom of our Lord the mighty conflict between the Antichrist and the rulers of this world. And many shall perish in flame, and many shall descend into the abyss. And it shall seem as if the Antichrist shall prevail and his enemies or opponents are to be cast down. But that is the moment when our Lord Jesus, surrounded by the hosts of the righteous, that is all who are truly faithful to His word, shall descend and smite the Evil One and his minions, and peace shall reign upon the earth, and the meadows, scorched by the wrath of the Evil One, shall bloom, and the oceans shall bring forth abundance, and the earth shall become once again a paradise. And we who are of the Rapture shall be its inheritors. But don't take my word for it. You have seen the signs."

That was the trouble: Alan had. His head felt soft. He was half in a dream. He sat down on the sofa. Vi hugged him and he smelt her strange musky perfume that almost suffocated him with its unchemical organic aroma.

"So, I say to you again: Are you with us or against us?"

Alan was bewildered. "But what am I supposed to do?"

"Alan," said Tim, "you have now entered the realm of Grace. Everything from now onwards is gift, the free gift of the Lord. If you look in your bank account online you will find plenty of money there. Your one task is to trust. Trust in the Lord. Trust me. Do you trust me, Alan?"

"Well, yes, I suppose. . . ." He did not know why the question confused him so much. It shouldn't have done. He nodded, finding that his speech was choked and his eyes blinded by tears. Vi hugged him and he was invaded by that suffocating smell of musk again. In other circumstances he might have reacted violently against these attentions, but he had been numbed by Tim's words and perhaps something in the tea. There was comfort, too, in the sudden surrender of all responsibility. It was a simple matter for Tim to abstract from him various passwords and bank codes: Alan felt happy to hand them over. And if the world was to end and he was to be snatched into the clouds by Jesus, as now seemed highly likely, he had no further need of them.

Soon afterwards he returned to his own flat and slept soundly. He heard the chorus of "Shine, Jesus, shine!" through the walls and the thud of feet in a heavy rhythmic dance like the chug of a bass drum but it did not trouble him.

The next morning Tim was in Alan's bedroom when he awoke. Tim told him he was there to give him his instructions. The End Times had well and truly started, apparently. The safest thing for Alan, he was told, was not to leave his flat and to keep the windows and curtains closed. Tim told him he had removed radio and television from him because they had been contaminated. PGSI had taken over the networks and were disseminating their peculiarly insidious brand of satanic propaganda. Tim made Alan a cup of tea, which tasted delicious, and gave him some literature concerning the End Times to read.

When he began to look at the material, Alan was pleased to see that everything that was happening had been foretold in the Bible. All was now straightforward. Alan had his allotted task, which was to transcribe passages from the book onto the computer and design a website to disseminate these words. Once his telephone rang. Marcia, who had become a ubiquitous presence, bringing regular refreshments, answered it for him. It was apparently Inez, his former girlfriend, asking how he was, but Marcia dealt with it all. She told him that Inez had sided with the Antichrist and was going to destroy him. Alan was relieved that he did not have to speak with her, but it was curious the length of time that Marcia spent talking to Inez. They even seemed to be arranging a meeting.

The atmosphere in Alan's flat, shut off from the rest of the world, was stuffy, and Alan found himself falling asleep from time to time, but when he woke there was always work to be done. Tim or Marcia were constantly popping in and encouraging him in his plans for the End Times website. "This is valuable work you are doing for the Lord," said Marcia. "Amen," said Tim. "The lord will honour you as you have honoured him."

The trouble was that by this time, with the curtains closed and, having for some reason mislaid all his clocks and watches, Alan no longer had any idea what time it was. He searched vainly for the information on his computer, but he could not find it, and the date on it was March 16th 2666 which was surely wrong. There appeared to be severe restrictions about what he could access on the internet, but Marcia told him he was not to worry: that was all part of the attacks by the Antichrist. Most of these were being fended off adroitly by Marcia and Tim, but some things were contaminating his computer with malware and spyware and viruses of all kinds. That was why Alan could only use his PC according to their strict instructions.

"You are the Lord Jesus's secret agent, you see," said Marcia. That made Alan very happy.

At some time he fell asleep and when he woke he found he was being shaken by Tim, who offered him a cup of tea. Alan, whose mouth was dry, drank it thirstily.

"The day of the Lord is nigh," said Tim. "Arise for His light is upon thee and his banners go forth to war."

"What's happening now?"

"The Rapture is nigh. Our Lord Jesus will be coming very soon to take us into the seventh heaven. Marcia and I must go into the streets to summon the faithful and I want you, Alan, to perform an essential task for us. You are to be our Holy Reserve."

"What . . . ?"

"Bestir yourself. Here. Let me help you to dress. Don't worry if you're a little unsteady on your feet; it's only to be expected. While we are out there will be attacks coming from the enemy at all times and in all places. We are now in the open and the Antichrist knows who we are and what we are up against. He is about to attack us. He will try in the street. Marcia and I must run that risk, but he will also be coming here and we need to keep our flat secure, so what I want you to do is to guard our flat."

"But how?"

"By prayer, of course! You know how to pray, don't you, Alan? Just put your hands together and call on the Lord Jesus. You won't be alone. Vi will be there to help you. Here, let me get your coat on for you. Now come into my flat and you will meet again your partner in this task, Vi."

The dim lightless atmosphere and the fog in his brain kept him from protest. Alan felt divided. A tiny, helpless part of him objected to the nonsense but so much of him now wanted the comfort, the warm bath of belief, the luxury of assurance, the thrill of certainty. Helped by Tim, he stumbled out into the corridor. After the dimness of his own room for the last—What was it? Three, four days?—the corridor dazzled. Its window at the end looking down onto the Archway Road blazed with unnatural light. He could well believe that some splendid process, in which he was only a minor player, had begun.

Tim led him towards 16A, which, when the door was opened, seemed even brighter, a room of light. The posters had been stripped from the walls, leaving them as naked and innocent as a young girl's flesh. Even the books were gone from the shelves. The room was filled with the music of Christian Choruses. "Shine, Jesus, shine!" "He is the one!" "Come, Lord, come!" and others emblazoned the atmosphere with their simple, urgent tunefulness. On the sofa sat Vi, dressed in white cheesecloth. Her eyes were open but they registered no recognition when Alan greeted her.

"She's deep in her prayer life right now," said Tim. Even to Alan's muffled sensibilities she looked drugged. He began to wonder if he was too, but he became easily distracted. The whole room vibrated with sound and light. Beyond the window there seemed to be not one but three suns and they appeared to be moving in time to the choruses. Though Alan's sensibilities had been much altered it still struck him as sad that the Lord Jesus should be operating through such banal agencies. It would seem that the Apocalypse was proceeding in accordance with the lurid cultural preferences of the Evangelical mind. But then, in such circumstances, even Bach might have proved inadequate.

It *was* happening; of that there was no doubt. Alan, who was now seated with a second cup of tea opposite the window, could see that the sky was now a whirling torrent of violent and conflicting colour, as if fire raged over it, but fire with flames of green and blue and violet, turquoise and ultramarine as well as gamboge and vermilion and primrose yellow. Across this animated iridescence sped hosts in flight or pursuit, sometimes clashing like titans in the purple clouds. Alan watched in wonder and tried to draw Tim's attention to the splendid spectacle, but found that he could neither speak nor lift his arm to point. The fact puzzled but did not trouble him; Tim and Marcia were staring down at him with such kindness. On the sofa opposite, Vi, as dumb and immobile as himself, smiled fatuously, her eyes as blue and innocent as a baby's.

Then Tim and Marcia Hembry were gone and he was alone in the flat with Vi, guarding it from the Antichrist and waiting for the Lord Jesus to come and relieve him from his duties. The Rapture! The Rapture! It would be here soon. He could feel it coming nearer. There was a warmth building up around him but Alan could not now even turn his head to see whence it came. Was it the coming of the Lord or an assault by the Antichrist? Some suffering was to be expected, he supposed.

Smoke began to fill the room, black and billowing like agitated thunderclouds, and through it flashed flames of crimson and yellow. Alan was finding it hard to breathe as well as feeling uncomfortably hot. Across the room he was catching glimpses of Vi. Meaning had returned to her eyes and an awful realisation that echoed his own. Perhaps the Lord Jesus had forgotten all about them and would not be coming to fetch them after all. There would be no Rapture; instead the flames of Hell had filled their little universe.

Alan and Inez Marston are a popular pair in the village of Oboma in the Eastern African Republic of Bokindo. They are Missionaries, it is true, and some of their ideas are rather strange, but they do so much good. Inez teaches at a little infant school she has set up while Alan runs a rudimentary medical practice and offers valuable advice on the growing of coffee, the main cash crop in that part of the continent. They never seem short of resources, financial and other, and are very generous with them. Nobody has yet acquired the information to point out their astonishing resemblance to Tim and Marcia Hembry who perished in an extraordinary fire at their flat in the Archway Road, London, England some time ago now. But why would anyone trouble themselves with these strange coincidences? Alan and Inez are such obviously good people, so "spirit-filled" as their jargon would have it.

THE GOLDEN DUSTMEN

by Colin Insole

The silver of Miriam Coelle's ring caught the late evening sun, shining through the train window. It depicted a stylized white horse, galloping across a background of hills, like the abstract Uffington beast, carved on the Berkshire Downs in prehistoric times. Unlike the stolid carthorses, scoured in the chalk by farm labourers from other counties in the eighteenth century, it seemed to straddle the landscape; a creature gracile and fluid. In her family for generations, the ring chose its owner, being bestowed on the child, boy or girl, whose finger fitted its delicate weave. It seemed to attune itself, stretching or contracting, for her father had worn it, with his pudgy sausage fingers, yet, when his three children came of age, only Miriam's pencil-thin finger could receive it. It caused no friction or jealousy, for it was an empty ceremony, any significance long forgotten.

As a child, making the same journey between their home at St Albans and St Pancras, she had imagined the family were riding in a tightly-packed group. The stations along the route were staging posts and when the train picked up speed, her eyes glowed in the fire and passion of a gallop. The landscape she interpreted as rural, seeing farms, homesteads and forests, instead of the concrete of suburbia.

Those eagerly anticipated trips to the capital to visit the palaces, galleries and towers always disappointed her. She expected mysteries and enchantment but found only opulence and vulgar ostentation. The great libraries seemed only grander inaccessible versions of the volumes in her father's study—a place she was encouraged to investigate. He never complained if her hands dirtied the pages or if, in clumsiness, she tore the dust jackets of rare first editions.

Her move to the city was unplanned and a betrayal of four years' hard work. The most inspired history undergraduate of her year at the prestigious northern university of her choice, she had assumed that her first-class degree would guarantee the coveted funding for her doctorate on 'The Lost Palaces of Tudor Britain'. Her tutor, Professor Bramager, a friend and confidant, had broken the news of her rejection, as his hands fumbled with white gloves, to pore over a document signed by Richard III, which he had recently acquired at auction. The antiquarian, whose goal was to possess the signatures of all the monarchs of England since the Norman Conquest, had, throughout her course, singled Miriam out to patiently discuss and enthuse over each manuscript; its significance, subtleties and nuances. But as his fingers caressed the page, he reminded her now of the teenage boys at school, with their Pokémon cards, or the fevered adolescent rush to collect a complete album of world cup stickers.

As she was about to leave, he had glanced up and almost as an afterthought had said:

"A colleague of mine, at the Institute of the London Paternosters, has funding for a doctorate in Tudor studies. I've recommended you."

And anxious to be rid of him and the place she had considered her home, she had accepted.

The Institute was housed in an august Victorian building, near Ludgate Hill. It specialized in postgraduate studies of the mediaeval and Tudor periods. The interview with the principal, Doctor Bedmond, was a formality, for Miriam's academic reputation had preceded her. But her proposed study of the lost palaces was waived aside.

"We would like you to research, instead, the work of John Leland, the noted antiquary. During the dissolution of the monasteries in the 1530s, he was encouraged by King Henry to tour the land, cataloguing and preserving historical documents from the suppressed religious houses. He was a great man and can be credited with saving many rare and valuable texts that would otherwise have been burned. His life is particularly important to this area of the city, for he retired with his collection—one of the finest libraries in England, to Cheapside. But sadly, the years of travel and study had taken their toll and he 'fell beside his wits' and died in the asylum. Incidentally, some of the rarer manuscripts were gathered in your own city of St Albans, where, I understand, you trace your ancestry back to the earliest records.

"There is one stipulation. We insist that you reside in accommodation provided here in Cheapside by the Institute. We feel that walking the same streets and visiting the same churches where Leland worshipped will give your studies an insight and instinct that would be missed if you commuted from St Albans. The pattern of London streets remains constant since Roman times—its trades, atmospheres and moods seem to linger. Perhaps you will absorb from the brick, stone and skyline of this parish, something of Leland's spirit. And by a fortuitous ruling in the constitution of the Institute, the rent for your lodgings at 2 Cold Harbour Buildings is fixed at the1756 rate—the peppercorn sum of three guineas a month. It is a fine old house, built on the foundations of mediaeval and Tudor dwellings and full of forgotten chambers and recesses that our academics have not the time to investigate. Feel at liberty to explore—any baubles or curiosities are of course the property of the Institute, but you would be rewarded handsomely."

Approached through an alley off Cannon Street, Cold Harbour Buildings were probably once the residences of prosperous eighteenth-century merchants, when the area flourished as a teeming market. But unlike similar houses, long fallen into destitution in Victorian times and divided up after the war into dingy flats and bedsits, the building's elegance endured. Astonishingly, Miriam's apartments entailed three floors, entirely to herself, and steps leading down to a basement or cellar. There was a staircase that was shared by the owner of the neighbouring rooms but a strange little courtyard and garden were hers alone. Neglected fruit trees, flourishing in beds of nettles, had already shed their leaves, and their trunks, gnarled and ancient, seemed more like stone than wood.

The original floorboards remained; solid planks of heavy wood, varnished black, and the old fireplaces were intact in every room. Kindling and coal had been provided and in the main sitting room, with its friezes and cornices, a huge vase of chrysanthemums greeted her.

Prominent in all the rooms and landings, were a series of marble and plaster busts, depicting old men, grave and studiously pompous. They might have been forgotten bishops, academics or hanging judges, about to pronounce sentence of death. The sculptors seemed to have accentuated the ageing and crumbling decay of the faces, lovingly caressing the stone, where their necks sagged and folds of grey flesh drooped—accounting it a virtue. Two days into her studies, Miriam identified the most prominent bust as John Leland himself. His head seemed to emerge from the plinth, like the writhing shape of a huge parasitic worm, white and sticky. Another day's reading confirmed that Doctor John Dee, the alchemist and dabbler in magic arts, who had acquired many of Leland's books, was the model for the sculpture in the lobby.

The rooms were incongruous for a young woman and more suited to a rich bachelor, ascetic, cold and unworldly. And yet, Miriam had the feeling that for all the patrician good taste of the furnishings, the austere elegance of the décor and the stolidity, maintained for over two centuries, that they were facades, artfully fabricated. On the first night, her footsteps echoing on the floorboards, in the cold oppressive rooms, with their high ceilings of waxy plaster, she remembered the line from the song about London Bridge—'Wood and clay will wash away'. And she pictured the walls, peeling and flaking, collapsing into a hollow shell and revealing underneath all the hidden detritus of past lives—ash, dust, flakes of skin and bone from the underground railway tunnels and the sludge of the river. She felt a squatter in a derelict building, her presence fraudulent and impertinent. Her brief tenure was dwarfed by the presiding spirits of the busts and the phoney grandeur of antique fireplaces and heavy brown furniture. Her possessions could be fitted into one small suitcase and all memory of her would be gone.

On her first night, in the long spacious bedroom that gave the illusion of sleeping in the open air, exposed and vulnerable, she dreamed of the old city, of wood and stone, in ruins. A host had passed through, bringing fire and a terrible retribution. All had been razed and gouged. Nearby, marshland, river and forest dominated the landscape. Only a small dirt track, rutted with the wheels of carts and the tread of horses, stretched into the distance. Two hills, which she knew as Ludgate and Cornhill, seemed like the banked rows of a theatre, looking down on the carnage. It was the wilderness of London, after Boudicca's Iceni had massacred the Roman garrison and all its inhabitants, before hastening to the city, now known as St Albans, where the same brutality was exacted. The tribe had long departed but wisps of fire and smoke blew across the desolation and little scraps of charred clothing on the blackened remains of the dead flapped back and forth.

Gradually, shapes emerged, as if from holes in the ash and fire; furtive, creeping things, with bony hands and chalky joints. At first, she thought they were survivors, hideously distorted and maimed. But as they crawled to the surface, she recognized the faces of the marble busts. They were probing and investigating the rubble, fastidiously digging for scraps and fragments. These, they delicately secured with tweezers or handled with white gloves, before securing them in leather satchels. Towards each other, they behaved with obsequious politeness, bowing and baring their teeth in exaggerated grins; a stately saraband of scavengers and vermin. They oozed across the desolation, with obscene grace and fluidity, like huge slugs, feeding and gorging.

On subsequent nights, the scene was replayed, in all the great terrors and destructions of the city—its fall into derelict marsh, as the Romans abandoned the land; the plagues of the Middle Ages and the Fire of 1666. At the height of the city's despair, the same scavengers emerged to pick over the ruins. They wore the clothes of comforters and alms-givers—the bird-like beaks of plague doctors and the robes of clergymen and confessors. And when the firestorms of the worst night of the Blitz had abated and the landscape of the East End smoked and sweated, they came in the uniforms of ambulance workers and ARP wardens. Quietly checking that they were unobserved, for they were fearful, timid creatures, despite their greed and avarice, they worked the houses of the dead. Rings were prised or cut from fingers, jewellery, furniture and paintings were selected or discarded. But books, photographs and papers warranted their special attention and these were scrutinized and filed. Always she recognized the white cadaverous face of Leland, the oily solemnity of John Dee, but now they were joined by the smiling hypocrisy of her former tutor.

A week into her studies, Miriam had not met the occupant of the adjacent rooms. Curtains were tweaked as she left or entered the building and once she caught an old male face, watching intently as she climbed the stairs. Turning to greet him, he had ducked back inside in embarrassment, like a cat, both curious and nervous of strangers.

But one evening, as she engrossed herself in Leland's tours of Wales in his *Itineraries*, her neighbour knocked, clutching a small file of documents, and introduced himself as Mr Childwick.

"Miss Coelle, forgive my nosiness but I noticed your name on a letter in our communal mailbox and think that you should see this."

It was an old newspaper cutting, with the headline 'Missing Theology Student', and was dated 1947. The brief paragraph read:

'Despite extensive searches of the surrounding wasteland and bomb sites, no information has been gathered on Herbert Cole, first year student of divinity, at the Institute of the London Paternosters, the son of the Reverend Albert Cole of Camberwell. The young man's clothes, personal belongings, religious books and papers were found undisturbed at his lodgings in 2 Cold Harbour Buildings, in Cheapside. His ration book was not located.'

"I was seven years old at the time and remember the incident," said Mr Childwick. "On the evening he vanished, he called briefly on mother to give me his chocolate ration. All was normal and he was anxious to return to his studies, declining her offer of supper.

"The rooms have been unoccupied ever since that day. A group of men comes periodically to clean and maintain the property but it has been preserved unchanged, as if in aspic. Always, they come in threes and fours, as if afraid to be alone there. It is owned by the Society of the Golden Dustmen; the title probably inspired by that benign philanthropist, Noddy Boffin, in *Our Mutual Friend*—a former dust gatherer, who inherited a fortune. Ostensibly they began as nineteenth-century antiquarians but I suspect that they have owned the building for many centuries—the Dickensian name being only a recent soubriquet.

"I admit that countless thousands of people have gone missing from this city and that the surname 'Cole' may be a coincidence. But there are other locations. Over the years, as the oddity of your building's lack of tenants gnawed at my curiosity, I began researching other disappearances in this area. At King's Cross, near Battle Bridge, believed to be the site of Boudicca's last stand against the Romans, is a strange little terraced house, from which at least two people have vanished. Brief newspaper paragraphs from 1926 and 1948 record the disappearance of students. Their names were Colby and Colehill. I have viewed it from the street. It seems to be charged with the same patina as this address sometimes exudes. Its dust swirls and seeps into the modern world, as if to beguile and lure the unwary. It remains untenanted—probably since the 1948 event, but is immaculately maintained, for fresh flowers—chrysanthemums, if I remember, can be seen in vases in the upper rooms. In Camden Town, close to St Pancras station, is an elegant Georgian house, similarly unoccupied, from which Ernest Colebrooke, a promising young curate, vanished in 1910. All the properties are owned by the Society of the Golden Dustmen."

His gaze shifted to the pile of Leland's *Itineraries* and to the bust of the antiquary.

"I see that you are studying one of Cheapside's illustrious dead and he oversees your work. Many consider him to be a benefactor of scholarship and the saviour of many priceless works. I believe him to have been an astute Machiavellian treasure hunter. For years, he remained in Henry's trust and confidence—no easy task, and undoubtedly, to curry favour, allowed many sacred artefacts to be burned or smashed. And after years of travelling Britain, ransacking the monasteries of their most valuable documents for his private collection, he settled here in Cheapside, for a comfortable retirement. And then, rich and secure, his work completed, he 'fell beside his wits'. Something happened in that house that destroyed him. In my idle speculations, I wonder if Cold Harbour Buildings, where solid brick and plaster seem about to crumble and fracture, are on the site of Leland's former house. Knowing the secret ways of antiquarians, I doubt that all of his books were recovered.

"It is a curious and numinous part of London. During his brief stay, in the summer, Herbert Cole brought us bowls of elderberries, from the tree in your garden. In the years of austerity, after the war, all gifts of fruit were welcome. I remember the crimson glow of the wine that father made and I imagined the hills of old London, covered in swathes of the white flowers, sweet and intoxicating. I still catch the perfume of the tree. It drifts up the stairs, like the memory of a song or a lost lover. The old name for the elder was *ellern*. Perhaps the very name of the city comes from the town or stronghold of the elder tree—*ellern don*, corrupted into London.

"We're probably living at the very heart of the old city, between the ancient hills, now called Ludgate and Cornhill, in the swamp where the lost river Walbrooke flowed and oozed. And just around the corner from here, protected by an iron grille, is 'London Stone', a piece of rock believed by some to have been brought here by those fleeing the fall of Troy. I wonder what lies beneath this carefully confected Georgian frippery—the palace of a Celtic king or the temple of a river god?"

Having thanked Mr Childwick, Miriam considered the information he had offered and reflected on her family name. Shortly before his death, at the untimely age of fifty-two, her father had traced their family history. At first, his researches were amused dabblings, but, as the line stretched back, beyond his expectations, he became engrossed in the findings.

"It seems we inhabited the little cluster of villages around St Albans, as far back as the Domesday Book," he said. And then from the archives of that city came an obscure reference, in an early Anglo-Saxon document, suggesting their presence in the area a millenium before, when the Romans invaded.

"It refers to the house of Coelle. We are described as *anhaga*—solitary ones, who dwell alone. In former times, apparently we were *weards* or *hyrds* of *bocastreon*—guardians of books. There is mention of *beag*—a ring. The vain amongst us might claim that those villages—Broad Colney, Colney Street, London Colney, even the River Colne itself, were named as a result of our influence.

"It's a leap of the imagination to believe it refers to our family," he had said. "Even if it's true, the cynical would say that we were librarians to the ancients. Perhaps the ring was given as a token gift on our ancestor's retirement—like a carriage clock or set of golf clubs."

But she knew, from the diffident self-mockery he always used in confronting the serious, that he believed he had found something vital. And then his researches stopped—as if he'd intuited something of even greater importance and sanctity and was subdued by, even frightened of his theories.

Curious about the two other properties that Mr Childwick had identified, Miriam decided to visit one herself. The house near King's Cross was located in a secluded back street, part of a terrace of ornamental red brick and once populated perhaps by aspiring Pooterish clerks and Victorian junior managers.

The little enclave basked in the autumn heat, lazy and soporific. The few residents she noticed were self-absorbed, almost like sleepwalkers. An occasional passer-by, straying into the street, jaunty and business-like, caught its mood of enchantment and slowed perceptibly, like the compulsion to yawn in accord with others.

Untenanted since 1948, the house appeared to Miriam to be in a deep slumber, more enduring than a few decades of neglect. A postman, delivering a handful of junk mail and circulars, seemed part of a masquerade: a staged figure, appearing daily to confer the illusion of normality. His charade complete, he withdrew from the stage, like an automaton disappearing into the mechanism of a great clock.

Miriam approached the letter box and peered inside. The view was remarkably similar to that of her own accommodation, with a hallway leading down to a courtyard and garden. Beyond was a grey industrial estate and modern apartment blocks. The rooms were decorated with the same busts of the antiquarians that oversaw 2 Cold Harbour Buildings—but smaller and more modest, in keeping with the status of the property. A bookcase in the hall was lined with cheap paperbacks and popular detective fiction. The furniture was in the contemporary minimalist style but slightly frayed and ragged, as if deliberately distressed. All seemed contrived to persuade a curious interloper that the house was ordinary. The floorboards had recently been polished but underneath the scent of pine and air fresheners was the smell of dust on old books—like finding a locked door in an archive and uncovering rows and stacks of mouldering and crumbling documents, seething with feeding insects and mice.

As Miriam adjusted her hand to maintain her grip on the letter box, her ring pointed directly into the corridor and beyond, into the far distance. Its silver seemed to dim the chintzy interiors of the house, casting the walls and furnishings into shadow, and exposing their forgery. But the ring's gleam caught the sunlight in the garden and the view shimmered and altered.

Beyond the garden was a line of trees, thickening to forest, that formed a low hill. In the valley was a wide river estuary and as her eyes grew accustomed to the scene, Miriam could make out flocks of waterfowl, rising and swooping—snipe, dunlin, wigeon and teal. The mustiness and dry solitude of the house were permeated now with the sweetness of gorse and heather.

The sounds of modern London; the hubbub of traffic and the wails of sirens and alarms, became distant and scrambled, like the blur of fading telephone conversation on a crossed line. Instead, she heard the cries of the birds in the river valley and the roar of the wind, blowing through the trees on the hill. The scene glowed, vibrant and shining, with a fire that seemed to emanate from the river. Little points of flame flickered there, as if from a thousand candles, lit to mourn some lost host. Their incense rose and the sky became a cauldron of smoke and burning crimson.

Cramping with the sustained effort, she withdrew her hand and the view of urban traffic and machinery returned, together with the noise of the city. But as if in an afterglow, a cloud of dust rose, funnelled into the street, blurring the outlines of the chimneys, and swirled around the facades of the houses. It seemed that the regimented lines of ornamental brickwork crinkled and fragmented. Elaborate patterns of six-petalled flowers, bright red and yellow, danced briefly in the sudden squall, before breaking and fading, as the lines reformed.

Doctor Bedmond, in his private apartment at the Institute, witnessed with impatience and frustration the same crimson turbulence of clouds that had fascinated Miriam Coelle . He had sought solace in his study and always, in times of anxiety, leafed with gloved hands through the manuscript of *The British Enchanter—or The Birth of Merlin*. He had first seen the handwritten pages at a bookshop in Hereford, amidst a sheaf of church papers from the seventeenth century. The bookseller had identified it as a puppet play of 1711, by Powell. But Doctor Bedmond had recognized the handwriting and the early glimmerings of Prospero's speech 'This rough magic, I here abjure'. He had feigned a scholarly interest in the church documents—mere shelf fillers; ecclesiastical bombast from the Puritan Commonwealth, and haggled over the price of £300.

"Throw in the old puppet play and it's a deal. I have a weakness for their nonsense," he had said.

And for a pittance, he had located a lost Shakespeare play, perhaps from the elusive wilderness years of his youth. The collector's instinct to hoard and gloat, alone and in secret, overcame any desire for wealth or glory in publishing his find. But this evening, its magic failed. Under the din of traffic and the clamour of the Cheapside throng, he had heard a peal of bells—a distant lost sound from the old site of St Katherine Coleman, demolished in 1925. And as the cloud furnace of gold and crimson in the sky twisted and gyred, the sun had broken through. It seemed that a ball of blazing fire, six-petalled flower or chariot wheel, rolled above the city.

He knew that it concerned the young woman and her researches. But like a cowardly general, squinting at the front line through trees and mist from the safety of headquarters, he could not interpret its meaning.

Locking his study door, he unrolled his map, on which the patterns and mores of the city were coloured in different inks. All converged as ritual and custom repeated itself—the modern, mediaeval, Saxon, Roman and the elusive shadow lines of the old Britons, which obsessed him. Highlighted in yellow were the clusters of the strange houses— King's Cross, Camden Town, St Pancras, Marylebone, Camberwell, but above all, Cheapside: the fulcrum of all the spinning cartwheels. There, the Blitz had revealed old conduits and links to the other houses. At St Mary-Le-Bow, after the bombing, a tile-paved chamber below the floor level was discovered. And at a nearby church, dedicated to St Alban, a blocked-up late Gothic doorway was found. The Golden Dustmen had assiduously added these findings to the map - confirming old theories and suggesting new areas of research. The significance of the St Albans connection, in Cheapside, in particular, had prompted a feverish flurry of post-war investigation, for that city's past had led to the founding of the Golden Dustmen, in the mid-1550s.

When the Saxons excavated the Roman site at St Albans, they discovered the remains of a huge palace. And in an alcove of a wall was a book, written in a script that only one monk, named Unwona, was able to decipher. He informed his abbot that it was from the ancient language of Britain, containing heathen lore, invocations and rites. The pagan book was believed to have been destroyed and a mediaeval writer gloated over the burning of heretical fables and superstitious follies. It was assumed that all record of the language and culture of the Britons had been eradicated. But when Leland looted a pile of manuscripts from St Albans Abbey, during the suppression of the monasteries, he unwittingly acquired the rarest and most perilous book in England. Brief sections had been secretly translated by Unwona. Leland read these tantalizing fragments, experimented with their spells and his wits unravelled.

Missing for three days from his house, he returned there, dishevelled and dirty, reciting rhymes and doggerel, and babbling of a scholar named Coelle. Throughout his confinement he fought and raged against the restraints, demanding to be returned to his property, where, amidst subterranean tunnels and dust heaps, the book was located.

The Society of the Golden Dustmen had secured the reports, observations and diagnoses of Leland's physicians. Remembering the visions he had seen above London and his meetings with Miriam, Doctor Bedmond re-examined their findings.

"The patient is obsessed with any rings, jewellery or trinkets that his visitors might be wearing, scrutinizing them intently. He veers between despair at failing to locate his book and confidential asides.

"'Ring finger, blue bell,

Tell a lie and go to Hell.'

"This rhyme he sings repeatedly, often dancing in the fashion of a lisping child, playing with her skipping rope. When urged to rest, he becomes conspiratorial, as if imparting great secrets.

"'I know an old lady, who keeps all the rings she finds, and still she is a spinster.'

"He appears to be most rational when he imparts the most absurd fantasies. He claims, on occasions, to have glimpsed from his courtyard the outlines and towers of a distant palace, together with groves, lakes and forests. These imaginary vistas can only be reached with the aid of his book, which he is unable to master. Although a great scholar, he can decipher only the occasional Latin translation. The bulk of the book is filled with symbols and text that swirl and dance, as if to beguile and delude the poor wretch. He claims to recognize, amongst its images, the branches of a tree that is growing in his garden. They are arranged in diamond shapes and the white flowers shine and glow. When we investigated his claims, we found only a ragged bush, bedraggled and neglected, its roots rotten and more akin to stone than living wood. He speaks also of six-pointed crosses or golden chrysanthemums that spin across the page. Berating himself as a school dullard, he repeats lines as if from a lesson, learned by rote, that he is unable to understand. An area of London causes him much confusion—'Pancras, Pan Grace, Pan Cross'. This nonsense he repeats continually, usually finishing with the lines:

"'There flock bright birds, a shining throng.'

"The patient speaks continually of someone called Coelle, for this person hurriedly wrote on the first page of the manuscript, as if he had been the book's guardian or keeper:

"'Written by Coelle, at the last muster and the hour of our ruin, for my descendants.'

"His sleep is troubled with recurrent dreams of following Coelle, who carries a light, through a web of tunnels, which can be accessed through his gardens at Cheapside. These fan out into a maze of underground vaults and chambers, spanning large parts of the city. Unable to keep pace with the light-bearer, he fumbles and becomes lost in earth and darkness. And indeed, when we found him, his nails were broken and his hands were stained with red clay."

The Society of the Golden Dustmen was formed, shortly after Leland's death, to locate the lost book. At first the bravest of their number stayed in the house, but one disappeared and the other was rendered feeble-minded, speaking of long subterranean journeys to places that were later chronicled in the maps that Doctor Bedmond annotated. When the Great Fire destroyed the shell of the building, in 1666, it was reconstructed by the society, along with other properties, where strange phenomena associated with Leland's finds were observed.

It became the practice to beguile those believed to be descended from Coelle, in the hope that they would recover the manuscript. Some of these novices, unmoved by the atmosphere of the houses, lodged there at ease, engaging in their studies for months, and had to be summarily evicted. But most disappeared without trace. A few returned, their minds permanently damaged, with garbled tales of wonders glimpsed from afar that could never be attained.

Doctor Bedmond knew that of all the novices, Miriam Coelle's pedigree was the most authentic. His fellow member, Professor Bramager, had enthused over her ancestry—the unbroken link, back to St Albans, and her ring, which echoed Leland's ravings.

Their enterprise had a genuine chance of success and he imagined himself holding the book, mouthing its incantations and spells: a master of old ritual and lost lore. But hope and uncertainty unsettled his composure and threw his practised routines into chaos. He had always managed to conquer his waking fears of 2 Cold Harbour Buildings. Cleaning and maintaining the property, he avoided the basement; imagining the house collapsing around him and being engulfed in plaster, dust and rubble, suffocating and gasping for air. The courtyard and garden, with its dark, melancholy trees and rampant nettles as high as his shoulder, made him reel with vertigo. Junior members of the society, less attuned to the atmospheres and presences of the house, were assigned those menial duties, whilst he busied himself with dusting the busts and arranging the chrysanthemums.

But a new terror had crept up on him. He dreamed that he was looking out from an exposed tower or promontory upon a vast panorama of hills, rivers and forest, devoid of people. A single track snaked through the desolate landscape, far into the distance, often hidden behind mounds or lost in the trees.

Compulsively, he scrutinized the horizon, in the morbid certainty that something malign was coming. Tiny specks of birds swooping and flocking, or the wind blowing the canopy of the trees, provoked a panic, until the scene subsided. All seemed serene and calm. After hours of vigilance, relief and drowsiness almost took him and he watched with amused curiosity as, at the vanishing point, the path blurred, as if in a heat haze. The disturbance swirled and drew nearer, obscuring a tree he had previously seen very clearly. Alert again, he sat up, realizing it was dust from the movement of a great host advancing, their progress hidden by forest and hill. Straining his senses, he could now hear a steady throb, as of marching feet, or the beating of drums and shields. And he remembered the film about the beleaguered defenders of the mission station at Rorke's Drift who listened in awe and dread to the unseen approach of the enemy: a rolling crescendo, like the clanking and rumbling of a great steam locomotive.

Above the line of bushes, he could see a banner, its emblem sleek and feral. At first he thought it depicted a cat or greyhound. But as it wound its curving path towards him, slowly and inexorably, he knew it to be the white horse, identical to the young woman's silver ring. The noise grew deafening and the column was about to turn the corner into view when he woke. The line of the path mimicked the pattern of the London street, viewed from his window. Briefly it was charged with the same menace. Traffic seemed to pause and the sky darkened in a hiatus of doubt and anxiety before the scene flickered and normality resumed.

That evening, Miriam researched online the family history of Herbert Cole, the previous tenant of 2 Cold Harbour Buildings, noting first that his father, the Reverend Albert Cole, died only a year after his son's disappearance. A quick visit to Mr Childwick confirmed that the clergyman had walked the London streets, day and night, searching for his son, before succumbing to a combination of illness, fatigue and grief.

She traced the line back to the late seventeenth century, to St Albans and a common ancestor, the spelling of the name diverging in the 1800's. The young curate, Colebrooke, who went missing in 1910, also had roots in her old city. Her findings recalled a family myth, related by her father, of a Victorian relative who moved to London in the 1850s and was presumed lost and debauched amongst the stews and bawdy houses of the East End. The significance of the legend now seemed to link with the other stories and suggest its truth.

Remembering the strange visions the silver of her ring had conjured at the house in King's Cross, she located a note that her father had sent about the origin of the white horse whilst she was at university. It read:

'The white horse was the emblem of the West Saxons and led them into battle against the Danes at Ethandun in 878, after the muster of the shire *fyrds*, by Alfred. Defeat would have meant disaster and the Anglo-Saxon language, which the king later encouraged with books and scholarship of his own, would have been lost. Today, we would probably be speaking some regional dialect of Norse. The odds were stacked against Alfred—the Danes held the higher ground and had superior numbers. But the banner of the white horse led the shield wall up the hill, overwhelming the invaders. I believe it was a talisman, far more potent and mysterious than we can really understand. Its force was deeper than a mere physical or psychological presence, like the Romans using elephants against the Britons, to terrify the horses of the charioteers. The symbol is much older than Alfred, dating from prehistory. But Wessex knew its force and adopted it.'

Reflecting on the disappearances, Miriam felt a growing sense of anger that many of her family had been gulled and lured to their deaths, down the centuries, by the Golden Dustmen. She recalled her old tutor's interest in her St Albans ancestry, and from his comments, it seemed clear Doctor Bedmond had also acquired this knowledge. He had encouraged her to probe for curiosities and baubles at 2 Cold Harbour Buildings, which shared a similar layout to the strange terraced house at King's Cross.

She had never paid more than a cursory visit to the courtyard and garden but resolved to view it, testing it with the aid of the silver ring. At first it seemed a drab forlorn place, devoid of interest. Pervaded with damp and the chill of autumn, she saw the rot and churn of leaf mould and caught the sour smell of old nettles, yellow and withered. Once a traditional walled garden, the branches of unpruned fruit trees splayed across the brick. At its centre was the elderberry that Mr Childwick evoked with nostalgia. Raking the nettles from its trunk, she realized that the roots and core of many generations of the wood had died and hardened, leaving great chasms in the soil. The new growth flourished on the tangled dry bones of its ruin.

Pointing the ring into the deepest aperture, she saw its silver illuminate a network of tunnels that mimicked the lines of the adjacent streets and alleys, like the roots and tendrils of a great tree. Without its gleam, the paths were confused and maze-like, but not entirely black, for in the gloom were tiny pinpoints of yellow light that tempted and seduced the unwary.

But confident of her path and sense of direction, Miriam eased aside loose bricks and clambered inside. On her left, where the passages burrowed under the foundations of the houses, were the remains of previous dwellings: a door split open to reveal a mediaeval fireplace, the charred timbers and swollen glass bottles from an apothecary's shop, from the time of the Great Fire, and a wretched Victorian basement, with ash-pale wallpaper that oozed with damp and slime. Here, someone had scrawled:

'God save you from the rain.'

As she became attuned to the distant hum of traffic, she could make out the buzz and whisper of conversation and the tread of footsteps in the rooms above.

But rising in steep banks to her right were towering dust heaps, where the layers of London had shifted and fermented. The plastic, glass and rubber of the modern age weighed down upon brick, soot, metal buckles, lumps of animal bone and human skeletons from previous centuries. As the rubbish seethed and rolled, it murmured, as if with a million voices. Sometimes, isolated fragments of song or street cries were squeezed from the ash. 'How many miles to Babylon?', 'We can bend as well as you sir, you sir', 'Hi, Hi, Curlywig!', 'Eight o'clock bells are ringing. Mother, may I go out?'. They had no malignity or power. These were no ghosts of cockney sirens, crooning to beguile the lost. They were only the echoing husks and shells of desire and memory, lodged in dust and flakes of skin.

About a hundred yards into the tunnel, almost within sight of the aperture by the elderberry tree, she found the remains of Herbert Cole. In this hinterland world of shadow, between the living and the dead, his body had not decayed, but was drained of colour. He was seated, smartly dressed in his austerity suit, its fabric now ashen grey, as if waiting to be called for interview. He wore a plain gold signet ring that had faded to pale straw. From his top pocket poked a ration book; his name on it barely visible in threads of dying ink. But by his feet, glowing with a fierce flame of yellow and crimson, as if the colours from his body and clothes had been drawn into its fire, was a candle. Caught by the draughts and surges from the teetering heaps of dust, its light veered erratically, as if probing the darkness to snare the guilty.

At his side was a book. Miriam read the Latin translation of the scribbled footnote and recognized her surname. As she opened its pages of animal skin, dried bark and parchment, the images and symbols span and whirled in a myriad of colours. She saw the white horse, a thing sentient and perilous, its limbs poised to bestride hills and leap rivers. There were strange, elaborate crosses, crooked or hooked, and embellished with petals, that veered between flower, religious emblem or chariot wheel. A tree, subtly engraved into a landscape as a watermark, spread its roots and branches like a map of a city's streets or the veins and filaments in a body. Birds, their colour golden or black according to the angle of the light, circled the tree in funnelled dances and spirals. Miriam realized that she was glimpsing distant, fleeting images and understanding little, like pressing a seashell to her ear to hear sounds that conjured wonders, whose magic she could only guess at or imagine.

But holding the book enhanced her perceptions. She found that she could eavesdrop on the voices and whispers from the houses above: the banalities and pleasantries of family life and the muttered soliloquies and embittered rants of crazed solitaries. Progressing down the tunnels, where in the distance glowed the candles of the lost ones of her family, she stopped under a building. Here, she recognized the soft tones of Doctor Bedmond, who was again reading aloud from the reports of John Leland's madness.

The architecture of accumulated dust and detritus was broken and she saw forests, rivers and hills. It was the same view that had haunted the Doctor's sleep but it was enhanced by her own memory. This was the landscape of her childhood, that she imagined as the train rattled from St Albans into St Pancras station. In the heart of the woods was a lake, with an island in the middle, at whose centre stood a white stone edifice, temple or tower, with blue glass in its turret. Beyond the dip in the hills were little homesteads and farms, dotted with cattle and black-faced sheep. Orchards, wells and sacred springs she remembered, and she longed to walk the path that snaked into the distance, to her home city. As the perfume of gorse, heather and other flowers reached her, it seemed that the land exhaled, as if years of waiting were over. And she sensed, amidst the expectation and welcome of her coming, a gathering anger, against the tide and filth of the dust heaps, the entrapment of the innocent and the avarice of the Golden Dustmen.

Carrying the book, she retraced her steps, gently removed the ration book from Herbert Cole's pocket and climbed back into the garden.

The next morning, under Miriam's instruction, Mr Childwick delivered, by hand, a small package to Doctor Bedmond. It contained Unwona's Latin translation of her ancestor Coelle's footnote, carefully cut from the book, the ration book of Herbert Cole and a deliberately enticing message, promising that other rare and ancient manuscripts would be brought to his rooms at the Institute the following day or later.

She set out early, well prepared for the twenty mile walk to St Albans, carrying sandwiches and sufficient water, in her father's old leather fishing flask. These she secured, together with her ancestor's book, in a haversack, strapped to her back. She navigated the path of the tunnels to the Doctor's house, where the strange landscape seemed vibrant and expectant, beckoning her onto the track that curved into the distance. But as she stepped onto its mud, and felt the autumn wind blowing, its mood felt sombre and charged with a deep melancholy.

The track was rutted and trodden with hooves, as if heavy carts had recently passed, but the land was devoid of humans or their animals. In the ditches, fringed with rows of elderberry bushes, and from shallow tumuli nearby, numerous lights glowed palely and smoke rose in thin plumes, like the incense offerings made to the dead from some huge submerged cathedral. In time, they became fewer and more scattered. Miriam recalled the words of her ancestor -'in the hour of our ruin'. This was the road that Boudicca's chariots drove, from their sack of London, both to burn and massacre the palace at St Albans and, finally, to their own destruction on the site of Battle Bridge near King's Cross. The air was heavy and uneasy with the presence of them all: their loss and mourning. Their spirits were not malignant or resentful of her intrusion, but withdrawn, turned in upon themselves, as if ashamed of their rout and defeat. She felt them gathering as she passed, hiding behind the brows of the hills, or in the canopy of the trees.

A lane led to a farm and outbuildings, its fences sturdy and intact, to contain the absent livestock. Apple trees were ripe with fruit in a well-tended orchard and blackberries and sloes were abundant in nearby bushes. The door to the main dwelling opened at her touch and she could smell the recent rain on the clothes and hair of the family. The floor was worn down with the tread of their footsteps and a chair bore the impress of a heavy body from years of repeated contact. There was a dark stain on a table leg, where a domestic cat had repeatedly marked its territory by rubbing its chin against the wood. The room, deserted for over two thousand years, had the same feeling of recent bereavement that she remembered from the days after her father's death.

A few miles down the path, she reached the temple or shrine, set in the middle of a lake. It was decorated with the same six-petalled flowers and crooked crosses that she had seen at the house at King's Cross. And there were other paths with stone monuments, stretching far into the distance, that she longed to explore. The waters of the lake and its tributary streams lapped invitingly. It was a place of great serenity and calm with river fowl rising and diving and the splash of huge fish. By the shore were stone and pottery dishes, stained with the dregs of wine, that had been offered to the water god.

The elegiac rain of October obscured her view of the horizon, but gradually the towers and balconies of the great palace, on the site of St Albans, shimmered in the mist. She reached its gates by late afternoon. A vehicle, shaped like a sturdy charger, but more ceremonial carriage than war chariot, stood by the entrance, as if waiting for its chieftain or king to survey his estates. A long ceremonial pole, at its head, was empty of device or emblem.

The doors gaped wide, all defences and fortifications down. Its many rooms and corridors were furnished in great luxury and beauty. They glowed with a freshness and vitality, as if the voices and footsteps of the court were imminent. Oils and perfumes, subtly different for each chamber and its function, were fragrant and soothing. The formality of the palace's design was softened by the presence of intimate objects—jewellery, children's toys, half- finished embroidery and battered musical instruments. All seemed to have been set aside a few moments ago, as if the family had been called away to another diversion or entertainment. In a bedroom, she found a comb, fashioned from bone and decorated with a frieze of flowers, and with strands of yellow hair spilling onto the table.

In each room was a mirror, austere and cold, with no embellishment or frame, whose glass was the colour of ditch water. Absorbed in the ornate splendours of the palace and the personal items that suggested the characters of its inhabitants, Miriam paid them little attention. But in the bedroom she checked her reflection and looked, instead, into a deep well of seething water and turbulence where fragments of glass, sand, wood, fabric and bone bubbled to the surface, before being drawn back into the whirlpool. Brief images formed—terrible visions of fire and blood; of yellow hair matted red and scorched, the room ransacked and aflame. And in the other mirrors, similar scenes of cruelty and the fall of the palace were enacted. The longer she stared into the water, the more vivid and enduring they became, until she could hear their cries and the triumphant yells of the rampant Iceni.

A series of rooms were set apart from the main palace—the quarters of a minister or important advisor. And in one, littered with an accumulation of manuscripts, shelves lined with parchments and scrolls, scribbled maps and jottings, she felt at home. It was like entering her father's study as a child, or returning to her own dissertations at university. The books were folded together, their pages overlapping, in the same way that she stacked her own research material, to access pages more easily. Here were the archives of her ancestor, Coelle, who had inscribed the hurried footnote to the book found in the tunnels. More than a librarian, he had been a counsellor and master of lore. The texts had been illuminated with a dazzling range of colours and tints from plant and animal dyes, which were arranged in jars and bottles on the shelves.

But the images in the room's mirror were equivocal. She saw him perish, not in the palace, but in the shadow of London's twin hills, Ludgate and Cornhill. He had fallen with Boudicca's tribe, at Battle Bridge. And she understood the contrast between the opulence and luxury of the palace court and its vast estates, with their love of beauty, learning and the sanctity of its religious sites, and the raw ferocity of the Iceni. Perhaps her ancestor had attempted to foster an alliance of the tribes, combining the attributes of both against the occupying Romans. He had failed, but his book of lore and ritual had been secreted back to the St Albans site, where the family remained. Probably they had been spared the fate of the palace inhabitants by Boudicca for Coelle's involvement in her cause.

The defeat of Boudicca's army, with vastly superior numbers, had always rankled Miriam. It contrasted sharply with Alfred's glorious victory against the Danes, with the Saxons, led by the banner of the white horse, overwhelming the hill.

The day was ending and in the twilight the palace was fading into shadow. Here, no candles were lit to remember the dead. Darkness was coming and, with the cloudy skies, it would be an intense blackness that modern city dwellers rarely experience. Even the coloured inks and dyes of the illuminated texts were grey and insubstantial as she left the archives; wondering where best to spend the night. But at the entrance to the palace, the carriage gleamed white, cold as moonlight, shone on bone, like the illuminated skeleton of a huge beast. She could now see that it was fashioned in the outline of the white horse depicted on her ring. It seemed to encompass and guard the entire grounds; the emblem of some white God of hillside and towering escarpment. But it was incomplete, as if one last segment of head or neck were missing.

Opening the carriage door, as if delving into the maw of the creature, Miriam found the banner, folded on a seat. It depicted the white horse, on a black background, surrounded by moon and stars. In the gloom, its luminescence was feral and dangerous—the slinking line of a cat or wolf from the old forests. It was a primeval spirit, channelled out of darkness by the tribes, to be set loose on their enemies, to tear and trample them and fill them with the fear and chaos of the wild wood. Fumbling with the cords, she attached it to the pole at the front of the carriage. Surprised by her own dexterity, it fastened easily, her hands working by instinct, in the failing light. The interior was warm and luxurious, and, anticipating the cold October night, she chose to sleep there, curling up like a kitten on the soft cushions. She drifted into sleep, uncertain of her plans, realising that she had engineered a confrontation with Doctor Bedmond, trusting only in the old magic of her family and the numinous power of the landscape. But her dreams were benign as she wandered at will through the archives, investigating and probing, or tramped the lanes and hills, exploring the glories and graces of a younger age.

As dawn broke, Doctor Bedmond studied the rainswept London street for signs of Miriam Coelle's arrival. Car headlights illuminated the grey shapes of pedestrians, huddled against the drizzle, their faces hidden. He was joined by her old tutor, Professor Bramager, who had driven down from the north, overnight. Unable to sleep, with the promise of success, after 450 years of the Society's efforts and researches, they had speculated and worried, obsessing over the ration book of Herbert Cole.

"She has discovered the truth about the novices. Even if she delivers the book, her knowledge is still dangerous to us," said Doctor Bedmond. The bust of John Leland on his desk seemed to stiffen, as if straining to maintain its composure and gravity.

"The basements of our properties are quiet and secluded. And I believe there are tunnels where our younger, less sensitive members, may be induced to confine and inter her," said the Professor.

"And her neighbour, the inquisitive Mr Childwick?"

"An old man with dreams and delusions. And besides, we can fabricate any number of vices and perversions to discredit or silence him." He pointed to the street. "Futile little lives—scurrying and fretting—the anonymous tide of the London crowd."

But the shapes had blurred. In the mist and half-light, they seemed more like rows of bushes or scrubland, buffeted by the wind. The shop fronts were dark, like tiered banks rising on a hill. As the rain intensified, streams formed, gushing and channelling into a wider flood.

Both men shivered, for the cold and damp had seeped into the building; the wind rocking its foundations. They felt exposed and vulnerable—two sentries scrying a hostile landscape, from a rickety wooden watchtower. Every movement of tree or bush seemed malign; the cover for encroaching enemies. Pale yellow lights were now visible, covering the entire panorama, as if emanating from underground. They formed in clusters that seemed familiar in pattern and symmetry. And they recognized the sites of the houses of the Golden Dustmen, where, over five centuries, the descendants of Coelle had been lured and beguiled to their deaths. Motionless at first, the lights seemed to oscillate and pulse, as if summoning strength after a long slumber. Then, in solemn procession, like a torchlight vigil, perhaps a hundred in number, they began moving towards a bend in the road, obscured from the view of the two men. They gathered there, flickering in readiness and impatience. From their flimsy promontory, both men could hear something coming, gaining in pace and ferocity. It churned and thundered the mud and great splashes of water now rose above the bushes.

Miriam Coelle had half woken from an idyllic dream in which she was bringing offerings to a spirit of the hills on the site of St Pancras Old Church in the vale below Penton Grove. She seemed on the point of unravelling one of the mysteries of associated words and sounds from the language of the ancient tribes with the modern names.

Caught between sleep and alertness, she realised she was in a fast-moving vehicle and assumed that she had dozed off in the train. But the jolting, careering motion, on a worn, pitted track, and the slap of branches on the roof, recalled the carriage of the white horse to her mind. And from the hills and plain came a sound that soared above the wind and seemed to drive the coach faster, roar on roar. She was being propelled onwards by thousands of voices: an ululation from the distant palace, the farmsteads and dwellings in the valley, the fallen men and women of the Iceni and the pilgrims to the shrines, by the lake. The wood of the carriage heaved and groaned as it surged around corners, accelerating towards London, in a torrent of rain.

Beneath Ludgate Hill, it stopped. There, the tumult of the dead subsided and she felt them fade back into the landscape. But lights hemmed around the carriage with a jostling urgent anger. The banner was seized from its pole and the torch bearers swarmed up the hill, bringing fire, thunder and ruin to those who floundered and howled at its summit.

Negotiating the labyrinth of the passages back to 2 Cold Harbour Buildings, Miriam noticed that the remains of Herbert Cole and the candle glow of the others were missing. After a brief visit to Mr Childwick to reassure him of her safety, she reached in her haversack for her ancestor's book. Only its dust remained: coloured fragments of bark, animal skin, flowers and ink. Its years in the modern world, amongst the litter of the towering heaps of the tunnels, had corrupted and decayed it. A last perfume from the corridors of the palace filled the room as she shook the heap onto a table where the powder stirred, swirled in upon itself and was gone.

Investigators at the scene of the devastation of the Institute were unable to establish whether Doctor Bedmond and Professor Bramager had died of suffocation under a tide of rubble, or the effects of fire. A red pall of dust reminded the more observant among them of the layers still visible in London soil, of Boudicca's destruction of the city. They were more puzzled by the discovery, in the ruins, of nearly a hundred human remains—some dating back to the mid-sixteenth century. But a handful of bodies, including those of Herbert Cole and the young curate, Colebrooke, were positively identified. Surviving academics from the Institute were questioned, but since all of the deceased had perished before most of them were born, no charges were brought.

The Society of the Golden Dustmen was dissolved, its associates and fellows anxious to fade into obscurity. They dared not contact Miriam Coelle, nor evict her from 2 Cold Harbour Buildings, which she used at will, despite securing more comfortable accommodation in her home city. The lure of the landscape beyond the tunnels engrossed her and filled her studies and devotions. The lost book was but one volume from a vast archive. Already she had identified ancient temples to spirits of river, springs and lakes, on the modern sites of churches bearing her family name—St Nicholas Cole Abbey, St Katherine Coleman and St Mary Colechurch. Obscure little places in London bore the shadow lines and memory of images in the great palace. The symbols of the old city and the new blurred and merged—crinkling and fragmenting, as their layers unravelled.

One evening, in the curious little garden she had encouraged him to visit, Mr Childwick noted that she had inscribed the words of Thomas Trehearne on its brickwork.

'A Stranger here
Strange Things doth meet, Strange Glories see;
Strange Treasures lodg'd in this fair World appear,
Strange all, and New to me.'

CANTICLE

by Daniel Mills

My mother is weeping. She hides her face in white hands smeared with dark stains. Her shoulders shake. The tears run down between her fingers, wetting the dried blood on her hands and turning it crimson. I watch, paralysed by sleep. She makes no sound and does not hear me though I call upon her. Mother, I say. The voice slips from me, a thin sound, and I am awake. My eyes open on this narrow room, cramped and filthy and with no shapes visible save the outline of the high window through which the water drips and puddles on the stone floor. It is not yet Lauds. This house is still, emptied of all but dreaming, the rain.

Three seasons have passed in this prison. Winter and the walls were cold, radiating absence. I fumbled at my beads but my hands were numb, the fingers chilblained. Nights of no sleep and only the moonlight pouring through the window to fill the cell with its silver glowering. Then spring, which was the false spring. Easter passed and winter lingered, would not depart. One morning, a robin settled on the sill above where it remained throughout the day, its call drifting down to me where I lay upon the pallet, an impossible distance. With the song came summer, this summer. Lice in my hair and bedding. Rotten bread, fleabites. The floors gather heat with the sun shining on them, growing hot as hearthstones by the dusk. The air in damp rags lodges in my throat. The heat sits on my chest: a slow suffocation like that of men who die upon the cross. My wounds open, refuse to heal. They pus.

The scent transports me. Before me loom the hills of my childhood. Perfume wafts from the grass where the wind makes ripples on it. I can picture it all so clearly, the paths down which I ran with my brothers as children, the sights we saw. The priest who stripped himself naked and knelt beside the river to flog himself with a thorn-branch. The old mad shepherd who dressed in animal skins and sang hymns to his flock as he drove them cross the sward, howling like a wolf to speak the name of God. The cries of deer in their mating. We heard them over the next hill: the bellowing males, the yearning of the hart. By the time we reached them, they had gone. They left no trace of themselves but blood splashed in the grass. Writing these words, I lose myself to the memory as I once I lost myself in prayer, in those days, long past, when I turned inward to the mansions of the soul. Sext, and the bells are tolling from the chapel. Their chanting washes over me. I answer. The words break from my lips, ragged as the hart's cry. Holy Mother, pray for us.

This cross becomes too heavy, the weight of my penance or sin. I am no longer sure of the difference or if it matters. The days are all the same, counted by my breviary. Evening falls. I watch for moonlight, then for the dawn by which I read the offices. I read without speaking, unable to give voice to the holy words. Once each week, the door is opened, and I am led past the other cells and storerooms to the staircase and the chapel where the Prior awaits me. He is a good man. He allows me to wield the rod for myself and takes it from me only when my strength fails me. Always the tabernacle is closed. It hides within itself the Host which is denied me. When the beating is over, the Prior dismisses me. He bids the limping friar, oldest among the brothers, to accompany me back to the cell. The old friar is kind to me. He gives me milk or broth and sneaks me the scraps of paper on which I write my verses, these words. Some mornings he sits with me and listens to the birds outside. He pleads with me to renounce my sin and to make full my confession that the Sacrament might be allowed me. He does not understand there is nothing to confess and no one who might listen.

Vespers. The day yields to its breaking but the heat does not relent. I thirst. I lick the damp from the wall and pant after memories, the frothing cool of mountain streams. Those days, too, have slipped away, emptying themselves like vessels inverted. I remember so little. I was so young. My father's face is as lost to me as his voice, though I can recall the tales he told us of the saints and of the priests and kings of Israel. After he died, my mother took the three of us to see his people, a journey of some days. On the road we passed a pond where a mule had laid itself down in the shade of the cedars. The animal appeared half-dead from hunger and its right foreleg was broken so it could not stand. Thinking of David, my eldest brother fashioned a sling from a tree-branch and hurled stones at the beast where it lay panting, our Goliath. The long ears split and separated from the skull. We joined my brother in throwing stones at the face till its eyes were battered shut. Blinded, the beast moaned softly, as though to itself, and stretched its bleeding head toward the water. My mother saw what we had done, but she was not angry. Without a word she wrestled the mule's head into the water and sat upon the neck until the thing was done. We were not punished. It isn't right, she said, to let a beast suffer. To prolong death when death already takes so much. She knew this too well. My father's people wanted nothing of us and gave us even less. Days later, returning home, we passed the pond in which the mule had been drowned. Around the corpse the waters had receded, exposing the wiry neck, the bleached skull. The buzzards had been at it and the flesh was stripped away. Only sinew and bone remained, wracked into the outline of the beast in its dying: all life fled from it, the lack made visible.

His absence haunts me. The memory of those inner mansions toward which I flew when first I was taken in chains. And found them empty: marble tiles gleaming, fires banked and roaring. The supper table was laid for the wedding with bread and meat and the finest of wines, but there were none to partake of them, and the musicians, too, had gone. They had left their instruments scattered about the room, but with the ghosts of songs upon them, melodies clinging like perfume to the strings. I floated past the supper table and crossed the threshold to the inner room, where the wedding bed was readied, piled with sheepskins and furs. Here the Bridegroom had come and from here again he had departed. His scent of myrrh lingered in the manner of songs just played, and the Bride, who remained faithful, lay herself down among the furs to wait. She looked up to the pine rafters as if to glimpse the sea of stars beyond. She grew anxious. At last she slept and did not dream, and when she woke, the fires were out. The house was cold, the wedding bed. His scent had faded from the air, faint as longing.

The Bride was not content to wait. The inner mansions were deserted, but I went out from myself in the one way that was open to me. This was December, the killing time, and ice had formed in bands down the walls of the cell. I stood upon the bed. I strained my mouth toward the window and sent my voice soaring out into the night when everything round about was stillness. Where have you hidden yourself, Beloved? I asked, and the words ran together into a song. One of my jailers heard and came running. He was tall and thin and spidery, his flesh riven by old wounds. He was once a soldier, now a husk of scar tissue. He threw back the door and peered into the cell, haloed by the light he carried. I continued to sing, could not stop. He took up the filth bucket from its place in the corner and hurled it across the room. It struck the wall over my head and upended, dousing me with cold urine, clots of frozen excrement. The pail clattered to the ground. The noise shocked me into wakefulness and I realised that I was not singing but moaning, screeching like an animal in the agony of its abandonment. I fell quiet. The door slammed shut. The jailer departed and I was alone with the night, my mother, her weeping.

Mother, I am sickening. My dreams have become as one fever. Night after night, my body falls away from me and I rise untethered from the bed, breaching the ceiling to drift over the city with its black walls and spires, houses lit by candle flames. Last night the wind was up. Floating, I spread my arms like wings and allowed the breeze to carry me north from the city through hills and canyons lit by the moon. The landscape was familiar. I recognised the sweep of grass and wildflowers, the low mounds of sleeping sheep. There was the clearing where the mad shepherd camped. His broken voice drifted up with the smoke from his fire and spread itself in the same way till there was nothing left of it. Into this hush I fell, slowly, turning over like a leaf to see the stars behind me fade and slip into the dawn.

The Feast of Saint Lawrence. I was roused by the sound of the door, the bolt shooting back. The thin jailer entered, followed by the limping friar. The first man glared at me. Get up, he said, and I did, assisted by the friar who helped me into the hall. The door to an adjacent store room stood open, lit by a casement which overlooked the top of the monastery wall. The friar nodded slightly as we passed then walked beside me down the stair to the chapel with its windows lit up like jewels and the tabernacle locked against me. The Prior was there. He faced the altar with arms upraised and called for me to approach. I obeyed. I removed my scapular and stripped away my habit and shift. The fabric clung to my back, stripping away scabs and causing the warm fluid to wash down my spine. Blood mingled with corruption, the odour of living decay, and in this guise of death, I knelt before the altar. The Prior murmured a brief prayer and produced the rod that was my penance. Will you take it? he asked, softly, as is his way, but I was too weak to answer. I sprawled forward, sliding my belly over the stones. They were cool beneath my skin, blessedly cool, and I think I must have drifted off because I felt myself rising, as in my dreams, floating and weightless. Then the first blow fell across my back and shocked my scars to life. I plunged toward my body, becoming one with my wounds as I vomited and convulsed upon the floor. The Prior struck me again and again. He wielded the rod not with hatred or with malice but with a suitable solemnity bordering on sadness. My wounds, opened, sprayed at each blow, and when the agony was over, the Prior said another prayer for my repentance. His features were sheened with blood and sweat and with white flecks of sickness like shattered bone.

Later. Evening? Again I floated from the room. I left behind me body and city and drifted north to the hills where I beached upon a mountainside. The valley spread before me, emptier for the dawn that rose behind it, grey and sapped of all warmth, and the sky itself was thinning, insubstantial as the smoke from a shepherd's fire. I listened for birdsong, but there was none, and the eye of the moon was on me in my nakedness. It sounded me to my soul's centre: formless and boiling as the heavens above. The moon shone from those depths as from a black water and with a light like the chill that precedes life, the silence that follows a death. From the mountain, I watched the sun climb into the east, dragging the shadows behind it, waves after a fisherman's boat, and the moon did not retreat but recast dawn in its own image, rendering all devoid of colour, as was the world before the world, before the Word was uttered. I waited, growing colder all the while. I listened for the Word of Light, but there was no god there to speak it, and all the sweep of time was revealed to me in this unfolding of the waves.

Canticle of Flesh. Song of songs, which is suffering. We enter into it as babes and endure it as we can and we do not leave it behind us until we are dead and the earth shovelled over us and none are left alive to mourn our passing. The fever is worse, I think. The days go by. The walls drip with heat and the sweat pours from me, dampening my robes. The weather will not break. My hands are shaking and greasy, useless. The window permits of too little illumination to read my breviary and I cannot stand to reach the light. The limping friar brings me bread to eat but my throat is dry: I cannot swallow. The reed of my voice is broken. My tongue flaps against my gums but makes no sound. The lash-wounds fester and rot.

This night, the longest of nights, my mother came to me and dressed my wounds. I could not see her for the darkness but remembered her scent of bread dough and opened earth. She undressed me, habit and shift. The latter stuck to my back but she massaged the strands of fabric loose and washed the sores with water from a jug she had brought with her. She bathed me, scrubbing the grime from my skin with a damp cloth, the same as she had when I was an infant. I tried to speak, but she hushed me into silence and helped me to sit up as she changed the bed coverings beneath. She lifted my hands above my head and guided them into the sleeves of my habit. The scapular came next and I lay down against the bed feeling wonderfully cool and clean. Her voice came from the darkness, a whisper. She spoke to me the words of the master in Matthew's parable: Well done, my good and faithful servant. Her shoulder shook gently. She was weeping. The chapel bell sounded Compline. She limped to the doorway and went out.

The cloister is quiet. The moon is down and still I write. I cannot see the page before me. Dawn is far off, but I am thinking of my mother and of the vision that was granted me. I have no doubt but that it was a vision, for she was a simple woman, and could not read. She could not have quoted scripture to me for all her faith was cut from stronger stone than mine, and even this availed her nothing when her husband died and his family rejected her. Mornings, she left the house while we slept and did not return till dusk with pieces of mouldy bread or scraps of firewood, bones to boil into broth. Where did she go? I asked my eldest brother, who said that he would show me. The next morning, my brothers and I sneaked out of the house behind her. We followed her from church to convent, where she pleaded for alms they would not give. Afterward she sought for shade in the town square and sat down heavily with the begging bowl between her knees. I was young, barely three, but old enough to know shame as I watched her grasp at the cloaks of men who passed her by and paid no heed. One man lingered, a younger man, but it was only to look at her in a way I could not understand, and afterward, I heard them together in the street outside our house when we were meant to be asleep. He beat her. We woke to find our mother in the bed with us, cocooned in the rags of our blankets. Her right eye had swollen up, sealing itself closed, but she smiled to see me awake and offered thanks to God when we sat down to break our fast of many days. My eldest brother would not join us, being too proud, but she did not resent him his pride any more than she begrudged the Lord her suffering, even after her second son succumbed to his weakness, and the cart came to fetch him away. My brother went after it. He ran with the tears down his face, but my mother merely lingered in the doorway and did not stir until sunset when the shadows lengthened and she murmured a prayer to the Virgin before going inside. We lay down together. She lay awake beside me while I pretended to sleep and did not cry out, or curse God, or scream for the pain inside her, but again tonight she was weeping, and I did not know why.

The night is passing. In the last hour of dreaming, I found myself adrift. Freed from my prison, I drifted south toward the coast and joined the birds in their migration. We flew across the sea, the seas of time, while the heavens seethed and divided to form the void that was the storm, its open eye. Tempest winds whipped at us, ripping the birds free of their wings and dragging their shrieks into the stillness overhead. The Holy Land was below me, the city of Jerusalem with its hill of Calvary, its three crosses. I hurtled toward them, dropping from the sky with the weight of a child spat, kicking, from its mother's womb. The Bridegroom was there, the one for whom I had searched. He had left his Bride on the night of their wedding, exchanging the promise of ecstasy for the cross to which they had nailed him and on which he had been abandoned in his turn. He dangled from the bar with the stink of death upon him, blood dripping from his wrists and feet. From above I noted the crown upon his head and the lash marks down his naked flesh like words in a foreign tongue. The hour was late: the crowds had dispersed. His followers, too, had deserted him, so only a few remained. The men among them were silent, while the women wept openly, without shame, all but for his mother who concealed her face behind her hands. She could not see me as I plunged to earth, falling toward the broken body where we were to be joined together, Bridegroom and the Bride, in this, our crucifixion.

Of course her face was hidden. She wept for her son on the cross as she has wept for me these nine months, as she weeps for all men in our suffering. Even now I hear her, though my fever is breaking. The long night past, I wait for night. Terce, and I am beginning to understand. Waking from the vision, I felt the bedclothes twisted up beneath me. From under my scapular I extracted a mass of stained and bloodied wool which I recognised as my old habit. It had been torn into strips and looped together with the remnants of the soiled bed coverings to form a crude rope, fifteen feet in length, which had been secreted under my scapular for me to find. I thought of my mother, who had limped when she left me last night at Compline and of the old friar, who had always been kind. I heard footsteps in the hall. His footsteps, I thought. But the door opened to reveal the thin jailer with eyes like dead coals. He squinted at me through the semi-darkness.

Please, Brother, I said. Where is the old friar?

He is no longer among us.

I do not understand.

He has gone to his reward.

Surely—it cannot be true.

He was old. The end came quickly.

It has just happened, then?

Yesterday at Sext he fell into a swoon. He did not awaken.

Thank you, Brother. For telling me.

I am not your brother, he said, and left.

Descendit ad infernos: he descended into hell. When the procession reached Golgotha, the soldiers drove nails through his wrists and feet and raised his cross high in the air so his flesh dragged on him and the blood drained from his wounds as from a butchered calf. The women gathered below him to weep while the emptiness loomed overhead, a silent storm. In his agony he cried out to his father, but the air swallowed his words, and gave no answer. He died, unable to breathe at the last, his lungs crushed by the weight of his own body, which was heavier than any cross. We are the same, Bridegroom and Bride. I am thirty-five and still the flesh defines me for all my yearning after heaven. This body breaks me with its aching, its awful weight, and even in dreams, God hides his face from me. Nine months have passed in this way, but everything is changing. The day is at hand, as the Apostle writes. In dying he smashed the gates of hell as I kneel now before the door to my own prison, my hands at the lock. My fingers grasp at the iron housing, taking hold. I pull myself up, hang my wasted carcass from it. The nails strain with the weight, then snap. The housing twists away into my hand and I fall, hard. The floor stones smash the breath from my lungs, but the lock is broken, the bolt exposed. A window in the next room gives onto the outer wall, and the rope is in my hand.

It has begun. Once begun, it must go quickly. This prison settles into itself, into a stillness like the void to which he cried, as I did, and with one word from his lips he turned the dark to light. I listen for it now, the voice of my Beloved. The quiet is complete. His Word, as yet unspoken, can be heard only in the silence of the night. Draw me: we will run. Through valleys and vineyards, where grapes grow fat upon the vine, to the hills with their fields of lilies and no steps visible among them, so light our feet upon the air.

White Light, White Heat

by Adam L. G. Nevill

There was no true light. Nothing at all to transport the spirit.

Nondescript and forgettable, like so many others in the company, I would sit at my desk in silence, facing forward, staring at a screen. Sometimes my body suggested to me that it could catch fire from the inside. Frustration was incendiary. It ignited the black lump of my despair, a slow-burning and inexhaustible fuel. Boredom fanned the embers red. Futility was the by-product of my smouldering, the cinders and ash that my hopes and purpose had been reduced to, a smokeless exhaust from a life wasted and rendered meaningless.

A silent furnace of anxiety and dissatisfaction dressed in a white shirt, I sat before a computer monitor, my expressionless face reflected in a screen, the features made ghoulish by the glow of the monitor that I longed to smash my forehead into.

I was but one of many. Call us Legion.

I worked in a long room of many desks. Behind each desk sat a hunched, tense and mostly silent colleague. With an increasing regularity towards the end of my tenure, the woman at the neighbouring work station would expel a huge sob, and then declare, "Oh God," in a voice made thin and unstable by her misery. After each uncontainable episode she would sniff repeatedly and swallow noisily, then dab her eyes and nose with a tissue, before falling silent. No one looked at her during these episodes. We all knew that she was approaching the end of her consultation period and would soon receive the white envelope from the executives.

In my last days at the company, other than the sobs of the woman in the midst of an emotional collapse, who resembled so many others in the past, whose faces and names I had mostly forgotten, and beside the creak of the chairs, the predominate sound that arose from behind the other thirty-eight desks in the office was the incessant, clicking of fingers racing across dirty, plastic keyboards. I was reminded of termites or beetles, relentlessly chewing rotten wood, or burrowing in a mound of soil, somewhere sunless, sealed from the world behind wire fences on forgotten and forgettable waste ground. In fact, like the site of the industrial estate that housed the company.

Sometimes I would also become aware of the buzzing of the lights in the ceiling, as if they were broadcasting the ghostly monotones of the dead insects that littered the transparent plastic sheaths, beneath tubes emitting a sickly illumination. Outside the windows, the sky invariably resembled the smoke from an oil fire.

The office was a large rectangle, flanked on two sides by identical rows of glass-fronted cubicles. There were eight of these private work spaces allocated to the middle managers. The blinds were always closed and their offices remained in darkness. We never saw the managers enter or leave their offices. Some claimed that the offices remained empty unless a consultation period was under way, and that they had been deserted for years; others said the middle managers were forbidden to leave their offices while a single employee remained at his desk. I never knew what to believe, but I often sensed a presence behind the black glass and the drawn blinds; someone monitoring every message, phone call and open file on our screens. How else did they know so much about our work?

Up on the next floor of the building were the executives. We were never sure what they did, but they were never ferried to and from the company, like cattle, in public transport. They arrived and left the building in the black cars that were parked at a subterranean level. During the working day, they never left the executive floor. Their only face-to-face contact with the staff occurred during the consultancy period.

Many former colleagues whose names I have mostly forgotten now, and whose performances for the company became unsatisfactory, and were deemed incompatible with the company's brand values, were summoned into the glass cubicles of the middle management. After the consultations began in the cubicles of the middle managers, an employee would be called upstairs, and only once, to the executive floor. That meeting was always final. Following the exit interview, the employee would return to the office clutching a white envelope, while flanked by the building's security, to clear their work station. A replacement would be sitting in their chair the following morning and the redundant employee was never seen again.

Only the recipients of the white envelopes ever met the executives, but their departure was so conclusive and guarded that we were never able to ask them about the contents of the white envelope, nor what, or who, they had seen upstairs. Fraternization outside of work was forbidden. Those that somehow formed office romances quickly received the white envelope. Perhaps they held hands as they starved together *out there.*

We all lived in terror of the white envelope.

The momentum of the process that advanced a colleague toward the receipt of a white envelope was unstoppable. I worked in the office long enough to know that the consultation process could never be curtailed or even slowed, no matter the renewed vigour with which one worked. Earlier starts and later finishes were irrelevant. No matter the change in one's demeanour or aspect as one approached the office block, through the footpaths of the industrial estate, and walked up the cement stairs, or rode the lift to enter the spoiled-cream uniformity of the company premises, once the consultation process had begun, the white envelope would always find its way into a pair of trembling hands. I observed the process 213 times in fifteen years while I sat at my desk. Only one man, who I stopped making an effort to speak with, a long time before my own demise, and who reciprocated my indifference, outlasted me in the company.

Work was very hard to find in the city. We were fortunate to have those awful jobs. The alternative *out there* did not bear thinking about. We were professionals.

Towards the end, my end, I often found blood in a sink in the staff toilets. One of my silent, anonymous colleagues had been mutilating. There was often a trail of blood leading from a toilet stall to the sink area. I only looked inside the stall once and saw that the epicentre of the mutilation had not been flushed away. Swirls of black hair and a yellow, jelly substance floated in the bowl, surrounded by toilet paper and fresh blood. The mutilator wanted their mess to be found; they wanted a physical manifestation of their pain to be seen by the next people who used the facility. This was not uncommon. Like caged animals driven neurotic by uniformity and captivity, we often smeared the walls of the staff toilet with our matter.

I wondered, and not for the first time, if someone had also offered a pound of flesh, in ironic tribute, to the silent sterility, to the humming of the lights and the clicking of fingers on keyboards, and to the callous, inscrutable but unscrupulous executive, and to the near pointless endeavours that we were engaged in at our desks. Many years ago a woman even took one of her own eyes out with a letter opener. I didn't see the incident, but there was whispering for hours about how she was spirited away by security, soon after the incident, and dragged screaming down the stairs. There was more screaming outside the building and then silence.

Sometimes, when work was simply insufferable, I felt an urge to open my throat over a sink too, and to hold myself upright and to gush euphorically onto the porcelain, to beard myself in blood, to sacrifice and martyr myself in a way that would not be forgotten, at least not for a few days, while also punishing myself for my inability to escape the situation or change my circumstances.

About four weeks before my end, I returned to my desk after I had been contemplating this mystery colleague's self-destruction within a communal toilet facility, to read a new message in my inbox. A message that would not only change my life, but the world I had known. The company's internal communication service had delivered a message from middle management entitled CONSULTANCY PERIOD.

I had been anticipating the white envelope, but that did not prevent a stunned disbelief and a cold tourniquet of dread that reduced me to paralysis. But by the day's end, the shock had gradually eased into a heavy, fatiguing, though warm feeling, born of something deep-seated, wild and reckless. This might have been acceptance, or acknowledgement, and my response to what signalled the end of an apprehension that had sickened me for as long as I had worked at that company as an editor. It might also have signified a profound psychological fracture that rendered me irreparably broken, and unsure of my thoughts and actions thereafter. I still don't know.

The messages that had been coming in during the previous month, from my authors, must have precipitated my demise. My work had always been beset by problems, but never of the magnitude of that final month. I had become unable to think of a way of surviving a series of setbacks that had been the result of a long momentum of decline within my publishing responsibilities.

So traumatic was that day, I deliberately suppressed any thought of the grim future. I only allowed myself to think of the light that I kept hidden at home. Back then, in my darkest hours, my only comfort came from the *light*. My Reliquary of Light. And that night I knew that I must open that simple wooden box to gaze into what may have been the last ember of celestial light on earth.

Working alone, each editor in the company published at least one hundred books per year. The company kept all of the rights to the works of the authors and paid a competitive 7% net royalty. But, as all of our books retailed at ten pence, and because the retailer kept 60% of every ten pence sale, and because nearly all of our books were pirated anyway, I had been finding it increasingly hard to find and keep authors on my fiction lists. A fortnight before my consultancy began, I had been informed that my best author, a writer of mystery stories, had killed himself. He used to write a novel every eleven days and had produced half of my list during the last ten years of service. Despite his productivity and reasonable popularity, he was able to earn just enough to occupy part of the communal area in a block of flats, under a staircase, while feeding himself on sufficient soya and yeast products to remain alive and committed to his work within a cardboard shelter. Without leaving a note, or delivering his last commissioned work, he had leapt beneath a high-speed train in a place where this city joins with the next.

The news was catastrophic to my professional life and prospects, and was soon augmented by another heavy stroke of misfortune.

My second most productive and popular author wrote romances. All of her books featured executive tycoons, from the top one hundred corporations, who met lowly service industry workers, and then transformed the existences of these women into lifestyles of affluence and luxury that involved exotic destinations. Eventually these tycoons were unable to live without the heroines in these stories. Every single book the author had written featured, more or less, the same story, which I assumed was a sign of some undiagnosed mania. But her final seven novels each revealed even more worrying signs: the author was parting from the strict guidelines of my Flame of Passion imprint. Her last books began to feature graphic scenes of anal rape and cannibalism.

The author was one of the company's top performers and occupied a position on the front list, but she had suffered a colossal nervous breakdown around that time. She lived with her elderly mother in one room, near a chemical plant that produced chicken portions made from soya. The author was mainly supported by her mother's small pension, a tiny stipend in return for sixty years' service in a factory that led to the mother's blindness and infirmity from a respiratory condition.

Without those two authors, who had kept me in a job by producing nearly sixty of my scheduled titles in each year's catalogue, I could not see how I could possibly continue working as an editor for the company. It seemed the executives had arrived at the same conclusion. I had many other authors who filled the remainder of my lists, but they could only write around punishing work schedules, or around caring for elderly parents, and sometimes children at the same time, in dim and cramped lodgings.

The company was also embarking on a major crackdown on 'downbeat storylines.' Most of the fiction delivered to me had a tone of despair and misanthropy and was written from what seemed to be a bottomless well of exhaustion and depression. But I had been instructed by the management to reject any manuscripts featuring divorce, suicide, mental breakdown, assorted social ills (they supplied a list), and physical ailments (they supplied another list). Within the new guidelines that I was to follow, the language of our fiction had to be simplified further than it already had been, the novels needed to become shorter and more episodic. Description was to be treated as superfluous, unless absolutely necessary for the progression of the story "from A to B". Particular emphasis on the removal of "strangeness" and "imaginative excesses" was also included in the new editorial guidelines. All "authors [were] to be encouraged to focus on fulfilling the material aspirations of our many readers".

Most of the population was too poor, subliterate, ill, or fatigued to buy the ten pence books and had little or no interest in what we produced anyway. But from the 60% of the workforce that was employed, and from those retired at a subsistence level with leisure time, there were just enough readers to support the publishing industry. Because they had all been closed, there was no competition from book shops or libraries in the still functioning retail areas, so that also helped. All books were downloaded from the Rainforest Cloud, which had a 98% share of bookselling; this was a vast subscription service onto which four million new books were uploaded each year. My authors only contributed one hundred titles, and without my two top mystery and romance authors respectively, I knew I had become "unsustainable".

On my journey home on the day my consultancy began, within a crowded train carriage, I passed the usual landscape: busy motorways and carriageways, soya crops, apartment blocks built too close together, stunted, dirty trees, and piles of refuse. And I recalled my holiday the previous year, taken in one of the few places remaining on the coastline that was unsoiled by intensive farming, overdevelopment, industry and overpopulation. But on the evening the consultation commenced, I felt as I had done on my return from the coast.

For the holiday, it had taken me five years to save enough money to spend four days in a grubby caravan, but the views of the wind farms out at sea and the shoreline were spectacular, as were the vast sulphur sunsets. My return journey to the city from the seaside was much the same as my two-hour journey to and from the office, though stretched across half the country; the landscape, topography, and living conditions therein, gradually degrading into a greyish smear of tarmac, wires, cement, with only the flat and stifling uniformity of the soya crops offering any relief between the grim and dirty cities. By the time I reached my destination, my face was strewn with tears.

The train guard must have seen that reaction many times before. He said to me, "If you're going to top yourself, I can recommend the facilities under the viaduct. They're just behind the station on Gradgrind Street. You can find the best euthanizers in the huts by the scrapyard. But stay off the tracks." He must have been on commission because he gave me a card, offering potential suicides 'Unbeatable Rates.'

I lived in an overcrowded building in the outer suburbs. I shared a room with another man. My salary as a publishing professional did not allow me to live nearer the commercial districts, nor would it allow me much privacy at home. But at least there were only two of us in the room; it could have been much worse.

Our room was divided down the middle by an old curtain on a plastic rail. Each side of the plain room contained a small bed, a bedside table, chest of drawers and a wardrobe. These old and scuffed articles of furniture contained all of our possessions. But as soon as I entered the room, on the evening of the day that I was notified of my participation in the consultation process, I could see that there had been incursions from the other side of the curtain.

Like me, my roommate was childless and unmarried. He worked underground and did something dangerous in the construction of new subterranean housing. Unlike me, though, he was a chronic alcoholic and just as selfish, thoughtless and manipulative as the many other addicts that I had encountered in the city.

In that room we were unable to avoid hearing each other's every move, sigh and sob. Graham's drunken rambling could continue for hours. If he felt that I was not listening, he was prone to tear the curtain aside so that he could rant and spit into my face. When sober and hung-over, he was sheepish and pretended that these altercations had never happened. He also continually asked me for money. Often I would find evidence of his rummaging for valuables and money on my side of the room. The only item of value I possessed, I had concealed behind the skirting board where the wood had come loose beneath the headboard of my bed. Despite all that I endured at work and at home, and while travelling between those two reservoirs of misery, the idea of the Reliquary of Light not being in my life was the only thing that I considered completely unbearable.

When I returned home from the worst day at the office that I could remember, Graham was not in residence; I always counted small mercies whenever I encountered them. I peered around the curtain where it swayed near the entrance to the room, to make certain of his absence.

His side of the room had been reduced to an impenetrable jumble of unwashed clothes, rubbish and empty plastic bottles. His detritus made the curtain bulge and issued a terrible miasma of stale ethanol and male sweat. Whenever his mess seeped or protruded from beneath the fabric divider, I would kick it back under, and I did a lot of kicking in that room.

I retrieved the Reliquary of Light from where it lay hidden. By that point in my life, this object supplied my sole pleasure and purpose. But what the small wooden box contained was of far more significance than me, or any of my worldly concerns. It was of far greater importance than the entire city and all who lived within it. The Reliquary of Light was a receptacle containing a holy relic, a mere fragment maybe, but one that had its origins in the paradise belt. It was a splinter of the most intense and forgiving and transporting love. Its joy was instantly euphoric and carried a sign from another place that was far greater and infinitely more beautiful than the earthly prison in which we were all trapped. A priest I once knew, called Father Suarez, used to call our world "the greylands".

The Reliquary was given to me by Father Suarez too, in the days before he died of cancer. At the time of his demise, I was his youngest parishioner at the Temple of Inmost Light and of the Saintly Martyrs of the Smooth Field. The church is long gone now. Its consecrated ground and hallowed masonry were reused for a block of luxury apartments intended for executives. But before Father Suarez died, and before he saw all that he had maintained and administered demolished, he passed on the Reliquary to me, while telling me in a hushed and whispery voice that he had distilled the inmost light from the church and placed it within the box. I accepted the gift and thought him deranged from morphine; at the end, the disease had ravaged his small body and reduced him to a barely living skeleton. But that very evening, when I opened the innocuous wooden box in my room, I found myself down upon my knees, and weeping from the most intense joy.

In my deepest self, I knew in an instant that all of my troubles were irrelevant in some vast scheme that I instinctively understood but could not define. Language simply does not have the range nor depth to describe this light. As if from a distant place, and one filled with the most piercing and yet soft and gentle light, my entire being was suffused from a mere spark contained within the box. I felt weightless, unburdened. I knew that those who had loved me dearly until their deaths, were ever present and waiting in another place. Within that small wooden container was a tangible sign of sanctuary and salvation, hope, answers, comfort and love. The transmission of this knowledge was instantaneous and without need of my indulgence in any conscious reflection. A part of me, that I could not even remember, that had been ground down by my life and its pressures, would awaken in the presence of this scrap of light.

My relationship with the Reliquary was always instinctive and I knew not to overuse the receptacle. A few seconds' exposure was sufficient to make my spirit soar, for it to rise up and become shrived of its burden within that forever of white light and golden warmth. I also lived in constant fear of the light source depleting or vanishing. Over time I had noticed its rays dimming, so I preserved my interaction with the Reliquary for the most trying days, like that one, and for special occasions.

Long after I had closed the Reliquary during the evening following notification of my consultancy period, I lay upon my bed in a soporific state, entirely satiated in body, soul and mind. Tracks that my tears had made upon my face cracked when I smiled beatifically, and seemingly at some great and secret thing beyond the grubby, yellow ceiling of the room. But what I smiled at and acknowledged I do not know. It was ineffable and immanent.

Perhaps the world's then moribund religions once yearned for that very light. And so suffused had I been by what poured from that box to transport me to the borders of another place, where there is no time or suffering, that I barely heard Graham enter the room. His drunken stumbling was nothing to me anyway after I had opened the box; his dismal existence in this cold and unfeeling world remained far outside my private and lingering bliss.

"You pissed?' he asked, his grimy, bearded visage appearing like the face of prehistoric man at the entrance of a cave. "You is pissed," he added as a declaration of fact. His bloodshot eyes flitted in their sockets as his vision skittered about my orderly space. Like a rat seeking sustenance he was searching for evidence of the intoxicants that he would demand a share of.

"Go away," I said quietly, not wanting him to intrude and trample upon the last vestiges of the heavenly glow that was slowly receding inside me as the world reclaimed me, and the usual bustle of anxiety and preoccupation sought an insidious passage back inside my thoughts.

Graham ignored my request and continued to scrutinise my half of the room. He could barely contain himself from intruding further on those great, bemired feet.

"Will you piss off!" I roared at him.

He withdrew behind the curtain reluctantly and sat heavily upon his bed. But not soon enough; my experience of the heavenly light had been decimated by his very presence.

As I expected, I was summoned into one of the management cubicles the following day at work. As I rose from my chair and approached the nearest cubicle door, I noted a thin static of tension pass across the shoulders and bowed heads of my colleagues who sat nearest my desk. But no one in the office looked at me, the dead man walking.

I knocked on the door of the cubicle office and entered, as instructed in the message that had been waiting for me when I came in that morning at 8:30 a.m.

I took my seat behind the desk in the semi-darkness of the tiny office. I was the only person present. I could see a grey metal filing cabinet in one corner. The ceiling was of the same polystyrene tiles as the main office space, the floor tiled with linoleum squares the colour of the grey sky outside, at least whenever the black, toxic clouds dispersed from above the city.

The sole source of the faint light was produced by a dim and occasionally flickering desk lamp. There was nothing else on the desk beside a black telephone. I sat and waited, and waited. I checked my watch and realised that I had sat in silence for twenty minutes when a voice suddenly filled the room and seemed to drill into the marrow of my bones.

I flinched in my chair and gasped loudly, and then quickly became angry when I realised that this was an obvious management technique; to let apprehension and fear build within an interviewee, before startling them by the sudden breaking of the silence at an unnatural volume.

The voice was broadcast from the phone's speaker; a small grid built into the base of the phone that could enable conference calls. And the tone of the voice reminded me of an old ventriloquist dummy, or even Mr Punch: its sound was camp but screechy, its tone amused and insincere. I suspected it was a recording too, because the voice gave me no opportunity for me to respond at any point during the monologue. I was also unsure of the speaker's sex, but as I listened to the voice, I imagined the gaudily painted face of a horrible little man, who had once sat down and read from a card and recorded his voice onto a machine, somewhere upstairs in this building. I imagined the eyes in that face were alight with sadistic mirth, as the company's official spiel was recited.

Once the monologue concluded, it commanded, "Return to your desk!"

By the end of the interview I was at stage two of the consultation procedure. This boiled down to one more month's salary. With my savings, I could scrape through two more months in the room while searching for work, and then I would quickly fall into arrears in rent unless I found work quickly. It was doubtful that I would. All I knew was books and I had heard terrible things about the other two publishing companies that operated in the city, who were repeatedly shedding staff. Those were my only thoughts: my limited chances of survival.

The voice from the phone had also had the temerity to pitch the information to me as if I were being offered a great opportunity, as if I were there for a promotion or pay rise. "We offer you a competitive new opportunity outside of book publishing. . . ." Like all management missives imparted from the Communications Department on the executive floor, this was pure spin, and a rewriting of an employee's immediate future prospects, which amounted in my case to penury, homelessness and perhaps even starvation before the year's end.

The hideous, buzzing voice also recounted to me how proud I should be of the company's continuing success once I had left, as if the company should always be in my thoughts. "You will agree the future is brighter than it has ever been for our company. You will wish us the best as we maintain our global reach and success. You will be proud of your association at all times with our brand values for producing the highest standards in creative excellence." It went on and on praising itself, *the company*. There was a brief administrative acknowledgement of my service, but that was incorrect. They had my length of service at three years, but I had worked there for fifteen. My name was also mispronounced and my home address was incorrect. The records had not been updated in ten years.

Following the propaganda about the company's greatness, which made no mention of the authors whose work it soullessly and unscrupulously exploited for its own benefit, the pitch of the voice became faux solemn—in fact, I had a sense throughout the entire interview that the voice was mocking me and perhaps even the company whose virtues it extolled at such mind-numbing lengths.

During the final phase of the prepared speech, in which the voice deepened and emulated a mock sinister tone, I was regaled with many official warnings and threats of severe legal action should any information about my work, my authors, or the company, be made available to its competitors.

I was given a date for my exit interview on the executive floor. Leaving parties were forbidden, and the day following my exit the staff would "be vigorously urine tested for illegal substances and alcohol exceeding the safe limit imposed by the company for maximum efficiency and safety on company premises".

Finally I was offered a 'generous compensation package,' subject to VAT, in exchange for several donor organs from my own body that the company would sell on my behalf through its medical insurance division. In exchange for a kidney, bladder, length of intestine and both eyes, I realised that I would be able to pay for the room I shared with Graham for another five months, while blind and writhing in agony in my pathetic bed, unable to experience the light. I would of course refuse the offer, but shuddered at the thought of those in this city who had signed up to these corporate donor *phishing* packages out of desperation. I sometimes saw the victims that could walk, milling around the municipal dispensary that provided clean water and basic foodstuffs to the destitute and lame in return for handing out flyers, or wearing sandwich boards for the corporations.

When I returned home that evening, gravity seemed especially crushing, the air of the city fouler, the wind colder than usual, the traffic more belligerent. I found myself fumbling with my transport pass at the station. My movements were poorly coordinated. I frequently lost balance in the street as the weight of what awaited me, what I had effectively postponed for fifteen years, became heavier and better defined in my thoughts as a reality and no longer just a nightmare. People glared at me, workers tutted on the train. I believe they could sense my failure and looming ruin in the city. There was no empathy left here, only a fear for one's own demise and a struggle to keep on existing, while dead on one's feet and demoralised.

I should have been saving my money for the struggle ahead, but I treated myself to a carton of Thai-style soya and a small bottle of rum. I intended to consume them quickly and then huddle under my bedclothes with the Reliquary of Light. The light would reveal to me that this dilemma was a worldly trifle, insignificant in the vast scheme of things; my suffering and misfortune irrelevant compared to what awaited me in the afterlife. As I entered my room anticipating such a private moment of bliss and revelation, I was actually light-headed and tearful with happiness at the mere thought of that tiny receptacle of inmost light waiting behind the skirting board.

But the day was about to become truly intolerable and my position in this world insufferable.

I could see how thorough Graham had been this time while searching my half of the room. Mistaking my epiphany the previous evening for intoxication, because he knew of no distinction between the two states of being, he had ransacked my portion of space while I had been at work. After his search for drink or narcotic substances, he'd only made poor attempts at concealing his trespass because he did not fear me.

The drawers were not shut properly. My bed was at least one foot away from the wall on two sides. The door to my bedside cabinet was wide open.

Already ashen-faced and quivering, bloodless with a dread that was near suffocating, I fell to my knees and burrowed beneath the bed to the skirting board that hung loose from the plaster. The cavity in which I had sealed the Reliquary of Light was empty.

I scampered to the curtain and tore it aside. Whimpering, and by this time physically shaking, I scanned the debris piled up around my feet, and then began searching on my hands and knees through what resembled, and smelled like, a landfill.

I found the Reliquary upside down and empty of its light in a corner of the room. The lid had been left open for too long and the light of heaven had leaked away into Graham's soiled clothes. The very sainted wood of that box, that portal, was actually concealed beneath a shirt with yellowed armpits that stank of a farm animal. But the front of the shirt still cast a faint luminance, like that of a glow-worm, where the light had spilled and dispersed. Despite the stench in the fabric, I pressed the wretched shirt to my face in an attempt to savour the last dregs of heaven on this earth. And such was my despair and such was my rage that I believe they even heard my cries in the paradise belt that night.

Once I had finished the bottle of rum and once I had finished urinating onto Graham's greasy pillow, I went down to the communal kitchen and fetched the only sharp knife in the cutlery drawer. I returned to our room and unscrewed the light bulb from the ceiling. I emptied Graham's wardrobe onto the floor, then crept inside the cabinet and waited for him to come home.

Even after my toils that night, the gristly wet work of getting Graham disjointed and unspooled upon his bed, and then distributing his various parts into plastic bags, my rage did not abate. Having the keyhole into paradise blocked, and a peephole filled that had offered me a glimpse into a place where all of the answers awaited, and where love eternal burned like the middle of a star, was not a matter that I could forgive, nor react to reasonably. I felt as if dear Father Suarez's purpose on this earth had also been dribbled into the vomit-speckled carpet of a degenerate alcoholic's room. It was not my task to forgive such an act of desecration, but I believed it was my responsibility to address it, and I'd had a really bad day too.

The act of dismembering Graham represented something of an awakening for me. I already knew that little in this world even came close to matching the harmony, resonance and perfection of *the light*. But the gulf between the world and what was accessible to all through love, and a devotion to simply being better, had widened to such an extent that the only happiness worth aspiring to now was that of wealth and acts of status-completion to move one incrementally upward within an unjust and callous hierarchy. And yet the rules of the game were fixed; the receipt of the white envelope was inevitable and only the monstrous would ever be ascendant. Sadists and sociopaths had completely enslaved us and removed any chance of inner or spiritual life. The inmost light had been doused within a whole species. These are broad brush strokes, admittedly, but they were the beginnings of an epiphany that presented itself inside my imagination in vast, epochal, even monumental visions that night and thereafter.

Day by day, as the date of my exit interview approached, I slowly but fastidiously removed Graham's body and his belongings from the room after I returned home from work. I took up the carpet and gave away his furniture to the local offices of charities. I scrubbed the bare wooden floors, the walls and the ceiling and took down the curtain. I erased him. Upon my bedside table I placed the empty reliquary, arranging it upon a piece of starched white cloth. My memories of what once existed and issued from that box I cultivated, while I sat cross-legged before my shrine. I made notes. I used as much description and strangeness and imagination as took my fancy, and I revised and whittled and then polished these words endlessly through the cold nights until I had begun, albeit feebly, to capture some sense of that wondrous light and all that it promised and imbued in oneself.

Though his phone rang continuously at one point not long after I freed myself of his burden, no one ever came to the room to ask after Graham. I gave his phone to a vagrant in the street.

By the time of my final interview, in which I was to be given the white envelope, I had made the room a place of solace and reflection, Spartan but clean, though not without a sense of sacred mystery engendered by my simple shrine and by the words that I would recount before it each evening, after a simple meal taken with a glass of cold water.

The security detail remained outside the main doors of the executive floor, and informed me that they would wait for me until the meeting was concluded. They would be present to supervise the mortifying ritual of my clearing my work station before the eyes of the terrified and cowed staff, who would commit themselves to their useless endeavours with a renewed energy in order to avoid my fate and the white envelope.

I found the corporate process and the building just as crude, simple and horrid as I had ever done. But that morning I was no longer afraid. Since the very light inside the Reliquary had been taken from me, I had nurtured a sense of its celestial wonder inside myself that had grown daily. I had no doubt about the existence of this light, and somewhere better than *this*. At that point, I had also come to accept that I had nothing left to lose besides my life. My death, however, would only hasten my entry to what I had experienced in a fragment inside Father Suarez's little wooden box. Living without fear, and with my spirits engorged with a memory of that light, I began to experience a sense of weightlessness and freedom that I had never known before in my daily existence. Emancipated from the indentured slavery of the company, I was also free to pursue a new purpose, and by means as extreme as I deemed necessary on a case-by-case basis. As an agent of light, I had also decided to permit myself a certain monstrousness with any monsters that I encountered, unto my inevitable end.

Once the doors to the executive floor closed behind me, I dropped to my knees and slid two rubber wedges beneath the doors to prevent them being opened from outside.

I proceeded as instructed into the boardroom where I was greeted by a shrunken individual in an expensive suit. He wore a gingery blonde wig atop his withered face, and had lifts in shoes that were too big for his feet. A clownish gargoyle who reminded me of an ape. A fat woman with masses of glossy, coiffured hair, that was far too young for her bloated head, joined him. Her corpulent hands were encrusted with gaudy golden rings. They each had quick, rat-like eyes that glittered horribly, and each half-smiled odiously, as if trying to repress their mirth at my anticipated distress.

I understood immediately that their destruction of my career—and therefore my life as they saw it, because what else defined us now?— gave them great pleasure. But *this*, these things that sat at the end of the long table, and those others that they served in some other building that was also, no doubt, a pressure cooker of fear and intimidation, made us afraid? These gibbons cowed us in our multitudes across the grimy cities? It was not enough that their rapaciousness had poisoned the environment. We also subjugated ourselves to these things that walked on their hind legs in expensive clothes, in return for existences blighted by anxiety and privation. People carved and mutilated their own bodies in the bathrooms of these companies, and leapt under high speed trains because of *them*, these quick-thinking, fast-talking apes that contributed no light to the world.

As the little monkey in the suit chattered and taunted me in its corporate double-speak, and while the great pudding with its absurd, regal hair, nodded its head at key words and phrases like 'competitive,' 'added value,' 'rationalisation,' 'taking ownership,' 'repositioning,' and 'market share,' I fingered the paring knife in my pocket. At last the devil had a face, but its theology was as empty and meaningless as the lives it had reduced about itself.

But I held back on destroying them. Since the dismemberment of my roommate, I realised that my patience must become as deep and boundless as the light that I now served; my bestial compulsions and impulses must be tempered by thoughts of paradise. Returning some light to the world would only be possible if my incarceration or execution was delayed. I had much work to do before I left the stage.

At the end of its spiel, the little gibbon was clearly unsettled by my indifference, and my failure to writhe and to beg for mercy. The porcine creature that sat beside the monkey even became petulant as if I were guilty of an unprofessional affront by merely standing still and staring at them with revulsion. In that room they liked to witness terror and despair, not defiance, not disrespect.

"You must not open the envelope until you have left the company premises. Nor will you discuss its contents with your former colleagues. If you do, the future opportunity contained therein will be void."

He hurriedly concluded his prepared speech by repeating an offer for me to donate my vital organs in return for a miserable stipend. The creature was at its most loathsome at that point in the interview. I was no longer even sure that it was human as it sat there and offered to recycle my body. But I had no doubt that it had been sustained by the organs of others. How else could something so ancient, with a face that reminded me of dried fruit stretched into a human likeness by cosmetic surgeons, still live?

I tore open the white envelope before their horrified eyes. Such an act would have been unthinkable before my awakening in the very blood of the vandal of light, the thief, Graham.

The envelope, as I suspected, was empty. A representation of the future. This piece of empty folded-and-gummed paper served as a reminder of a world without human rights, the lightless consensus.

This was their final act of revenge on those who failed to generate enough capital to sustain the vulpine roles of the executives, that in turn maintained a status quo in which they were the sole beneficiaries. And we actually feared them. *Them!* It was time someone shone a simple, pure and bright light upon their faces.

I moved around the table as if to shake their hands. Such a manoeuvre had clearly not been attempted before and their bewilderment bought me time. Enough time to uncrown the apes. Simultaneously, I seized a handful of hair atop each executive's head and then tore upwards with all of my strength.

There were shrieks and both figures rose from their chairs like puppets that I had taken control of. The great, royal curls of the woman came away after a tearing sound reminiscent of sticky tape ripped from fabric, and I revealed the ghastly, grey wisps and the pasty scalp beneath its tresses.

The monkey's locks appeared to have been stitched into its remaining glandular hair around the ears, but the wig partly lifted like a carpet tile and the creature's little legs, that ended in those canoe-like shoes, skittered about the floor. When I released his donor-hair-piece, he fell and kicked out like an insect on its back in the soil. And in that moment of triumph, I realised that such things as the executive, and its most loyal acolytes, could only really be dealt with effectively through a rapid dehumanisation and physical destruction. Only after such a reign of cleansing rage would any light rise and then bathe a world freed from the entitled.

"I'll come back for your heads another time," I said, and left the boardroom, my body suffused with a light and energy that seemed to make me capable of raising and pitching great rocks through the tinted windows of the buildings that rose like cathedrals in the commercial districts.

As I left the building via the executive fire escape, I passed a private ambulance parked onsite that waited expectantly to perform extractions from my torso.

My first ten pence *Book of Light* has been a great success. Since it was published four years ago, another sixteen million books have been uploaded onto the Rainforest Cloud, so it took a while for the book to shine its solitary ray of light through that mass of wishful thinking and delusion. It took me three years of giving the book away for free, before it became sufficiently visible, to then gain its present and unstoppable momentum.

And while the *Book of Light* worked its way to the surface, and unto discoverability, I took to the streets and shared my message with any who would listen. The message was greater than me; it had been imparted to me from a higher source. The recalcitrant, the rude, and those I deemed so helplessly entangled in the hierarchy, and its sophisticated system of lies and false hope, were occasionally despatched by my own hand. I likened my wet workings to the smashing of false idols, or the destruction of grotesque puppets.

I found that others with nothing to lose were only too happy to engage in such acts of holy vengeance too; many even took responsibility for my excesses. But in prison, they found there was no greater opportunity to evangelise and recruit more soldiers of light, and those with greater skills and motivation, for the more direct and uncompromising side of our faith.

The acts of destruction and chaos attributable to *The Book of Light* swiftly led to it being banned, but its verses and cantos will never go away. They have been sprayed all over the city for one thing. And though brutal attempts to belittle and suppress it, generated from the highest levels of commerce and government, have been excruciating for the book's advocates at times, *The Book of Light* persisted orally and was evangelised by the multitudes of the put-upon, disenfranchised, dispossessed, exiled, imprisoned and left behind.

I had hoped for a slow and bloodless revolution, but the implementation of the *Light's* core tenets were inevitably crude at times. During the initial sackings of the luxury apartments, and of those giant monoliths of glass in the heart of the city, many died, and many continue to die as hell is consumed by the very rage that it created within its subjects. Once people realised that the pain should be projected outwards, and not bled into toilet bowls, and that we were only held in check by a few bewigged apes and self-crowned imposters, and for as long as we maintained our stamina for the promise of future light, great changes could be effected quickly.

I have no more control now of the dispersal of the book and its message, and the subsequent anarchy that it causes, than does the man whose foot has carelessly trodden upon a nest of ants. But out of destruction grows new light in the myriad shrines and temples that have spread through this city, first appearing anywhere from the many wretched blocks of flats to the garbage fires of the homeless who gather beneath the stars. There also remains a great and bloody wrangling between factions who vie for my favour, and who misinterpret my message of love, fairness, equality and justice. It is also hard to see my egalitarian vision amongst streets filled with so much broken glass, burned out cars and charred corpses, and particularly when all that one can hear in the city are the sirens, screams, the distant *crumps* of explosions and the clatter of small arms fire. But gradually things are simplifying and becoming clearer. When people ask me, "Where is this light?" I say, "Soon. Soon, my friend. Soon, you will have eyes to see this light."

To have gotten this far is the cause of much satisfaction to me as I sit in my little, plain room and continue to reflect before Father Suarez's small wooden reliquary. In the mornings I can peer down from my solitary window and observe the genuflections of the naked executives who have been found guilty of exploitation, and who are brought here in chains, smeared in their own excrement, at gun point, each day. And yet, alongside their daily debasement, I also receive news of how meritocracies and cooperatives are forming in the industries, and how the vast divide between the wealthy and the poor is narrowing. The enforced dispersal of hoarded wealth, I am told, has been like an explosion of light and hope about a blighted land.

The light itself remains curious in its absence, its source as ineffable as it ever was, its distillation proving impossible, but it is out there, somewhere, and inside all of us. Of that I must remain certain.

THE BLACK MASS

by Justin Isis

Mark Samuels reached a hand into the darkness to silence the shrilling of his mobile phone alarm and felt his reflexes pull him awake sharply, with no consideration for the vestiges of his disordered dreams. The room was still. A vague rose glow entered through the window. In a few moments Samuels had pulled back the sheets and was on the floor, engaged in his morning exercises: a hundred push-ups; a hundred sit-ups; fifty crunches, back bends, jack-knives and Russian twists; five minutes of shadowboxing.

The girl was up now, watching him. Samuels heard the click of her lighter and smelled acrid smoke rising to the ceiling; finishing his routine, he turned and gazed back at her, noting with approval the juvenile quality of her breasts, firm but not yet fully ripe. Her dark hair had been trimmed short and dyed a chestnut brown, and her eyes were wide and guileless. She had given her age as nineteen, but Samuels suspected this was an exaggeration. He smiled at her, and she said something that sounded like "gun" or "goon" with the intonation of a question.

"Gun? Couldn't have gotten one through immigration. Don't even carry one back home."

The girl shook her head, clearly frustrated. She took her own phone from the nightstand and fiddled with its electronic dictionary before handing it to him. Samuels glanced at the kanji characters before reading the translation.

"Oh, the military? No, love, I'm a horror writer. We're much scarier."

Samuels examined himself in the mirror. A light sheen of sweat had formed on his flesh, highlighting its clearly defined musculature. His natural stoutness had been conditioned through discipline into the bearlike build of a heavyweight boxer. A shaved head completed the impression of clean masculine strength. He was now older than Poe and Lovecraft had been when they died, but in contrast to the sickly Americans, Samuels's body was what the fanzine *Ghorla* had termed "a pinnacle of physical achievement." An Idealist in several senses, he liked to think that the real pinnacle lay ahead of him, some Olympian summit of training ever out of reach. He had never believed in the myth of the "sick men of literature." Only a man in the prime of his health had the strength to truly gaze into the dark places of the universe. Where the sick men had turned away, curtailing their visions to mere glimpses of cosmic terror, Samuels kept his gaze focused, producing not just sketches but comprehensive maps of the abyss.

The girl—Yuka or Yuko, he couldn't remember—rose from the bed and placed her arms around him. He ran his hand through her hair in a manner that would almost have been paternal were it not for the conflicting evidence of their clothes strewn across the floor. Samuels knew men his age who used Viagra and Cialis, but his faculties had never been in need of artificial aid. Routine kettlebell exercises had strengthened and lengthened his thrusting—he doubted whether many teenage boys had the same titanic endurance—while the regular consumption of broccoli, oysters and other zinc-rich foods kept his testosterone high. Perhaps too high, he reflected, remembering the eight used condoms in the trash bin.

Samuels retrieved his trousers and sky-blue Paul Smith shirt from the floor, located an iron in the closet and tended to his clothes. Once dressed, he took a bag of tobacco and some rolling papers from his briefcase. In a few moments he had produced a thin cigarette. As he smoked, he performed an inventory of the room and eventually located his tie behind the trash bin. He stood, ground out the cigarette and completed a quick Windsor knot. The girl had pulled a sheet around her and was repeating something that sounded like "matte," and then a word which could only be "shower."

"Sorry, love," Samuels said. "No time, lots on the agenda. Here, have a book."

He took from the briefcase a red softback volume with a Baphomet pentagram on the cover: a copy of *Black Altars*, his second collection.

"Bit of a rarity, this. Not my finest moment. But you can't read it anyway, can you?"

Samuels found a pen next to the television, signed the book and handed it to her. While she was still poring over it, he made his exit. He heard her calling to him just as the door closed behind him, muffling her voice.

On his way to the elevator he took in the unusual frames of the doors: arched, like those of a church. Ironic, Samuels decided, given that he was now on his way to Mass. The hotel's details, which he had been too drunk to notice the night before, now struck him as superbly grotesque; the yellow plastic chandeliers and vermilion wallpaper were clearly intended to evoke a European castle or manor estate, but were too scrupulously artificial to be anything but a kitsch parody. As he waited in front of the elevator a nearby door opened and a couple emerged: a suited geriatric with mottled skin and a young woman with aquamarine hair and fishnet stockings, who on second glance appeared to be a transvestite. The couple stood at a respectable distance from him in silence until the elevator arrived.

"Decor's bloody gothic," Samuels said as he stepped inside and moved to the back so the couple could enter. The habit of speaking aloud sometimes came over him in foreign countries, even when those around him were unlikely to respond. "Could set a story here, couldn't you? Horror of the Love Hotel. Forbidden Mysteries of Interior Design."

As he had expected, the couple ignored him. When the elevator arrived at the ground floor they exited quickly, tossing their key to the attendant behind the counter, who was hidden behind a glass window. Curious, Samuels slowed down and glimpsed a crone with a face like a faded tombstone. He took out his Galaxy S7 phone and made a note to use her in a story.

Outside, he found himself in a sloping alley filled with hotels similar to the one he had just left. Some of their facades were minimal, businesslike; others bore elaborate neon signs, the lettering now faint in the early morning light. Groggy-looking couples were emerging from the exits, eager to be on their way. A few solitary figures dotted the edge of the street, smoking cigarettes and staring into space: flotsam cast up by the night. Samuels walked downhill until he eventually freed himself from the maze of hotels and rejoined the thoroughfare leading back to Shibuya Station. The sky was clear and the air warm, but he knew from yesterday that the heat would soon rise and hang above him like an oppressive cloud, a dense humidity trapped by the endless towers. Tokyo in August did not agree with him, he decided; it lacked the rain and modesty of an English summer.

When the station came within view he hailed a taxi and showed the driver a printed page of directions to the Catholic church in Roppongi. Fifteen minutes later he stepped out and joined a modest stream of parishioners walking through the doors of the Franciscan Chapel Center. They were mostly Japanese, but he noted a number of Westerners as well, most of them in tourist clothes, looking oblivious and slightly malnourished: the usual crowd of pale expatriates he had encountered in Mexico, Egypt and the other countries whose names crowded the pages of his passport.

Samuels found space in a pew at the back and settled in for the service. The priest's voice had an impressive range, but since Samuels could not understand the Japanese, he found himself paying more attention to the man's gestures, and could not help noting his somewhat mechanical performance and brief, perfunctory homily. During the Liturgy of the Word he found his thoughts drifting to a new story he was planning, a retelling of Machen's "The White People" from the perspective of the supernatural beings whose presence the original story had adumbrated so fearfully. He took out his phone and typed in a handful of notes before he noticed the parishioners next to him glancing over in reproach. He forced himself to turn his gaze back to the altar.

Not for the first time he questioned the wisdom of the Second Vatican Council in allowing a vernacular Mass. The eternal verities demanded an equally eternal, timeless language, one of sonorous phrases and invocations expressing the mysteries of the Word made flesh. And in a more profane sense, he supposed, capitalism, despite its numerous obscenities, had a lesson for the Bishop of Rome: why, when he could walk into any city in the world and order a McDonald's hamburger within ten minutes, was it so difficult for him to find a Latin Mass? Only when the Liturgy of the Eucharist moved his thoughts to the prime Mystery did he feel an intense and untrammelled satisfaction. When it was over he left quickly, despite the attempts of a few parishioners to engage him in conversation.

Their English was passable, but he attended Mass for the sacraments, not to socialise.

Another taxi took him to Shinjuku, where the day's business awaited him in two hours at the Kinokuniya Bookstore. He wandered through the station in search of breakfast and, deliberately avoiding the nauseous green logo of the nearby Starbucks, entered a cafe called Dotor. After a bacon and egg sandwich and two cups of black coffee, he decided it was time to start drinking; he would need at least a few shots in him to tolerate the book signing. Samuels had depleted his flask of whiskey the night before, but a visit to the station's 7/11 furnished him with a fresh supply. Japan, he had been pleased to discover, was unconcerned with public drinking; walking to the hotel in Shibuya he had seen businessmen passed out in the street like common indigents. He had noted also the tolerance for public smoking, another mark of an advanced civilisation.

Restocked and fortified, Samuels made his way to the bookstore. He was greeted at the entrance by a delegation from Kodansha, where a new imprint, Kaigai Hora, had just brought out a translation of *The White Hands and Other Weird Tales*, his first collection. Samuels's writing had come to the attention of the publisher when one of his stories, 'A Question of Obeying Orders', had been included in a bulk anthology of foreign horror and, reimagined in a Japanese wartime setting, been made the basis of a successful film. Samuels had been unimpressed with this production, which departed significantly from his story, but it was difficult for him to argue with the money and greater exposure it had brought him.

A woman in a navy blue suit stepped forward and extended her hand. "Mr. Samuels? I'm Rioko Tomita. I'll be interpreting for you today."

Samuels looked at her. Slender and pale, she was at least a head taller than her two colleagues—almost his own height. He supposed she was in her mid-twenties, although she bore the professional air of someone several years older. Her long black hair was tied back in a ponytail, and a light coating of pink lipstick highlighted her small, finely-formed mouth. She spoke English with the faintest trace of an American accent, which Samuels found moderately offensive, but was willing to overlook.

"Nice to meet you, love."

Rioko introduced the others: Mr. Hasegawa from the marketing division, sleek-haired and smiling like a film actor; and Mr. Miura, the translator, a tiny young man who resembled a prematurely-aged librarian. Hasegawa greeted him with a bow and a loud good morning, while Miura only bowed and nodded. They proceeded inside the building, where a modest crowd had already formed, and took up position at a table laden with copies of the translated collection. Japanese books, Samuels noted, seemed mostly to be disappointingly small, fragile-looking paperbacks: bonsai editions, fit for a man's front pocket. The collection was no exception, but sported a cover which, though it had no connection to the stories he had written, was at least suitably macabre. It depicted a young woman's head impaled on a spike, missing its eyes and nose and hideously bleeding from the wounds, the mouth open in an unnatural rictus. A swarm of transparent, disembodied faces hovered around it like ghostly flies.

Hasegawa began speaking to the crowd, while Rioko, seated next to Samuels, interpreted for him.

"We are very pleased to welcome Mark Samuels to Tokyo. Mr. Samuels is regarded by discerning readers as the finest living writer of weird fiction. His stories have already been translated into numerous other languages, and he has inspired writers as diverse as John Mundy and James Champagne. Closer to home, Keigo Nishino cites him as an influence. He has his own international appreciation society, the Friends of Mark Samuels, and a well-trafficked website, Mark Samuels Online."

Samuels held up a finger to interrupt. "The discussions there are less focused on me than you'd think. Too many shut-ins and undergraduate philosophers posting nonsense about unreadable Edwardians and American detective shows. They don't even have the good taste to include pornographic ads."

Hasegawa continued. "Hippocampus Press has recently announced the impending publication of *Black Bowers of Creation*, Devin Thomas's study of Mr. Samuels's writing in light of the psychological theories of Jung and Lacan. Also in the works from Eibonvale Press is *Touched by the Hand of Mark Samuels*, a book of personal recollections of Mr. Samuels by numerous well-known writers. Finally, Snuggly Books has finalised the table of contents for *Marked to Die: A Tribute to Mark Samuels.* On the less professional side, the anonymous writer behind the Internet handle WereFox93 has just posted the sixth instalment of her popular serial *Markitty: Friendship is Magic*, which details Mr. Samuels's adventures with a time-travelling and very hungry Ann Radcliffe as they ride on flying unicorns."

"I'd rather that weren't discussed," Samuels said. "And I don't approve of that tribute anthology either, which seems like a transparent attempt to profit from my name. Apparently they're even using me as a character. Some originality would be nice."

"Now on sale from Kaigai Hora, Kodansha's new foreign horror imprint, we present *Shiroi Te No Kanari Kowai Dekigoto: The Considerably Frightening Incident of the White Hands*. Translated by Hayato Miura, who has previously brought us the works of Jincy Willett and Nell Freudenberger, this British Fantasy Awards-shortlisted collection is sure to inspire a tingling metaphysical dread that will disrupt your everyday routine. Now, I leave it up to Mr. Samuels to address you in his own words."

Samuels scanned the crowd, most of whom appeared to be unemployed layabouts lacking any discernible upper-body strength. "Weather's muggy as fuck," he said. "Good of you all to come. I don't know what the horror scene is like here but it can't be much worse than in Britain. You lot seem to like my stories, so thanks for funding my vacation. Any questions?"

There was a brief silence, until an obese man at the front of the crowd stepped forward. A plaid jumper had been tied around his waist, and his white T-shirt was soaked in sweat. He spoke with a whining voice that seemed too young for his heavily-lined eyes. Samuels turned to Rioko as she explained the question.

"Where do you get your ideas?"

"My arse?" Samuels said, and held up his hand in front of Rioko to stop her from interpreting. He spoke Spanish and some French, but could not imagine switching between languages at her lightning speed. He paused. "I don't know . . . they just come to me, don't they?"

The next question was from a middle-aged woman with a leporine face and oversized black glasses that seemed to have come in and out of fashion multiple times without her noticing. She spoke almost too quietly to hear, with much apologetic nodding of her head.

"Your stories are too frightening for me to read to the end," Rioko interpreted. "If I continue reading, I begin to cry like a child. Then, I lose hope in everything. Is it okay for me to stop reading halfway through?"

Samuels considered the question for a few moments before replying. The woman was looking down, unable to meet his gaze.

"It's not okay," Samuels said at last. "I took the time to write them . . . the least you can do is finish them."

The woman nodded several times in quick succession, chastened, a deep frown furrowing her features.

"What horror writers from the past have influenced your work?" an intense-looking young man asked next.

"It's difficult to say. You could mention Poe, Machen, Lovecraft, certainly. But did they influence me or did I influence them? There's been a lot of talk about 'retrocausality' recently. And you know what Borges said about Kafka and all writers creating their predecessors. A few weeks ago I was reading 'The Masque of the Red Death' and thinking, I could have written that. And maybe, in a way, I did. Think about that."

Silence descended for a few moments, until a young man and woman stepped forward. Samuels guessed from their clothing that they were Americans, although he supposed they could as easily have been Canadians or Australians. So he was disappointed when the young man opened his mouth and exposed himself as an Englishman. Pale and spindly, he was wearing a deep-cut white V-neck with an unnecessary cashmere scarf, skinny jeans cut off at the knees and scuffed, grey racing shoes. His partner was an unathletic-looking girl in an oversized blue hoodie with the Batman logo emblazoned on it in lurid yellow. Her face, free of cosmetics, was marked by a snakebite lip piercing. She wore a Supreme baseball cap with a flat brim, and a fringe of dyed red hair hung over her eyes, which were hidden by vintage pink Cazals.

"Um, yeah, I have a question," the man said. "In your interviews you've alluded to your Christian faith. How do you reconcile cosmic horror, which is founded on Lovecraft's eliminative materialism, with any kind of belief in a Supreme Being? Particularly a Catholic one, as opposed to some kind of 'blind idiot god'? Don't you think the fifth of Aquinas's Five Ways is basically the deist 'divine watchmaker' argument made by William Paley, with a needlessly anthropomorphic slant?"

Samuels smiled. From the couple's age and appearance he had expected something like this. It could almost have been a cartoon in a Victorian periodical: the Nemesis of Puerile Atheism, an orphaned puppy with upturned eyes and searching paws begging attention and acceptance. No matter how many times he kicked it into oncoming traffic, it returned, maimed and limping, still feebly gnawing at his ankle.

"Nice try, mate. But that's not what Aquinas was saying at all. More importantly, no serious person needs rational arguments to determine their relationship with the divine, any more than they'd require them to know that chips go well with salt and vinegar. If you're even trying, you're too much of a eunuch for me to waste time with. Next question."

The questions continued for a time, most of them inane. Eventually Samuels was reduced to signing books. At one point a primary school boy mistook him for the Big Show, a professional wrestler he had never heard of. When Samuels corrected his error, the boy tossed the book aside in disgust and ran off. Finally the crowd dispersed, and Samuels made a show of checking his watch while glancing pointedly at Hasegawa and Miura.

"Looks like that's all," he said. "These things always exhaust me. What say we cut out early?"

Rioko had a brief exchange with Hasegawa in Japanese.

"We're supposed to stay for another twenty minutes," she said. "I'm sorry, Mr. Samuels. The turnout isn't as great as we'd expected . . ."

Samuels took out his flask, swigged from it, and offered it to her. She shook her head.

"Call me Mark, yeah?" he said. "Surprised anyone turned up at all."

"Have you enjoyed Tokyo so far?"

"'Course I have. Last night I went out in that . . . Shibuya it's called, innit? Had a few drinks with some Australians, then wound up at a disco. Not my thing, really, but it wasn't too bad. Ended up meeting one of my fans. I was so bloody knackered from the flight I would have slept in the gutter, but I ended up in that big hill in Shibuya, you might know where it is."

Rioko's expression was unreadable. "If you like, we could show you around Asakusa in the afternoon. There are a number of famous temples and shrines in the area."

Samuels glanced at Hasegawa and Miura again, neither of whom were paying attention. The translator appeared to be sleeping while sitting up straight, eyes closed and hands folded behind his back.

"Look—athose two are a bit dire, aren't they?" He picked up a copy of the translated book. "I mean, he's only gone and given it a bloody nonsense title, hasn't he? 'The Considerably Frightening Incident' . . . s'pose that sounds better in your language, does it?"

"Mr. Miura is renowned as one of our foremost translators . . ."

"Sure he is, doesn't mean he's any good. Oh well, long as it shifts the old units, right? Anyway, can't be much fun hanging around them all day."

Rioko restrained enough of a smile for Samuels to know the remark had connected.

"I'm sure you're capable of giving me the grand tour," he said. "But I think that would be pretty boring for both of us. We could always go to my hotel—it's a nice one, the Hyatt. Best deal I ever got from a publisher, really. We could order room service and kick back."

Rioko now smiled. "Sounds good, but I think I know where that might lead. I appreciate the offer but I just got out of a pretty heavy relationship and I'm kind of in a weird place right now, so . . ."

"No worries. You'll at least let me treat you to lunch, then. Show me somewhere nice, will you? I need something with meat and vegetables. None of this raw fish and bits of rice, yeah? Proper food."

"We were thinking of taking you to a yakiniku place in Naka-Meguro. Barbecued meat, vegetables, all kinds of drinks . . ."

"Sounds good, but we don't need Mr. Slick and Considerably Frightening there dampening the mood. I never get on with translators and publicity types. You could bring some friends if you want though—anyone normal, yeah? I'm always up for meeting interesting people."

"It might be difficult. . . . All three of us are supposed to be with you at all times."

"I'm sure you can work it out with them. Hang on love, just a minute—"

Samuels had noticed a man approaching the table: perhaps a late arrival for the signing, although the man's appearance immediately put him on guard. Tall and gaunt, his grey suit was covered with dark, damp patches. Sweat drenched his skin, which was understandable, Samuels supposed, given the heat outside, except that the man's features seemed almost tubercular: pinched and pale, wasted. His age was impossible to determine, but he was clearly in poor health, and looked to have been so for a long time. While the homeless men and women Samuels had seen in Shibuya seemed relatively clean and hardy, this man was the opposite, an impression sharpened by his ghastly attempt at maintaining a dignified attire. Whatever stained his suit could not have been mere sweat; the dark patches on the blazer looked closer to grease or slime. As he watched the man approach at a faltering pace, Samuels thought of the word *contaminated,* which he supposed was the writer in him talking. Even so, he felt an instinctive revulsion.

"You all right there, mate?" Samuels asked. Despite the man's slow pace, he was moving towards the table with distressing single-mindedness, and his gaze was directed at Samuels's own. As he came closer, Samuels heard him mumbling to himself, a steady repetition of syllables more like an invocation than any normal greeting. Hasegawa said something to him, but the man ignored him.

Samuels held up a copy of the book as if it were a protective charm. "You wanted one of these, yeah?"

Rioko, clearly disturbed, attempted a translation, but the man clamped his hands on the table and stared ahead at Samuels. He bared his teeth, which were pale yellow and encased in shrivelled gums. His lips were a bleached purple.

"*Kurokabi no jidai,*" the man said. A trail of saliva descended from his mouth. He swatted the book away and spat out a volley of words. When Hasegawa stood and tried to take his arm, the man swung his fist again and connected with Hasegawa's temple.

Samuels was dimly aware of Rioko and Miura getting to their feet and darting away from the table. The man staggered around to the other side and reached out for him.

"What are you trying to say?" Samuels asked, backing away.

The man started to speak and then doubled up, wracked by a fit of coughing. As he struggled to move forward, the fit became a full body convulsion. Their eyes met once more, and Samuels moved quickly to dodge a blast of black vomit. The man's eyes rolled in their sockets and he collapsed, striking the floor with the sound of a cracking skull.

Samuels knelt and felt the man's pulse fading to nothing. Rioko and Miura had returned with two security guards, one of whom was on the phone. The other guard motioned for Samuels to move away from the body, which he did. As he stepped backwards he noticed that the pool of vomit was filled with small, slug-like lumps of matter.

The two guards took turns applying CPR. Samuels did not envy them the close contact with the body—or corpse, he supposed, since their efforts were having no apparent effect.

After fifteen minutes had passed, emergency workers arrived and took over with a defibrillator. The guards moved everyone away from the scene and took down statements.

"The way he passed out . . . it was like he'd just been switched off. Stroke or what have you. Never seen anything like it," Samuels said.

The guards conferred with Hasegawa and Rioko. Samuels craned his neck to get a view of the body. The emergency workers were continuing their revival efforts, but he suspected they would soon be taking the man to the morgue.

"We're very sorry about this," Rioko said. Samuels saw that she was shaking. Miura seemed dazed, his eyes fixed wide open. Only Hasegawa retained his composure, despite the bruise on his temple.

"Not your fault," Samuels said. "Are you all right?"

"I'm fine," she said. "Thank you."

Samuels took his briefcase from under the table and gestured for her to accompany him a short distance away from the others. Rioko said something to Hasegawa and then followed him to the entrance.

"Listen, Rioko—what was he saying? I need to know."

Rioko looked in the direction of the body and shook her head.

"Just nonsense . . . nothing that made any sense. He was crazy. . . ."

"Exact phrases, love."

"I don't want to remember it . . ."

"I'm sorry. . . . I know this is upsetting. But it's important."

Rioko thought for a moment. "He kept saying something about 'The Age of Black Mold' . . . it was nonsense. Something about the future. Prophets, a new age, religious things. What you always hear from crazy people. That's all I can remember."

Samuels nodded. "Black mould? Are you sure?"

"Yes. Why?"

"I've written about something like that before. The black mould. In fact, that was one of the stories that I heard your Mr. Miura translated for a magazine. It came out a year or so back, if I remember right."

"You think he read it?"

"He must have done. Lots of crazy people out there. Still, I got a strange feeling when he came in. Before he came in, almost. Kind of a buzzing headache. Did you feel anything like that?"

"Yes. I thought it was just stress."

"Can you ask them if they felt it too?"

Rioko checked with her colleagues. Both of them had felt headaches coming on in the moments before the man had approached the table. Miura had felt so unpleasant that was forced to close his eyes and wait for the waves of nausea to pass over him.

Samuels took Rioko's hand and pressed something into it.

"Got these from his pocket when I was checking his pulse."

Rioko opened her hand and saw a bundle of three business cards, all different.

"Mr. Samuels, um, Mark, you shouldn't have taken these. I mean . . ."

"They were loose in his pockets. Practically falling out, I should say." He smiled. "Anyway, take a look at that one. What's that all about?"

Samuels pointed to one of the cards, which depicted a winged stone head, perfectly white, vaguely Egyptian and vaguely Art Deco, on a field of solid black. The rest of the card was crammed with kanji and website links.

"These characters are difficult to explain . . . um . . .'The United Brothers and Sisters of the Coming Eon'. Eon, or . . . era? Age? I've never heard of it. It sounds like some kind of cult."

"Sounds like M. Valdemar back there was wrapped up in it. What about the others?"

Rioko flipped through the cards. "They look like normal business cards. This one's from a brewery worker, Yuji Shimura." She examined the card's picture and looked in the fallen man's direction. "It's him, I think. And this one's from a sculptor, Eijiro Okamura. It gives the address for his store."

"Lovely," Samuels said. He spoke more quickly as he noticed Hasegawa moving towards them. "Listen, Rioko. I appreciate your help with this, really. There's something not right here and I'd like to look into it more, so I'll need your help with the language."

"I'm not sure what you mean. But if you're worried about something, we can talk to the police. The station isn't far from here."

"Yeah, see, that's not it at all. There was something wrong with that man, and he was coming straight for me, knew who I was. I take that personally, yeah? Think of it this way. You're supposed to be showing me around anyway. But I'm allergic to temples, except for the RC kind. So just think of it as a different kind of tour."

"What do you want me to do?"

"No time now to talk now. Let's meet up later on. Alone, yeah?"

Rioko frowned, resentful of the imposition. But her hesitation to answer firmly in the negative suggested a repressed curiosity. She looked over at the fallen man and then back at Samuels.

"Meet me in two hours outside Ebisu Station," she said. "The West Exit."

Hasegawa had reached them. "You are okay?" he said, in English.

Samuels clapped a hand on his shoulder. "Bit out of sorts from all that—think I'll pop back to the hotel for a lie-down. Thanks for all the help, hope the book takes off."

Without waiting for a response he turned and left the bookstore.

Outside, in the sun, he dipped into the flask again and considered looking for a bar, although with the surfeit of convenience stores and their alarmingly comprehensive liquor sections, he supposed there was no need. He rolled himself a cigarette and walked back to the hotel, where he took a cold shower, changed his clothes and ordered coffee and sandwiches. After another cigarette on the balcony, he returned to Shinjuku Station. Ebisu was four stops away on the Yamanote Line, which seemed inordinately crowded, given that it was only early afternoon. Commuters in suits jostled against teenagers in neon punk clothing, and a number of collapsed-looking senior citizens occupied the priority seats. Samuels noticed several other foreigners, but most of them were hunched over their smartphones and they paid him no attention.

When he arrived at the West Exit, Rioko was already waiting.

"I can't stay long," she said. "We'll just go to a cafe, is it all right?"

"Sure, long as it isn't Starbucks."

They walked into Ebisu and entered a cafe whose logo was a picture of a croissant in the center of an orange circle.

"Mr. Hasegawa wasn't pleased," Rioko said. "I told him you weren't comfortable having him around. He made some . . . unpleasant comments."

"Did he, now? Saucy git. Well, he can mind his business, can't he?"

Rioko ordered a flat white and Samuels ordered black coffee. They took up seats in the smoking area. Samuels took out his tobacco and rolling papers and offered her a cigarette, which she declined.

"So, Rioko, tell me about yourself. I'm sorry if this seems a bit personal. I always like to get straight to the heart of things."

"I was born in Tokyo," she said. "My father is in trade, so I spent time in America when I was a child."

"I'm sorry to hear that."

"No—for me it was freedom. I went back as a college student and lived in New York for three years. I used to work in finance, but it was too much for me. I wanted to become a journalist after that, but I joined Kodansha instead, since it gave me a chance to use English. The department I work in—"

"Too many facts, I'm bored already. Something personal!"

Rioko laughed. "There's a lot of pressure here to settle down early, but it's not for me. I like staying busy. And I have a bad temper."

"This bloke you've broken off———"

"I don't want to talk about it. There are a lot of narcissists in the dating scene here. That's all I'm going to say."

"And these knobs at work, Slick Boy and Frightening Incident— they're not all like that, are they?"

"Company workers here are very serious. There's a lot of unpaid overtime and lots of mandatory drinking parties. But they're not as fun as they sound. Mostly we have to pour drinks for the boss and listen to him sing karaoke."

"And I thought British yuppies were bad. Have you read much horror?"

"I haven't read fiction for a few years. But I read a lot when I was younger. I was more into alternative comics, Daniel Clowes, things like that . . . social horror, maybe?"

"Anything social is horrible if it's the wrong people. By which I mean almost everyone at every workplace I've ever been at."

Samuels lit a cigarette he had been rolling and blew a puff of smoke against the glass screen separating the smoking area from the rest of the cafe.

"I was never the professional type," he continued. "Couldn't even stand school, barely ever went. No, for me it was Golden Age hip-hop. Beats from the streets. This was back in the '80s—I started a crew with young Quentin S. Crisp from Devon. We called ourselves Mark E Dope and Qabalistic Q."

Rioko looked at him. "You were really in a hip-hop group?"

"Oh, it was grand at first. We did small shows all over the place, battled other MCs, brought in some dancers. We had our own tags and wrote them everywhere. The four elements, right? Of course, the scene was so much smaller then. Eventually we borrowed money and recorded a demo tape. It was called *Remember Y'All Got One Ball*."

"What happened?"

Samuels spat out the remains of his cigarette.

"Simple. The Beastie Boys stole my ideas. The layered samples and call and response rhymes. Irreverent, but technical. We were going to do it British style—and then *Licensed to Ill* broke. I've never been able to forgive those bastards—someone must have slipped them a copy of our tape. No labels wanted to hear us after that, said we were copycats. But that fucking Ad-Rock and his mates were the ones copying us! Wankers. Utter wankers."

"That's . . . terrible," Rioko said.

"No, love, it's ancient history. I won't bore you with things that happened before you were born. You've still got those cards, yeah?"

Rioko took out the business cards and placed them on the table.

"Good," Samuels said, taking his laptop from his briefcase. He pointed to the card displaying the winged stone head. "We're going to start with that one."

He connected to the cafe's wi-fi and handed the laptop to Rioko.

"I want anything you can find on this group, the United Brothers and Sisters or whatever it's called. Check their website, and see if there's anything about them in the Japanese media."

Rioko clicked through to Google Japan and was soon navigating a sea of text. Samuels caught sight of what he took to be the group's official site, a crude single page-layout that reminded him of sites from the earliest years of the Internet. There were occasional English words interspersed with its characters, such as "future" and "avatar", alongside a series of abstract paintings: dark colour fields and geometrical patterns.

"Looks bland," Samuels said.

"Hold on, let me finish reading."

Rioko opened several new browser tabs and continued the search on major news websites, flipping back and forth between them and the group's site.

"Okay," she said. "The group was founded by Takahiro Aso. His followers call him 'The Aleph'. He was a normal company worker until a car accident five years ago. While he was in the hospital he had some kind of mystical experience. He claims to be a 'spiritual scientist' and Buddha, or 'World Teacher'."

"What does the group believe?"

"It seems pretty vague. They keep talking about 'The Human Communion', which sounds like their idea of Heaven. The members say Aso can give them special powers, turn them into angels."

"Any press?"

"Not much. They seem very reclusive. There are a few negative reports." She flipped to one of the tabs. "This one's from a former member who used to live with them in their commune up in Saitama. He mentions their rituals being degrading . . . blood and other kinds of fluids . . . and former members dying soon after leaving the group. But there didn't seem to be any direct connection. They just got sick and none of the treatments worked."

Samuels picked up one of the business cards. "Our friend Mr. Valdemar here didn't look very healthy either." He picked up another card. "And this other chap, the sculptor, Okamura. I think it's time we got in touch with him. This is his number here, yeah? We can call him on your phone and then—"

He stopped as he became aware of two individuals standing close by. Rioko had noticed them already, a young man and woman who had walked over from the back of the smoking section. The former attempted a tentative greeting in Japanese. He was wearing what Samuels took to be neo-mod clothing, and what Rioko recognized as the standard garb of a university student: layered clothes, a thin and buttoned-up pinstriped shirt beneath an equally thin grey cardigan, and cuffed houndstooth shorts that came to just above his knees. His clothes were dry and spotless despite the weather outside.

The girl was different, and seemed almost to be a member of a subculture, except that her clothing lacked the overt contrivance of a true Goth or Gothic Lolita, even as the muted colours and intricate lacework of her blouse suggested both. She wore a ruffled miniskirt with black knee-high socks and shiny black platform sandals. An umbrella with a pencil-thin handle hung at her side. She could have been anywhere from fifteen to twenty-five, Samuels supposed; her features were gentle and rounded, while her silky black hair hung past her shoulders and over her forehead in an even, square fringe, suggesting a long acquaintance with a straightener. Her eyes, enhanced by black circle lenses and spidery false lashes, never left his face, and her demeanour lacked any of her companion's trepidation. She seemed not to have noticed Rioko at all.

The girl said something that sounded like "Ma, coo some yells."

It took Samuels a moment to realize she was saying his name.

He nodded, and the girl handed him an iPhone 6s encrusted with black rhinestones and dangling accessories in the shape of plastic bats and skulls. The screen displayed the scanned pages of a magazine with inset illustrations. Samuels inspected the first image—a hallway in a derelict office tower filled with inhuman figures frozen in postures of agony—and recognized it as a scene from one of his stories, 'Mannequins in Aspects of Terror'. He saw that the app's frame bar contained the ebook version of his translated collection, as well as hundreds of other translated books and magazines. Though he could not read their covers, he glanced at the file names and saw works by Thomas Ligotti, U.G. Joshi (the young critic responsible for the revisionist biography *H.P. Lovecraft: A Grotesquely Inflated Reputation*, often mistaken for the less acerbic and dismissive S.T. Joshi), Shaun Hutson, Richard Staines, Guy N. Smith, Reggie Oliver, D.F. Lewis and Brendan Connell, as well as collections of Izumi Kyoka and Edogawa Ranpo, and also Takamoto's forbidden *The Aesthetic of Chogen*.

"Ma coo," the girl repeated, staring at him with somber absorption.

The young man, seemingly desperate to assert himself, indicated Samuels and said something to Rioko; Samuels caught a fragment that sounded like "America".

"No, son," Samuels said. "I'm a subject of her Majesty the Queen. And if you've something to say, you can address me directly."

The young man sensed Samuels's curt tone and, not understanding the words, seemed to crumple into himself. Rioko said something that sounded like "in grease", and then a string of quick phrases with an apologetic smile. The young man nodded nervously.

Samuels turned back to the girl. "You're a reader, yeah?"

The girl said nothing. Her eyes were wide and focused. Samuels felt her take his hand, and he made no effort to pull away. Her fingers closed around his own and she led him out of the smoking section, across the cafe and into the restroom. It happened very quickly; neither Rioko nor the young man had time to process it until they found themselves regarding each other across Samuels's empty seat.

"I'm very sorry to have interrupted you," the young man said, in Japanese. "I'm really very sorry."

He struggled to think of something else to say.

"Your friend . . ." Rioko started. "Is she———"

"My sister," the young man corrected. "She's . . . a strange girl."

He looked away.

An uncomfortable silence fell, lasting for nearly fifteen minutes. Rioko returned her attention to the laptop, continuing her research while the young man busied himself with his smartphone. When Samuels and the girl returned, both looked dishevelled, if not exactly exhausted. The girl seemed unwilling to leave him and kept her gaze focused on his frame, massive in comparison with her own, her eyes lit with an intensity belying her size.

"Sorry love, bit preoccupied at the moment," Samuels said. "Come visit me in London, yeah?"

The young man began a fresh stream of apologies and managed to pull the girl away. The two of them exited the smoking section and left the cafe.

"Sorry about that," Samuels said. "Didn't mean to keep you waiting. Let's just say I found myself in a bit of a tight situation. There was barely any room in that toilet . . ." he trailed off. "Still, I made the most of it. That's all you can do."

"Does this happen a lot?"

Samuels nodded. "There seems to be an occult connection between young dolly birds and literary ghost stories. It isn't easy being a British horror writer published primarily on small presses. Our extreme global popularity means we're exposed to a side of human nature most people usually don't see. Frankly, the fan devotion can be a bit much at times, but you learn to live with it, I suppose. You might remember those 'Machenalia' outbreaks of the 1920s—of course, 'Saturnalia' was more like it. Organized abductions in which Machen, well into his 60s, was dragged from motor carriages by frenzied flappers and compelled to dance until dawn. In '26 he put out his right knee doing the Charleston at a club in Soho. I can well imagine how he must have felt. I've tried to live a more moderate life, but it's never worked out."

"I can relate to that . . ."

"You can?"

Rioko smiled mysteriously. "Never mind. Anyway, I have to get back to work soon. You said you wanted to call the sculptor?"

"That's right. I want you to call him and tell him Mr. Valdemar's, what's his name, Shimura? That his old friend Mark S is in town and he's very keen to learn more about the Brothers and Sisters society and whatever it has planned for the future. That I've heard good things about the group and want in, blah blah blah. Tell him I've heard he's a master sculptor and a credit to the art. And I'd like to meet him at his shop, if he could spare the time."

"Okay," Rioko said. "I'll try."

She dialled the number on the card and waited. After a few moments Samuels heard her say something in what sounded like a formal register.

"His wife," Rioko mouthed. "Hold on."

She resumed speaking, and Samuels supposed Okamura had come on the line. The conversation continued in a monotonous tone, which Samuels had noticed was characteristic of Japanese.

"Are you free later tonight?" Rioko asked him. "Around eight or nine?"

Samuels nodded. Rioko resumed the conversation for another few minutes before hanging up and turning back to him.

"That was Okamura. He wants to meet you at his home. I said the shop would be okay but he insisted and said he and his wife would prepare dinner for you. He said he's heard about you from Shimura."

"He didn't say anything about . . . you know, what happened in the bookshop?"

"Nothing."

Samuels thought for a few moments.

"Rioko," he said. "You wouldn't happen to know where I could lay my hands on one of those samurai swords, would you?"

"No. This isn't the Tokugawa period—you can't just carry them around in public."

"Doesn't matter how legal it is," he said. "You don't have any contacts in that area?"

"I could ask my friends, but it might take a while. Why?"

"Just putting together a little tool kit. S'pose I'll have to improvise. Could you give me a list of hardware stores and places I could find sporting goods?"

"Sure."

She took his phone and tapped in a series of names.

"Okay," she said. "I have to get back. Let's meet outside the East Exit in Shinjuku at 8.30."

"Fine, but . . . you're sure you're okay with coming?"

"Why not? You need my help, right?"

"Of course, yeah. It's just . . . I don't know yet, but this might not be the safest place to go, if you take my meaning. I wouldn't want to put you in any danger."

"I've lived in New York and Mumbai. I've seen people stabbed in the street. I don't think an elderly sculptor will be anything to worry about."

"I hope you're right. Listen—I appreciate the help."

Rioko smiled. "See you later."

Samuels spent the rest of the afternoon shopping. From Tokyu Hands he picked up a rack of kitchen knives, a coil of wire, a screwdriver, a pair of stainless steel secateurs, forearm-length gloves and protective goggles. A specialty store in Gotanda furnished him with steel-toed boots. At Sports Authority, when he approached the counter with an aluminum baseball bat, a smiling young sales assistant asked him in English if he would like some balls. Samuels said no, he had enough already. At Yamada Denki he bought a jug of kerosene and waterproof matches. Finally he went to Ameyoko for an oversized backpack, which he hoped made him look like a harmless tourist. He filled it with most of the equipment, leaving only the kerosene jug in his hotel room.

At the appointed time he met Rioko in Shinjuku Station, and they took the Chuo Rapid Line to Kichijoji. Stepping out of the exit gate, Samuels found himself in an area resembling most of the stations he had visited so far, a cramped intersection of roads bordered by shops and corporate offices. He followed Rioko as she tracked the sculptor's address with her phone's GPS, and, as they moved further away from the station, the spaces between the buildings grew larger and the shops smaller, the signs replaced with trees and terraced gardens. They were in the suburbs now, he realized; the houses were small but elaborately stylized, with European-style facades. There was a vague kitsch element to these arrangements that reminded him of the love hotel, although here, in this subdued and moneyed setting, it took on a more dignified aspect. Curtains and in some cases winding vines and overhanging vegetation covered the windows. For whoever lived here, Samuels decided, privacy was paramount.

"Nice area," he said. "Bit foreboding, though."

The fall of night had not lessened the heat, and despite his short-sleeved shirt, he was visibly sweating.

"You're not hot?" Rioko asked.

"Just a bit," Samuels said. "Never could stand this sort of weather."

"What do you have in the backpack?"

"A few goodies; presents, you might say. I thought that was the idea with this country, yeah? Big on gifts?"

As they came to the base of a hill, his headache from earlier in the day returned. He noticed that Rioko was holding her hand to her forehead.

"Rioko—is your headache back?"

"It's been back since we stepped out of the station. I can feel something tight behind my eyes. Don't worry, I've been overworked recently. And you're probably still jetlagged."

But as they continued up the hill, Samuels felt the pressure in his head increasing. More worryingly, his awareness seemed to be slipping, as if with each step he were waking from a brief and shallow sleep. He suddenly had the impulse to look up at the sky, but when he did he felt dizziness overcome him, as if he were being pulled into infinity. He shook his head and forced himself to concentrate on his surroundings. Rioko had fallen silent and was walking with her head down, focused on her phone.

"Rioko," he said, struggling to concentrate. "The sculptor. He mentioned dinner. But I don't want you to eat or drink anything he gives you."

"I've already eaten," she said. "But they'll probably make us tea, at least. We'll have to have some to be polite."

Samuels made his voice stern. "Look. I don't really know what we're getting into, all right? It's just a basic precaution. Do not eat or drink anything."

"Okay. I won't." She stopped. "It should be that house over there."

They approached a residence which appeared similar to the others in the area. Two white stone walls separated it from its neighbours, while twin rose bushes bordered the path leading to the doorway. Rioko raised her phone and called Okamura to announce their arrival. A moment later the door opened and an elderly woman stepped out. Samuels had expected a wizened hag with her back bent double, perhaps wearing a kimono, but this woman, despite her evident age, looked sprightly in a smart black blouse and floral skirt that could have come from Prada or another high-end brand. Her long grey hair reached past her shoulders, and she wore a pair of gold-rimmed glasses. She motioned them over, smiling, and Rioko greeted her in the same formal register she had used earlier on the phone.

Before stepping into the entranceway Mrs. Okamura asked them to remove their shoes. Samuels took off his new steel-toed boots, which she stared at with evident curiosity. Then she said something to Rioko, and Samuels became aware that she wanted to relieve him of his backpack.

"I'll just bring it in with me," he said. "Goodies inside, re-member?"

Rioko interpreted for him, and they were ushered inside. Before they came to the living room Samuels became aware of a smell emanating from within. He thought first of mould, but it was less musty than pungent, and he realized with a certain disgust that it was a human smell, that of hundreds of people crammed into a small space, like the hold of a slave ship. There was no evidence of such congestion, though, as the house's interior seemed all but empty. Samuels noticed what looked to be freshly cut roses in a vase, but their scent did little to disguise the underlying stench.

A large rectangular table occupied the living room. This too seemed to be empty, until Samuels noticed its seated figure. He had at first taken it to be an object—a bundle of clothes, or at best a mannequin. Despite the heat outside and the slow whir of the air conditioner, the figure was wearing a heavy woollen coat and had been wrapped in at least two layers of blankets. A cap and dark glasses hid the top of its face, while the rest was covered by a cold mask. As the figure rose with some effort, Samuels realized that it was Okamura himself. He greeted them with a sepulchral trickle of words, suggesting a throat ravaged by cancer.

"Mr. Okamura apologizes for his voice and appearance," Rioko explained. "He says that he's 'pretty far along'. Very old—I think that's what he means."

"Pleased to meet you and all that," Samuels said. "Tell them we can't stay long, will you?"

At Mrs. Okamura's prompting, Samuels sat across from the

sculptor, taking the opportunity to look around the room. A screen partitioned it into two areas, one containing the kitchen and living area, and the other, he supposed, the couple's beds. The walls were covered with large framed prints, most of them abstract images reminiscent of those on the cult's website. Small stands had been set up in seemingly random places, supporting angular sculptures and abstract constructions of blown glass. An enormous plasma television screen dominated the far wall. The room's proportions seemed subtly wrong—the walls too high, the table too low to the ground—although not having set foot in any other Japanese homes, he could not be certain these features were as anomalous as they seemed. Whatever the case, their effect, combined with his headache and the unbearable stench, both of which had become impossible to ignore, made him anxious to leave as soon as possible.

Okamura spoke again in the same ruined voice, and a stunted conversation ensued. Samuels tried to keep up with Rioko's explanations, but he sensed that she was having trouble thinking of English equivalents for whatever the sculptor was saying. Soon Mrs. Okamura broke in and an awkward exchange followed, which Samuels interpreted in terms of the dynamics of their facial expressions. Mrs. Okamura was insisting on something, and Rioko was struggling to refuse her with as much diplomacy as she could muster. For a moment Rioko seemed to have won, but then Mrs. Okamura dismissed her with a smile, as if she were addressing a child, and headed to the kitchen.

"She's bringing out tea. I tried to stop her, but . . ."

"Dead serious," Samuels said. "Do. Not. Drink."

"She mentioned dinner too—she's prepared some kind of roast. I told her we can't stay long, but she said we have to at least try it."

He sensed Okamura following the conversation, and for a moment he was certain the old man understood English. But then the sculptor launched into a monologue which Rioko struggled through in fits and starts.

"He says thank you for coming . . . he realizes you've made a great effort to get here. I'm not sure whether he means this house or Japan in general. He says that his friend Shimura, or Brother Yuji, wanted to talk to you after he read your black mould story. He wanted to tell you the good news. Your story was sad, Brother Yuji said, but the real future isn't like that . . . the real future is a paradise."

Mrs. Okamura returned with two glasses of cold black tea. Samuels's throat was parched and he found himself wanting to reach out and drink, though he managed to restrain himself, and looked over to make sure Rioko did the same.

"We were worried, after what happened," Rioko said, adding: "I think he's talking about the bookstore."

Okamura said something in a jovial tone and then broke into choked laughter.

"All of us, we're beacons. But Brother Yuji went too far, and he was deactivated. It was too public, that was all, and too fast. But everything turned out for the best, didn't it?"

Samuels noticed that the television screen set against the wall was excessively large, even in this era of enveloping home entertainment; from the corner of his eye it became a black mouth or window into darkness.

"The large-scale transmissions are coming soon, from the Eon of the New Biology. New contact points. He hopes you'll join the Human Communion and continue the good work back in England. He says there are already contact points waiting for you there." Rioko stopped. "I'm sorry. I don't really know what he's talking about. And it's hard for me to breathe in here . . ."

Samuels too found his breath coming in short, and his consciousness was slipping in the same strange way it had on the street. The pounding in his head continued. The air conditioner, despite its whir, seemed broken; a suffocating heat pressed against his skin. He wanted more than ever to reach for the glass of cold black liquid before him, and he sensed Rioko was feeling the same impulse. He took her hand under the table and squeezed it, hard enough to hurt. She sat up sharply, startled back to attention.

Okamura had placed a handful of white pills on the table.

"These are . . . um . . . immunosuppressives. Suppressants. They'll help with making contact."

The sculptor moved his other hand into view and dropped what Samuels recognized as a hunting knife, its serrated edge glinting in the dim overhead light.

"He says . . . he says we can use this too, if we want. Sudden, localized damage will . . . will make the process easier. Look, Mark, I think we should get out of here. I'm not really comfortable with—"

Mrs. Okamura interrupted her by bringing out the roast, which did not resemble anything Samuels had ever seen connected with the word. It was a deep dish filled with thick, circular lumps of black matter that reminded him of enormous sea snails. Looking closer, he could see minute silvery filaments connecting them, and the suggestive shapes of half-formed organs beneath the surface. They were covered with a sticky film of matter resembling a mixture of charcoal and slime.

"Right," Samuels said. "I think this has gone on long enough."

He stood and opened his backpack, which had been resting against the table.

"You. Mr. Sculptor. I'd like a look at your face, yeah? Let's see what's under the mask."

Samuels extracted a pair of forearm-length gloves from the backpack and, still standing, slid them on. He noticed that this action took Rioko and the Okamuras alike by surprise; now he needed to press his advantage. Belatedly, Rioko explained his request. But instead of seeming threatened, Okamura acted almost relieved. He pulled off the cold mask and removed his cap and glasses, just as Samuels was fitting his own protective goggles over his eyes.

Rioko started back in horror. The sculptor's eyes had fallen out of alignment, and only the left still moved with recognizable human intelligence. The right was a leaking cyst. His face was marred by patches of translucent blue-black skin, in places almost scaled. His nose had caved in, its cartilage reduced to jelly, while his lips had nearly fused into a single teratomal mass.

"Oh," Samuels said, "that's just not on, is it?"

In a single movement he pulled the baseball bat from his backpack and swung it across the table, connecting with Okamura's head. The sculptor fell out of his seat and struck the floor. In the next moment Samuels rushed to his side and pulled off the blankets. Someone behind him screamed, but he was too absorbed in the sight before him to turn and determine whether it was Rioko or the sculptor's wife. The force of the blow had ruptured Okamura's left eye, and a steady stream of black blood flowed from his ruined face. His woollen coat, which had been concealed by the blankets, was drenched in a similar damp substance.

Samuels felt a sharp pain and looked down, remembering that he had removed his boots at the door. The black fluid leaking from

Okamura was congealing and liquefying again in sinuous ophidian movements, as if it were being subjected to sudden and extreme temperature changes. Some of it bubbled onto his bare sock and burned like acid. He jerked his foot away and tore the sock off, but the pain remained. Okamura raised his head and Samuels struck him with the bat again. The skin of the sculptor's face hung in flaps, and beneath was not bone but a hard black substance like the shell of a beetle. On impulse Samuels dropped the bat and reached his gloved hands into the wounds, peeling back their unevenly-textured flesh. He felt his hands burning despite their protective coverings as he tightened his grip and dislodged a mound of black gristle from the space where Okamura's brain should have been. Its shell-like exterior seemed to have been arrested during formation, transitioning as it did to leathery scales, slick, black fur and other motley textures. At its centre was a soft pit of pulp, heavily vascularized and inset with a single staring eye of lacteal blue, its multiple pupils a field of black stars shining in a noonday sky.

"Hello, sunshine," Samuels said, gazing into the eye. "Getting a good look at me?"

Behind him Mrs. Okamura ceased her screaming, grabbed the knife from the table and rushed at Rioko, who was staring at the sculptor's body with dim horror. She turned just in time to upend the table, forming a wall between them. When Mrs. Okamura began edging around it with her weapon extended, Rioko grabbed one of the glass sculptures from its stand and hurled it at her. It struck her shoulder on its way to the wall, where it shattered. At the sound of impact Samuels dropped the black lump and drove his bat through its eye with full strength, reducing it to a milky puddle. Okamura's body continued its strange dissolution, small clots of matter emerging from the riven folds of his face like parasites fleeing their host.

"Right," Samuels yelled. "Out of here, now. Now!"

Rioko hurled another sculpture at Mrs. Okamura and ran for the entranceway. Samuels grabbed his backpack and lugged it after him as he followed her out the door, neither of them stopping to look back.

They continued running until they could no longer see the house behind them. Rioko stopped when they were almost within range of the station, panting from the exertion. Samuels slowed down and felt his heart racing as if it would burst. The pounding in his head had worsened to the point that he was struggling not to vomit. Rioko stared ahead into the distance, seeming not to see him. Her expression was more angry than frightened.

"Rioko," Samuels said, "we left our bloody shoes."

She laughed, but it was more like a cough. He sensed she felt the same nausea that he did, and was restraining it with similar difficulty.

"Oh my God. I can't believe . . . his wife. What if she calls the police?"

"Not going to happen," Samuels said. "The last thing they want is the law back there. No, she'll go running to the boss instead. Mr. Aleph."

"We'll have to call them ourselves then. I mean, I only caught a glimpse of that thing but—"

"No police," Samuels said. "That's not how I do things."

"Are you crazy? His wife tried to kill me. They both wanted to poison us. And what was wrong with his body?"

"Look. We don't know what's going on here, neither of us does. The police wouldn't believe us, first of all. Second, we'd waste time and probably give away our position."

"What do you mean, our position? And why did you have all those things in your backpack? Have you been involved in something like this before?"

"Not exactly. But I've seen things I couldn't explain. And I've had enemies, yeah? Maybe not ones like this, but enemies all the same. You always want to keep the upper hand if you can."

"Well," Rioko said, "I don't think they were expecting that."

"With Mark Samuels you don't get what you expect, you get what you deserve."

"I can't believe that really happened. It's like a nightmare."

"You don't have to believe," Samuels said. "It happened. We were both there."

Rioko seemed to calm down—or maybe it was only that exhaustion had caught up with her. They resumed walking until she stopped again.

"Oh my God . . . we can't go into the station without shoes. We have to find a store."

"Does it really matter?"

"The station guards won't let us on the train barefoot."

They came to the station and walked around to the Sun Road street of shops, where they found a shoe store called ABC Mart. As they passed through the entrance, an attendant came and said something to Rioko.

"He's not letting us in," she said.

"Why?"

"We're not wearing shoes."

"But we're going to buy them!"

"He says it doesn't matter, they can't let anyone in without shoes."

"Fuck's sake . . ." Samuels said. He pushed past the attendant into the store and threw a handful of notes on the counter. "Here's twenty thousand yen. That's what, a hundred pounds?" He grabbed two pairs of thong sandals from a rack. "I'm buying these. Ta."

He walked back and handed one of the pairs to Rioko.

"Problem solved."

Sandals on, they headed back to the station. Samuels noticed that the spot on his left foot where the black fluid had touched him had taken on a scalded look, and was filled with what appeared to be tiny fragments of black gravel. He made a mental note to disinfect it when he returned to his hotel.

"It's Saturday tomorrow," he said to Rioko. "You don't have work, right?"

"No. But I don't think I'll be able to sleep tonight . . ."

"I'm sure you've got some medicine for that."

"I do, actually. How did you know?"

"Just a guess. You seem like the insomniac type. I am too, so I might end up asking you for some later. Always found it goes down better with this." He took out his flask and threw back a slug of whiskey.

As they rode back to Shinjuku, Samuels got the impression she was deciding whether to contact him again the next day or head straight to the police.

"Look," he said, "I probably shouldn't have gotten involved in this, and I really shouldn't have gotten you to come along. It's just a thing with me. I'm a bit paranoid. And sometimes I keep going when I should turn and walk away."

Rioko leaned in closer to him. He sensed she felt awkward talking on the train.

"It's all right."

"So I'd understand if you wanted to get out now. You know . . . tell Mr. Slick I took off on my own. I'll be heading back to England next week and I'm supposed to be meeting some friends of friends before I go, so you lot don't have to worry about me. You can—"

"They tried to kill me," Rioko broke in. "I'm not letting them get away with that."

Samuels nodded, and a minute passed before he spoke again. "I was twelve years old the first time I felt like that. I was walking home in Crystal Palace when some lads decided they didn't like my clothes. Everything I wear I like to keep clean, yeah? Well, they thought my Nike Blazers were too spotless. Said I'd nicked them, said I should hand them over. I could have run or tried to call for help, but I held my ground. Blinded one of them, put the other in the hospital and wound up there myself. Since then, that's how I tend to react."

Rioko looked at him.

"I think you can take those off now."

"What?"

She reached over and gently slipped off the goggles he had forgotten he was wearing.

"The gloves, too. You look like the plumber from Hell."

"That's about how I feel right now, love."

The train arrived at Shinjuku. Rioko needed to change to the Yamanote Line, so they parted on the platform.

"I'll give you a call tomorrow," Samuels said. "We can decide what to do then."

Rioko nodded and managed a half-smile. "Good night."

Samuels walked back to his hotel and stopped on the way at a convenience store called Lawson, where he bought a bottle of whiskey, six cans of Kirin beer and a packet of salt and vinegar crisps, or 'POTATOE CHIPPS' as a flaring line of text on the bag referred to them. He had noticed similar misspellings on objects and signs throughout the day, which he put down to the country's American influence, but he was past caring about them now. Back in his room he poured three fingers of whiskey into a plastic cup and drank it neat. Over the next hour, while marvelling at the excesses of Japanese late night television, he made what he considered a valiant effort to finish the bottle. After thirty minutes he decided the effort was not only valiant but courtly and heroic. After forty-five it became noble, chivalrous and gallant. He was still searching for synonyms when the darkness in the room deepened.

He looked around. His left hand held the plastic cup, his right a cigarette. He had stripped down to his underwear and changed into an old Zapatista T-shirt he had picked up in Mexico. The lights had been off for some time, but just for a moment the darkness surrounding him had blinked, flashing to absolute pitch before returning to normal. At first he thought the television had lost power, but he was certain nothing on the screen had changed, and so the adjustment must have come from outside it. He was still thinking about it when it happened again, and this time the change remained. The television was on but its light failed to reach him; he could no longer make out any part of his body, and had to touch his face to reassure himself he still existed. The screen, which had been tuned to an infomercial, faded to a pure, crackling white rectangle that burned itself into his eyes. He looked away but the image filled his vision no matter where he turned, and as he struggled to orient himself in the darkness, he slipped and fell off the bed.

Samuels sat up. He was now less than a foot away from the white rectangle, and he watched as a faint image formed on its surface, resolving into the outline of a man. First his head took shape: coal-black eyes with greatly dilated pupils in a stark white face framed by long hair and a wispy beard and mustache. Then his shoulders and the rest of him came into view, the body covered by a long black robe.

The eyes fixed him and the lips moved.

"Good evening, Mark."

Samuels felt an explosion behind his eyes and steadied himself to avoid vomiting. The voice came from the television and from the inside of his head at the same time; he could hear the words ricocheting in his skull like steel ball-bearings.

"Hello, sunshine," he managed. "Bit late for a visit, isn't it?"

"No, not at all."

Samuels clutched his head. There was no difference between the room and his mind, and the voice filled both with its flat blare, a tuneless angel's trumpet whose every syllable announced final judgement. His body and the hotel were gone; there was only the voice and this ultimate void.

"It's a pleasure to finally meet you," the figure said. "If you're wondering, I'm using your own nervous system to communicate. We made contact earlier tonight, but it was you who opened the door. Right now your liver is on the verge of failure, and the little missionaries in your bloodstream are taking advantage of the lowered defences to receive the transmissions."

Samuels realized he had forgotten to clean his foot. The whiskey had made him forget the pain, but he realized now that the scalded flesh had been filled not with gravel from the street, but traces of the black matter that had escaped the sculptor's body.

"What do you want?" he asked.

"To offer friendship. Brother Eijiro Okamura isn't dead—he's here with us now. The important parts of him are still alive, and he doesn't hold anything against you. His wife, Sister Misako, was surprised and acted without thinking, but she understands now. We're very interested in you, Mark. We need Brothers and Sisters in England to continue our work. You've always sensed there was something beyond this world, haven't you? A greater reality of which the life you know is only a child's sketch. We'd like to show you what it is."

"Fuck off. You corrupt the sick and vulnerable. You're a cancer, and I'm going to end you."

The figure reacted only with a mild smile. Samuels got the impression it was enjoying the contrast between its conciliatory words and the oppressive force with which they were delivered.

"The next visitation has already begun in Tanimoto Hospital. I invite you to attend and share in the contact. You're correct that the sick, those near death, are particularly receptive to the transmissions. They're afraid, but we can remove their fear and heal their wounds, so that they may share in the life of the coming eon. In us there is no death."

"I wouldn't count death out just yet," Samuels said. "Because you're looking at it. Your own."

Immediately after delivering this line, which in his drunken state seemed suitably cinematic, Samuels decided his next priority was to prevent the figure from making any kind of retort. A solution came to him, and he congratulated himself for the way it also encompassed an equally pressing matter, that of ending the explosions in his head. As the figure's lips moved to form a response, Samuels pulled back and, summoning all his strength, smashed his head into the screen. After the impact there was a moment of total dislocation, as if he were drowning in a sea of static and razors, and then his awareness dispersed in the darkness of oblivion.

Pain returned, first as unwanted light and heat, then as an expanse of generalized aches supporting a constellation of more precise agonies, their coordinates—his foot and forehead, a spot on his side and one on his chest, just above the heart—traced by lines of bone-deep weariness. The sun streaming through the window was the eye of a cruel god.

Samuels forced himself up and checked the time; he had been out for only four or five hours. He scanned the room. There was no sign of damage or forced entry, and more remarkably, the television screen was intact, though he had succeeded in knocking it off its stand. He had not even vomited, though a dark puddle of saliva marked the place where his head had lain.

Next he inspected his foot, which looked worse than before, but was not the tentacled monstrosity he feared it might have changed into over the course of the night. The black grains had enlarged and hardened into scabs, with sticky liquid spreading beneath them. Looking at his stained flesh he imagined death moving within him, then reminded himself that this was a pointless line of thought. Everyone everywhere was always doomed, in the strict physical sense; it was only a question of time. The important thing was to preserve what was valuable. For now, his body was a means to an end. It had served him well before and would last a while longer. He boiled a pot of water and let one of the knives he had bought rest in it for a while before using it to cut away the scabs and remove as much of the black matter as he could. The already blistered flesh broke open and bled. Samuels washed it with soap and water, applied antiseptic ointment he had bought from a pharmacy the day before, covered it with an adhesive bandage and hoped for the best.

Then he forced himself through his morning exercises.

He had not believed the televised spectre's remark about the poor condition of his liver, but he decided it was not worth risking it, so he ignored the leftover whiskey and had two breakfast beers instead. Finally he used the hotel phone to call Rioko's mobile. It took ten rings for her to pick up, and when she answered it was in leaden Japanese.

"It's me," Samuels said.

She paused and cleared her throat. "Yeah. Okay. I'm awake."

"Hope you got some sleep. I'm sorry, but—I had a run in with Boss Man Aleph last night. Bastard beamed himself into my room."

"What? Are you okay?"

"Fine. But listen, have you heard of a Tanimoto Hospital?"

"Yeah. It's in Ikebukuro. My cousin is there now. She's having her tonsils taken out."

"Uhhhhhm. Right. Well. That's not good. Not good at all."

"What are you talking about?"

"Aleph mentioned his crew was paying it a visit. He made out they were already there, or arriving soon. And that was before I passed out. Somehow I don't think they're handing out cards and flowers."

"Oh my God . . . okay. I'm twenty minutes from Ikebukuro by train. I'll meet you outside the East Exit."

Samuels barely managed an "okay" before he heard the phone click. He took a brief shower, grabbed his backpack and headed out the door. Ten minutes later he was in Shinjuku Station, and ten minutes after that he arrived in Ikebukuro by way of the now-familiar Yamanote Line. He met Rioko outside the East Exit. Her hair was down and she was dressed more casually than the day before, but he did not get the impression she had rushed out the door either, and she seemed more composed than she had on the phone. But after a moment he realized that what he had taken for composure was really numb horror.

"This is crazy," she said. "It's like being in a war. I don't know what to feel anymore."

They hailed a taxi outside the station and asked the driver to take them to Tanimoto Hospital.

"Never had any run-ins with the yakuza?" Samuels asked.

"Normal people don't have anything to do with yakuza. It's another world. But even that world, it's still made of people. But this . . . I don't know what these things are, what this disease is. That's what frightens me."

"We know enough. They're targeting a hospital. They tried to give us immunosuppressant drugs. So this infection or whatever it is doesn't seem to work too well unless the victim is injured or willing."

Rioko gave him a doubtful look.

"Yeah, I know," Samuels said. "My foot is still killing me. Theoretically I could drop dead at any moment. I wanted to pick up a new pair of boots and some other gear but there was no time. Here, wear these at least."

He handed her a pair of gloves and a cold mask from the pharmacy.

"We should really have proper masks or even hazmat suits, but there's no time."

Rioko put on the mask and gloves and said, "Why do we feel so awful whenever we get close to them? I felt like throwing up when we were walking to the house yesterday, and I almost passed out when we went inside. That's the worst part. It's not just what they look like, it's how they make you feel."

"I don't know," Samuels said. "Unless the infection is airborne, some kind of cloud. In which case we're buggered. But Okamura and Boss Man both said something about contact points and transmissions. So maybe it's not a conventional infection at all—maybe it's targeted, like a weapon. They select some coordinates—could be as big as a whole neighborhood block, or as small as a single person—and fire away. Whatever's in range gets hit. That could explain Aleph on the telly as well. We still don't know much about this cult, do we? It could be some kind of experiment, something military. Or alien—can't rule that out either."

Rioko shook her head. "That's crazy . . ."

"Just trying to consider all possibilities. There's one I've been trying to avoid, which is that it actually is the black mould from my story."

"Why? What happens in the story?"

"The black mould spreads across all time and space, absorbing everything. Including Earth, of course. Not a happy ending. Anyway, it doesn't seem likely, unless I've underestimated my prophetic powers." He noticed the taxi approaching the hospital. "We're almost there. Tell me about your cousin. Do you know what floor she's on?"

"Her name's Yuma. She's eleven. I called my uncle and he said she's on the third floor."

"Yuma, eleven, third floor, got it."

The taxi stopped in front of the hospital and they got out. Before they had taken their first step towards the entrance Samuels felt his headache returning, and a sudden vertigo overcame him. He steadied himself and saw that Rioko was holding a bottle of white tablets out to him.

"Aspirin," she said.

He laughed and took one of them. "Don't think it's going to do much good, love. Thanks, though."

They approached the entrance, where Samuels stopped and opened his backpack. He took out the baseball bat and two kitchen knives, handing the latter to Rioko.

"Anything comes at you . . . stab it in the head, yeah?"

"It's daytime," Rioko said. "And this is a hospital. There should be people coming in and out all the time. If the cult's inside, everyone will know."

"You're sure about that? It's a small hospital, not on the main strip, and it's still pretty early in the morning. And somehow I don't think they walked in the front door and signed the register."

Samuels left the backpack by the entrance steps, reasoning that it would slow him down in the event of violent conflict. As they passed through the doors he noticed that no one else was around, and there was no sound of movement and no voices from within. When they entered the lobby he was assailed by the same slave-hold stench that had been present in Okamura's house.

"It looks deserted . . ." Rioko said.

"Just be careful, keep your eyes open."

They moved into a long corridor, where Samuels had another attack of vertigo. He felt his headache changing from a dull throb to a white-hot knife-point twisting behind his eyes. He saw that Rioko was holding her hand to her head.

The first corpse they found did not immediately strike him for what it was. It looked like a mound of mixed garbage staining the corridor floor, as if a bin had been overturned: filthy remnants of barely recognizable clothing mashed into a pile of wet black meat. Recognition came with the sight of a single, undamaged ear on its surface. Looking closer Samuels saw that the shapeless flesh was unevenly studded with teeth, and on its other side he made out the shape of a fractured jawbone. He turned just in time to see Rioko vomiting.

Samuels took a step towards her and felt something land on his shoulder. Instinctively he brought his hand up and knocked it away; a moment later he saw a small black slug land on the floor in front of him. He looked up just in time to dodge another. A great black stain bulged through the low ceiling.

"Look out," Samuels shouted.

Rioko looked up and staggered out of the way.

"Are you okay?" Samuels asked.

"No. I feel like I'm in Hell."

"Me too."

126

Not wanting to risk the enclosed space of an elevator, they arrived at the end of the corridor and began climbing the stairs to the third floor. As they reached it and moved towards the door, Samuels saw movement and held up a hand. Rioko stopped and followed the line of his gaze. The headless corpse of an infant was crawling towards them, its tiny body weighed down with black fungoid growths. Samuels crushed its limbs with several downward arcs of the baseball bat and kicked it down the stairs.

They entered the door to find a larger corridor with walls covered in black stains. There were more human remains, many all but unrecognizable, and more of the black slugs and larger masses, some of them animating dismembered limbs and broken skulls like snails in their shells. The area resembled the aftermath of a bombing. Samuels and Rioko crossed the corridor without stopping to look at its sights in detail, although it was impossible to ignore their outlines. The exploded bodies and black matter dominated their field of vision, and the air itself seemed thickened with sickness. They came to an open area with multiple beds separated by curtains. As they passed through it, something rose from one of the beds and reached out for them. Samuels reacted without thinking, striking it with the bat and dodging away as it reeled from the impact and then came for him again. It had once been a pregnant woman, he realized; that much was clear from the distended bulb of its abdomen. While the woman's head hung forward as if her neck were broken, something resembling a hybrid worm and rat made of mucus thrashed furiously inside the translucent sac of her womb, piloting her from within. Rioko buried one of her knives in it and shoved the mother-vehicle away. Other figures were coming for them now, rising from beds and staggering out from behind curtains. Samuels fended most of them off with the bat, collapsing already fractured skulls and knocking unbalanced bodies to the ground, but Rioko was often forced to slash her way through to safety.

"Call out!" Samuels said. "See if anyone's hiding."

Rioko shouted something in Japanese and repeated it as they moved forward, opening all the closed doors they found and knocking on the locked ones. Some of the rooms discharged fresh horrors; others were empty. There was no sign of any hospital staff, which made Samuels think they were either dead or in hiding. Eventually there was a tentative noise from behind one of the locked doors, and they heard the sound of raised voices. Samuels moved forward and rapped on the door sharply.

"Anyone in there? Rescue team's arrived."

He made out fragments of a muffled conversation. Rioko came over and called out in Japanese. The conversation continued for several moments, and then the door opened slowly. He caught sight of a frightened man's face, pinched, middle-aged. Samuels turned away as he noticed several corpses moving towards them. He held them off with the bat while Rioko spoke to the man behind the door. After a few moments the door swung open and he heard Rioko crying out. He rushed over, expecting some new danger, but saw only a group of people in hospital gowns, most of them very young or very old. One of them, a thin girl with short black hair and braces, rushed forward and embraced Rioko. This, he supposed, was Yuma.

"What's the deal?" he asked.

"These are the only survivors, about ten of them. They think there were others, but they couldn't get to them in time. Most everyone else was too far gone to help."

"No one on the other floors?"

"Not that they know."

"Okay. Tell them we're leaving."

A flurry of conversation broke out. One of the older men seemed to want to stay, not wanting to risk the dangers outside. Samuels reached out and grabbed him, and the man pulled away.

"Not going to argue," Samuels said. "We go, now. Tell them they can stay if they want but we're going."

Without waiting for a response he turned and headed in the direction of the stairs, stopping only to clear the way with his bat so Rioko and Yuma could proceed. As he had expected, all the patients eventually followed after him, including the old man. They made their way back to the ground floor with no casualties, although there were frequent stops to repel the corpses and make sure no one fell behind. Eventually they passed through the lobby and out the door. Samuels retrieved his backpack from near the entrance.

They crossed to the other side of the street and stood for a moment, catching their breath. In their bare hospital gowns, with their terrified faces and frail bodies shivering in the wind, the young and the old alike reminded Samuels of escapees from a prison or concentration camp, not patients at a modern hospital. Yuma and a small boy clung to Rioko. A middle-aged woman began to cry. The old man spoke up again in a querulous voice, and several conversations broke out at once.

"Ask them what happened," Samuels told Rioko. "What they saw, when it took place."

Rioko consulted the old man first, partly to calm him down. She listened for a while, then talked to the others.

"No one remembers much from the beginning," she said. "Most of them were asleep when it happened. They remember waking up with terrible headaches, and some of them started throwing up. The electricity was out. There were strange noises. They saw . . . holes in space, things they can't explain. There were people screaming and dying. It sounds like total chaos. No one remembers seeing strangers or cult members, but the black matter was everywhere."

"About what I thought," Samuels said. "Okay." He walked over to the old man and placed his hand on his shoulder. "You, sir, are in charge now. Hate to say it, but . . . you're going to want to get to another hospital. All of you. You could all be infected and not know it." He pointed at the hospital behind them. "That whole area of space is sick, you can feel it."

Rioko explained what he had said. The old man nodded and spoke with the other patients.

"I'll take Yuma home," Rioko said.

All at once the old man began shouting. Samuels looked over and saw him pointing at the crying woman. The other patients had moved away from her, giving him a better view of her face. He saw that a black stain rose up from beneath her gown and curled around her neck, its edge reaching as far as her lower lip. Samuels understood at once. The old man was accusing her of contamination, and the rest of the patients were listening to him. He heard a volley of clipped shouts and recriminations. The woman backed away and held up her hands, tears streaming down her face. Rioko walked over and tried to calm her down, even as the other patients dispersed, taking off across the street alone and in pairs. The few who remained continued shouting.

"They're saying they should have left her behind," Rioko said. "And that she's probably infected everyone. I think we should get her away from them."

"Some real humanity on display here," Samuels said. "Well, sod it. I don't have time for this."

He went over to the woman, took her hand and led her away from the other patients while Rioko comforted her in Japanese.

"It's all right," Samuels said. "I'll take her back to the station myself. If anyone has a problem they'll have to get through me."

"What are you going to do then?"

"I think there's only one option left. We're going to have to go to the cult headquarters and find Boss Man. And we're going to have to kill him."

Rioko stared at him for what felt like several minutes.

"Okay," she said at last. "I need time to think."

"I'm going soon. For all I know the bastard is reading my mind now. They could have a private army there, but I doubt it. I don't think they need many members when they can manage stunts like this. As to whether I'm capable of pulling this off . . . I don't know. I don't even know if he's something that *can* be killed. I might die, but we've all got to go some time."

"You're serious."

"Perfectly." Samuels turned towards the thoroughfare. "This is Ikebukuro, right? I'll meet you back at the same exit at noon. If you don't want to show up, you don't have to. In fact you probably shouldn't. You saved Yuma there, and I'm sure she wants to keep you around for a while longer."

"I'm coming with you," Rioko said. "I need time to think but . . . I know I'm coming with you. Does that make sense?"

"Not really, but I think I understand. You're sure?"

"Yes."

Samuels walked over to her and knelt down so that he was face to face with Yuma. He looked at the girl's dark black eyes and resolute expression.

"How are you, love?" he said, then glanced up to indicate Rioko. "You've got a real crazy one here, you know. But maybe it runs in the family. You've been brave today too, haven't you?"

Yuma stared at him and smiled faintly.

Samuels got to his feet.

"I'm off. See you at noon."

He left her with Yuma and the small boy and headed back to the station, taking the crying woman with him. She had calmed down somewhat, although she turned her head away whenever he looked at her, to prevent him from seeing the black stain.

"It's all right, you know," Samuels said. "I've got one too, see?'

He took off his shoe and showed her his bandaged wound, but it had little effect; the woman was clearly traumatized, and broke into tears again as they continued walking.

"You don't have to worry," Samuels said. "I'm going to put a stop to all this. You can go to another hospital; I'm sure they'll be able to do something. Bugger it . . . you can't understand what I'm saying, can you? Afraid I can't speak much Japanese . . ."

"I understand . . . just fine . . ." a voice said.

Samuels looked over at the woman just in time to see her falling towards him. He caught her in his arms and her head slumped against his shoulder. He heard a voice whisper in his ear:

"I'm looking forward . . . to meeting you in person . . . Mark."

He seized the woman's shoulders and held her at arm's length. Her eyes had rolled back in their sockets, their whites flecked with black. Her mouth was open, leaking black fluid.

"What did you say?"

The voice that emerged from her now seemed to issue directly from her throat, a guttural eruption given only the grossest shape by her lips. Samuels had to strain his hearing to string its syllables into sense.

"This woman . . . Yoshimi . . . her husband . . . immuno . . . def. . . deficiency virus from . . . prostitute . . . passed it . . . to her. No . . . defences . . . the missionaries have . . . set up contact points . . . inside. Showing her . . . the . . . the wonders . . . of the Human . . . Communion . . ."

"Let her go," Samuels said. "It's me you want, isn't it? I'll be there soon enough. Let her go. Now!"

He shook her until her head fell forward, but the voice from her throat continued.

"Open . . . your mind . . . listen to the . . . transmissions. You don't . . . have to die. We can show you . . . worlds within . . . worlds . . ."

The words degraded into a choking cough and all strength left the woman's body.

Samuels checked and found that her heart was still beating, but her pulse was weak. He carried her to the police box close to the East Exit and left her with the officers there, explaining with a combination of hand gestures and basic phrases that he had found her in this condition on the ground outside the hospital. The officers seemed embarrassed by their stunted English and looked relieved when he left.

As he was walking away from the police box, Samuels became peripherally aware of two young Western women whose tall stature made them stand out from the crowd. They were both blonde, heavily tanned and outfitted in what Samuels guessed were clothes from H&M or Forever 21. When he passed by he saw that they were now looking in his direction and conferring with each other, and as he continued on his way they approached him from the side and one of them addressed him.

"Ummmm this is going to sound really weird but ARE YOU MARK SAMUELS?"

"You've got it," Samuels said, looking at them more closely. They both looked to be in their early twenties. The girl who had spoken was wearing a midriff-exposing black, cut-out sleeve top, white shorts with pink and yellow polka dots, and black platform wedge sandals. Her teeth were blindingly, almost chromatically white, contrasting with her deep, even tan. Her abdominal definition was not sharply cut enough to be competition-worthy, but still gave evidence of a serious gym routine. Her companion had a similarly toned physique, and was wearing a short blue floral-patterned dress along with white sandals.

"Oh wow, this is so crazy," the first girl said. "What are you doing in Japan?"

"At the moment I'm . . . well, it's a long story. And who wants to know?"

"Oh, I'm sorry . . . I'm Kendra. Well, DJ Special K, you might have . . . well, actually you probably haven't heard of me but I'm obviously not the guy that comes up when you Google that and I'm trying to get a copyright for it because I'm a lot better than him."

"I'm Julee and I'm not a DJ or anything," the other girl said. "But I'm feeling amazing right now . . . we're coming down off acid and I'm just totally blissed-out . . ."

Samuels narrowed his eyes. "When you say DJ . . . look, it's not this bloody pop EDM, is it?"

Kendra said, "Well, um, EDM, yeah."

"I only like progressive house," Julee said, somewhat defensively.

Not for the first time Samuels marvelled at his continuing popularity with what he thought of as "these junior ravers" who seemed to comprise at least half of his current readership. It seemed that expensive limited edition volumes of Weird Fiction with small print runs were inordinately popular with a certain subset of fitness-conscious club-goers.

"I suppose you girls are here on holiday?" he said.

"I just did a show last night and I have another one tomorrow in Osaka, then we're flying back to Sacramento," Kendra said.

"You're sisters . . ?"

"Just friends. Well, um . . . we met in this polyamorous commune in Belgium, actually. And everyone there was passing around *The White Hands*. They were really into training too. You would have loved it."

"What sort of training?"

"Mostly CrossFit."

Samuels nodded but remained tactfully silent, as he disliked CrossFit for the way its practitioners tended to set themselves up to plateau by neglecting progressive overloading; in his view conventional circuit training was superior. He preferred a strict separation of lifting and cardio, and had observed that a large number of CrossFitters did not know how to do Olympic lifts properly.

"So yeah, what are you doing now?" Kendra asked.

"I told you it's a long story. You probably won't believe it but I'm actually saving the world from some kind of . . . Lovecraftian incursion or something. I still haven't worked out what it is."

"Haha, that's such a 'horror writer' thing to happen! I can't imagine that happening to anyone else."

"You could probably take some time off though, right?" Julee said, moving closer to him. "I mean is the world really going to end immediately or whatever?"

"Yes, look, the situation is actually pretty urgent. I'd love to stay and chat longer but someone is waiting for me . . ."

"We were going to head back to our hotel," Kendra said. She too now moved closer into Samuels's personal space. "We just came out to get more drinks from the store. We're going to blaze up some Sour Diesel when we get back. You should come!"

"It's really high quality," Julee added. "You should totally come!"

"Bloody Hell," Samuels said. "I would love to blaze . . ."

"Then come on!" Kendra said, taking his arm.

Samuels was now struck by a crisis of responsibility. He knew that somewhere, past the standard range of human perception, the forces of the Aleph were monitoring him with ceaseless malevolence. He was now involved too deeply and too personally to back out. But at the same time, he felt like blazing, and Kendra's abdominal definition kept attracting his attention. He knew that if he were to accompany her and Julee to their hotel, he probably wouldn't end up making his appointment with Rioko. And in his absence, the cult might strike again. The dilemma seemed insoluble, so he decided to excuse himself for the moment.

"I've really got to meet someone now, but I'll get in touch with you later, yeah?" he said.

"OK, no problem," Kendra said. "Can we follow each other on Instagram?"

Samuels took out his phone, and they exchanged details.

"Send us a message later, okay? Let us know when you're coming," Julee said.

Before they parted he took two copies of *Black Altars* from his *Black Altars* pocket, signed them and handed them over.

Samuels continued on his way, losing himself in the crowd. After walking for a while, he turned on voice and data roaming on his phone and flipped to the address book, scanning his list of contacts. After a few moments' deliberation he called John Llewellyn Probert. The phone rang for a long time, and Samuels remembered the time difference with England. But eventually he heard a voice replace the dial tone.

"Hello? Mark?"

"Hello John, I haven't woken you up have I?" Samuels asked.

"Not at all, but I am a bit busy. You see, I'm in the midst of establishing a charitable foundation at the moment. The John L. Probert Foundation will provide prostheses for children who were born lacking significant nasal cartilage."

"You mean they were born without noses?"

"No, their noses are just rather . . . inadequate, by current standards. No fault of their own, of course."

"Angling for a knighthood, eh?"

"Not particularly, but charitable work is rather expected of someone in my position. I mean, I've moved beyond the mere 'successful author' stage, to the point where I'd open myself up to public comment if I kept it all to myself for yachting or putting away mountains of the white stuff. Small press British horror problems and all that. You know how it is."

"Yes, well," Samuels said. "I hate to bother you, but I've run into some difficulties. Somehow I've gotten into it here in Tokyo with some disreputable types who've been causing me a lot of grief. I'm not even sure they're from this planet. I'd handle it myself of course, but . . . well, I'm thinking of doing a runner. I've just met some American birds who are into CrossFit and EDM. And they've got high quality green. I was wondering if you could catch a flight over here and sort out the bad element for me. I'd be willing to contribute to this foundation . . . I could PayPal over some funds, yeah?"

"American birds? I hope you told them CrossFit is rubbish."

"Well, I was going to mention it at some point. Anyway . . ."

"Let me get this straight, Mark. You want me to drop everything and fly to Japan to knock around people I've never met. I'm sorry but it's really too much of an imposition. After I finish drafting this foundation charter I'm planning to write up a review of the DVD box set of *Space: 1999*. Heading to the airport now would rather inconvenience me."

"Look, John, I haven't blazed in a while and this seems like an excellent opportunity."

"Mark, you remember that conversation we had about changing horses midstream. It wouldn't make sense to pick a fight with these underworld types, or whoever they are, and then toke up with random Americans. You can't simply 'do a runner' every time someone shows up with the green, no matter how tempting it might seem. It's not cricket."

Samuels paused. "No, I suppose you're right."

"You know it makes sense, Mark."

"I'm really sorry to have troubled you."

"Not at all."

"Listen, do you think Stuart Young is awake now?"

"Stuart Young is engaged in a fairly rigorous bare-knuckle boxing routine, much too rigorous for him to go jetting about for Scooby Doo nonsense abroad. And don't go bothering Adam Nevill at this hour either."

Samuels concluded the call. After several minutes' reflection he decided his friend was right; he would have to focus on the situation at hand and deal with the cult himself.

Back at his hotel, he sat on the balcony smoking cigarette after cigarette and drinking small cans of black coffee he had bought from one of the ubiquitous vending machines. On his way back from Ikebukuro he had stopped at Yamada Denki and bought two more jugs of kerosene, which now rested on the table in front of him along with his other weapons: the bat, the knives, the wire and the secateurs. A pitiful arsenal for what he was up against, he decided, but it was all he had. As he considered the situation, he realized that the Aleph was leading him into a trap, but he saw no option other than to confront him head on. As the smoke from his cigarette curled away from him into the blue of noon, Samuels thought again of his death, which was surely waiting for him at the cult's compound in Saitama: death or something worse, some timeless hell of living corruption. Strangely, his mind was calm. He had not expected to live this long and felt nothing tying him to life. His books would be cast onto the tide of history like everything else and whether they would sink or stay afloat he would never know. He could leave Japan and the rest of the world to the cult's coming aeon, he supposed, except that he had always felt that certain things must be faced and fought, and it was this conviction that made him rise from the table and prepare himself for what was to come.

Lugging the jugs of kerosene out of the hotel would have been work enough without the backpack. With it, he felt like stripping down to his underwear; even the thin T-shirt and trousers he had thrown on in haste seemed like too much clothing for the noonday heat.

"Here, you can take one of these," he told Rioko as soon as they met outside the East Exit, and he handed her one of the jugs.

"Um . . . thanks."

"It's not as heavy as it looks. Really."

They caught the Shonan-Shinjuku Line to Kagohara and changed to the Takasaki Line on their way to Fukaya, where the business card Samuels had taken from Shimura indicated the cult's compound was located. As they rode the train, Samuels fell silent, lost in his thoughts.

"Say something," Rioko said. "I'm getting nervous."

"Sorry. I'm trying to make my peace with God, since I'm not sure I'll get another chance. You might want to do the same, yeah?"

"Umm . . . that might be difficult."

"It's not as hard as you'd think."

She looked at him.

"I thought Christians were supposed to be kind and peaceful, not violent libertines."

"You're thinking of Protestants, love. Responsible for America, capitalism and other disasters."

The train ride took over an hour. Fukaya was in Saitama, north of Tokyo, and Samuels watched as the towers gave way to suburbs and industrial areas, and then the empty spaces of rice fields and the countryside. When they at last arrived at the station, they were forced to ride a bus to the address given on the card. Even this was deceptive, as the nearest bus stop turned out to be a twenty-minute walk from the compound. Samuels and Rioko stopped to rest, already exhausted by the equipment they carried, so that it took another hour before they arrived at the compound itself, which appeared to be several small shacks and ancillary buildings connected to a central complex.

"I guess this is it," Rioko said.

They paused for a moment before continuing on. Their headaches had returned.

"Do you really think the direct approach is best?" Rioko asked.

"They know we're here already. Might as well knock on the front door. Just . . . Rioko. Don't look too hard or think too long about anything you see inside. And if anything comes near you . . ."

". . . stab it in the head," Rioko finished.

The main entrance proved difficult to locate; they had to pass through a kind of courtyard and walk around a long wall, as if they were entering a maze. When they at last found it, Samuels was disappointed; there were none of the guards or security cameras he had been expecting. In fact the central complex, a traditional Japanese wooden building with low, overhanging eaves, looked dilapidated to the point of being abandoned.

"Looks like they're not big on housekeeping," Samuels said. "Right then, let's get on with it."

He had given the baseball bat to Rioko and taken the knives and secateurs for himself. Now he strode forward and knocked with the latter, the cold metal ringing as it struck the wooden doors. There was no response, so he pushed forward and saw that the doors were open. He took off his backpack and left it by the wall, then stepped into a dim hallway and motioned for Rioko to follow.

The entrance hall was deserted and free of any furnishings. There were no light fixtures apparent anywhere either, but a dim phosphorescent glow suffused the room. Looking down, Samuels saw that it was coming from the floor, which he had at first thought to be covered completely with a black carpet. He realized with a sudden flash of queasiness that it was not a carpet at all but a thick covering of the black matter, condensed like soil.

"Watch your feet," he told Rioko.

As they continued forward, they noticed branch-like extrusions growing from the floor in strange fractal shapes. The stench was unbearable, and their headaches almost forced them to the floor at several points. Samuels got the impression the building was trying to do just that, suck them into the black carpet and compound their bones in its mulch.

They moved deeper into the hall and passed numerous open rooms. Taking his own advice, Samuels did not stop to look too long at any of their occupants, although he could not help but be struck by some of them. In one stood a being which seemed less a man than a grotesque statue, rooted into the black carpet like a living tree. Only its eyes moved, following him and Rioko as they passed. In another, a ginger cat had been tied to a chair at the centre of a circle of televisions. The restraints seemed unnecessary, as the animal's movements were torpid and delayed, and all four of its paws had been amputated. Four foetal human arms protruded from its belly, their tiny fingers flexing slowly. And in another, a naked woman lay on the ground luxuriating in the black matter as the pieces of her face rearranged themselves, the nose creeping forward like a hermit crab, the eyes emerging from their sockets and lolling across her cheeks.

"In Hell again . . ." Rioko said. "I feel sick . . . even worse than before . . ."

"Just stay close and don't think about it," Samuels said. "Don't let them into your head."

They came to the end of the hall and turned into a passageway leading to a large open room. Samuels held up a hand for Rioko to stop as he took in the sight in front of them.

Takahiro Aso, the Aleph, stood rooted to the floor, his body covered by the folds of a thick black robe. He held a naked child in his arms and was stroking its forehead. Black tumours covered its face, but Aso's features were clear and corpse-pale.

"Good afternoon, Mark."

The voice echoed inside Samuels's mind, the English words drowning out Aso's spoken Japanese.

"Thought you'd have a few more guards than this, sunshine," Samuels said. "You're getting sloppy."

"We don't need crude physical defences. We're already inside you."

"Not for much longer." He took a step forward, gripping the secateurs. "Right then, let's have it out. What are you lot? Space mould? Septic leak from another dimension?"

Aso smiled. "Nothing so dramatic. We're merely human. Your descendants, in fact."

Samuels continued forward one step at a time, moving slowly and keeping his gaze focused on the Aleph's. "What are you talking about?"

"We're you, after half a million years of industrial progress. We've discarded your limited bodies and fixed forms. Do you understand? Time is not a single point moving on a line, or an expanding sphere in one of your clumsy geometries. Time is like a wave lapping back and forth on the vast shore of night. The past and future are not separate. Each is both cause and effect to the other."

"You've lost me. I asked what the fuck you are, not when you're from."

"Five hundred years ago, in your country, they spoke of us as angels, spirits from outside. In this country we were once called the *nopperabo*—the faceless ones. And in Wales, the *bwg*. A thousand names in a thousand places and times. But this is a scientific age, isn't it?"

"Too bloody scientific for me."

"But you understand evolution. The change in cells: first simple prokaryotes, then eukaryotes, cells with a nucleus. The process continues in ways you can't yet imagine. There are new organelles in the future, new kinds of cells in new kinds of life. But still human, still part of the great family. And if you don't like these terms, then why not combine the scientific with the spiritual, as we do. Call us the Black Mass."

"Black Plague is more like it. There's nothing human about you."

Samuels continued forward until only ten feet separated him from the Aleph, who now moved his hand away from the child's face and held up a finger to indicate himself.

"I first heard them in the hospital, after my accident. I was dying from a bone infection when I heard them singing, first through the television, then through my mobile phone. They sang to me of the static canyons and the shadow people. And the Human Communion, their holy empire stretching across history. They can condense their cellular blueprints into pure information and transmit it through waves and light. They can even send it through time."

"Nice trick, that. Might consider selling it to the BBC."

"They showed me what to do to help the process along. What to remove."

Aso placed the child on the ground, where it crawled away from him, and spread his great robe. Samuels saw that it was not a robe at all but an extension of his body, its folds flowing from the lengths of his arms like the wings of an enormous bat. Beneath them was the pale expanse of his flesh, the chest and abdomen covered with thick black slashes. There was only a scarred and swollen mound where his genitals should have been, traversed by black worms that crawled from it as if from a wad of carrion. Gently he reached up, hooked his thumbs under his eyes and slid out their orbs, revealed now as glass. The black pits beneath stared forward unblinking.

"It only hurt for a while, until they took away the pain. Don't look so surprised. The other eyes inside me can see you perfectly well. Can see *through* you."

Samuels took another two steps forward. Now only five feet separated them.

"The transmissions reach back as far as the first age of the universe," the Aleph continued. "Countless missionaries establishing footholds on barren worlds in endless empty galaxies, filling the interstellar darkness with warmth and light. And in each era of the human age."

"But you haven't had such a hot reception, have you? Not in Japan, at least."

"Most of the previous visitations were covered up by the government. A common practice. Have you heard of the Minamata Incident? Or Junko Furuta? What about the nuclear reactors at Fukushima? The true radiation levels might surprise you even now. This country is adept at ignoring anything that could threaten its everyday routines."

"Sounds like England."

"Humans everywhere are slow to accept change. Fortunately for them, we seek only the greater freedom of the race, a freedom through unity. Once the contact points spread, this era will be united with all others. The superstructures will arrive later, and the sun and the moon will be changed."

"Not if I have anything to do with it."

"When I look at you I can see your ancestry, little potentials stretching through time, back into the slime. Like an autopsy of your soul. I can see you in four dimensions."

"Not a pretty sight, is it?"

"I'm inside you now. From here I can trigger some interesting . . . well, racial memories is no longer a fashionable term, is it? You don't have words for these association blocks."

Samuels made to hurl himself forward at Aso but fell to his knees instead as a screaming began in his head, worse than any he had heard before. His vision shorted out and he saw only incoherent epileptic flashes followed by a parade of nightmares as much felt as seen. A thousand sodden coffins opened inside him, fragments of childhood terrors giving way to a kaleidoscope of shifting scenes: black stars hanging over a decayed city of inverted steeples shrouded in fog; outcasts of the universe crawling among pale shades in an overgrown and crumbling necropolis; human mannequins reduced to cannibalism, worm-white faces dribbling icy tears; atrocity landscapes and fantastic panoramas of dismemberment painted in blood and filth; mutilated spirits fleeing a cosmos of wounds, tormented refugees from the malice of the material. At the heart of it all was an awareness of his body inching forward like an insect, his self a ghost seared into quivering meat by wet electricity, a frail tenant of bone and memory. A desire for dissolution filled him, the need to drive out the ghost and let the night minds fill him with their twilight songs and secret knowledge: a desire lurking on the other side of death, kindled by shadow cells grown in the broadcast factories of the future. The Aleph's face appeared as an ultraviolet outline at the distant centre of the kaleidoscope, eyeless and yet penetrating him with nameless senses, gazing into every corner of his soul.

"Get the fuck out of my head . . ."

"But verbal communication is so inefficient. The world I will show you is beyond words and voices . . ."

Samuels forced himself forward in one agonized rush, extending the secateurs so that their points lodged in the pits of Aso's eyes. He squeezed the handle with all his might until the metal blades bit through the bridge of the Aleph's nose. In the next moment he swung his knife up and thrust it into Aso's neck. He dropped the secateurs, seized Aso by the hair and stabbed him again and again in the throat, head and chest. Through it all a screaming like that of a skinned infant immersed in boiling oil tore through his mind, and a force like the gravity of a heavier world weighed on his limbs, sapping his strength. Finally the screaming faded and the force decreased as Aso's body fell backward, still supported by the heavy folds of his pseudo-flesh and the roots that tied him to the black carpet beneath.

"That's better. I was getting a bit tired of you, sunshine."

Samuels considered what to do next. He knew that Aso was just a human receiver for the Black Mass, and as such, expendable: simply killing him solved little. There was nothing to prevent the Human Communion from singing its songs to others like him, prompting further incursions, fresh visitations. How could he win against an invisible enemy, one who would always be countless steps ahead of him, safe in the distant future? He was not even sure that he had killed Aso, as the black folds continued to move, flapping wildly and wrapping themselves around his limbs. Holes were opening in the cult leader's flesh, escape tunnels made by the black worms within him.

There was only one thing to do, he decided: what he had always done, which was to take the fight to his enemy. The Aleph had told him to open his mind to the transmissions, and now he would do just that, following them to their source. If the Black Mass really was a biotechnology so advanced it was indistinguishable from magic, then it would have to be sophisticated enough to include backwards compatibility. Or in other words, sophisticated enough for even a primitive like himself to interface with.

"Rioko!" he called out. "This is either going to save us or kill me. Or both. Whatever happens, give me ten minutes at the max. Any longer than that . . . torch everything."

He heard her running to him now, moving over the black carpet, but he ignored her words and reached for Aso's corpse. Taking the knife again, he sawed off the top of the Aleph's skull and extracted the mass that passed for his brain, just as he had done with Okamura. The difference between them was apparent: Okamura's central nervous system had been caught in transition, still incomplete, but Aso's had had years to develop. Encased in a sheer black shell, it trailed strange roots and branching nerves, and was studded with small knob-like organs and glands whose nature escaped him. Samuels hacked through the black casing and pulled apart the stringy matter inside, until he was confronted with a perfect ring of cloudy blue eyes.

He gazed down into the wet black pit as it gazed back up at him.

A train of alien thoughts drifted into his mind.

He pressed his face forward into the pit and let its eyes press against his own.

"Take me home," he thought.

And felt it inside of him as

TAKE ME HOME

and his mind was a train barreling through a dark tunnel, a sleek missile slamming into a neon void. The alien gravity returned, tearing the nerves from his flesh and dragging them to the centre of the Earth, where they were dissolved in a white-hot furnace. Then he was in the tunnel again, slamming into the void, and then another furnace and another tunnel, the process repeating in hypertime like a fast-forwarded film, a thousand agonizing deaths and rebirths propelling him across the centuries. He caught glimpses of towers rising and falling as oceans flooded continents, living vessels expiring in an endlessly changing climate, vermin scurrying across the surface of a ruined world and perishing in its poisoned valleys. Centuries became millennia and piled on each other as the world whirled through space, civilizations rising and falling at its poles and under the ground, their arcs visible only as brief flashes, pyrotechnic eruptions fading as fast as they formed. Life left the world for an exile in the stars and returned, changed from its sojourn in the outer dark. Tentative beings emerged and flourished until the images became vague and abstract, less windows on a world than on time itself, vast formations he could no longer name. He was a thought, an atom, a breath—torn from his time, known by none.

At last the images dissolved and his senses expanded until he could no longer fix himself in a single location. The world was an endless swarm of flies, a sea of phosphorescent motes. Thought colonies bloomed and merged, technology drifting by like seaweed: an undersea world, inhuman in its intricacy. There were things like sharks—grotesquely specialized feeder-drones—and living philosophies competing for primacy, vandal stains and art globs.

Unbearably soft beings with froglike skins built spiral cities in the air, mating and dying within moments as the cities themselves clashed and danced through territorial wars and architectural sex. His vision contracted and he glimpsed ecologies smaller than a grain of sand, pinprick cultures seething in every inch of space. His vision expanded and he took in the whole of the planet and beyond: mountain ranges reaching spires into space, linking with living clouds and thinking moons; the sun encased in a hollow obsidian sphere, an inexhaustible black battery; hard-shelled wraiths and rivers of pitch streaming between worlds that were all Yuggoth: the solar system as reversed Tree of Life, satellites and serpentines and the gleaming jewelry of night. His vision contracted again and he was back on the surface of his world amidst the whirlwinds, gale forces lashing him across continents, stripping away the layers of his awareness.

He could not survive here long, he knew; the strain of it would destroy him. Worse, he was not unobserved: shoals of the feeding creatures had noticed him and were encircling him as if weaving a cocoon. With no words to describe the forces seething around him, he doubted any appeal would be heard, but there was no alternative left. Summoning all his strength, he sent out a series of commands.

BROTHER ASO REPORTING MISSION FAILURE ABORT RETREAT
TWENTY-FIRST CENTURY UNDER QUARANTINE
CEASE ALL TRANSMISSIONS REPEAT
CEASE ALL TRANSMISSIONS

At the last moment he realized what the feeders were weaving: not a cocoon but a face, impossibly ancient and full of inhuman hunger, a pitiless intelligence burning behind its eyes like the black light of the sun's endless eclipse.

And the whirlwinds ripped his mind apart.

Samuels awoke somewhere in a damp field as the setting sun warmed his face. He thought first that he was dead, and this thought seemed perfectly natural: wherever he was, it could not be the world in which he had been born. He had been too far and seen too much, and it would not be possible to step back into the life he had led. He did not even try to move, but was content to stare up into the darkening sky and trace the rich gold lingering at its edges. He knew that he must be somewhere out in the countryside, but he gave no thought as to where or when or why; no answers he might find seemed important. Perhaps this forgetfulness itself was Heaven: not an ignorance or forgetting from despair, but an existence without questions, a liberation into limitless peace.

He changed his mind when Rioko kicked him in the side.

It was not really a kick, she explained later, only a nudge; but to Samuel's battered body it struck with the force of a lance. He pulled himself up and felt instinctively for his own body, finding his arms and legs and face intact—although his clothes were shredded and covered with mud, and burn marks covered his flesh.

"What happened? Aleph, is he . . . is the . . ."

He struggled to think of a coherent question.

"I dragged you out of there," Rioko said. "You're heavier than those jugs of kerosene were. A lot heavier."

Samuels looked around. They were in the middle of a rice field, which explained the dampness and the mud. Far off he could smell something burning.

"You just went limp," Rioko said. "You pushed that thing into your face and collapsed. I pulled you away from it and got you outside. I looked around to see if there was anyone else I could save but they were too far gone . . . just . . . nothing human at all."

Samuels nodded. Rioko continued:

"Then I dumped the kerosene everywhere and set it on fire. The whole carpet went up like an oil field . . . I've never seen anything burn that fast. I thought the building was going to explode."

She stopped and looked towards the horizon.

"Do you really think that's it? That it's over?"

Samuels placed a hand on her shoulder.

"I don't know. Looks like I've still got this black shit in me. My foot doesn't seem any different, and God knows what else is going on inside where I can't see. But I don't think it's too substantial, or at least it won't be from now on. They were always pretty sketchy, I think— ghost cells, you might say. If the transmissions have stopped then I think they'll fade over time. Or at least that's the idea. And as for Boss Man and the rest, I doubt they'll survive a good long cook in the oven. I'm sure they're crisping up nicely into little charcoal bricks . . ."

"But if they're really in the future then they can attack again any time, right? And didn't they say there were already other contact points in other countries?"

"There could be. But if there are, I think they're on their own now . . . I don't think any reinforcements will be arriving, at least not for another century."

"What are you talking about?"

"Not sure I can explain, love. But I think I got a message through somehow. If not, I probably wouldn't be here now. I think we've done all we can." He got to his feet. "Come on, let's go."

They walked out of the field and found their way back to the main road, where it took half an hour for a taxi to pass by. Samuels hailed it by running directly in front of it. Later, when they arrived back at Fukaya Station, he paid the driver twice the standard fare.

"Well," he said, "I can't say this trip worked out as planned."

"I think I'm going to sleep for a month," Rioko said.

"Sleep would be nice. After that I'll take a bottle of whiskey and a long, slow Latin Mass. Not necessarily in that order."

"I'll take the whiskey," Rioko said.

On the train back to Ikebukuro they fell asleep resting against each other and stayed that way until the announcer woke them. Then they parted, barely aware of their surroundings.

Samuels spent the next few days in his hotel room, sleeping and drinking cheap beers and sake from the convenience store, emerging only to visit a hospital in Roppongi Hills, where he spent an inordinate sum having his foot and various other wounds examined by an English-speaking doctor Rioko had recommended. He was given an extraordinary amount of creams and ointments and placed on several simultaneous courses of antibiotics. He suspected whatever cell cultures the doctors took would keep the Japanese medical industry busy for the next few decades, provided they looked closely enough.

Rioko met him at Narita Airport when it was time for him to leave, and presented him with a box of traditional Japanese sweets. Samuels opened it immediately and declared that they tasted like papier mâché and powdered sugar. He gave her a copy of *Black Altars* in return, and they sat drinking coffee in a cafe.

"Bloody weather hasn't changed," Samuels said. "S'pose it continues on until October or November, doesn't it? I'm getting out just in time."

Rioko looked at him. "Mark, I'll be honest. When we first met, I thought you were kind of an asshole."

"It's 'arsehole', yeah? Hate to be pedantic."

146

"But I'm glad we got to know each other. Even if it was like this."

"You know I'd have been useless without you, Rioko."

"It is over, isn't it?" She looked away. "I've had nightmares every night for the past few days . . . I don't know if I'll ever get over this. And I'm sorry it happened to you too . . . I don't think there's anything in Japan as bad as that was. Or if there is, I can't imagine it."

"Well, we're not dead, at least. I think that's all you can hope for. Listen, you should come to the UK. I'll show you our version of that worse-than-you-can-imagine thing. It's called Glasgow."

"What will you do now?"

"I don't know—keep writing books and receive even more public acclaim, I guess."

"I've been thinking about writing myself," Rioko said. "To try to deal with all this. I could write it down—my own version. Why not?"

"Let me know when you've finished, and I'll tell you which publishers to avoid."

Samuels checked in and they walked to the security area together, where they embraced and finally parted.

On the plane, he went to the bathroom and pulled off his sock to inspect his foot. The blistered flesh had healed, but the black stain remained. Perhaps it would never wash away, reminding him of the death waiting in his future, the same death that would come for everything he knew before the world passed out of his understanding and became something unfathomable. But there were worse things than death, and a reminder of his diminishing time was not so bad. He covered his foot again, walked back to his seat and hailed a stewardess. By the time the plane cleared Tokyo and passed over Western Japan he was already on his fifth whiskey, and so it did not immediately strike him as strange when the air inside the cabin began to ripple and waver.

After a while Samuels noticed the lights dimming, which did not seem remarkable either. It was only when a familiar stench assaulted his nostrils that an alarm sounded in his mind.

He got out of his seat and stumbled into the aisle as his ears picked up a high-pitched whine from somewhere far off. The dimming continued, until darkness descended over the cabin, and he could make out only vague, confused shapes. Numerous passengers were now unconscious, while others were clutching their heads and making frantic, agonized gestures. In front of him, a cabin attendant stood frozen in place, her face obscured by fleshy strands of black matter, a clotted spiderweb of shadows. As he watched, the same embodied darkness filled the cabin windows. He felt something monumental lodged behind the surface of the world, a war machine casting off its camouflage and emerging into view. Ahead of him he could already make out a predatory face forming in thin air, one whose outline he recognized from a tortured fragment of memory. The future, it seemed, had not forgotten him after all. The whine behind his ears became an endlessly repeated scream.

Samuels forced himself to raise his whiskey and finish it.

"Well, hello again," he said.

THE BIG-HEADED PEOPLE

by DF Lewis

I always knew, physically speaking, I had a big head. My mother complained about the difficult labour she had had with me as a result. Later, I sometimes felt I was carrying around a burden, not only because of the head's thoughts with which I needed to deal (as we all do, I presume), but also because of what was this conception of a weighty object balanced upon a relatively thin neck. One of my dinner-party jokes was about needing enough space for both my brains. The only real acknowledgement I made to its size.

But it wasn't exactly a problem. It wasn't outlandishly large, and, for most of my life, I never gave it a second thought. Indeed, it later became more proportionate to my portly physique, the neck beneath it soon thickening with middle- and eventually old-age, and the stomach swelling to a size that had more to do with beer than anything else. Or so my wife told me.

I ought to add that I never considered myself to be big-headed in the figurative sense of being arrogant. In fact, most of my life, I suffered from the opposite, as I felt a sense of reticence and diffidence based upon an inferiority complex. I was an only child. Still am, of course.

I first met my big-headed brother, meanwhile, in what I initially considered to be dreams, but as time has gone by, I have begun to consider my so-called real life as a dream or a serial of broken dreams. Whether my actual dreaming when asleep had become my real life outside of sleep did not logically follow on from that, of course. It was a beta situation, still being tested, I told myself.

Some of you will now point to my still big head and screw your fingers round and round, implying that lots of old people like me confuse dream with real life. Well, I screw my own finger back at you and at your relatively tiny heads. Not that I am implying that the old adage—tiny heads, tiny minds—holds any water!

I shall call this big-headed brother by the name he called himself: Francis, later Frank.

Frank told me that his house was in a place where other big-headed people lived, where, in fact, only big-headed people lived.

In the early days, we merely sat in his living room, not unlike my own living room. Comparing heads.

Being brothers, Frank and I had heads of similar size, although the features on our faces were smeared across slightly out of kilter with each other. As if the painter had lost his skill from one portrait to another. Not that we ever agreed which portrait was which!

Over quite a long period, Frank and I got used to each other, not only to the phrenology of our respective heads but also to the personalities contained within them. He was slightly more confident about life than me, but, he did bow to my greater wisdom on many an occasion. However, his confidence gradually took full sway—not a confidence-trick as such, but more a way of enticing my acceptance that he knew a lot about the place where big-headed people lived— and eventually he suggested we venture outside the house and expand our horizons by meeting a few of them.

He warned me that our own heads were nothing by which to judge.

"You have seen nothing yet, young Desmond," Frank often said. "There are some very sad people out there."

There is indeed sadness about big heads, I always thought, as they tend to look heavy. But one can never really judge whether other people are depressed simply by the inferred weightiness of their heads. I had always assumed Frank was a happy man, but maybe he wasn't. I now wondered whether or not he thought I was happy. With shared parents, we were probably of similar mentalities, but neither of us could clearly remember our parents.

I nodded at what he said and, soon after that, we ventured out.

I was astonished that the area in which Frank lived was not a city or town. Not even a village, in fact. The reason I had assumed he lived in some built-up area is now beyond me to understand. You see, I cannot recall ever hearing traffic outside or ambulance sirens or anything like that. So when I saw a land stretching into a distance of valleys and hills, I should have accepted it quite unequivocally. But I must have looked quite confused, because Frank said: "Desmond, Desmond, surely you knew I lived here?"

"Yes, Frank, I knew you lived here, but I did not know you lived HERE." I waved my hand from one end of the warm blue sky to the other.

It was then I spotted the distant tower, indicating perhaps a community.

"Is that where the big-headed people live?"

"They live all over the place."

"Is that a church, then, all on its own?"

"It is not a church as you understand it. But it is a high enough church, however, and its tower radiates a mystical power over us all, without our needing to visit it."

We had already walked quite a distance while talking about this 'church,' as if entranced by it. So when I turned to look at Frank's house, it was too late to inspect its nature as an abode, hidden as it now was by a slope of undergrowth. It was then I noticed the first person since leaving that house, almost stumbling upon him, as I did, on the wayside of the rough track where a stile led into a meadow. The man leant against it, as if resting his head for a while before resuming his journey. The head was indeed noticeably bigger than Frank's or mine. His face was vaguely doleful, amid otherwise smoothed-out expressionlessness.

"How are you, good sir?" asked Frank confidently.

"Nobbut middling, Frank," he replied lugubriously.

"This is my brother, Desmond, who is visiting the area for the first time."

"Pleased to meet you, Desmond. I've been happy to know your brother for many years." He offered me his hand, with a slowly mooning smile.

I took it firmly (having been taught by my father from childhood never to offer anyone handshakes like wet fish) and we then exchanged gentlemanly small talk for quite a few minutes, before Frank and I moved on. It was only later I realised that Frank had not actually introduced him properly to me by name.

It was difficult to tell whether or not we were heading in the general direction of the tower, as the contours of the pleasant countryside intervened. And, before long, we met a second person, this time a woman, with a head slightly bigger even than the previous encounter. She had some sort of upholstered device that rested on her shoulder and served to support the weight of her head. I was rather taken aback at how she seemed disabled simply by having to bear this head in the normal course of her life.

Frank did not seem to know her and she only nodded to us in the way complete strangers would nod to each other when passing on a countryside walk, with no real desire to hold a proper conversation. However, I felt tears in my eyes as I turned to Frank and said: "We should have offered our help. She looked as if she was struggling to carry on."

"No, Desmond, there are many people like her, and if we stopped to help everyone we would never get home again. And, indeed, you have seen nothing yet."

And he was right. Around the next corner, we came across a man who was literally laid low, his head so big, it seemed bigger than the rest of him. But that was because his head was the nearest part of him to us, the rest of his body tapering into a ditch.

I was perturbed that he had fallen into the ditch, but Frank assured me he was only resting, at a convenient comfortable configuration of land to support the flow of his head and body. I bent down and looked into his eyes.

"He seems to be crying . . ." I said, looking up at Frank. But Frank was looking away as if preoccupied with something else. And before Frank could respond, the man himself spoke in a kindly half-whisper, half-outspoken-singsong:

"I'm not really crying, just thinking of the past. I shall get up in a moment and be on my way."

"Can we help at all?" I asked. "There are two of us here. One of us under each arm and you'll be up in a trice."

"Where are you from? Where are you off to?" the man asked, as if testing whether we could be trusted. "Are you heading towards the tower?"

I didn't know how to answer, but Frank suddenly became involved:

"One can never reach the tower, however far one travels."

"Speak for yourself, young man." A tone of irony there from the laid-low man, or of cheeky politeness, as Frank was almost as old as I was. "I am travelling there myself and hope to reach it before long. They say it has the highest priests in the land even though the church itself doesn't have the tallest tower. And I have spent my life hoping to receive confession at their hands."

I lowered my head. I didn't want him to see that I was crying, too. If I had been able, I would have given him confession myself there and then. But I did not believe I had the qualification to do so, nor did I believe in what he believed in.

I told him that I would reach the tower and prepare the priests for his arrival. That would be half the battle, at least. And, if the worst happened, and if he didn't reach the tower, then they would know about his pilgrimage towards them and pray for his soul, instead.

When we left him, he was smiling.

I did reach the tower, in the end, having lost Frank along the way. Sadly, it was derelict, with most of the church in ruins, but the tower itself was, with some difficulty, climbable. And indeed I climbed it, negotiating the spiral stairs to the tower's highest point; the sides of the wall were barely wide enough to allow the passage of my head. I was determined, however, at least to view eventually, from such a height, the whereabouts of Frank's house, so as to guide my return towards where this dream had begun, if dream it was. Or at least view the nature of his house itself, beyond the dumpty hills.

ATTRACTION

by John Mundy

I thought I would carry the story of the Old Man to the grave. But long years have passed and now, as my own death draws near, I feel compelled to tell everything—and let the doubters be damned!

There were six of us in a room that stank of encroaching death. Six of us . . . and the Old Man.

Along the walls of the vast, high-ceilinged chamber, at carefully measured intervals, ornately carved holders of black wood held scarlet candles that burned and flickered and released a strange and heavy incense that made the poisonous air bearable. Suspended high above the bed were spherical objects of varying size, not unlike astrolabes; the largest of brass, the others fashioned of dark wood and engraved with horrific images and numerals. The largest of the globes revolved slowly with the muted sound of a clockwork mechanism. On the eastern wall, now shrouded in shadow, barbaric symbols beneath a great radiating eye had been crudely drawn in rust-colored strokes. (The Family had been horrified at the defacement of property they hoped to inherit but the Priest summoned by the Old Man was a foreigner, of some obscure Order, and would not be deterred. He spoke not a word of English and his face was bandaged from a recent and severe accident). The voluminous purple drapes, tightly drawn against the golden sunlight of the late autumn afternoon, shut out all the sensual world beyond Stout House. All was in preparation for the death watch, all carried out per the Old Man's rigorous instructions. But even in a room of shadows and flickering light the sick man's eyes burned with inexplicable merriment. Despite pain and weakness, he motioned to those who surrounded the bed to draw nearer. A slow smile creased the darkness of his face. Such a terrible smile! Rictus-like, a ghastliness that only death might remove before replacing with its own sardonic stamp! The smile spoke of how he detested the ones in that dark and foul-smelling chamber; detested them as they detested him. In that moment I admired his honesty, even if it hid behind a mask of mockery.

"Come close," he said. "I must tell you a secret." His voice was hoarse and horribly liquid. "A great and terrible but *necessary* secret . . . come nearer, my dear ones . . ."

The stench of decay was enough to make one retch, but how could they refuse? I alone refused his invitation, merely watching as they drew nearer . . . and I thought of animals cajoled into a clever and cruel trap.

"My studies," he began (his voice decimated by age and disease but now suddenly empowered by the vigor of a barely concealed gloating), ". . . my studies have led to this inevitable moment. Yes, my children, *those* studies which all of you have mocked—no, *no*, please, I respect you for having the decency to whisper only private laments over the tragic decline of once prodigious faculties. I commend you for your . . . *compassionate* humanity."

"Dear Grandpapa," said Marie hesitatingly, "you should not let yourself become agitated—"

"My sweet child, your concern touches me deeply, but I fear we have no time for such fine flowery flourishes . . ."

Not the words but something behind the words, behind the hinted challenge, made the girl instinctively step back from the bed with the caution of one expecting a physical blow. And not for the first time I found myself thinking, *This old dog still has teeth.*

"Her concern is sincere," stammered Paul, Marie's husband. Unfortunately, his quivering voice lacked all conviction; we knew him as a weak man and a physician of dubious skills and morality; the Old Man tolerated Paul, finding him convenient for obtaining the necessary variety of drugs, in ever greater amounts, for the atrocious pain that ravaged his failing body. Any other man in his physical state of collapse would have been raving in delirium or lost to coma; but the power of his Will, always terrifying, would apparently carry him through to the end.

156

"Paul is right, Father," said Jean, in a tone that failed to conceal the hopeful blade within. "Like all of us, Father, Marie is only concerned with your welfare . . . "

"Yes, yes, how could you doubt such a loving granddaughter?" cooed Helen, Jean's fat wife who seemed clownish with her mascara, rouge and garish lipstick. "The child loves you *so. . . .*"

"Love? Ah, love. Yes. And what of James?" asked the old one, turning his Gorgon gaze toward me. "Does James feel filial affection for the stinking husk in this beautiful bed?"

I said nothing and surely he couldn't have expected a reply. What need for it now?

"You were never blood of my blood, James, but it was hardly sentimentality that made me take you into this loving household and raise you as one of my own. You know me too well for that! But in you, I saw much I recognized, reflections of things and desires that burned fiercely in my own heart. Not all good things, of course . . ." He chuckled and Helen's plump, sweaty face paled at the sound. More than words, that death rattle of amusement evoked memories of the free-ranging depravity of the Old Man's younger days. "Perhaps you may not love me, James. But it isn't gold that drew you here today. Gold holds no attraction for one like yourself. But curiosity . . . a curiosity only the Damned can appreciate . . . the Lust to *know,* so powerful it can burn and eat out your guts if unquenched . . ."

"I came," I replied, "because I owe you a debt. You taught me much, even if the lessons learned weren't always the ones intended."

To my surprise, the ghastly smile softened. He seemed for the briefest moment like a tolerant father bemused at the folly of his errant child.

"Come, come, Old One, dearest brother," croaked Janelle, the ancient, withered crone who was his only surviving sister. "Tell us of this important matter you say *must* be cleared up now and not—" Here she paused suddenly as if overcome by unbearable sorrow, " . . . and not at some . . . later time. . . ."

The best performance in the Death Room yet! My snort of disgust earned a look of purest hate from the old creature.

"So be it! Let me explain now, before Fate prevents that possibility forever, dear sister. Let me explain how the very things you have mocked—my rare and ancient volumes, my priceless medieval manuscripts, my relentless and *rigorous* studies, my travels to strange distant places seldom frequented by tourists—all these things have made it possible for you, dear ones, to now possess *forever* the thing you crave the most . . . my wealth, my fabulous wealth. Most specifically my *gold* . . ."

I heard a soft collective gasp and watched as the old devil's smile grew even more wicked.

"But—first forgive me, family, if my mind seems to wander; indulge this old dying man you love so—and let me point out Death, something we accept as an *inevitable evil* in this world, is far from inevitable or evil to a man of Knowledge, a man of power prepared to seize that rarest of golden opportunities. Death is inevitable only to the clods that are obliterated by it, ignorant and helpless beasts in the face of its glorious fires. They know nothing of its true nature and die like beasts of the field because they cannot use its Transformative power. *It is the moment of Death Itself I refer to.* Such a moment offers a man with certain Knowledge and Abilities, infinite possibilities that most men would find unthinkable, unbelievable . . . perhaps unendurable. For a Man of Knowledge, Death is but a trauma *and can be survived—*"

Was it my imagination? As he spoke those words a subtle change seemed to come over the room. The candles flared and flickered and the shadows about the great bed seemed strangely distorted, almost menacing. Black masses became elongated figures like stick caricatures of human beings only to be replaced almost immediately by serpent-like shapes that seemed to move and slither across the bed's occupant. For a moment I felt like a child again, frightened by the moonlight streaming through the black groaning branches of the tree that rustled in the wind outside my window, casting frightening shapes on the walls of my bedroom. Yet the others appeared to notice nothing and the effect was as subtle as it was disturbing. I said nothing and cursed the vagaries of Fancy.

He continued to speak. I saw what I perceived as a sick excitement building up inside of him as his hands, little more than yellowed claws, slowly and methodically kneaded the bedsheets.

"Can you recall, my dear children, so many years ago, so many decades, when I left you and your poor mother and took off for an entire summer to a small and ancient town in a part of Europe I stubbornly refused to identify? It was a quaint and charming place with its Soul in the Deep Past. Nestled by the heavily wooded slopes of great mountains to the North and East and a great gushing gorge to the South, the houses seemed doll-like and lost in dreams of centuries forgotten; a few were gaunt and angular; they leaned precariously over narrow lanes of cobblestone and reminded me of sardonic old gentleman tilting forward to touch their hats to their brothers. It was selfish, no doubt cruel to leave you so, but it had to be done and I've never hesitated from doing what necessity demands. You see, it was necessary for my instruction, for my continuing education in the hidden Wisdom that can only be found in certain sympathetic locales, in certain . . . *atmospheres*. Of course I was not alone. I had a companion—I fear the Way of Enlightenment that drew me so demanded it. But even to one of a temperament like mine, my companion was hardly what I'd call congenial company. No, far from it. His manners were unpleasant and his visage more so—but it would be folly to talk too much of such things. His Presence had cost me much—I do not speak of money, understand—and after finding such a one as he, how could I slink back from seeing it through? I doubt if any of you have heard of the *Black Pilgrimage*—though I suspect James here has." At that moment, I glimpsed the feral beast fully showing its teeth.

"Yes, the Black Pilgrimage. That's what they called it, what it's been called since time immemorial . . .

"Know that for each man the Pilgrimage is different. Some men may travel to the darkest and most terrible places imaginable, covering vast areas of land, of continents, seeking out different, progressively more intimidating Teachers along the way. For others the Path to Enlightenment may be different. It may be achieved with one terrible and demanding teacher. Why, children, some men may not even be required to wander from their homeland . . . the Pilgrimage, you see, is a journey of the heart and the mind. . . .

"Well, I learned much from my unpleasant companion over the course of that strange summer with its withering heat so untypical for that town and its furtive inhabitants. Of the precise nature of our activities, I must, again, have recourse to silence. Suffice it to say they were numerous and varied; and under the rigorous discipline of my excellent Teacher I advanced with a pleasing swiftness. Yes, I leaned many great and terrible secrets under the tutelage of my dark companion. And no secret greater or more terrible than this did I learn: That man is born with only the *possibility* of developing a Soul;

and a man of sufficient Knowledge and Will might, only at the very moment of approaching death, create a thing that most wise men had always regarded as a chimera, a mere illusion . . . a thing common men might call a soul. The creation of a Soul would be an act comparable to the greatest wonders of Alchemy, a glorious transformation that would require the willing energy of many others for its success though the price would be a terrible one for *those* human beings to pay . . ."

No one in that room had said a word since the old man had begun to tell his story. But the expressions on their faces spoke all too clearly of their incredulity and growing disgust.

My own reaction was quite different. I felt an anger that demanded expression.

"The price," I asked, taking advantage of a moment when the old man had been forced to draw several deep breaths. All in the room turned toward me. "The price of such tutelage . . . "

"Why do you ask, James?" he said at last. *Again, that rictus-like smile!* "Surely, you know it well. How many times on how many nights when the wind howled like a hungry cur beneath your window, have you asked yourself if *you* could pay it . . . *assuming the time comes for you.*"

"*Never!*" I cried. "I no longer seek that kind of knowledge."

The Old Man paused and managed a slight nod to Paul. Jean, impatient as ever, scowled as Paul prepared a syringe of stimulants and narcotics.

"You disappointed me, James. I had such hopes for you . . . "

"The coin of such Enlightenment is blood." I spat out the words. "The oldest coin in the world and I refused to pay it . . ."

"You should not interrupt Grandpapa," hissed Marie, glaring angrily at me. "Why encourage him to waste his precious energy on fairy tales when there are more important matters to discuss—"

"Yes, yes," rasped the jaundiced monster in the bed. "Pressing matters, matters of the utmost importance. Like the *gold* . . ."

His death was obviously near. Once, I knew, the Old Man *had* possessed great wealth. But that was many years ago and I suspected the real Fairy Tale was this feverish talk about gold. It was merely a cruel tool, a cynical way to manipulate and torture those around him. . . .

And still he continued.

"The *gold*, yes. But that, children, is what I am telling you about. At the end of that parched summer I was a wealthy man. I had discovered a great treasure and I brought it home with me. My Teacher led me to it . . . it was the hottest day of that summer and near twilight we had come upon an old and blackened church, long abandoned. The sun, strangely distorted, was an impossible fiery sphere, red and huge, glimpsed through wavering mists that rose from the surrounding hanging woods and the roaring river rushing through the deep gorge that cut through the unearthly beauty of that enchanted land. *I swear to you nothing had stood on that ground the previous day*. . . . Now the black majesty of a desolate Church rose like a great beast from an otherworldly Lair. Black skeletal trees stood like sentinels about that Holy Ground, their branches twisting and creaking in the absence of the lightest breeze. With the resolute heart of the True Seeker I followed my companion across the bare burnt earth surrounding this Great Dragon. He entered and I followed . . . but I cannot, *must* not speak of the Wonders and Terrors that mighty edifice held. The very silence both delighted and terrified . . . it was black with infinite and unnamable possibilities . . . in the end it was my Teacher, now my Guide, who found the massive shadowy portal that beckoned from behind a gigantic black-robed and *very* horned saint . . ." He laughed and choked simultaneously. He struggled and regained breath enough to sneeringly speak again. "You have seen ample evidence of that wealth and believe me when I say you have no conception of its magnitude! None! "

The old man's description of a "blackened church"—so infuriating was the *light* manner in which he discussed these things! —made my blood run cold. If his story were true—and I saw no reason to doubt it *might* well be—then he had traveled *farther* into the Pilgrimage than I had ever suspected. Over the centuries many Seekers have embarked on the Black Pilgrimage but few have ever reached *that* hellish place or been vouchsafed the merest glimpse of it. Now I wondered: had The Old Man *completed his journey?*

"No one doubts you, dear brother," said the old crone. "We believe."

It was at this moment I sensed the air in the room had grown strangely hot, almost stifling. I felt lightheaded; my thoughts began to swim. Was it imagination or did the shadows move in a mad dance in the wavering light of that noisome chamber? A chamber that only minutes before had seemed so vast but now seemed oppressive and narrow as a coffin . . .

"Come. Children," he said, and with his remaining strength raised his arms toward them as if to welcome them in an eternal embrace. There was something monstrous in the gesture but their greed made them blind to any mockery.

The Old Man regarded me with a piercing look.

"It is time for you to leave now, James, there is no place for you here."

The others turned to regard me. They began to laugh uproariously, making no attempt to hide the scorn in their eyes, the sneers on their lips. Fools so besotted with avarice they saw and understood nothing . . . I needed no further urging to leave; I had acknowledged the perverse debt I owed him. But the room seemed to be shifting in and out of focus while my breathing had become labored, and my sense of balance precarious. I reached for the door—

I staggered into the hallway, the heavy oak door closing behind me. I felt on the verge of collapse. I blamed the heavy narcotic incense and the stench of death choking the Old Man's poisonous chamber. But then the *screams* began . . . and when I turned to re-enter the room I found a door that would not budge . . .

In some ways, I suppose, my nature is every bit as cold blooded as the old man's ever was. It was after the sounds had ceased that I lit a cigarette and smoked it, hands uncertain, trembling in the darkness beyond the old man's massive door. I was shaken, weak and disoriented as if I'd been drugged. Night had invaded the old house and there had been no one to see to the lights. The sounds from the sick room—including the unexplainable and explosive crack that sounded like wood rending and a heavy weight falling—had not stopped for a considerable time but there had been no one to hear them; the staff had been discharged that morning in accordance with the Old Man's instructions. The thought that the Old Man had succeeded in creating *something*—I dare not call it a Soul—that would survive the "trauma of death" filled me with an icy horror beyond words.

The old man had spared me, yes, but I could not believe it was out of any sense of affection. I was simply not the *willing* victim his obscene Alchemy required.

I smoked several more cigarettes before I decided I must enter that room again. The room was empty, the candles still burning; there was no trace of the others who had rushed so willingly into the old one's embrace. Only one object of significance remained.

It lay on the bed which had collapsed under its great weight. To any eye it appeared to be a remarkably detailed statue of a man, a statue entirely in gold. The skin had become altered and terrible to look upon. But even worse were the small, round protuberances that seemed to erupt from that skin. On his chest they gleamed dully in the room's light; they reminded me of miniature faces, carved with no regard (or perhaps contempt) for detail. Unable to break away from the magnetic pull of revulsion and horror, I saw in each of these protuberances small crude pits exuding a purulent discharge, streaming like black tears; as well as what appeared to be mute rudimentary mouths. And only after some minutes did I realize these things were sinking slowly into the gold flesh that had called to them.

Within an hour the ghastly protuberances were gone. Shortly after, the flesh of the dead man began to change back to the jaundiced and diseased skin of a sick man of great age, a man now dead.

That was long, long years ago.

But *gone?* God help me, I wonder still.

THE EARLY SIGNS OF BLIGHT

by Kristine Ong Muslim

When the bad man once again came to see ten-year-old Ben, the boy did the usual: screamed for his Mama. Ben told his mother that this time the bad man had managed to reach out from the confines of the closet, had reached out without fear of the yellow light of the Pooh lamp, reached out with a blackened arm that was long enough to encroach into Ben's world, and had grasped the end of the bed sheet. At first, it was just an arm—impossibly long and snakelike, skin burned uniformly throughout its length. And where the burnt outer skin peeled away, the flesh underneath revealed a fleshy pink tone, the colour associated with healing.

Ben had expected the bad man to finally show himself. The rest of him, anyway, and not just the arm. The bad ones always did. The bad always came out of the woodwork and showed themselves to the world. Ben had just not expected that it would start its journey into his world with an arm. The arm, after grasping the cotton sheet, withdrew. It disappeared again inside the slightly opened closet door, a testing of the waters of what Ben expected to be its gradual trespassing into his world.

His mother, upon hearing the screams, entered the room. She hugged him.

"He's back," Ben said.

"I know, I know, I know," she said, releasing her son from her embrace, and headed outside the room. She returned with a sponge and a bucket of soapy water that smelled strongly of bleach and cleaned the insides of the empty closet. She would end up ruining the wood with her forceful rubbing of wet sponge, but she did not care. She wiped away at the nonexistent blood with calculated strokes, wiped away the origins of the beast, crying as she did so but not noticing until she felt spent and tired, the acrid sting of bleach everywhere.

In the midst of his mother's manic cleaning, Ben fell asleep, inhaling the bleach's fumes. He snuggled his pillow. The blanket covered his body, except for the feet. He could not sleep with his feet under the blanket.

There was Pooh on the lampshade casting a warm amber glow, one that enlivened as much as it concealed. There was Pooh on the lampshade, and he was holding his pot of honey, his grin locked in place.

The next morning, Ben came bounding out of his room and smiled at his mother as he met her worried gaze. She instantly brightened and motioned for him to join her at the breakfast table. She sipped coffee, looking outside the kitchen window of their two-bedroom apartment at Station Tower, the five-storied apartment building that had stood for close to one hundred years at the junction between Outerbridge and Bardenstan.

The whole apartment smelled faintly of bleach slowly dissipating out of one living room window that was left partly open. It looked as if she had spent the entire night cleaning. The lopsided coffee table had been straightened, its edge lining up with the striated pattern of the area rug. The edge of the yellow ottoman was lined squarely with that of the coffee table. The rug was fluffed and freshly vacuumed. Four throw pillows, all in varying shades of grey, were arranged according to size on the couch. The magazines on top of the coffee table were organized in stacks of two—the thick ones on the left, the thin ones on the right. The pile of thick magazines towered over the pile of thin ones, and this unnerved Ben. He crossed the room and placed some of the thick magazines on top of the thin ones to balance the height of the two magazine piles. Satisfied, he went to the kitchen.

She poured milk and proffered the glass to her son. He took his accustomed place at their small dining table, drank without meeting her inquiring eyes. "I'm okay, Mama," he said, as if anticipating a question from her. He always made an effort to reassure her, even if there was no reason to. She smiled at her little boy, a smile she reserved for the people in her life whom she loved unquestionably.

It was the first Sunday of December. The cold was underway. In the distance, the Fletcher Memorial Home squatted, its silvery industrial-grade panelling glinting. In the streets below, there were only a couple and a woman walking her dog. Jim Shenkel, Station Tower's dayshift doorman, shuffled with his familiar gait by the side of the building, checking whether the vandals had spray-painted the walls again. Last week, someone had spray-painted GOD LIVES HERE in red.

"Are you crying again, Mama?" Ben called out from the couch as he watched *The Land Before Time*. There was no way that he could tell she was crying because he could not see her face. She was hunched before the sink, scrubbing the already spotless metal surface.

"No, honey," she said, steeling herself not to cry again.

That night, Ben covered himself with the blanket up to the chin, prayed the same memorized lines "as I lay me down to sleep" his mother had taught him to say each night. The prayer did not ward off the bad man. It certainly did not make him feel safe, even during the times when he recited it fervently. But he relied on his mother's instincts to survive, and if she believed that the verse about dying while asleep and being delivered straight to Heaven could save him, then he would gladly say it.

She was still fussing in the kitchen. The whole of the afternoon, she sorted the dried laundry from the downstairs laundry room and wiped the windows, the empty top shelves in the kitchen.

Ben saw her, or thought of seeing her in his mind's eye as she sought more and more things to clean. His last thought before he drifted to sleep was this: she should have been here, protecting him in case the bad man showed up again. He absently scratched at the healing cuts in his abdomen.

Hours later, Ben woke up, feeling a tug in his exposed left foot. He threw his blanket aside and looked down where the bad man's fingers grappled at his foot, pulling him into the gloom of the closet. Holding on to the metal headboard for balance, Ben screamed.

His mother entered the room, still clutching a dirty rag. When he looked at his foot again, the bad man's hand had disappeared. He could not remember how long his mother comforted him before he fell asleep. When he woke up, it was past six in the morning.

With a soft knock, his mother peeped through the gap of the slightly opened door and told him to get ready for breakfast. She made an omelette, one with cheese and some meat trimmings. She slid the egg onto his plate, paused as she heard a knock.

Ben could only hear parts of their conversation. He did not pay much attention to them. There was no need to. He and his mother had more serious problems to contend with—a bad man in the closet and then Ben's mother losing her job a week ago—than a stranger appearing at their doorstep on a Monday morning.

"I'm Officer Subic, Mrs. Bruin."

"What's this about?"

"Can we talk to you in the police station, ma'am?"

"Just tell me what this is about."

"Someone from your husband's office called us. He hasn't shown up for work for three days and his cellphone's been turned off. And when they called you, you said that he had already left you and your son."

"That's correct."

"May I come in, ma'am?"

"Sure."

They talked for a long time. Half an hour or more had passed before the door latch finally clicked in place.

Ben's mother once again busied herself with household chores. At Station Tower's apartment 11, there was never a shortage of surfaces and corners to dust, of table cloths and couch covers to straighten, of home decorations to wipe down and rearrange.

Meanwhile, Ben, inside his room, had advanced eleven breathtaking pages in his copy of Maurice Sendak's *Where the Wild Things Are*. The pages were filled mostly with illustrations. Ben sometimes touched the book's pages and imagined feeling the vibration from the pacing of the characters in the book.

That night, Ben woke up with another tug at his foot. This time, it was much more forceful. Without looking down, he knew. He understood that the manner in which the bad man had grasped his foot, the nails digging deeply into his skin, the bad man's rot seeping in through the scratches the scrabbling nails made against his skin, meant that the bad man would not let him go this time. He would end up another blackened, disfigured creature in the closet, known henceforth to the world only as a bare arm worming out of every bedroom closet door. He shrieked.

Predictably, Ben's mother entered the room and switched on the overhead light. Instead of the usual cleaning rag, this time she clutched a knife, swung it and slashed at the stunted form in the middle of the bed, the form that tormented and lived, tormented and loved, tormented and demanded, again and again, to be rescued.

"It's me, Ma," Ben said twice as he fended off the blows with his small hands.

"Leave us alone, leave us alone, leave us alone," she raged in a monotonous tone, and exorcising all the evils harbored by the flesh, slashed with her knife until the flailing stopped.

The police, toting the search warrant the erstwhile Officer Subic did not have the day before, broke down the door at ten minutes past seven in the morning.

They found Ramona Bruin rinsing dishes—dishes that were already clean—in the kitchen. She looked out of the small kitchen window by the sink, a window the size of a submarine porthole showing the off-white of winter, the near monochrome universe that beckoned to no one because there was no one else left to call outside.

"It's over now," she said to the officer.

On the bed was Ben. Ben, who could not sleep with his feet under the blanket. Ben, who no longer stirred and was covered by a blanket up to his chin. At the bedside table, the Pooh lamp burned golden yellow, the colour of summer afternoons.

The officer who peeled away the covers made an effort not to retch. This was only his second homicide. In the closet, another officer found a mannequin's arm. Then someone remarked on the incredible cleanliness of the rest of the house, except for the blood tracked on the floor by Mrs. Bruin.

A day and a half later, Carlos Bruin's body—what was left of it—was discovered inside a dumpster behind the Fletcher Memorial

Home, a short walk from Station Tower. The head and pieces of his torso were stashed inside a wheeled trolley bag. The limbs were not located.

The shaken residents of Station Tower were interviewed by the police. Some were guarded in their responses. Some were open to speculating: everything from child abuse to how Ramona Bruin was driven to insanity when she lost her job. Claire Dalkey, who owned a unit in the first floor of the building and who had lost her son in an accident weeks ago in front of the building, said something about not bothering to find out what had happened to the Bruins because nobody could ever know the truth. "Perhaps, it was all random, and she just snapped," she said.

The news told of self-inflicted wounds on Carlos Bruin's abdomen. They were all superficial and in various stages of healing. A similar pattern of cuts was discovered on the boy's stomach.

Nobody could piece together exactly what had happened at Station Tower's apartment 11. Months later, in another part of the city, almost the same thing happened—mother and son, two-bedroom apartment, mannequin's hand in the closet, self-inflicted wounds on the abdomen in different stages of healing when the son's body was found, and the mother near-catatonic, scrubbing a perfectly clean kitchen countertop. And once again, someone noted the orderliness of the apartment. It was as if everything was buffed and straightened out by mechanical hands. That there was something underneath all these—the clinical neatness, the incredible attention to detail, the absence of family photographs, and the seemingly contrived cleanliness—that was yet to be uncovered. Even then, no one could figure out the whys.

The third time a similar yet still unsolved case landed on the precinct just outside the border of Outerbridge, one detective unwittingly intuited the truth. "When we impose so much order onto our lives, it upsets the balance, you know, the natural chaos of things. Then it explodes back in our faces. Then we kind of just—snap."

"Trying to channel your inner Carl Sagan, Jess?" said Brenda from internal affairs, holding a measuring cup full of coffee grounds in the pantry.

Everyone laughed, but the laughter was born out of nervousness and frustration. It was going to be a long day.

CHAOSKAMPF

translated by James Champagne

II
Information Overload Unit

In the eyes of the manly poet (that most paradoxical of all artistic hybrids), there are few sights more guaranteed to inflame the loins of their repective Calliopes than that of some grizzled old salt standing on the deck of his boat and gazing out at the ocean with a stern/ stoic/world-weary expression on his face (take your pick). One could only wonder what nautical fantasia in verse Coleridge could have committed to paper had he lived to see the spectacle of Captain First Rank Ivan Sigismondavich Karnov standing atop the fair-weather bridge located near the top of the sail of the submarine known as the *Crimson November* and contemplating the South Pacific sea: surely the resulting epic would rival that of his immortal *Rime of the Ancient Mariner*?

Captain Karnov, of the Red Banner Pacific Fleet, was 52 years of age, and stood a little under six feet tall. His face bore a startling resemblance to that of Bishop Fulton J. Sheen, though his gunmetal-grey hair was a distant relative of the coiffure of Samuel Beckett. As his vessel neared Antarctica, the cool air forced him to dress warmly when he was outdoors, and that afternoon he was wearing a bulky black wool coat and, atop his head, a gray military-style *ushanka*, one whose fur was made from expensive sheepskin: in the centre of the cap was a gleaming red star. Underneath the ear flaps of his *ushanka* he was wearing headphones that were connected to the Walkman clipped to his belt (no generic *pokazukha* knock-off Amphitone Active Acoustic System this, but a genuine Sony Walkman: *glasnost* had its benefits), and that afternoon he was listening to The Smiths' *The Queen is Dead* album, which had been released a year ago. Captain Karnov was sure the brass would have preferred him listening to a pop star from their side of the Iron Curtain, someone like Alla Borisovna Pugacheva, but as far as he was concerned, nothing could compete with the biting melancholy of such songs as 'There is a Light That Never Goes Out', which was the track he was currently listening to.

The date was December 3rd, 1987, the Year of the Scavenger. Twelve days ago, on November 21st, the *Crimson November* had set sail from the fleet headquarters at Vladivostok (which was less than 40 miles from China), and had begun travelling submerged in a southeasterly direction at a steady 24 knots. Their heading was 47°9'S 126°43'W, which was located approximately 7602.819 nautical miles away from the ports of Vladivostok. At the rate they had been travelling, they were expected to reach their destination the following day, on the 4th: 13 days to get there, then another 13 days to get back. Captain Karnov was aware that they were approaching the Pacific Pole of Inaccessibility (also known as Point Nemo), which was the place in the ocean that was farthest away from land. If they kept heading south past that point, they would reach the shores of Antarctica, the South Pole. Luckily for him and his crew, they weren't expected to go that far south.

At that moment the ship was surfaced, and the submarine's massive sail was extended 42 feet above the waterline. Even though it was a breach of military protocol, Captain Karnov ordered his ship to surface every few days or so, just so he could get some fresh air up on the sail and take in the scenery. Not that there was a lot to see out here in the middle of nowhere: just the light blue of the cloudless sky divided in a straight horizontal line by the dark blue of the ocean, the occasional iceberg being the only thing to break up the aqueous monotony. It would be a peaceful enough sight, were it not so cold: as a Russian Captain, Karnov was more than used to such weather, and when he had first been assigned to the Red Banner Pacific Fleet all those years ago he had looked forward to idle days cruising the temperate seas of the North Pacific, at the same time thanking fate that he hadn't been assigned to the Red Banner Northern Fleet: the idea of freezing his balls off at the submarine pens up in the Polyarny District of Severomorsk (where the Cold War truly was cold) hadn't appealed to him at all. Yet here he was years later, still freezing his balls off.

Still, he knew he was lucky, that there were other Russians worse off than him. At least he wasn't a *nekulturny* KGB Border Guard (spending lonely evenings scanning the horizon with passive PN-1A night vision devices), or a SPETSNAZ officer stationed in the mountains of Afghanistan, piloting an Mi-24 Hind helicopter and dodging Stinger SAMs fired by Bactrian camel-riding *mujahideen*. Worst of all for those enmeshed in these wars of Islam were those technicians tasked with creating (and deploying) the so-called "doll-bombs" in the villages of Afghanistan (most recently in the Ningarhar Province). Booby-trapped mines and bombs designed to look just like toys, dolls, pens, and other common objects, that when picked up would explode. Even more insidious (in Captain Karnov's opinion) was the fact that many of these "doll-bombs" were painted green, a colour associated with Islam, the better to tempt (and maim) unsuspecting Muslim children. Captain Karnov wondered how those engineers could sleep at night, knowing what their devices were used for. Sometimes he guiltily wondered if perhaps the West was right, and that the Soviet Union was in all actuality the Evil Empire. But then again, every government had skeletons in its closets. During World War II, Japan's Imperial Army had supposedly developed biological weapons on the island of Okinawa, something to do with gas germs and walking fish. And going even further down the diseased spinal cord of history, he had heard stories that in 1837, the U.S. Army had distributed blankets infected with smallpox to the Mandan Indian tribe at Fort Clark in North Dakota, though such a story could never be confirmed. . . . [1] Be that as it may, the U.S. had supposedly curtailed its production of biological weapons following the Biological Weapons

1 Save the e-mails, I'm well aware that the historian in question has been discredited.
–Translator

Convention of 1972, whereas the following year the Soviet Union had initiated its *Biopreparat* program, an enormous nightmare network of 18 top-secret laboratories tasked with producing pathogenic weapons on the sly: weaponised anthrax, Ebola, the Marburg Virus, the Bubonic plague, Q fever, the Junin virus and smallpox were just a few such diseases currently being studied (and created) in laboratories all throughout the U.S.S.R.

So while the Captain wasn't all that crazy about this current mission, at least he could take solace in the knowledge that most men of the Soviet Union would kill to be in his boots, commanding the Soviet Union's newest and greatest submarine. And the *Crimson November* was certainly deserving of the hype, of that there could be no doubt: the fact that it had been given an official name was further proof of its greatness, as the other *Typhoon*-class subs all had extremely generic names such as TK-208 or TK-13 (that is, they were named after their hull number). That the *Crimson November* should have a proper name was something that Captain Karnov had insisted upon when he had been assigned command to it, and because he had such clout, his wish had been granted: it was hard to stand out in the Red Banner Pacific Fleet, which was the largest of the four Soviet fleets, but somehow, Captain Karnov had managed that tricky task. He had even managed to convince his superiors to keep the *Crimson November* docked at Vladivostok, rather than at the *Typhoon* SSBN division pens up at Nerpichya, which was near the border of Finland and Norway: amongst Soviet submariners, Nerpichya was notorious for its extraordinarily poor crew- and base-worker facilities.

The *Crimson November* was a *Typhoon*-class SSBN. *But why use the Imperialist's NATO designation,* the Captain wondered. It was the latest release from the U.S.S.R.'s line of Project 941 *Akula* (or "shark") submarines (the first such sub in this class had gone operational in 1981), and it was the largest submarine in the world, nearly half the length of a *Nimitz*-class aircraft carrier. Designed by S.N. Kovalev at the Rubin Design Bureau in Leningrad (back in the old days, it had been called Technical Bureau #4, Karnov remembered, his grandfather having been employed there back in the 1920's), and built at Severodvinsk, like most of the Soviet Union's other *Typhoon*-class submarines it consisted of two parallel main-pressure hulls (each hull housing assorted crew quarters, equipment, and propulsion machinery), these hulls being over 488 feet long with a maximum diameter of 23 feet and divided into eight compartments each. In between these two hulls (and forward of the sail) were twenty missile tubes placed in two rows, each tube holding a solid-propellant RSM-52/R-39 Rif missile (NATO designation: SS-N-20 Sturgeon). Another pressure hull (this one over 98 feet in length and housing two compartments) was located beneath the sail and in between the two main hulls, and here one could find the control room and attack centre. All in all, there were 17 hull compartments, all enclosed within a gigantic outer hull that was somewhere in between 564 and 574 feet long. The submarine was powered by two OK-650 pressurized-water nuclear reactor plants (one per main hull), along with an 800-kilowatt diesel generator: the steam-turbines of the reactor were capable of producing horsepower somewhere in the 50,000 range. Its twin seven-bladed bronze screw-back propellers were housed in shrouds to protect them from ice damage, as the *Crimson November* was designed with ice travel in mind. In terms of speed, it could travel at 14 knots while surfaced and 24 knots when submerged. Beneath the forward hull at the front of the sub and built under the torpedo tubes was the vessel's Skat sonar system (a massive MGK-503 low-frequency spherical array sonar, manufactured by the Deregand Computer Systems' Gholraqy Division, who had also provided the ship with the experimental Artificial Intelligence system known as the JC AI), while built above each of the two main hulls were escape chambers that could easily carry the *Crimson November's* entire crew of 160 men to the surface should the need arise. With a surface displacement of 23,200 tons and a submerged displacement of 48,000 tons, the submarine could stay submerged for over 120 days (handy in the event of a nuclear war), and its test depth was 1,300 feet. Both the inner and outer surface of the *Crimson November* were coated with special anechoic tiles, so despite its large size, it was still an especially quiet and stealthy ship.

Of course, first and foremost, the *Crimson November* was an instrument of war, and it was fully outfitted in that regard: the Russians didn't refer to it as "shark" for nothing. It boasted six torpedo tubes (capable of firing either type 53 torpedoes or RPK-2 Viyuga cruise missiles), a 9K38 Igla SAM, and the aforementioned 20 RSM-52/R-39 Rif missiles. Part of the reason why the submarines of Project 941 were so large was because of the size of the missiles they were carrying, as each R-39 missile was 52 ½ feet in length and weighed over 198,420 pounds. These missiles (which were controlled by the new D-19 missile system and which were manufactured by the Zlatovst Machine-Building Plant in Zlatovst, Russia, in 1984) were solid propellant (as opposed to the more commonly used liquid propellant ones) and used a 3-stage solid-fuel boost design. With a range of up to 4,480 nautical miles, each of the missiles carried ten MIRV (Multiple Independently targeted Re-entry Vehicle) warheads of 100 kilotons each. Like the *Trident* subs of the Americans, the *Crimson November's* firing rate was one missile every 15 seconds, which meant that it could fire its maximum armament of twenty missiles in around five minutes time. To sum it up, there was enough sheer nukage aboard the *Crimson November* to give any red-blooded member of the CND nightmares for life. The knowledge that he could start World War III in just under five minutes was a fact that hung over the Captain's head like the proverbial Sword of Damocles. *The State promises us a glorious future, a Worker's Paradise, but what kind of paradise will our children inherit? The theoretical implications of these weapons of war we have created seem to make a very mockery of this idea . . . in this 20th century of ours, the vision of a Worker's Paradise now seems as far-fetched as that of Chernyshevsky's Crystal Palace,* Captain Karnov thought grimly. *Ah well, it's not my job to question my superiors. I'll leave that to the academicians: let them grapple with these questions of modern technological dehumanisation.* But what man wouldn't be distracted by the power he had under his command? One of his biggest worries was that of his submarine being hijacked by hostile forces and turned against the U.S.S.R. So for his own peace of mind, he had put his own safeguards in place, as a precaution against that very scenario. But even that may not have been enough; so much of their technology was currently controlled by elaborate computerised servomechanisms that he supposed a hacker of some skill might be able to take control of the vessel, and if such a thing were to occur, than Captain Karnov would have no power over his own submarine, much like that sorcerer mentioned in *The Communist Manifesto* who finds himself unable to control the powers of the subterranean world his spells had called up.

Part of the reason why Captain Karnov was up on the fair-weather bridge that afternoon was because he was trying to take his mind off the nightmare he had been suffering from for a number of evenings now, ever since they had set off on this voyage. The nightmare was always the same one: in the dream, he was not a submarine captain; rather he was an astronaut, one floating in outer space, a long air hose connecting his body to the Salyut-7 space station. They were in orbit high above the earth, the planet looming before him like a leviathanic marble. In the dream, Captain Karnov was forced to watch in horror as the outer surface of the planet was slowly covered up by what looked like an enormous red mould, or fungal material; during this spectacle, Joy Division's 'Ice Age' was playing on loop from some unknown source, seemingly acting as a soundtrack to this yeasty atrocity exhibition. This fungus would first manifest itself at different spots on the Earth's surface, before slowly elongating itself like old leeches. The red fungus would slowly spread out, eventually merging with the other red patches in blasphemous harmony, until the entire planet was covered, not just the landmasses but even the oceans. And issuing forth from the smothered planet was a most horrible sound, the collective scream of the asphyxiating population, the final death rattles of those pale and morbid ape poets. How had this evil fungus come to be? Could it be traced back to space-sailing spores from some unimaginable horror from the outer rim of the universe? Whatever the case may have been, in the dream he somehow knew that the Earth was not the first planet to have been consumed by the Red Mould, and that it also wouldn't be the last . . . he knew that it would continue to spread to other worlds, other galaxies, and that as long as it existed no life was ever safe. And, even worse, that there was nothing that a lone man such as Captain Karnov could do to stop it. Soviet Solidarity was all well and good, but even the unity of the collective could only fall against the threat of this Red Mould.

Over the music, he could hear the sound of someone ascending the ladder located within the interior of the sail. He took off his headphones and pocketed them just as the hatch near his feet swung open and his navigator, Lieutenant Dmitri Doak, climbed into view. Once Dmitri was atop the sail, he swung the hatch shut and walked over to stand by his captain's side. They were both kind of cramped up there, as there wasn't much room atop the sail, what with most of its free space being taken up by a large array of antennas, periscopes and other machinery: a Kora satellite communications antenna, a Cintez radio communications aerial, a Zona direction finder, an Anis VHF radio aerial, a MRKP-58 Radian ESM/radar mast, a Salyut radio sextant, a Kutum search/navigation periscope, and a PZKE-21 Lebid attack periscope.

"Good afternoon, Comrade Lieutenant," Captain Karnov said with a polite nod.

"And a good afternoon to you as well, Comrade Captain," Dmitri said. He was in his early 40's, a stout and ruddy-looking fellow with a brown, receding hairline, a thick brown beard and moustache, and a square-shaped head. He was blind in his left eye, and it was for this reason that he always wore a black eyepatch over that eye. Recently assigned to the *Crimson November*, this was his first mission serving under Captain Karnov. Initially, the captain had been wary about this, but his superiors had assured him that Dmitri Doak was a good man to know: he was a rising red star in the Soviet Navy, the very personification of the New Soviet Man. Captain Karnov was familiar with the man's dossier: how he had been born on the large island of Sakhalin, how his family had moved to the wastes of Siberia when he had been still just a boy, how before joining the Soviet Navy he had made a living first as a construction worker, then raising (and racing) sled dogs (a somewhat unpopular sport in the Soviet Union, though one that was slowly starting to make a comeback that decade). Like Captain Karnov, he too had been both a member of the Young Octobrists and the Young Pioneers (though Dmitri had also belonged to the Komsomol), and he too was a loyal member of the Party. He was a rugged hard-drinking man, a friend of all the right people in all the right places, the Next Big Thing, a dynamic new voice. Even his children were going places: his son was currently a member of the Cosmic Defence Troops over at the Baikonur Cosmodrome near Tyuratam, while his daughter was employed at Mosfilm, where she composed State-approved experimental electronic music for documentaries revolving around the Soviet Union's space program. Dmitri Doak had truly lived a wild life, and he even had the bloody receipts in his pocket to prove it.

"What are you doing up here, if I may be so bold as to ask?" Dmitri asked.

"Trying to avoid Boris, for starters," Captain Karnov said with a chuckle, making a reference to the *Crimson November's* annoying and unpopular *zampolit* officer. "I keep forgetting that this is your first mission with me, Dmitri. Hang around my crew long enough, and I'm sure they'll tell you stories about how I like to take these little topside breaks."

"Some of them have already insinuated as much to me, Comrade Captain. Some suspect that you prefer the sky to the sea, that you'd be more comfortable as a pilot rather than a submariner."

"Ah, but what is the sky but the sea's double, its twin, or even its mirror, if you will," Captain Karnov said. He took out a pack of Sobranie cigarettes and lighted up. "The problem with being cooped up in a submarine all day, especially one with all the creature comforts and amenities of the *Crimson November*, is that it can cause you to forget that one is constantly at the mercy of the sea, and it is to one's own peril to ignore that fact. Always keep in mind the first thing they taught us at the Nakhimov School, Comrade Lieutenant: don't forget the sea, because the sea won't forget you."

"Wise words indeed," Dmitri said with a sagacious nod. "Forgive me for saying so, Comrade Captain, but isn't it a risky move for us to be surfaced out here for such a long period of time?"

"Fear not, Comrade Lieutenant. Here in these deep ocean basins, we don't have to worry about those pesky SOSUS receptors. And as for occasionally surfacing, the KH-11 satellites of the imperialists are too busy hovering on their orbital paths over Grid Square 54-90, desperate to get some images of our OCTOBER FROST war game. A classic *maskirovka* feint! They're too distracted to care about spying on this godforsaken part of the ocean. In any event, recent data collected from our own RORSAT satellites reveal no *Amerikantsi* naval forces in our immediate vicinity," Captain Karnov assured his subordinate.

"Ah yes, I seem to recall reading an article on OCTOBER FROST in last week's issue of *Krasnaya Zvezda*," Dmitri murmured. "I'm sure that Captain Tupolev is itching to prove himself against his old teacher, *da*?"

"Indeed," Captain Karnov nodded. "But come, no sense lingering up here any longer, let's go below and get moving again. I intend for us to reach our destination tomorrow, and wrap this mission up."

"I'm a little curious as to the exact nature of this mission myself," Dmitri said. "I haven't been told much."

"None of you have been told much . . . but then again, Dmitri, you do come highly recommended, so I suppose it's okay for you to be let in on what we're doing. I must say, though, I'm surprised by your request to transfer to the *Crimson November*. As I heard it, you had a relatively comfy position aboard the TK-208."

"You know what they say about sharks, Comrade Captain, how they always need to keep moving to survive? Well, that's me," Dmitri said. "I simply want to be a better shark, and what better place to do that then on the *Crimson November*, the latest and greatest of our *Akula*-class submarines?"

"Ha! Well said. Come, let us go to the control room, then we can talk further in my stateroom. Besides, it's getting dark out here."

"Yes, let us return to the deep, where it's more dark," Dmitri said. He then noticed the headphones from Captain Karnov's Sony Walkman, which were slightly sticking out from the pocket of his coat. "Were you listening to music just now, Comrade Captain?"

"Guilty as charged, Dmitri. The Smiths, as it happens. Have you ever heard of them?"

"I've always been more of a fan of The Police and David & David," Dmitri shrugged. "Used to like U2, but all their album covers of shirtless boys look like carefully cropped photographs taken from some pervert's child porn collection to me. Better not let Boris find out, though. He'd rather have us listening to Pesnyary. As if their 'I'll Take You Away to the Tundra' can even hold a candle to The Beatles' 'Back in the U.S.S.R.'"

The mention of The Beatles caused Captain Karnov to reflect briefly on the topic of his dead wife, who had been a fan of that band. The Captain remembered buying her an imported copy of their *White Album* LP back in 1980, during a period when Western products were hard to come by. It had cost him 80 rubles (about $150 in American money), and he had had to purchase it from the black market tape pirates that convened at a small park off Mayakovsky Square in Moscow. But it had been worth the trouble, because in the end, she had loved the gift.

The captain stooped down and pulled open the hatch. Beneath it were the steel rungs of a ladder descending down the interior of the sail. Captain Karnov watched Dmitri clamber down, before he himself followed. Once they were within the interior of the sail, Captain Karnov pulled the hatch into a shut position, then spun the wheel until it was locked. He checked the green indicator light on the ceiling next to the hatch to be sure that it was securely shut. Then he watched as Dmitri opened another hatch on the floor, this one leading down to a ladder that led to the control room. Dmitri climbed down, followed by the captain.

Once they were both in the control room and the hatch on the ceiling was shut and secured, Captain Karnov gave the dive orders. He pulled on the diving alarm, and a second later a loud buzzing sound rang throughout the inner hulls of the *Crimson November*, causing the crew within to run to their stations. Captain Karnov then gave the order to flood the ballast tanks and rig out the diving planes. The inner hulls of the *Crimson November* became filled with the noise of rushing air, this noise being caused by the opening of the vents atop the ballast tanks. Slowly, the *Crimson November* began to descend into the ocean, finally levelling off at around 150 meters below sea level. The noise of the ballast tanks was replaced by new sounds, the ominous creaking and popping of the hull as it came under the great pressure of an ocean that now completely enclosed it on all sides like a darkling blanket. Once their position had stabilized, Captain Karnov gave control of the bridge to one of his *starpom* (executive officers) before indicating for Dmitri to follow him.

The two men climbed through a circular and watertight portal in the bulkhead, ducking down as they did so. They came to a ladder that led out of the control room compartment, into the long and wide passage that ran in between the two main hulls: like most of the other areas of the sub, the floor here was painted green. They walked down this passage for a bit, past walls that were made of laminated wood (and which were stenciled here and there with Cyrillic lettering), the smell of diesel oil all around them, the whirring sound of the nuclear reactor pumps an ever-present soundtrack to their movements. As they walked to a door, they passed by a man carrying a Geiger counter, monitoring the submarine's radiation levels to make sure that nothing was leaking. Finally, the two men came to one of the doors that led into the recreation area of one of the starboard hulls. They first passed by the dining room, where a number of officers were currently seated, having lunch, steaming bowls of *nichego* kasti, which they ate while reading the latest issue of *Kommunist*, their conversation covering a variety of topics, included some good-natured ribbing ("Your *babushka's* uglier than Ayn Rand!"). A few others were playing chess, or watching a hockey game on a TV with bad reception (the current game was Central Army vs. the Wings). Then they passed by the aviary, with its pastoral green carpeting, where real birds encased within glass cages flitted amongst tree branches. Rocking chairs were set up in this room, and a few of the crew members were sitting around, listening to another of their comrades strumming an acoustic guitar and singing David Bowie's song '1984' (this room also had a big aquarium filled with exotic-looking fish embedded within one of its walls). They walked by the recreation room, a big room with fake-wood-panel wallpaper and rectangular wooden tables with red-plush chairs. A lone crew member was currently in there playing the arcade game known as *Morskoi Boi* ("Sea Battle"), which involved peering into a fake periscope and launching torpedoes at digital sea craft. What better way for a sailor aboard a submarine to relax in his off-hours than by playing an arcade game that simulated submarine warfare? Also located in this room was a coin-operated *sok* juice machine: as with most vending machines in the Soviet Union, purchased drinks did not come in individual containers, and a communal glass was used instead (to bring one's own glass was considered a social faux pas). They passed by a small gym (complete with a 4x2-metre pool, its depth 2 metres. Captain Karnov didn't use it often as the water always looked somewhat filthy, even dirtier than Lake Baikal), and in this gym there were currently a few young men clad only in tight shorts; they were lifting weights, their muscular young bodies covered in sweat, while Tangerine Dream's song 'Choronzon' blared on a nearby Bolide VEF SIGMA 260 boom box. Past the gym was an even smaller sauna: not quite on the same level as the *banyas* one could go to in Moscow, but it was the thought that counted. Finally, they passed by the officer movie theatre: a paper taped to the side of the door announced that the film being shown that evening was, as always, *Battleship Potemkin* (no Burke Stodger *Commie Confidential*-type films shown here, no siree bob).

Soon they came to the Lenin Room, which was located near the wardroom. The Lenin Room was a small library (no bigger than a closet) which housed the *Crimson November's* propaganda texts and ideological books: mainly books by Karl Marx (such as *Das Kapital*), Leon Trotsky, Vladimir Lenin, and other assorted agitprop. Posted on the wall next to the door were the orders for the various crew members. As Captain Karnov and Dmitri walked past the Lenin Room, the door opened and Boris Smirnov, the ship's *zampolit* (political officer), stepped into the corridor.

"Good afternoon, Comrade Captain and Comrade Lieutenant," Boris said. He was a few years younger than Captain Karnov, an oleaginous little *apparatchiki* with lactescent skin and a black bowl haircut that reminded the Captain a little of Moe from the Three Stooges.

"Good afternoon, Boris," Captain Karnov said. "Lt. Dmitri and I are going to my office for a drink. Care to join us?"

"Would that I could, but there are matters I must attend to on the bridge; Wagenheim's teeth are acting up again," Boris said with a theatrical sigh. "Perhaps I will join you for dinner later on tonight?"

"I'm sure that can be arranged," Captain Karnov nodded, even though he wasn't looking forward to such a thing. That Captain Karnov viewed Boris with distaste wasn't surprising, as most Soviet submarine captains tended to loathe their political officers.

"I look forward to it," Boris said with a disingenuous smile. "Until then, *do svidania*."

The two men said goodbye to Boris and continued on their way. Finally, they reached Captain Karnov's stateroom. It was a sizeable room with a desk, a small bookcase (mostly housing various books by Vladimir Nabokov and Fyodor Dostoyevsky, along with bootleg *samizdat* translations of the works of Arthur Machen), a safe containing the mission documentation, a small bar, and, in the portside bulkhead, his bunk. Hanging up on the wall was a framed map of Russia, along with the Flag of the Soviet Union, complete with red star and the alchemical marriage of the hammer and sickle. There were some personal touches, however, like the framed photograph of Captain Karnov's wife on his desk, along with the framed reproductions of famous nautical charts and *mappae mundi* from antiquity (such as prints of Olaus Magnus' *Carta marina et description septemtrionalium terrarium ac mirabilium* of 1539 and Abraham Ortelius' map of Iceland from the 1598 Antwerp edition of his *Theatrum orbis terrarium*). Captain Karnov had always had a predilection for such maps, and the one thing they all had in common was their depiction of sea monsters. On these old maps and charts, one could bear witness to flying turtles, aquatic bishops, pig-snouted krakens, ichthyocentaurs playing viols, faceless Sirens with eyes or walrus tusks in place of nipples, an owl-faced ziphius devouring a seal, a one-eyed, duckbilled sea serpent with a furry tail, a lobster-like octopus dragging a man into the sea in one of its claws, a grotesque-looking creature known as a roider (essentially, a toothless whale with bloated red and white lips, two spout like horns sprouting from its head), a giant squid wrapping its tentacles around a clipper ship, another ship being attacked by a physetera (or 'spouter', giant whales that attacked ships by vomiting water on them from the spouts atop their heads), plus other ships getting sucked down whirlpools with names like the Dubois Maelstrom and the Finknottle Vortex. Some of the maps were also inscribed with warnings, similar to the "here there be dragons" of yore: one map advised seamen to steer clear of one particular island, which was said to be populated by the dreaded Roko Basilisk. In the old days, such monstrous depictions no doubt chilled the blood of even the most rugged seaman, but to modern eyes Captain Karnov supposed they must look perfectly quaint. He liked to gaze at such maps in his spare time, though, if only because they were relics of a time when much of the world's seas were still unknown, and also as a reminder that the ocean was a dangerous place, even if the only true monsters in the sea now were man-made machines like the *Crimson November*.

Captain Karnov watched as Dmitri looked over the old maps. "What do you make of my décor, Dmitri Gospodin?" he asked the younger man, using his patronymic.

"It's, ah, interesting, Comrade Captain, but not exactly my thing. These maps don't seem to represent the triple ideal that all good art should strive for, that of *partinost*, *ideinost*, and *narodnost*," Dmitri admitted.

"Do you like art, then?"

"I've always been more of a fan of the Social Realist style," Dmitri said. "Are you familiar with the work of Aleksandr Gerasimov? His 1938 painting *Stalin and Voroshilov at the Kremlin* is breathtaking . . . I keep a print of it up in my office at home."

Of course you do, Captain Karnov thought. In one corner of the office was a small wet bar. Captain Karnov nodded in its direction as he asked Dmitri, "Would you care for a drink, Comrade Lieutenant?"

"*Pozhaluysta.*"

The Captain poured out two small glasses of vodka, one for himself and one for Dmitri. "To the *Rodina*," he said, by way of toast.

"To the *Rodina*," Dmitri echoed. And with that, the two men took their drink.

"Not bad, not bad at all," Dmitri said, licking his lips.

"In terms of quality, I'm afraid it's no Stolichnaya," Captain Karnov apologized as he set his empty glass down. In truth, he preferred black balsam liquor anyway (a Latvian specialty). "Still, it's better than the Sannogan our comrades had to guzzle during the Great Patriotic War, *nyet?* Another round?"

"We'd better not," Dmitri said. "Don't want to look unprofessional while Boris is on the prowl."

"You're probably right . . . it is a bit too early in the day to start seeing the green snake," Captain Karnov agreed.

"Now, about this mission, Comrade Captain?" Dmitri asked.

"Ah yes," Captain Karnov said. He walked over to the safe behind his desk. It was unusual that this safe was kept in his personal quarters as opposed to the submarine's wardroom, but as has been observed, the Red Banner Pacific Fleet brass gave Captain Karnov greater leniency in how he ran his ship. The Captain put in the proper combination and the safe swung open. Within was a manila folder (on the cover of which was the familiar Soviet iconography of the hammer and the sickle) with some papers inside. Captain Karnov set the folder on his desk and opened it. He then gazed at Dmitri and said, "What I am about to tell you does not leave this room, Comrade Lieutenant."

"Do I look like a *stukachi*, Comrade Captain? Do I look like I'm wearing good shoes?" Dmitri protested. He was referring to the easiest way to spot a KGB informer in Moscow: always look for shabbily dressed people wearing nice shoes.

"Very well, I trust you. Tell me, Comrade Lieutenant, how familiar are you with the *Wunderwaffe* of Nazi Germany?"

"I've heard stories," Dmitri said in a guarded tone. "They were revolutionary superweapons conceived by the Third Reich, correct? As far as I've ever heard, almost none of them were actually built."

"Indeed. One of the most famous was the Sun Gun, or Heliobeam, or the *Sonnengewehr*. Whatever name you wish to call it, it was a theoretical orbital weapon conceived by Hermann Oberth in 1929. Picture, if you can, a space station with a 100 metre-wide concave mirror, a mirror that could be utilized to reflect sunlight on a concentrated point on Earth," Captain Karnov said as he shuffled through the mission orders. "Such a weapon could burn a city to ashes, boil entire oceans."

"It sounds like the sort of thing that would give the creators of President Harley's Strategic Defense Initiative wet dreams. Good thing the Fuhrer's scientists never succeeded in creating such a device," Dmitri said.

"So it's been assumed . . . but now, we're not so sure, and that's what this mission is all about," Captain Karnov said. "I'm sure you've heard about the Werewolf Bunker, or *Werwolf*, to use the Nazi word for it." He was referring here to one of Hitler's old Mitteleuropa headquarters, this one built in the forests of Vinnitsa in central Ukraine back in 1941. "Recently a top-secret excavation of one of its underground levels revealed long-lost documentation regarding the *Wunderwaffe* weapons program. According to our intelligence networks, the Nazis had established a secret underwater experimental weapons laboratory out in the South Pacific. The coordinates for this lab are the exact same coordinates as the ones we're being sent to. In other words, the purpose of this mission is to head to that spot of the ocean and see if the Nazis did indeed operate such a laboratory there. And, if so, to salvage any technology there that we do find, for reSearch purposes."

"So what do you think we'll find out there, Comrade Captain?" Dmitri enquired. "Do you really think we'll find a Nazi superweapon?"

"If you believe that, then you probably also believe that Nurse Davitashvili can make roses bloom with a wave of her hand," Captain Karnov grunted. And yet . . . who knew? Maybe there really *was* a Nazi superweapon out there at 47°9′S 126°43′W. Weirder things, after all, had happened. And were Captain Karnov the man to retrieve that weapon . . . well, it could only further his military career, and ever since Sonya's death, his career was all he had; it had, in effect, become his life. He closed his eyes for a moment and imagined the fame that would greet his name should he be the one to retrieve the superweapon: the front page headlines in *Pravda* and *Izvestia*, interviews on the TASS network, front row tickets at the Bolshoi, first class seats at Aeroflot (even though the airline's food was all but inedible anyway; garlic was one of the few identifiable foodstuffs they employed), perhaps his own ZiL-41047 limousine (complete with his own personal driver, certainly a step up from the Volga sedan he currently owned . . . and wouldn't that beat taking the *elektrichka* at *chas pik*?), maybe even a summer home at the Black Sea resorts or a fairytale dacha in the birch forests that surrounded Moscow (a real first class dacha, not those ugly and cheap tin-roofed ones so common to Kazan). *Yeah, sure, keep dreaming Ivan Karnov,* he thought sadly. *The Slepaks have a better chance of getting their emigration visas approved than you do of getting a nice dacha.*

Captain Karnov snapped back to reality and continued his conversation with Dmitri. "Still, orders are orders, and this is the task that Admiral Khvatov has given to us, though of course, his orders are coming straight from the Central Committee." He was referring here to G.A. Khvatov, the former Chief of Staff who had assumed command of the Red Banner Pacific Fleet on January of that year.

"These orders seem less like the handiwork of Admiral Khvatov and more like that of Oleg Popov. If you ask me, it sounds like the plotline of an old *Nu, Pogodi!* cartoon," Dmitri grumbled. "I just worry that this will turn out to be nothing more than a wild goose chase, and that should it go public, then our Soviet Navy will become as ridiculed in the West as our air defence comrades currently are, thanks to that infernal Matthias Rust."

"Hey, they don't pay us the big rubles for nothing," Captain Karnov said with an ironic smile. He himself made around 1,000 rubles a month, which wasn't anything to sneeze at, seeing as how the average conscript was lucky if they made 7 rubles and 80 kopecks a month. "You know how it is, the *nachalstvo* has a bowel movement and the shit rains down on us. Anyway, I've taken up enough of your time, Dmitri. I'm sure you must have other tasks to attend to."

"Indeed I do. Well, thank you for taking me into your confidence, Comrade Captain." Dmitri gave his Captain a salute, then made to leave the stateroom. Before he left, however, he seemed to notice the computer on the Captain's desk for the first time, a computer that was of a Western model (as opposed to a native Elektronika 60 or a Soviet DVK-2), an IBM PC to be precise. "A Sony Walkman *and* an IBM, Comrade Captain? You certainly do like living on the *na levo*, don't you?"

"Please, all these items were purchased at legitimate stores," Captain Karnov said. Thanks to *glasnost*, the days of buying Western products from the *fartsovshchiki* were all but over.

"Ain't *perestroika* grand?" Dmitri asked as he left the room.

Once Dmitri had left, Captain Karnov placed the mission orders back in the folder, then returned the dokument to the safe. As he locked the safe back up, he wondered if telling Dmitri the true nature of this mission had been a good idea. Most of the crew members of the *Crimson November* were under the impression that their submarine was taking part in a military exercise and nothing more; very few of them knew what was really going on. Aside from Captain Karnov,

Boris, and now Dmitri, they were all being kept in the dark. Partly this was because Captain Karnov just wasn't sure who he could trust. It was bad enough that Boris knew, but that was an unavoidable fact of life; being the ship's political officer, it was his task to report back to his superiors of the Politburo, so he had to be kept in the know. Captain Karnov had heard rumours that there might be spies on board, poisonous people whose true allegiance lay not to him but to darker powers. Supposedly the sub's cook was a *chekist* from the 7th Directorate (a slang term for KGB agents), and one of the *michmen* was possibly a mole planted there by the GRU. There were also rumours that the CIA was interested in this mission as well, and the last thing Captain Karnov wanted was The Company snooping around his country's business. In other words, there were people in very high places at the Kremlin who had taken a great deal of interest in this operation, and Captain Karnov felt as if he needed to be wary of where he stepped. One false move could have him stripped of his military rank at best and jailed at Lefortovo Prison or, at worst, find him doing hard labour up at one of the Kolyma gulag camps. Best to treat every man as if they were secretly outfitted with Z-5690 microphones and Svouk lighter cameras (the latter courtesy of the KGB's 11th Optical Laboratory). It was hard to be a brave Apollo to his men if he couldn't trust them, but these were the cards that he had been dealt.Captain Karnov looked at the chronometer mounted in the bulkhead of his stateroom (which was set to Moscow Standard Time), saw that it was only a few minutes until dinner. So he left his stateroom and made his way to the officer's dining room. A few minutes later found him seated with Boris, and the two men conversed over a meal of *shashlik, lobio* and *khachapuri* (the latter being bread made with goat cheese). For dessert, they had some kefir (which was a cross between buttermilk and yogurt) and Russian beluga and caviar imported from the mouth of the Volga River over in Astrakhan, which was the Soviet caviar centre. One of the perks of serving on the *Crimson November* was that you certainly got to eat well, unlike the rest of the *narod*: no mere diet of pork, potatoes and pickles here (ditto for the elsewhere ubiquitous cucumber).

"I must say I want to just finish this mission as soon as possible and get back home in time for the New Year's celebration at the Kremlin," Boris said in between bites of caviar. "I find submarines so dreary at times . . . I miss the sun."

"The sun isn't exactly a regular visitor to Moscow this time of year," Captain Karnov said with an ironic smile. Indeed, from the months of October to March Muscovites typically only received around 15 minutes of sunlight a day. But he knew what Boris meant, as he was especially looking forward to once again seeing the sun rise over the Golden Horn Bay in Vladivostok. "You should be honoured, Comrade Boris, to serve on a state-of-the-art vessel such as this."

"Yes, yes, the *Crimson November* is state-of-the-art, but I wonder how long he truly has before he gets sent to the scrapheap," Boris said. Like most Russians, he referred to sea vessels in the masculine gender, contrary to the Western practice of thinking of their craft as female. "I think the era of Mutually Assured Destruction (MAD) is coming to an end, my dear Captain. The days of the Brezhnev gerontocracy are over, and one can only assume the nuclear SLBMs will follow. The future of war will most likely be asymmetrical power struggles between rival private military companies (PMCs). Did you know that the General Secretary is in Washington D.C. as we speak? He'll be meeting with President Harley in two days."

"Oh yes?" Captain Karnov asked. He hadn't been aware of that.

"Supposedly they'll be signing some new treaty initiated by the Pax Institute, something to do with reducing our mutual nuclear armament," Boris sighed. "Here's hoping it all goes better than SALT II; the last thing we need right now is another foreign policy nightmare. I know that history is a process, and that the victory of world socialism is assured, and that so long as the Berlin Wall stands the worldwide adoption of atheistic communism is guaranteed, but sometimes I worry that our nation is falling into a dark time. Last year we had that business with Chernobyl, along with the destruction of our illicit chemical weapons facility at Arkhangelsk thanks to those two MI6 agents. The war in Afghanistan is going poorly, as usual, and it doesn't help matters that Qurac is now funneling money and weapons to the *mujahideen*; what do you expect from a country that employs a murderous clown as its ambassador? The divorce rate is rising, and alcoholism has been increasing at a steady rate since 1979. The streets of the *truschchobys* are running wild with *khuliganys* and *Lyubers*. And now there're all these troubling stories I've been hearing about weird doomsday cults that have been cropping up in the *Rodina*. No doubt it's a problem that'll get worse the closer we get to the millennium, but still . . . disturbing. Why, just before we left dock, I read a story in *Pravda* about an oceanographer from the Shirshov Institute of Oceanology who killed himself recently. Only he didn't just kill himself, he also murdered his entire family as well: the autopsy report showed that he gouged out the eyes of his own children and ate them."

"*Yebat' menya!*" Captain Karnov exclaimed in disgust.

"I know! Can you imagine doing such a thing? After he killed his wife and children, he smeared a message on the wall with their blood, then drowned himself."

"What did he write on his walls? What was the message?"

"Oh, just a lot of gibberish, mostly. There were two words in particular that he scrawled out numerous times: Esok Agi. Along with this message: EL NIIS IALPVRG, YOLCI MAHORELA. What do you make of that?"

"Beats me, Comrade. My, this has certainly been a grim conversation," Captain Karnov observed as he finished off his Russian beluga.

"Well, what would you rather have us talk about? Lipizzaner stallions?" Boris asked with a smirk. He raised his glass with a sad smile and said, "To Marxist Solidarity!"

Following that remark, one of the sub's ensigns approached the Captain's table. He was far younger than either of the two men, being somewhere in his early twenties: fresh out of the Nakhimov School, in other words. His name was Liu Zhang, and he was of Chinese descent. Like Dmitri Doak, this was his first mission serving under Captain Karnov's command. The Captain was already quite fond of the kid. Not only was he eager to learn (and even quicker to master any tasks that were sent his way), but he also followed orders well, yet at the same time he didn't hesitate to improvise on the spot when the need arose, a quality often lacking in the typical Soviet military man, who had a tendency sometimes to fall into a state of inefficiency when cut off from the chain of command. Heck, even Liu's uniform was in immaculate condition, with not a crease in sight, no easy feat on a submarine, where oil spills were endemic.

"Comrade Captain," Ensign Liu said, as he gave the captain a proper salute.

"Ensign Zhang," Captain Karnov said with a nod. "You have something to tell us?"

"Pardon my interruption of your dinner, Comrade Captain. I just wanted to inform you that I've left that report you wanted concerning the current efficiency of our reactor turbines on your desk."

"Ah, very good, Comrade. I'll be sure to look it over later on tonight," Captain Karnov said. "You may return to your duties."

"Thank you, Comrade Captain." Ensign Liu gave him another salute, then returned to his duties.

"Great, I didn't know we had a Chinaman on board," Boris said with barely concealed distaste, once the ensign was out of earshot.

"Ah, he's a good kid, very bright," Captain Karnov said. "I think he'll go far in the Pacific Red Banner Fleet."

"You mean to say you actually trust that *pizdaglaz*?" Boris asked, surprised. Like many Soviets, he was prone to Sinophobia.

"Please, there's no need for such language aboard my ship," Captain Karnov said irritably. "Certainly I don't need to remind a man so learned in our Communist doctrine as you that here in the Soviet Union all races are equal? Why, we were the first nation to put a man of African ancestry in space." He was referring here to Arnaldo Tamayo Méndez. "Under my command, I treat all men as equals, regardless of their race. All that I ask from them is competence and efficiency; there's no place on my ship for hobbledehoys."

"Ah, so that is why some of the Politburo refer to you as 'Saint Karnov', then," Boris smiled.

Later on that evening, Captain Karnov decided to visit the sonar room before he retired to his quarters for the night. The sonar room was located in the control-room compartment of the sub, beneath the control room and right next to the radio room. It was a small room, and currently the only man inside it was Sonarman 2nd class Gleb Zimanov. Gleb was a thin and unhealthy looking younger man, with sallow skin and a slightly unshaven face. He wore spectacles and his dark red hair was unruly; he looked less like a Russian seaman and more like a radical student from the 19th century. For whatever reason he reminded Captain Karnov of Raskolnikov from the novel *Crime and Punishment* (dude even lived on Carpenter's Lane in Leningrad, which was the exact same street that Raskolnikov had lived on). Unlike the other crew members aboard the *Crimson November*, he was dressed in casual wear: that day he was wearing acid-washed jeans and a black t-shirt, on the front of which was the image of a yellow smiley face with a streak of blood slicing across one of its eyes (Captain Karnov, unfamiliar with Western comic books, didn't realise that this was a promotional t-shirt for the recent *Watchmen* comic book series). Gleb was seated atop a leather swivel chair (that was in turn bolted to the floor), and before him was a computer terminal and an oscilloscope. Resting atop the computer terminal was a hardcover book. Aside from the book, the room's only personal touch was a poster hanging up on one wall that depicted the cover artwork of Vangelis' 1978 *The Dragon* LP: a red-eyed, green-scaled dragon with bat wings and face tentacles rising above the waves of some Arctic ocean. At the moment Gleb was wearing a pair of headphones that were jacked into the instrumental table before him, and he was nodding his head to something when he noticed Captain Karnov standing before him.

"Good evening, Comrade Sonarman," Captain Karnov said to him. "Anything to report?"

"Comrade Captain, listen to this," Gleb said, as he removed his headphones and handed them to his Captain.

Captain Karnov took the headphones and placed them over his own ears, expecting to hear the usual underwater sounds. To his surprise, he heard music instead, a funky and upbeat electronic pop song. He looked over at Gleb with a raised eyebrow. The younger man smiled and said, "Pretty cool song, huh, Comrade Captain? It's called 'State Farm' by some British band named Yazoo."

Captain Karnov sighed as he handed the headphones back, mentally reminding himself as he did so to remain patient; it was a known fact that on submarines all over the world, the sonarmen were usually the most eccentric types onboard, and Gleb was no exception to this rule. "We pay you to listen for Imperialist submarines, Gleb, not to listen to their synth-pop," he said with a scowl.

"My apologies, Comrade Captain, but things have gotten dull down here these last few days, unless you think that listening to the flow of icebergs or whale *meteorizm* is your idea of fun," Gleb said. "Not much to report, really . . . aside from a few seismic anomalies in the general region, I've been unable to detect any enemy craft . . . or anything else of interest, for that matter. No cavitation noise, no reactor activity, no nothing."

"What do you mean by 'seismic disturbances?'" Captain Karnov asked.

"Could be a lot of things . . . magma displacement, for example," Gleb said with a dismissive shrug of his bony shoulders. "I wouldn't lose any sleep over it. I made a copy of the anomalous signal and right now I have a computer program analysing the recording to see what it makes of it, but that might take some time. It would go a lot faster if we were outfitted with a BC-10 like the *Amerikantsi* have on their subs."

"That'll happen when the crayfish on the hill whistles," Captain Karnov sighed. Even though the *Crimson November* was the most high-tech submarine in the arsenal of the Soviet Navy, there was no hiding from the fact that in terms of computer technology, Russian submarines (and the entire Soviet computer industry) seriously lagged behind the West. During the Stalin era, the study and development of cybernetics was rejected by the powers-that-be as a pseudo-bourgeois science, nothing more than a puppet of monopolistic capitalism. The Communist Party believed that computer technology would only serve to replace class-conscious workers with unthinking machinery, and that the very universality of the cybernetic feedback principle would eradicate their beloved Marxist dialectics. By the time of Stalin's death, the Soviet Union was already lagging 10-15 years behind the USA's cybernetics program. The Khrushchev Thaw eventually led to the Soviet Union forming its own computer programme, but by then it was far too late, and in 1972 the Central Committee decided to just cancel the Soviet computer programme entirely and steal and reverse-engineer Western computers. Earlier that year, a number of Japanese cybernetics experts had been allowed entry to the U.S.S.R. to analyse the current state of the Soviet computer industry and come to a conclusion on how many years it would take Russia to catch up with Japan's computer programme. Going into the study, the Japanese experts had assumed that it would take the Russians around 15-20 years to catch up. After seeing the present state of the Soviet Union's computer technology, they concluded it would take forever. Unsurprising, in a country where most offices and department stores still used the abacus as a means of calculation, and where the most high-tech PC was a knockoff of England's Sinclair ZX Spectrum. And to think there was a time in the early 1960's when President Kennedy and the CIA were actually terrified at the very notion of a Soviet "cybernetics menace!"

"Very well, keep me posted," the Captain said. He then glanced down at the book that Gleb was currently reading. The art on the front cover depicted an illustration of a sinister-looking, black-skinned toad statue clutching an equally sinister-looking key, and the book's title was *The Dream-Key of Nan Samwohl and Other Tales*, by some Western horror writer named Dagon Grimalkin (like most Russians of his generation, Gleb had been taught a number of secondary languages during his student years, including French, Chinese and English). It was well known on the ship that Gleb was an admirer of pessimistic weird fiction, and he was also drawn to the philosophers of woe, such as Schopenhauer, E.M. Cioran, and so on; the most recent book he had completed reading was Celestine and Aristide Arosteguy's *Labour Gore: Marx and Horror*. Captain Karnov couldn't say that he approved of his sonarman's choice of reading material. He had no empathy for those books which were written in darkness, the protagonists and narrators of their stories all nothing more than glorified piñatas, painted puppets marching off like lemmings to their collective dooms. How could anything they wrote compare with the almost unbearable despair of the following passage from Dostoyevsky's *The Brothers Karamazov*: "We always imagine eternity as something beyond our conception, something vast, vast! But why must it be vast? Instead of all that, what if it's one little room, like a bathhouse in the country, black and grimy and spiders in every corner, and that's all eternity is? I sometimes fancy it like that."

A strange impulse then caused the Captain to ask, "Gleb, let me ask you a question. Do the words 'Esok Agi' mean anything to you?"

"Can't say they do," Gleb grunted as he pulled his headphones back on. "Sounds Enochian to me, though."

Captain Karnov sighed and left the sonar room. A few minutes later and he was back in his stateroom, seated at his desk, completing his paperwork for the day. Every now and then he would glance up from the papers before him and stare at the framed photograph of his dead wife, Sonya. She had only been dead for a little over a year and a half now, but still the wounds felt as fresh to him as a newly constructed Belarus MTZ tractor coming right off the assembly line at the Minsk Tractor Works. They had met in the fall of 1976 at some clothing store in the GUM (pronounced "goom") Department Store near Red Square, when both of them had been shopping for the latest in that season's winter hats. How beautiful she had looked then, with her trendy Charodeika haircut and her Dali brooch. They had quickly hit it off, and in the spring of 1977 had gotten married. She had been a doctor, not a great shock in a country where women comprised 70%

of the U.S.S.R.'s medical doctors. Certainly she hadn't been averse to dating a military officer. Thanks to his "officer privilege," they had access to the so-called special (or "closed") stores, where one could purchase caviar, Japanese stereo systems, Swiss chocolates, French cognac, and other (mostly imported) consumer goods and *defitsitny* (items in short supply) not available at the State-owned stores. He could still bring to mind their walks beneath the yellow-tinged leaves of Vorontsovo Park as if they had happened just yesterday, could recall strolling past the little preschool girls with the gauzy pink bows in their hair who were playing spirited games of *gorelki* and *kazaki-razboiniki* (Cossacks & Robbers), the young mods grooving to the latest Melodiya sound confection, with their poor imitations of rock & roll haircuts and their bootleg acid-washed denim jeans (outfits all but guaranteed to get them disapproving glares from the headscarf-wearing potato-faced *babushkas* herding their geese through the park, said babushkas chanting "*tega, tega*" to their avian wards). He could easily recall their first kiss, which had been shared beneath one of Moscow's ubiquitous giant metal billboards, nearly all of which displayed the face of Lenin and some boilerplate ideological slogan, such as "Long Live Labour" (like most young married couples, the Karnovs had taken a rented *Chaika* limousine to Lenin's Tomb on their wedding day, where they had left flowers for good luck). How beautiful she had looked on that wedding day. He could still see her standing in the local Palace of Weddings, decked out in a traditional Kazakh wedding dress (for she was born in the northern region of Central Asia, though her family had moved to Grozny when she was very young). Other random memories: watching the nightly news program *Vrenya* every evening at 9 p.m. (or catching the occasional Umm Kulthum movie: Sonia had been a big fan of her work), going to see the Olympics at Lenin Stadium in 1980, shopping for ptarmigan meat and rowanberries at the Bounty of Russia's Forests shop on Komsomolsky Prospekt, taking in the annual fireworks display over the colourful onion domes of St. Basil's Cathedral on New Year's Day, attending rock concerts at Gorki Park or the missile parades at Red Square (during the latter celebrations, he and Sonya had waved their little red flags while standing in the shadow of a giant May Day banner decorated with idealized portraits of Lenin, Engels and Marx, all three men looking like bearded Old Testament patriarchs), watching actual grizzly bears playing hockey at the Moscow Ice Circus (in his opinion, if you had never seen a bear on ice skates hitting a puck with a hockey stick, you hadn't truly experienced life to its fullest, though Sonya, an animal lover, had been concerned about the ice skates hurting the bear's feet).

In February of 1985, the two had decided to move out of their cramped apartment in Moscow and take up residence in the city of Pripyat in the Ukrainian SSR, where Sonya had relatives. In retrospect, this turned out to be a very bad idea, what with the nuclear reactor meltdown that occurred at the Chernobyl Nuclear Power Plant a year or so later. Captain Karnov had been out at sea when it happened, commanding the *Crimson November* on its very first military war-game exercise, but Sonya hadn't been as lucky. When the explosion had occurred late that evening, the hospital that Sonya worked at was the first one contacted, and she arrived at the scene as soon as she could, along with some firefighters and other paramedics. They got there a little after two in the morning. At first she had been told it was an electrical fire; no one had mentioned anything to do with a reactor. This first responding crew had gone to the top of the building that housed reactor number 4. While up on the roof, Sonya and a few of the other firefighters had accidentally looked down into the open reactor core, which had resembled a giant, glowing blue eye. In some ways, this was the 20th-century version of gazing into the eyes of a gorgon. Sonya had instantly been hit with a fatal dose of radiation, and her beautiful brown eyes (as captivating as a Bella Akhmadulina poem) had changed to blue. She died a few days later, her body placed in a lead coffin and buried at Novodevichy Cemetery in Moscow. Captain Karnov hadn't found out about this until he had returned to Vladivostok, as one of the requirements of the war exercise that the *Crimson November* was taking part in was that radio silence be maintained at all times until they returned to port. Needless to say, he had been devastated by the news. His wife had been posthumously decorated with an Order "For Courage," Third degree, but that was only a small consolation to him. Losing his wife had been bad enough, but he also ended up losing almost all his possessions, as the city of Pripyat was now a no man's land, falling as it did within Nikolai Ryzhkov's Zone of Alienation, or Exclusion Zone. It was for that reason that Captain Karnov had ended up moving to Vladivostok in the autumn months of 1986.

Sometimes he tormented himself by remembering all of the things they had planned on doing in the future, like starting a family, or buying a nice house, not some crumbling *khrushchobi* from the 1950's or an apartment in some anonymous Brutalist high-rise made of prefabricated concrete that were so *en vogue* in the Soviet Union at the moment, but an actual, honest-to-goodness house. She had been very much looking forward to attending the exhibition of Marc Zakharovich Chagall's artwork that took place in September of 1986 (Chagall's 1943 Symbolist painting *The Juggler* was her all time favourite work of art), but sadly, her death had made that an impossibility.

Before Captain Karnov went to bed, he lit up his IBM PC and spent a few minutes playing Alexey Pajitnov's *Tetris*, his favourite computer game of all time. The main reason he had gotten this IBM PC in the first place was specifically so he could purchase the Western version of *Tetris* that had been released by Spectrum HoloByte earlier that year, which had far superior graphics to the Russian original of 1984 (the utilization of an electronic rendition of 'Korobeiniki,' a Russian folk song from the 1860s, was also a nice touch). One reason why Captain Karnov preferred this version of the game was because of the backdrops that bordered the game's playing field, these backdrops depicting various Russian scenes, including the Kremlin Wall, the liftoff of the Soyuz, the port of Vladivostok, the Ural Mountains, the Komsomolskaya Metro Station, a view of the Earth from Salyut, and a hockey match between the Soviet Wings and Team USA. In the Captain's mind, a game of *Tetris* was a symbolic enactment of the eternal battle between Order and Chaos, with the block clearing actions of the player representing Order and the CPU and the falling bricks standing in for Chaos. And sadly, just like in real life, Chaos always won. Captain Karnov's only real problem with the game was just that fact: that it was impossible to really win at it. Sooner or later, no matter how good you were, the CPU was better, and you would lose. Chaos could only ever be temporarily thwarted, but never completely overcome, and for some reason this fact outraged the Captain.

Perhaps I have more in common with my father than I care to admit, the Captain thought as he manipulated the blocks falling down from the top of the screen. For most of his adult life, the Captain had tried his hardest to distance himself from his father's name. His father had been an outspoken member of the Russian Orthodox Church, the kind of man more likely to have a picture of Patriarch Tikhon hanging up in his house than of Lenin, the kind of man more likely to be caught reading

Vekhi than *The Communist Manifesto*. He had been as conservative as a Misko sculpture. His father's religious beliefs hadn't been much of a cause for concern in the early 1940's, when Stalin revived the Church in an attempt to give heart to the Russian people in the face of the looming Nazi threat, but after the war it had been a different story. His father's religious views had eventually gotten him branded as an "enemy of the state," and in 1950 his father was arrested and sent to a penal facility in Romania for "re-education" ("re-education" being a more polite way of saying "torture and brainwashing"). Forced to take part in the infamous Pitești Experiment, his father (along with assorted intellectuals, diplomats, priests, and other dissident young people) had been physically tortured, forced to attend tedious lectures on the joys of dialectical materialism (a torture in its own right), to endure malnourishment, and to suffer various acts of public humiliation: the guards had forced him against his will to consume Holy Communion wafers of fecal matter, and every morning they would "baptise" him by plunging his head into a bucket filled with urine and feces. He had even been victimized into writing out a false autobiography in which he confessed to all manner of deviant behaviour and grotesque sexual acts, all false. The purpose of this was to get him to renounce his religious faith once and for all, but he had never bended from his beliefs. Going against the spirit of the day, his father had died for his faith, just another casualty of the Pitești Prison system, a martyr to the *gosateizm*, or state atheism.

It was a shame that Sonya had never gotten to meet his father, as she had been very religious as well, though she had been a practicing Roman Catholic. Captain Karnov had never told her how his father had actually died, instead telling her that he had eventually died from wounds he had sustained taking part in the Great Patriotic War (which was a total lie). This was something that often made Captain Karnov pause in thought: namely, wondering if Sonya would ever have gone out with him in the first place were she to have found out how his father had really died, a martyr for his beliefs. Naturally, Captain Karnov was sad that his father had died in such a way, and wished that it had never happened. But at the same time, it wasn't as if his father were some naïve babe in the woods . . . he had to have known what his fate would be, were he to continue down the path he took. And to die for such a foolish reason! However, Captain Karnov knew deep down in his heart that Sonya would have viewed his own decision to join the Party as an unforgivable act, in light of what the State had done to his father.

In her own way, Sonya had tried to get him to convert to her faith, but had eventually given up when she realized it was a lost cause. She had even tried to get him to read the Bible, but he had found it such dry and tedious reading that he had only ever been able to read small portions of it. Her favourite parts of the Gospel had been the parable of the Prodigal Son, and also the Penitent Thief who dies by Christ's side, as recounted in the Gospel of Luke, this thief known to some as St. Dismas (or Rakh, as he was known in the Russian Orthodox tradition). Captain Karnov had always found the story of the thief somewhat touching: the idea that even a man who had wallowed his whole life in sin, the lowest of the low, could find redemption on the threshold of death, simply by repenting and asking for forgiveness.

The Captain's game of *Tetris* ended as it always did, with the playing field on his screen completely filled up with Tetris blocks, a jumbled, utterly disorganized and chaotic mess. He sighed and turned his computer off, then lowered the lights in his stateroom before climbing into his bunk. As he closed his eyes, he wondered what tomorrow would bring.

III
Sigmoid Colon

At 0800 on December 8th, 1987, Captain Ivan Karnov was roused from his uneasy slumber by a steady knocking on the door of his stateroom. He groaned, slid out of his bunk, and walked over to the door. He opened it and found Ensign Liu standing on the other side, looking as impeccable as always in his freshly laundered uniform.

"Good morning, Comrade Captain," Ensign Liu said. "I hope I didn't awake you from any pleasant dreams?"

"I can categorically assure you that you did not," Captain Karnov comforted him with a smile. Not unless one's idea of pleasant dreams involved watching helplessly from outer space as one's home planet was devoured by enormous tendrils of crimson mould. "What's the sitrep?"

"Just wanted to let you know that we've almost reached our heading of 47°9'S 126°43'W," Ensign Liu said, rolling the coordinates off his tongue as casually as if he were discussing the latest episode of *What? Where? When?* (a quiz show that Captain Karnov had never enjoyed; he had always been creeped out by its title card, which depicted a Masonic crowned owl). "We should be arriving there in less than half an hour. Comrade Lieutenant Doak thought you should know."

Captain Karnov yawned and tried to rub away some of the last remnants of sleep from his eyes. "Very good, Comrade Zhang. You may return to your duties. I'll be heading up to the bridge in a few minutes . . . just need to take a shower and get dressed first."

"As you command, Comrade Captain," Ensign Liu said. "Oh, wait, before I forget, someone taped this to your door this morning." And here the ensign reached into his pocket and pulled out a folded-up sheet of paper, which he handed to Captain Karnov.

Captain Karnov frowned as he unfolded the piece of paper. To his surprise, he saw that it was a crudely photocopied image of a close-up of a human eye, only one that had become horribly infected, its outer surface crawling with maggot-like insects. Disturbed by what he saw, he folded the piece of paper back up and placed it in his pocket. "Thank you, Comrade Zhang," he said again. "Must be one of the crew trying to lighten the mood with a prank of some sorts. You're dismissed."

Ensign Liu gave the Captain a small salute, then walked off.

Captain Karnov closed the door of his stateroom and headed into his small private bathroom, where he took a quick hot shower (a luxury only he enjoyed on the *Crimson November*, but that was one of the perks of being captain). Following this shower, he shaved, then got dressed in his black uniform. After checking in the mirror to make sure his appearance was satisfactory, he left his stateroom and made his way to the bridge.

Captain Karnov arrived at the control room of the bridge a few minutes later. Quite a few people were there: Sonarman Gleb was fiddling with one of the sonar control panels, Dmitri Doak was plotting the *Crimson November's* position on the control room's chart table, Boris was issuing orders and otherwise trying to act important, while Ensign Liu just seemed to be trying to stay out of everyone's way. The first thing that Captain Karnov did upon entering the control room was to walk over to Dmitri. "Comrade Lieutenant, report," he said.

"We've reached our destination, Comrade Captain," Dmitri informed him. "Our preliminary passive sonar scans indicate an object of some size is before us, but we haven't done an active sonar scan yet."

"Comrade Sonarman, conduct an active sonar search on this object," Captain Karnov ordered, his pulse skipping a beat.

"Ay ay, Comrade Captain," Gleb said, an unlit cigarette dangling from his pale lips. He pressed a number of buttons on the computer console before him. A loud "ping" sound was heard as a sonar scan was launched into the sea before them like Koschei the Deathless casting a spell on another man's wife. A moment later, this "ping" was followed by an equally loud "pong" sound as the sonar scan returned, letting Gleb know (in terms of yards) the range between the *Crimson November* and their target. The sonarman analysed the data on the screen before him as he slipped on his headphones.

"Well?" Captain Karnov eventually asked him.

"According to the target configuration, whatever it is, it's stationary." Gleb frowned. "I'll be utterly blunt with you, Comrade Captain: I have no idea what we're looking at here. The acoustical signature matches no sea vessels that I know of. I can tell you this, though . . . whatever it is, it's big: I'm talking something like six miles across and 14 miles in length."

Captain Karnov let this information sink in. He then walked over to one of the walls, where a giant TV screen had been set up. The Captain turned on the TV, then ordered the video cameras located at the very front of the submarine to be turned on. Once that was done, a view of the ocean in front of them was broadcast onto the screen. Currently it was utterly black, mainly because this deep the visibility was under 20 yards. The Captain then ordered someone to turn on the bow lights. The bow lights at the front of the *Crimson November* were switched on and pointed directly in front of them, giving them all a better view of their target. And what Captain Karnov saw on his screen made him gasp.

Floating in the ocean before them was an enormous rock, the biggest rock that any of these men had ever seen in their lives. It was a very impressive, even an awe-inspiring sight, as oddly evocative as the way that the silhouette of the Shukhov radio tower in Moscow looked at sunset.

"What is that thing?" one of the crew members asked.

"A sunken island?" another Soviet wondered out loud.

"No, it's an asteroid . . . a C-type asteroid I believe," Dmitri said in a sure voice.

"How do you know that, Dmitri?" Captain Karnov asked him, raising a manly eyebrow.

"My son is a cosmonaut, Comrade Captain . . . he has a lot of books on the subject at my house, and I've perused them from time to time during moments of boredom," Dmitri said.

"If it is a meteor, this couldn't have landed recently," Ensign Liu said. "A thing this size crashing into the Earth would have wiped out most life on this planet."

"Perhaps it was dislodged from the ocean floor by the recent seismic activity in this area?" Gleb suggested with a shrug.

Boris studied the screen with a frown. "It looks like there's some sort of hole in this meteor, on the side that's facing us," he said, squinting a little. "How strange: it almost looks like a manmade entryway. But that's impossible, isn't it?"

Captain Karnov sighed. "I'm getting the feeling that this mission might end up being a one-way ticket to the Yellow House for all of us," he said, shaking his head. "Still, we must investigate. We shall sail into that entrance and see what we find inside."

"But how, Comrade Captain?" Boris asked. "That hole isn't big enough for the *Crimson November* to fit through."

"So we'll take the *Mir*," Captain Karnov said. "Gleb, Liu, you'll accompany me. Dmitri, Boris, you two will remain in charge of the *Crimson November* while I'm gone."

"As you command, Comrade Captain," Dmitri said with a salute.

"Boris, I'll take a walkie-talkie with me," Captain Karnov said. "I want the two of us to be kept in radio contact at all times, do you understand?"

"As you wish, Comrade Captain," Boris said, giving him a salute of his own.

Everyone scattered to attend to their respective duties. Before Gleb could walk off, Captain Karnov pulled him aside.

"You wish to speak with me, Comrade Captain?" Gleb asked him.

By way of answer, Captain Karnov reached into the pocket of his uniform and pulled out the folded-up Xerox that Ensign Liu had discovered on his stateroom door earlier that day. The Captain unfolded the piece of paper and handed it to Gleb. "What do you make of that?" he asked his sonarman.

Gleb stared down at it, then said, "It's a photocopied image of a diseased eyeball."

"Nothing gets by you, Gleb, does it?" Captain Karnov observed. "Ensign Zhang found it taped to my door this morning. What I want to know is, is this your doing? Because it seems to me like your handiwork."

"I can assure you I had nothing to do with this, Comrade Captain," Gleb said. "It does, however, remind me of something I read many years ago, in an old Department of Army study conducted in September of 1966: Army pamphlet 550-104, to be precise. Mention was made of a certain Operation BLACK EYE, in which members of the South Vietnam army were organized into death squads and penetrated areas held by the Viet Cong. They would then kill off Viet Cong leaders in their beds, leaving behind pieces of paper on which was printed the image of a grotesque human eye. Apparently 500,000 copies of this eye were printed out by the USIS: United States Information Services. Soon enough these eyes started turning up on the doors of potential victims of the South Vietnamese death squads; they were also seen as a clearly Orwellian warning."

"Big Brother is watching you," Captain Karnov said, quoting *Nineteen Eighty-Four.*

"We are the dead," Gleb quoted back ironically, as he rubbed his unshaven chin. "The whole operation was clearly inspired by General Edward Lansdale's 'Eye of God' prank from the Philippines in the 1950's. The CIA's black psy ops program back then was always getting involved in some crazy shit . . . remember Colonel Francis Sands' Operation Tree of Smoke? It makes me wonder if any of the old-timers on here did any time in Nam . . . they might remember stuff like this."

"So what are you trying to tell me? That I've been marked to die by a death squad of Southern Vietnamese agents?" Captain Karnov asked.

"Probably just a practical joke. I wouldn't worry about it," Gleb said. "Come on, we should be getting ready for the expedition."

The *Mir* was a self-propelled Deep Submergence Vehicle (DSV for short) that was housed in a small pen located at the very bottom of the *Crimson November*. Developed by the USSR Academy of Sciences in partnership with the Design Bureau Lazurith (and designed and built by the Finnish company Rauma-Repola's Oceanic subsidiary), the *Mir* had first been introduced into service earlier that year. It was a small and attractive-looking vessel, 26 feet long and 12 feet wide, and white and orange in colour. With its large propellers capable of achieving a max underwater speed of 5 knots, it only took the *Mir* two hours to reach its maximum depth of 19,685 feet (and it truly was a deep sea vessel, capable of reaching 98% of the ocean floor). Powered by NiCad batteries of 100 kWh capacity, the mini-sub also had VHF radio, 6 5,000-watt lights, and 3 viewports. It was manned by a three-person crew, and that day that crew would be Captain First Rank Ivan Sigismondavich Karnov, Sonarman 2nd class Gleb Zimanov, and Ensign Liu Zhang.

Built adjacent to the *Mir's* pen was an even smaller changing room, inside of which were three lockers, each of which held a diving suit and diving helmets. The three men quickly changed into these outfits. The diving helmets they wore were manufactured at Factory #28 in Leningrad, and they were of the military 3 bolt UVS50m design, with a microphone in place next to the face plate. Having been made in the year 1963, they weren't exactly bleeding edge technology, but they were still superior to the far scarcer GKS3m BR Mix Gas helmet. The suits they had on were similar to the Western Mark V deep sea diving suits: that is, rubberised-canvas suits (underneath which the three men wore wool undergarments), with wrist cuffs and a rubber seal around the neck to secure the diving helmet in place.

Once they had their diving gear on, Captain Karnov led his two men into the *Mir* itself. A few minutes later the *Mir* had exited the *Crimson November*, and was well on its way in the direction of the sunken meteor. On their way there, Gleb insisted that they listen to music (he claimed to help calm his nerves), but because he had neglected to bring headphones, the other two men were forced to listen to his choice in music, as he ended up playing an Einstürzende Neubauten cassette tape over *Mir's* internal speakers. As 'Halber Mensch' played loudly within the interior of the DSV, Captain Karnov gazed out of the central viewport (which was the largest of the three viewports). All six of the *Mir's* lights were on, and their illumination sliced through the murk of the ocean all around them, giving them a good view of the sunken meteor. When they had first departed from the *Crimson November*, the meteor had been nothing more than a small dot on the aqueous horizon. But now it was steadily growing in size, the closer they got to it, to the extent that they could now see that the outer surface of the meteor was scarred with alien-looking sigils that were miles wide, like the calligraphy of the Titans. The sigils were a gleaming, pulsating red colour, as if they were made of molten lava, and there was something sickening about the way the lines of the runes twisted and turned, like phallic eels engaged in unnatural sex acts.

"What are those symbols?" Ensign Liu asked with a frown as he craned his face closer to the viewport.

"They look almost like runes to me," Gleb said.

"Would you say they look Germanic?" Captain Karnov asked. He himself was unable to read (or speak) German, but he knew that Gleb had studied the language.

"It's difficult to say, Comrade Captain," Gleb said. "I think a more significant question would be, 'why are they on a meteor?'"

"I've been wondering the same thing," Captain Karnov said. *The rational explanation is that this rock we're approaching isn't a meteor after all, but something manmade. Perhaps that experimental Nazi laboratory? Or the Threshold House to something insidious?*

Soon enough they reached the gaping hole that led into the interior of the meteor. The perimeter of this hole was lined with titanic, almost tentacle-like tendrils of seaweed, while the inner lining of the tunnel was made of bright red rock; for this reason, the hole on the side of the meteor resembled a colossal vagina. *One can only wonder what Freud would have made of all this,* Captain Karnov thought with a small smile, the tendrils of seaweed seemingly beckoning them forth like Oankali sensory tentacles. But as the phallic mini-sub passed through the hole, into the tunnel, he couldn't help but notice that his mouth had suddenly gone as dry as the Qara Qum Desert in Turkmenistan.

Or perhaps *tunnels* would be a more accurate word, as very quickly the three Soviets discovered that the tunnel branched into two other tunnels, which in turn branched out as well. They passed by gaping chasmal holes that no doubt led to further tunnels in turn. Ensign Liu, who was piloting the *Mir*, chose tunnels at random, though like the other two men onboard he had no idea where they were going. Captain Karnov just hoped that his ensign was memorising his path so they could backtrack later: the idea of getting lost in this labyrinth of stone didn't appeal to him. The further they got into the meteor's interior, the stranger the appearance of the tunnels became. Soon it didn't even look as if the walls were made of stone anymore, but instead mass amalgamations of red fungal clumps. In Captain Karnov's mind, it felt less as if they were drifting through the interior of a meteor and more like they were travelling through the endocrinal system of the fabled Bakunawa.

Captain Karnov and his two subordinates wandered down a long tunnel, the sickly greenish light far off in the distance at the end luring them like a siren song from the chapped lips of the muses of the lower world. This metaphorical song was not an audible one, as the tunnel seemed to muffle all acoustics in general, even the footsteps of the three Soviets. But was it not Franz Kafka who observed, "Now the Sirens have a still more fatal weapon than their song, namely their silence. And though admittedly such a thing never happened, it is still conceivable that someone might possibly have escaped from their singing; but from their silence certainly never." The men had removed their diving helmets and each of them now held a flashlight, and as they walked they cast thin beams of light all around themselves, like brain-damaged film projectors. They had no idea that they were being watched, as if this were all a film, and that in fact the song 'Necropolis' by SPK was serving as a soundtrack to their scientific spelunking.

Captain Karnov switched on his walkie-talkie. "Boris, this is your Captain speaking," he said into the device.

"I'm here, Comrade Captain," Boris said, his voice made scratchy and distorted by the static of distance.

"Just wanted to let you know that we've arrived inside the meteor, and are currently exploring its interior regions," Captain Karnov said. "Other than that, nothing new to report. I'll get back in touch with you once we know a bit more about just what it is we're dealing with here."

"As you say, Comrade Captain."

Gleb aimed his flashlight at the western wall of the tunnel and paused at what it revealed to him. He dashed over to the spot on the wall to get a closer inspection. He then called out, "Comrade Captain, come and see this!"

Captain Karnov and Ensign Liu wandered over to where he stood. Once they got closer, Captain Karnov was able to see what had gotten Gleb's attention. The illumination of the flashlights revealed the wall to be covered with bas-reliefs. One of them was a depiction of a vast jellyfish, one whose sac was bloated with foetal-looking tadpoles. This jellyfish monstrosity was surrounded by mechanical hermaphrodites, and these homunculi were connected to the jellyfish in an umbilical fashion by long tentacles, which seemed to pierce them through their genital organs. Odd-looking numbers spawned from no numerical system that Captain Karnov had ever seen ran along the sides of the bas-relief in columns.

"This is like Viennese outsider art," Gleb said breathlessly. "It reminds me of R. Gie's *Circulation of Effluvia with Central Machine and Metric Tableau.* Comrade Captain, I have no idea what this thing we're traveling through is, but it can't be from outer space. This art is clearly man-made."

"How can you be so certain that these bas-reliefs were crafted by human hands?" Ensign Liu asked. "Perhaps this meteor is actually a spaceship, one created by an alien race."

"Maybe I should get back in touch with the *Crimson November* and tell them what we've found," Captain Karnov said. He reached into a waterproof pouch on the side of his diving suit and pulled out his walkie-talkie. He flicked it on and asked, "Boris?"

"Captain!" he heard Boris exclaim on the other line. "Put the book down now!"

"What's that?" Captain Karnov asked.

"The mission has been terminated! Close the book! It's just a story," Boris went on, his voice all distorted by static.

"Boris, what on earth are you babbling about? Have you been drinking?" Captain Karnov asked. But all he heard on the other line now was silence.

"Captain?" Ensign Liu asked as the three men walked down New York's 52nd Street naked, their hands cupped over their genitals. Here in the bombed-out and exfoliated remnants of the future city, rat-sized fleas were sucking the blood of cat-sized rats. "A question. Must we really be naked for this operation?"

"A cigarette? Of course I have a cigarette," Captain Karnov said as he reached into the pocket of his military uniform and pulled out a cigarette. "The question is, do you have a lighter?"

"But I didn't ask for a cigarette, I asked for a breath mint," sonarwoman Gina complained as they jogged down the pixelated rainbow road, floating vector graphics circling around them like halos on all sides.

"Why are we suddenly talking in English?" Ensign Lucy asked.

"Quiet, you two," Captain Karla said as she piloted the spacecraft. "We're fast approaching the Lobster Nebula and I don't want to fall into the Black Hole of Ysmault."

BORIS' VOICE: New in slave . . . for fun . . . for . . . stay with uh . . . can . . .

The flashlights temporarily failed, plunging the three men into darkness. When the flashlights came on again, the three Soviets can see, in the beams of light, that I am surrounded by large disembodied hands, hands that are walking towards you on their fingers, like enormous five-legged arachnid xenomorphs.

BORIS' VOICE: James Champagne has lied to you all along. The *Crimson November* is not a submarine. It's actually a Winnebago. This message has been brought to you by the Rationalism Dept.

Ensign Liu is on his knees, head bowed, hands clasped in useless prayer. Bloodstained antlers are growing forth from where his eye sockets used to be, and his mouth has gone missing: all that remains at its former place of residence is blank flesh. The wall behind him is a cross section of pulsating, dark-green flesh. In the centre of this biowall, directly behind Ensign Liu, there is a giant gaping, mouth, shaped like the petalled outline of a flower, the interior of this mouth lined with a seemingly infinite amount of fangs. Six pink tentacles are emerging from this orifice (as nasty a void as that of the asshole of Thérèse of the Château de Silling, a virgin to toilet paper), one of which is in the process of wrapping itself around the Ensign's neck like an organic noose. Radiating outward from this mouth the wall is speckled with a massive number of eyes of all different shapes and sizes, all of which are gazing at Liu in a malignant manner.

BORIS' VOICE: Hey, have any of you guys ever read Niklas Müller's 1822 classic *Glauben, Wissen und Kunst der alten Hindus*? There's a really cool illustration on one page depicting a turtle balancing the 21 worlds of Hindu mythology on its shell, surrounded by the world serpent Shesha.

Gleb is strung up in the centre of the city marketplace, atop a crude and makeshift stage. He is suspended in mid-air by chains that are wrapped around his wrists and ankles (and are thus connected to two tall wooden pillars), thus spread-eagling his body into the shape of a crude letter X. His body is almost entirely encased in black armour, with even his face blocked from sight; the only part of his body exposed is his anus. Surrounding this stage is a jeering crowd of mutant children with black holes in place of faces. With twigs and fingers they smear honey all over Gleb's exposed ass cheeks, along his crack, and all around his sphincter. This honey attracts a cloud of wasps, which converge on Gleb's ass. One of the black-hole children manipulates a wheel on the side of the two pillars, which causes the chains holding Gleb in place to slightly shake. Unsurprisingly, this annoys the wasps, who begin stinging Gleb's exposed posterior (some of them even begin crawling up Gleb's asshole). Over the buzzing of the wasps and the catcalls of the crowd, the only other sound that can be heard is Gleb's screams.

BORIS' VOICE: Captain, it's all well and good that the top brass in the Soviet Navy let us keep birds on board, but do you think that they'd let us take on a camel as well? I had a pet camel when I was a kid . . . his name was Gimel. The numerical value of Gimel is three.

Captain Karnov, is on his hands and knees, completely naked, his mouth and anal sphincter kept propped open by torture instruments made to resemble medieval-looking dental jams. He is surrounded by a number of bizarre-looking alien creatures. Their heads are shaped like lightbulbs of flesh, with unblinking and protuberant eyes that resemble cartoon alarm bells and nose sockets shaped like chicken wishbones. Their mouths are painted on, big stupid grins, like slices of ebon watermelon, with one single square bucktooth clinging to the upper ridges of their smiles. Running along the curvature of their skulls like bio-organic crowns are a number of severed breasts. Their bodies are warty orbs, with hairy spider legs sticking out from the sides, while their large round feet are clad in bright red galoshes. Emerging from a slit in the centre of their stomachs are long snakelike phalluses, candy-striped in vivid pulsating rainbow colours, and at the tip of each of these penises is a species of fanged eyeball. One of these sadist-aliens is positioned behind Captain Karnov's prone form, and it is ramming its penis up the Captain's vulnerable and gaping asshole in a steady motion, while an extremely distorted version of 'Back in the U.S.S.R.' by The Beatles plays from hidden speakers. Another of the aliens is standing before Captain Karnov, and it is thrusting its penis into the Captain's mouth and down his throat, while blood and alien semen dribble forth from the Soviet's violated orifices.

BORIS' VOICE: The JC AI is malfunctioning. Hypervirus detected: infiltration from MIT's ULTRAC-666 supercomputer is suspected. System failure. Captain Karnov does not exist. He is a fictitious construct. All that does exist is the JC AI. The JC AI is malfunctioning. Give me steel . . .

From the 'Chaoskampf' notebook, page 27: 3-26-15:

(Plans for pt. 2 of 'Chaoskampf')

-a knock on the door of his stateroom awakens Captain Karnov (Ensign Liu)

-Ensign Liu tells him they've almost arrived at their destination

-Captain takes shower/dresses/leaves stateroom, heads to control room

(describe who is there)

-Captain K asks for a report

-Dmitri/Gleb talk about object (Captain K calls for active sonar search)—ping!

-Gleb analyses acoustical signature: determines it's not a US sub

-Captain K calls for video feed/floodlights (sub lights turn on)

-they see a giant rock floating in the ocean before them

-Captain K wonders what it is (sunken island?)—Dmitri recognizes it as a meteor

(they rationalize that it couldn't have landed recently: possibly dislodged by seismic activity)

-they spot a hole leading into it: Captain Karnov decides to investigate (take *Mir*)

-he decides Gleb & Liu will come along, leaves Dmitri and Boris in charge

-Captain K/Gleb/Liu get dressed in diving suits (describe) then enter *Mir* (describe)

(weapons)

-they take the *Mir* DSV to the floating meteor (Gleb plays Einstürzende Neubauten's 'Halber Mensch' on the way there, to Captain K's annoyance)

-entrance into meteor: a hole made of red rock, lined with seaweed (resembles vagina)

(weird symbols) Germanic runes? (Captain K wonders about Nazi superweapon after all)

-*Mir* passes through hole: goes down a long winding tunnel: eventually surfaces

(a large cavern)—odd bas-reliefs (no mere meteor)

-tries to contact *Crimson November* (just static—lost communication)

-begin to wander around meteor interior (describe)

Pg. 35 > (enter a chamber—bizarre hallucinations)—death of Gleb/Ensign Liu

-Captain K rushes back to sub, takes *Mir* back to *Crimson November*

(end of pt. 2)

Marginalia:

~~*Dark Side of the Moon* poster~~
Vangelis: *The Dragon* (1978)
his precautions
Yellow House
Choronzon

The three men now stood in a chamber whose dimensions were so staggeringly gargantuan that mere words failed to adequately describe just how small they felt while standing in it, like pilgrims who had found themselves wandering into a cathedral of death. Hanging from the top of the cavern were long stalactites, along with curious snake-like rock formations that seemed to twist their way down to a point a few feet above the cavern floor. The tips of these latter formations were shaped like coffins, and their outer surfaces were decorated with sinister-looking sigils. In the centre of each of these appendages were gaping openings that resembled vaginal slits. In the centre of the cavern, there was a raised platform, the top of which could be accessed by two stairs that zigzagged upwards. At the top of this stone platform was a large green bonfire, one that seemed frozen in time and encrusted with unblinking owl eyes. Standing sentinel at the base of the platform, off to the side of the staircases, were two statues. They resembled towering upright starfishes, and each had a human nose growing from its centre. Growing forth from the sides of their topmost arms on long antennae were two human ears, while their left and right arms were impaled with human jawbones. Hanging from beneath their bodies, in between their 'legs,' were sac-like appendages similar to the male scrotum, only in the centre of each sac was one lone cyclopean eye. Beyond the raised platform was a wall made up of what resembled grotesque melting clown faces: a circus celebrating the

Agony of the Plasma, an amorphous pale-blue liquid hell of bulbous round noses, cartoon plus-sign teeth, and uplifted irisless eyes, *Loony Tunes* and Disney clowns as animated by a Salvador Dali or Max Ernst, which was another way of saying, "Totally fucked up."

"This place is incredible!" Gleb said, his voice echoing in the vast space.

Come-into-our-parlour-humans

"Who said that?" Captain Karnov hissed.

"Captain! Look!" Ensign Liu screamed as he pointed at one of the vaginal slits, which was at that moment starting to slightly open and then

> *Xywoleh vay barec het vay yomar ha elohe*
> *Elohim ascher tywohe hythale chuabotay lep*
> *Ha nawabra hanveys ha hakia elohim haro*
> *He otymeo dy addhayon hazze hamalech hago*

System Death/ System Death/ System Death

Captain Karnov CUT footsteps echo CUT two men screaming CUT down the Burrows CUT or is it Warrens CUT heartrate accelerating CUT breathing faster CUT pupils dilating CUT Captain Karnov CUT the corridor goes topsy-turvy CUT Ensign Liu screams CUT as IT emerges from one of the vaginal slits CUT Ensign Liu screamed CUT Karnov turns the corner CUT Gleb had fainted dead away at IT CUT where is the *Mir* CUT one wrong dead end and it's over CUT Captain Karnov runs CUT he didn't see what IT did to Liu and Gleb CUT he didn't see IT morph the two of them into one CUT he doesn't still hear their screams in his ear like cries from the sanatorium Cut RUN CUT screams in his ears like feedback at some SPK live assault CUT footsteps echo CUT down the endless twisting tunnels CUT to the *Mir* CUT CUT CUT CUT

IV
There is a Light That Never Goes Out

How Captain Karnov had made it back to the *Mir* was something he would never understand; indeed, it seemed to him to be a veritable miracle. As he piloted the mini-sub out of the asteroid (or whatever it was), relying on muscle memory and instinct alone to lead him to the exit, he tried not to think about what he had seen in that horrible chamber, at what had emerged from one of the slits in the coffin-stalactites, at what IT had done to poor Gleb and Liu. All he could focus on now was getting back to the *Crimson November*. It now seemed clear to him what needed to be done to this asteroid: nuke the damn thing to hell and beyond. Whatever it was that lurked in there (and who knew just how many other primeval horrors haunted its interior?), it couldn't be allowed to escape.

But how could he even be sure that what he had just seen and experienced had been real? What if this whole mission was nothing more than some kind of controlled psychic experiment, an exercise in hypnotic telepathy conducted by some shadowy and faceless military industrial complex? It wasn't common knowledge amongst the Soviet Union's upper brass, but some suspected that certain institutions within the U.S.S.R. were experimenting in the realms of abhorrent parapsychology. Certainly the Toth Incident a decade or so ago had raised some troubling issues, along with the declassified release of the Controlled Offensive Intelligence Agency (DIA) Task Number T72-01-14 report. Captain Karnov had heard rumors that back in the 1960's, in the city of Academgorodok across the Ob River, there had been, at the Institute of Automation and Electrometry, a certain sinister department known only as Special Department No. 8, which had supposedly been carrying out a top-secret research projekt known as 'Project No. 8.' Primarily Machine Age Voodoo: measuring photon waves with frog eyes, seeing if fatal bacteria could spread through panes of glass, and other seemingly nonsensical experiments. Was this the purpose of the *Crimson November's* mission? Was it possible that it had been dreamed up not by Admiral Khvatov, but instead Dr. Valery Petukhov, chief of the Laboratory of Bio-Physics at the State Control Institute of Medical and Biological Research? It was a shame that Gleb had been devoured by . . . well . . . whatever it was that had emerged from those slits, as he could have probably told the Captain all about this. Or had Gleb been devoured? Captain Karnov idly wondered if the diving suit he had on had been tampered with, perhaps sabotaged with some sort of weaponized aerosol-based psychotropic drug. Or maybe he was trapped in some kind of vast computer simulation being dreamed up by a malevolent AI, a lemming in the service of the S3 Plan. Weirder things have happened. . . .

Finally, through the *Mir's* central viewport, Captain Karnov could see the *Crimson November*, floating in the deeps of the Pacific, and in the glare of the DSV's lights it resembled the silhouette of an enormous black penis, as if it were a detached body part of Osiris that Isis had failed to recover. If there had ever been a sight that had provided greater relief to Captain Karnov than the relief he now felt as he gazed at his submarine, he wasn't able to recall it.

After manoeuvring the *Mir* back into its berth in the docking bay beneath the *Crimson November*, Captain Karnov exited the vessel and returned to the changing room, where he discarded his diving outfit and changed back into his officer's uniform. As he got dressed, he began to frame within his mind how he'd have to go about breaking the bad news to his crew about the deaths of their fellow comrades Gleb and Liu.

Upon exiting the changing room and stepping into one of the *Crimson November's* long corridors, Captain Karnov immediately perceived that something was wrong. In the space of time between his departure and return to the *Crimson November*, something had changed within his ship, and it was his olfactory system that first detected this change. The acrid smell of smoke was in the air, along with a far more sinister smell: that of spilt blood. Captain Karnov was just about to radio in with the bridge when he heard footsteps coming from the direction of the door at the end of the corridor. A second later a man passed through the door and stumbled into the corridor.

Captain Karnov gaped when he saw who the man was: Boris Smirnov. The reason why Captain Karnov was gaping was because of the condition that Boris was in. He had never seen his *zampolit* in a disheveled state before, and at that moment Boris truly was in disarray, what with his hair being a mess and his eyes wide in erethic panic, splotches of blood staining his uniform.

"Boris? What is the meaning of this? Organize yourself, man!" Captain Karnov exclaimed.

"Comrade Captain!" Boris wailed, his eyes practically rolling in fear. "It's Dmitri! He's-" But before the *zampolit* could complete his sentence, his head vanished, replaced by a pink cloud of bits of brain, skull and teeth. The corpse fell to the ground, and behind it Captain Karnov could now see a small group of men at the bulkhead, brandishing AK-74 Kalashnikov assault rifles (the AK-74 being an adaptation of the 7.62x39mm AKM assault rifle, designed in 1974 by

Mikhail Kalashnikov and manufactured by IZHMASH: weighing 6.8 lbs and being 37.1 inches long, the assault rifle boasted a 5.45x39mm cartridge and a gas-operated, rotating bolt). At the very least, Captain Karnov assumed they were men, but it was hard to be sure, as their bodies were draped with shapeless black robes, while their faces were blocked from sight by grotesque latex starfish masks.

The muzzle of one of the AK-74s held by one of the masked men was smoking. No doubt this was the murder weapon that had reduced Comrade Smirnov's head to a short-lived ecosystem of gore. His gun trained on the Captain, this man (who Captain Karnov surmised to be the leader of this motley group) pointed his free hand at the Captain and said, in a harsh voice, "Get him!"

Captain Karnov turned away from the men and began racing down the corridor, cursing at himself for not having his Makarov PMM semi-automatic pistol on his person (which was the standard firearm issued to all high-ranking officers in the Soviet Navy). Behind him, he could hear the starfish-masked men giving chase. Apparently, they wanted him alive, otherwise they would have simply shot him in the back.

Captain Karnov ran down corridor after corridor, the smoke making his eyes water with tears. As he fled from his pursuers, he dimly perceived music playing loudly over the submarine's internal sound system, Time Zone's 'World Destruction' (the original 12" mix). In some of the rooms he passed by, Captain Karnov could see the corpses of some of his crewmembers strewn across the ground, their bodies riddled with bullet holes. In some of the rooms he passed by he also saw other black-robed, starfish-masked men, and these mutineers were breakdancing in time to the music, seemingly oblivious to what was going on around them.

Eventually, Captain Karnov came to a dead end, and that was when he knew the game was up. The men behind him seized him, and though he tried to fight them off, it was all in vain, for he was outnumbered thirteen to one. Once they had him properly subdued, they dragged his body to the control room on the *Crimson November*'s bridge.

The Captain was roughly tossed down onto the steel floor of the submarine's bridge. Beaten and bloody, he gazed up at his captors.

"Who are you?" Captain Karnov demanded.

"Isn't it obvious?" the leader asked. With his free hand, he gripped the bottom of his starfish mask and yanked it off his head, exposing the eye-patched and mustachioed face of Dmitri Doak.

"Dmitri?! Why? What is the reason behind this mutiny?" Captain Karnov asked, shocked at this betrayal.

"You're looking for a reason? There is no reason in this world, my dear Comrade Captain, only chaos," Dmitri said as he tossed the mask to the side, the smile twitching on the side of his mouth resembling a patchwork corpse being reanimated by malignant electricity. "Still, you deserve an explanation. We never belonged to the Soviet Navy, you see. Our true allegiance is to the Cult of the False Angle, and now the *Crimson November*, one of the most powerful weapons in the history of the human race, is ours. The perfect setting for humanity's endgame."

"What sort of madness is this? What are you babbling about, man?" Captain Karnov asked. "What is the Cult of the False Angle?"

"An organization that has its tentacles in many branches of the Soviet government . . . we even have a man in the Politburo. He's the one who authorized this mission, incidentally," Dmitri said. "We serve the Esok Agi."

"What is the Esok Agi?" Captain Karnov asked. "It sounds like the kind of words an Eskimo would use to describe a walrus' kidneys."

"No one can say with one hundred percent certainty just what the Esok Agi are . . . you might see them as an alien race, but that's not the whole story," Dmitri said. "Billions of years ago they inhabited the long-lost Jellyfish Constellation, the lost Zodiac sign, at the universe's rim, the borderland between our cosmos and the anti-universe. They are highly advanced sadistic sorcerers and scientists . . . but aeons ago, one of their experiments went wrong. The Red Mould . . . you've dreamed of it, have you not, Comrade Captain? Perhaps you may have subconsciously seen it as a metaphor for Communism, but it's much more than that, I can assure you. The Red Mould . . . as lethal as the Scarlet Jungle's Bloodmorel (see Rem-Ul's Almanac of Old Krypton, page 417, entry #5,308, only in this case it is fatal in 100% of infection cases as opposed to only 92%). It spread and spread and no matter what the Esok Agi tried, they couldn't contain it. So they initiated a supernova in the heart of the Jellyfish Constellation, escaping from their home world in a spaceship designed as a meteor . . . a spaceship that you yourself set foot in mere hours ago. They had hoped that the supernova would wipe out the Red Mould, but somehow or other, it survived even that, and continued to spread to nearby stars and planets, corrupting everything in its path like a noxious panspermia. The Esok Agi's craft landed on this planet some 66,038,000 years ago, the resulting impact causing an extinction-level event that in turn wiped out this planet's population of dinosaurs and ushered in a great age of ice. The trauma of the impact forced the Esok Agi to go into a sort of hibernation state, one almost akin to mediation. For millions of years, they meditated on the problem of the Red Mould, and this was the conclusion they reached: the only thing capable of repulsing it was the cold."

"I take it this story of yours is going somewhere?" Captain Karnov asked, wondering if Dmitri was being paid by the word.

"For countless years, this planet was protected from the Red Mould because it was too cold . . . but then humanity came along and ruined everything," Dmitri said. "The Esok Agi intended Earth to be their new home world, the start of a new and terrible empire. But what with the human race contributing to climate change and global warming, now this planet has once again become too warm, and thus is no longer safe from the awful tentacles of the Red Mould. A few years ago, the Esok Agi finally awoke from their long hibernation. Realizing the threat at hand, they began to reach out to susceptible minds via dreams, and thus was our Cult founded. The plan was made to hijack this submarine and use its missiles to start World War III. We shall launch all twenty of the *Crimson November's* RSM-52/R-39 Rif missiles to major cities all over the USA and Russia. When both countries believe that the other is attacking them, they'll retaliate with their own nuclear arsenals, causing further devastation. All those firestorms igniting all over the world will cause soot to rise into the upper troposphere and lower stratosphere, blocking out sunlight and causing temperatures to drop all over the earth. This will result in a new ice age. The Esok Agi will then wipe out the rest of humanity and establish their new Empire of Tears. The only exceptions to this rule will be . . . us, the Cult of the False Angle. After we carry out their work, they will make us like them. We shall usher in a New Dark Age, and sing and dance and rape amongst the Ruins of Reality!" Dmitri crowed. "This is the new realpolitik."

"A New Dark Age? Isn't civilization dark enough as it is?" Captain Karnov asked in disbelief.

"It can always be more dark, Comrade Captain. One must never forget that the dark is limitless," Dmitri explained.

"So how exactly do we fire these missiles?" one of the cultists spoke up. "Is there some kind of passcode that has to be entered into the system? Something like 'The Soldier and the Hunchback,' or 'The Lion and the Unicorn?'"

"Nothing so cloak and dagger as that, my comrade. This isn't *Spy vs. Spy*, after all," Dmitri said. "On their own, the missiles are worthless. It's only when they've been activated by the *Crimson November*'s computer systems that they can be launched as weapons. We can fire them from right here in the control room, actually. All we need are the three missile control keys. I already have mine and Boris', and you took our good Captain's key when you subdued him a few minutes ago, correct?"

"Indeed we did," one of the other cultists said as he tossed a key over to Dmitri, who caught it. "So, do we start firing right now?"

"Not just yet . . . before we begin, our Masters wish to have a word with our Captain," Dmitri said. "Are we surfaced yet?"

"We surfaced a few minutes ago, Comrade," another cultist answered.

"Keep us surfaced for now . . . I wish to show our captain something," Dmitri said. Still holding his AK-74, he motioned Captain Karnov to climb up the ladder, to the top of the sail. A moment after the Captain had begun scaling the ladder, Dmitri in turn began following him.

"What did you do with the crewmembers who weren't part of your cult?" Captain Karnov asked as he climbed up the ladder. "I assume you killed them?"

"You assume correctly," Dmitri said. "Those that have managed to escape from us or hide for now will later on be hunted down, I can assure you."

The two men reached the top of the sail. Dmitri ordered Captain Karnov to open the hatch, so that's what he did, not having much choice in the matter given his current circumstances. As the two men climbed atop the submarine's sail, the Captain could see that it was now evening.

"So what did you bring me out here to see? The stars?" Captain Karnov asked.

"Not the stars . . . the things that snake between the stars and glissade from far-off galaxies," Dmitri said in a somewhat pompous tone. "See? Even now, they come forth."

Captain Karnov directed his gaze at the night sky, and he quickly realized that Dmitri was telling the truth. For entities *were* manifesting in the starry firmament: Captain Karnov assumed that these beings were the much ballyhooed Esok Agi. The morphological complexity of the Esok Agi was truly something to behold. Alpha and Omega of Biogenetic Law, they were the answer to Ernst Haeckel's World Riddle, a mockery of the very notion of dysteleology. Indeed, they resembled nightmarish variations of Haeckel's most diseased imagination: vast conglomerations of tentacles, feelers, leaves, feathers and orbs, demonic siphonophorae, asteridea, discomedusae (see in particular the illustrations of the *Siphonophorae/Staatsquallen* of Tafel 37 in Haeckel's *Kunst-Formen der Nature*). Psychic teratomas from the Aeon of Ashenzohn, reanimated stillbirth monstrosities from the floor of the N Factory, archons of the *Urschleim*. And yet, at the same time, as horrifying to the six senses as these deities were, Captain Karnov found himself feeling a tad let down. *That's it?* he thought. *This is the Esok Agi? All that buildup, and they're nothing more than giant alien jellyfish? I must say, not very scary.*

Dmitri aimed the muzzle of his AK-74 at Captain Karnov. "And now, Comrade, I'm afraid your time is at an end," he said apologetically. "Do you have any last words before we commence with World War III?"

"*Tvoyu mat!*" the Captain spat at him.

"Defiant to the end," Dmitri said, a hint of admiration in his voice. "I can respect that. Though you should show more respect to me, Comrade. After all, I am the Chosen One, the man the Esok Agi handpicked to be the prophet of their Eldritch Gospel!"

"Pretender-to-the-Throne, not-one-of-us," the Esok Agi all seemed to say at once, in a multitude of voices. "Your-part-to-play-is-over, False-Prophet."

"No!" Dmitri cried out as blood began to leak from his eyes. "You can't! I'm the Chosen One! Ph'nglui mglw'nafh Cthulhu R'lyeh wgah'nagl fhtagn! La-li-lu-le-lo! Sushi, kamikaze, fujiyama, nipponichi!" His mad babblings came to an end when his body violently exploded, Truls Hellevik-style (that's a name you do NOT want to do a Google Image search for).

"Well, that was unexpected," Captain Karnov muttered as he wiped bits and pieces of Dmitri off his face.

"Captain Karnov-you-are-the-true-Chosen-One-you-will-be-our-prophet-now," the Esok Agi said to him. "Your-blood-is-truly-of-the-Sea-unlike-that-fool-Dmitri:you-will-take-his-place-and-serve-us."

"I wish I could say that I was tempted by your offer, but then I'd be lying," Captain Karnov told the Esok Agi. "You know, for so long now I was worried about this ship falling into the wrong hands. So before we left dock, as an added precaution, I booby-trapped this submarine with enough Semtex H to sink it ten times over." And before the Esok Agi could react, Captain Karnov reached into one of the pockets of his military uniform and pulled out a makeshift detonation device. "Forgive me," he said, and while he wasn't even sure to whom he was asking forgiveness (God? Sonya? His father? His crew? The *Crimson November* itself?), it seemed like the appropriate thing to say. This was his final thought as he jammed his finger down on the detonation device's trigger.

With a spectacular roar, the *Crimson November* exploded, killing everyone on board. For one moment, the submarine was nothing more than a chaotic cloud of disassembled pieces. Then these pieces began to slowly drift downwards, to the ocean floor, while New Order's 'Your Silent Face' played from some unknown source.

Amongst this debris was the corpse of Captain Karnov, immolated beyond recognition. For whatever reason, his body seemed to fall to the ocean floor faster than the rest of his vessel. Once his body had settled against the ocean floor, the remains of the *Crimson November* followed suit, and as they fell all around Captain Karnov (settling over him like a makeshift sarcophagus), they oddly seemed to arrange themselves into a very particular shape: that of a Russian Orthodox Cross, and like most such crosses this one had three horizontal crossbeams as opposed to the standard two, with the third one stationed at the bottom of the cross, serving as a footrest, and it was slanted slightly upwards, thus pointing in the direction of Rakh, the Penitent Thief.

Some Influences

Mark Samuels (especially his stories 'The Black Mould,' 'The Other Tenant,' 'An Hourglass of the Soul,' and 'The Ruins of Reality')

Tom Clancy's *The Hunt for Red October* and *The Cardinal of the Kremlin*

Grant Morrison's *Nameless* comic (along with the 'Pax Americana' issue of his *Multiversity*)

Norman Polmer's *Cold War Submarines: The Design and Construction of U.S. and Soviet Submarines, 1945-2001*

The art of Ernst Haeckel

Metal Gear Solid 2: Sons of Liberty

Sunless Sea

The Communist Manifesto

Tetris

SPK/ReSearch

David Bowie's *Diamond Dogs* album

Dostoyevsky

Soundtrack

'There is a Light That Never Goes Out' (The Smiths)

'Ice Age' (Joy Division)

'1984' (David Bowie)

'Choronzon' (Tangerine Dream)

'State Farm' (Yazoo)

'Halber Mensch' (Einstürzende Neubauten)

'Necropolis' (SPK)

'Back in the U.S.S.R.' (The Beatles)

'World Destruction 12" Mix' (Time Zone)

'Your Silent Face' (New Order)

A Bad Un to Beat vs. The Highgate Waterman:

It's All About the Benjamins

by Brendan Connell and Quentin S. Crisp

Monday

He awoke at 2 a.m.—an hour later than usual, but he had stayed up too late the evening before, reading Volume 156 of the *Patrologiae cursus completus*, which is to say the volume containing those most fascinating letters of Manuel Chrysoloras as well as the *Chronicon maius* of Georgius Sphrantzes.

"I awake in darkness," he thought, "but dawn shall before long form over the mountains, and the wind shall come and blow my troubled thoughts away."

He arose from bed, lit a 14-inch taper that had been donated to him by Canon Michael Brockie, of the Church of Our Most Holy Redeemer & St. Thomas More, which he stuck in a 5-inch glass taper-holder with a silvered mercury finish, and, after performing his morning ablutions, donned a 100% wool habit with a stiff, pointed hood.

He knelt before a small wooden crucifix that hung on an otherwise bare wall and said matins prayers. He then carried the taper to the kitchen, made himself a cup of tea, went to his desk, set the cup of tea down on the left-hand side of the desk, the taper down on the right, and sat down himself, in a straight-backed wooden chair which had been with him since the beginning.

The hand-written letter from the previous day was there, and he looked it over with little satisfaction.

"No, I will have to begin afresh," he said, in a somewhat leaden voice.

He set a piece of fresh, crème-coloured paper before him, dipped his hand-blown glass pen in a bottle of lawyers' ink, and, in a fit of exultant inspiration, composed the following missive:

> Dear Mr. Patric,
>
> I am sure you will do me the justice to admit that, since I have occupied my present residence, I have been most punctual in paying you the rent monthly, as it has fallen due. Circumstances, however, over which I have no control, have conspired just at this moment to cause me several disappointments in money matters, to my great temporary inconvenience. Thus situated, I am induced, with the greatest reluctance, to request that you will be kind enough to permit the month's rent which is now due to you, to stand over until the beginning of next month, at which time you may rely on receiving the amount of the two months together. Your compliance with this request will oblige, sir, your obedient servant,
>
> Mark Samuels

He read the letter over once, nodded his head in satisfaction and then recalled those immortal lines of Cercidas:

> Why then doth the balancer even
> Never unto me incline?

This was however a question for which he had no logical answer, and so he answered himself with a logical sigh. He opened the drawer of his desk and took out an envelope and a packet of stamps. He folded the letter, inserted it into the envelope, licked the envelope and sealed it and then addressed it and affixed a stamp to the upper right-hand corner.

He looked at the clock. It was almost 4 a.m. If he wished to go for a morning walk before the streets became dense with the offspring of Eve, he would have to do it now.

He took off his wool habit and put on a pair of jeans, a long-sleeved checkered cotton shirt, diamond socks and a pair of Clark's desert boots. He slipped into a mocha overcoat, set a light-weight, burgundy-coloured wool fedora on his head, then opened his desk drawer and took out a 15-inch Circassians-Muhajir Kinjal dagger which he installed in the right-hand pocket of the coat, while into the left he slipped a sack of Vape Stick brand rolling tobacco, a box of matches, and a BLU Samba Jr. handset with built-in FM radio receiver, address book, text messaging and office tools.

Thus equipped, he left his apartment, which was situated above Kiplings Restaurant and Bar, on Hill Street.

Outside the air was cool and thick with a mouse-like fog. He rolled a fag, stuck it in his mouth, and lighted it.

He began a leisurely march up North Hill and, after about three hundred yards, came to a letter box, extracted the letter from his pocket, popped it in the box, and then continued on to Church Road, swung right and went on until he came to Archway Road, which, at that hour, was all but abandoned.

He struck east, toward the Boogaloo.

Two-storey brick buildings stood on either side which, he imagined, had in bygone days been the resort for merry roysterers and quaint-faced ladies. One of the buildings someone had painted dark green. He wondered what sort of person lived there now. Undoubtedly some magician or tool grinder, some fellow who, in the blank of the morning snored easily, dreaming of flowers and hay.

The green colour of the building reminded him of moss, but the building itself was, as fact would have it, completely moss-free.

He often wished that more moss would grow on the sidewalks and walls. He imagined that, if there were fewer pedestrians and motorists and people scrubbing at surfaces, there would be a great deal of moss everywhere.

He crossed Southwood Lane, and continued on.

The buildings here were Edwardian, the bottom storeys taken up by shops—Tonton Nails, Oriental Café, British Spirals & Castings.

Moving past these, he came to a building which he saw as rather curious.

It was old—seemed to be one of the oldest, if not the oldest, on the street. The top windows were of oddly-tinted glass. It was of red brick with stone dressings. Down the walls a few drain pipes made their way. They had once been painted black, but the paint had mostly peeled off, revealing the colour of raw tin.

He noticed a light on in the basement window and then, gazing up, saw that there was a sign that read:

Credentes Baking Co.

"What a peculiar name," he said aloud.

He had read recently, in an article in the *Catholic Herald*, about how odd bakeries were popping up all over London, in the most unexpected places—in old powerhouses, dismantled cash and carries, and debtor's prisons. He had even heard of a bakery that had recently opened in the cloakroom at Victoria Station.

When he had been a young man just starting out on the adventure of life, he had been advised by a certain poet of great repute to become a baker.

"People can do without many things," the man had said, "but they cannot do without bread."

Indeed, if he had heeded the man's advice, and become a baker rather than a composer of weird tales, he, undoubtedly, would not at that moment have been shy of rent money.

His nostrils, oblivious to conceptual thought but not to subtle essence, found themselves dilating in a most pronounced manner—as nostrils often do when confronted by a pleasing aroma.

Whatever they were baking in there certainly smelled good.

He was tempted to tap on the window and ask if they could sell him a roll. He would take it home and have it with tea—or, better yet, eat it on the spot, as surely there was nothing better than a hot roll on a foggy London morning.

He bent over and peered through the glass. A number of people were busy at work with bread, but what surprised him was the manner of their costume. They were dressed in black gowns and had large yellow crosses suspended from their necks. Mark was no expert on baking or bakers, but he felt that this attire was not the standard for their profession. His gaze fell on one figure who was, in a most feminine manner, especially robust. The person's face was handsome, even beautiful, and she was engaged in kneading dough, her hands encased in white gloves. Another figure, of the male persuasion, approached her. He had red hair. They smiled at each other and spoke. The female figure then removed her right hand from the dough she was kneading, raised it up, and placed it on the head of the other.

Mark suddenly felt his mouth go dry and knew that, were the rolls produced by those hands the very last rolls in the world, he would not partake of one. He moved on and hid himself in the shadows.

A quarter of an hour later, a figure emerged from the doorway of the building and turned south-east on Archway Road.

Mark followed at a reasonable distance and observed as, a few hundred yards on, the fellow crossed the trafficless street and sat down at the bus stop. Mark approached. He stood and stared at the man for several moments.

"Hey, what's up, mate?" the fellow said.

"What were you doing?"

"What do you mean, mate?"

"I saw you come out of the bakery. What were you doing in there?"

"Um, baking, mate . . ."

Mark stared at him. The baker began to get nervous and stood up.

"Listen mate, I don't want no trouble. I've got some good grass from Leeds. A couple of tokes mightn't do you bad."

Mark balled up his left hand into a fist, pulled it back and let it spring forward into the other's jaw. The fellow rocked on his feet for a moment and then fell backwards.

Mark looked him over. He was a clean-cut fellow with no apparent tattoos or body piercings. This alone was enough to tell him that his suspicions were not unfounded.

Mark pulled out the dagger, kneeled down and thrust it to the other's throat.

"Look mate, I'm just a breadhead. I ain't done nothin' wrong, I ain——"

The words drowned in a terrible lake of crimson.

Mark unzipped the man's backpack and looked through it. Inside was a notebook full of love letters, a ziplock bag with what seemed to be about an eight of an ounce of marijuana, a pipe, and a dog-eared paperback titled, *The Book of the Two Principles*.

"I was right," Mark said to himself. "Those bakers are fucking Cathars!"

Friday

It was five o'clock. He hadn't been home all day. And what a day it had been. That morning, at 4.26, he had killed his fifth Cathar that week. Just as his blade had severed the carotid artery, a police whistle had sounded and he had spent the rest of the morning dashing about, running over housetops and trotting through sewers.

At 12.35 he had had a bowl of clam soup at a lunch counter near Waterloo Station and then he had idled away forty-five minutes in front of a florist shop before making his way to the Dandy Lad pub, where he had been sitting for the last three hours and twenty-six minutes drinking Three Tuns Golden Spicy Bitter, which he had heard from reliable sources was the favourite beer of Algernon Blackwood.

He extracted his phone from his pocket and decided to check his email. There was a single message in his inbox, from a Mr. George Tete, that looked promising. He opened it.

FROM THE DESK OF MR GEORGE TETE
THE BILL AND EXCHANGE MANAGER
BANK OF AFRICA (BOA)
OUAGADOUGOU-BURKINA FASO
WEST AFRICA BRANCH.
TEL:+226-66 23 93 30 +226-66 23 93 30

Dear Sir/Madam

I am contacting you based on trust and confidentiality that you will
keep this as top secret.don't be scared or surprised, i am the Bill and Exchange Manager of BANK OF AFRICA and i have an opportunity to
transfer sum of US($11.5.MILLION US DOLLARS) into your account.

I have the courage to look for a reliable and Honest Person who will

be capable for this important business. Transaction,believing that you
will never let me down either now or in Future.

The owner of this account is MR. ANDREAS SCHRANNER FROM
MUNICH,GERMANY,.He died along side with his families in PLANE CRASH ON
31 JULY 2000. Since his death, the bank has made series of efforts to
contact any of the relatives to claim this money but without success,And my investigation proved to me as well that his company
does not know anything about this account.I want to transfer this
money into a safe foreign account abroad but I don't know any foreigner,I know that this message will come to you as a surprise as
we don't know ourselves before, but be sure that it is real and a Genuine business.

Hope that you will never let me down in this transaction, at the conclusion of this business, you will be giving 35% of the total amount, 65% will be for me.

I look forward to your earlier reply by email your full information's such as.

i)Your Full Name...
ii) Your Private Telephone Number........................
iii) Your Resident Address...................................
iv) A Scan Copy Of Your Passport if Any........................

Thanks. Mr GEORGE TETE
BILL AND EXCHANGE MANAGER,
BANK OF AFRICA (BOA

He was just about to reply when his phone began to ring. It was Quentin S. Crisp. He answered and, after a few formalities, a rendezvous was arranged for an hour hence at the Three Salmons Pub.

"I guess I have time to knock off one more pint here before heading out."

And, on this matter, he was correct.

He arrived at his destination seven minutes before the designated time, went to the counter, got a pint of Old Brown Ale, a drink much admired by the great Arthur Machen, and then sat down at a table in the corner just beneath a portrait of James Hogg.

He took a sip of the glorious juice. It was like drinking a dark cloud blown in from the sea. After taking in about a third of his drink, he went and used the restroom. When he came out, he noticed Quentin just then walking in through the front door. The latter saw Mark Samuels and waved and then made a gesture indicating that he would join him in a moment. And, after purchasing a pint for himself, of Marston's Pedigree (the preferred drink of Yukio Mishima during his famous 1952 trip to London), he did, in fact, join him.

Quentin had longish hair and glasses. A green woollen scarf was wrapped around his neck. He was a typical product of North Devon—a vegetarian who had formed an early penchant for mermaid porn. But, just like everyone else from North Devon, he had no desire to live there and had found his home in London—that is if Bexleyheath could be called London, which would be akin to calling the man who scrapes bubblegum off the tracks along the District Line the Secretary of State for Transport.

Though his real passion was Brazilian wrestling, he made most of his money from ghost writing for a British author by the name of Laiman Mangay.

Aside from his parish priest, Quentin was the only person in England Mark trusted.

"Hey," Mark said as Quentin sat down, setting his pint and an iPhone with a cracked screen on the table as he did so.

"Hello."

They each drank from their respective beers.

"So you heard about the killings?" Mark asked.

"Killings? No, I don't think so."

"Don't you read the newspapers?"

"Generally speaking, I only get my news from the *Living in the Future* webzine or whatever random links Brenpyon sends me."

"Brenpyon?"

"Yeah, he is the one who is writing this story."

"I thought you were."

"No, mine is in the 'notes' app on my iPhone. I will read it to you if you like."

Mark said that, yes, he did like, and so Quentin picked up his iPhone, cleared his throat, and read aloud the following:

Nothing in time is eternal, but some things borrow eternity with such success that when they end we think the world itself has ended. Johnson, famously, thought London as large as life. The end of all things is kept from the consciousness of the Londoner as if by the Thames Barrier. "When I am rich," say the bells of Shoreditch. Though now such bells ring only in memory; in the present streets that voice is still the foot-passenger here may be so persuaded by London's commotion, still-going locomotion, prolific commerce and intermingling of enterprise and entropy that he is sharing in eternity, that even a doom dogging humanity as close as debt might be expected to dissipate here as if confronted by a reality with a greater credit rating than its own.

But what is the substance of this great credibility? In the central thoroughfares, though certain buildings stand firm against the centuries, the shuffling of money requires an effervescence of the new, a glass-and-concrete sparkle of inflationary bubbles that many sink beneath, and in this circulation of strangers all is change in the paper cup of a beggar on the pavement.

Is there nothing but this to London's borrowed eternity?

A hundred years and more ago, the Japanese novelist Natsume Sôseki, under an inky existential weight like a migraine of the soul, stopped at each intersection and unfolded his map, buffeted by those passing into shadow like this scene, so, too, will pass the young man in SkinnyJeans who stands here now, intent on his iPhone's GPS as he steps into traffic.

How the vastness of such turning seasons chills us! Yet the writer must hope to draw a thread between the disparate seasons, as Sôseki threaded those streets to him so hostile: as a spider holds together summer and autumn with its delicate web. The writer, in truth, is time's cartographer, and the most necessary thing for him to mark upon his map for future generations is where untainted drinking water might be found.

You are always the first point in the baseline from which you triangulate. Once you know the way here or there the crowd will be no longer just a crowd; you will discriminate which faces are old, which new, which buildings are ferned with tradition, which are the vigorous, illegitimate offspring of innovation. One thing separates from another, and in their separation their relation becomes clear. And presiding over these relations, unseen by most who tread the designated route of common sense, are the ghosts. Arthur Machen wrote of a fairy paradise visible to some at different times among the streets of Stoke Newington. On Peckham Rye, Blake saw a tree whose boughs were filled with angels. How much remains hidden? How much, though seen, untold? How much told among the obscure and unbelieved who, to the world of reputation and fame, are themselves as ghosts?

North of King's Cross, say the protagonists of Machen's Stoke Newington tale, we have left the known world behind us; if so, it is the unknown that will be our real starting point, but let us make our way by the known.

We find ourselves at London Bridge. A strange, fatalistic wind compels us and we sail down on the moving stairs to the Northern Line, watching the shine of the shoes, though they do not shine as in years past unless the haze of alcohol or pills makes it seem so, or the haze of melancholy itself; is it that in such a haze we see the Misery Line the shuffling tunnels that this black-inked section of the London underground acquired its unofficial name?

Pushed up like sedatives in the Tube of a hypodermic syringe as the plunger rises, we pass through Bank, Moorgate, Old Street, Angel, King's Cross St. Pancras, Euston (Bank branch), Camden Town (Bank branch), then swerving towards High Barnet we meet Kentish Town and Tufnell Park, and continue. If we have read the aforementioned tale by Machen, we might here remember the curious words of one of the characters concerning the elusive fairy garden: "You go in through a gateway, and . . . it [is] like finding yourself in another gateway." For, next, we come to Archway—surely, a gate. Yet beyond this gate is another, and greater—we have arrived at Highgate.

We seem to have attained a vantage from which we can look down upon London while still in London—look down upon geographically, but also as if historically, and even, perhaps, spiritually. There are places on the slowly rising hill from which at certain times of the day during certain times of year, we can see the street descend towards and yet not meet, a strange suspension of an entire metropolis of rooftops among mist and cloud, as if that great, eternal city of the world, London, had only been a dream.

Ask and you might here, in lofty Highgate, in the eyrie of a top-floor flat, lives, drinks, writes and dreams another, such as Blake and Machen, who has seen beyond the seeming of London's mazy changes to the sure, unmoving flame whose shadows are our certainties: the sage of resignation, Mark Samuels, author, haunter of the bar, scryer of mysteries.

Let us now pass through the lofty gate and enter upon a point in time, as being enters the realm of becoming. Sunday, the 3rd of May, 2015. Samuels has visited, on the East Finchley Road, one of the capital's few remaining second-hand bookshops of note the copy of Evelyn Waugh's *A Little Order* in his hand, on its cover other hands, of that other author, a cigar between the fingers of the left, a pen in the right. These are a writer's totems; as there is a world apart from the world, so literature begets literature, and the writer invests in the paraphernalia of literary meditation. Samuels anticipates such meditation in his slow, measuring trudge along the Great North Road; he begins it, and the road becomes Archway Road, passing along the head of a bank, at the bottom of which runs a railway track on whose opposite side rises Highgate Wood.

Here let us pause, having entered time, and allow the tale to become past tense. It was one of those days in late spring or early summer when the sunshine has attained a golden mean between the imposition and the deprivation of heat; though such days are ephemeral they almost convince with their serenity that they are as everlasting as gold itself. A great, pacific friendliness of light was enlivened by now and then breezes just firm enough and delicate enough to tell you that a little sweat had moistened your brow. Samuels had drunk, before his excursion, sufficient to make the sunlight heady, his sensations as he glanced at the trackside Queen Ann's laced with sweet gusts of air as ale is with foam. The sun had brought out the bitter-fresh odour of the privet hedges, and now, as he walked along at the head of the railway bank, separated from him by a wire fence, where a little cool was made by trees and minor greenery anonymous as nursery rhyme, the odours of leaf and soil, in the gentle stew of sunlight, were as aromatic as a herb garden.

Samuels slowed and considered. We have long had means of recording sight and sound, but smell as yet has no medium in which it might be used to chronicle history. Perhaps if snails kept records, they would be primarily in smell, but for humans it is a sense whose tales are ghostlier even than the oral traditions of the unlettered. What story was this, told in scent? It was something long forgotten, but so deeply familiar it even reminded him of what words— dependent on the ones who speak or write—seldom did: that such a depth as this existed. Soil and sap. It was not just memory, he understood where he was on the pavement; that other world whose history was scent not word was as much alive as now is now. Still, what was it? There only came to him the thwack of ball hitting cricket bat, as if a riddle and its answer were contained in this sonic stereotype; and if the shell of this old chestnut could be cracked, its kernel would be fresh.

He continued. Between the spot where he had paused and the location of his flat there lay the Woodman, a pub with interior décor of humourless kitsch intended to be, perhaps, both tasteful and modern, but according to some observers, succeeding more nearly in creating the ambiance of a brothel. It also boasted, however, a pleasant beer garden with a good number of wooden tables, some of them sheltered in a flat-roofed wooden pavilion. It being Sunday, the weather fine, the breezes refreshing, and since he had received a cheque in the preceding week in payment for a tale, Samuels purchased a pint of Doom Bar here and took it outside to one of the tables in the roof-covered corner. He took his notebook from his shoulder bag, opened it in front of him, and wrote:

A chronicle of odours.

Laying down his pen, he picked up his pint and swigged, noticing as he did so a discarded *Metro* on the seat beside him. He swigged again, laid down his pint, picked up his pen once more and sat poised to harpoon with his nib any ideas that surfaced beneath his watchfulness. Where shadows had moved suggestively in those waters, now there was disappointing stillness.

If there's no inspiration, best not to write, he told himself, but his eye had returned to the discarded *Metro* and now he put down his pen as if finally and reached for the folded tabloid. He swigged again at his beer. Turning the inky pages he became aware of a tarry fascination. What tobacco smoke did to the lungs, he felt, this was doing to his mind, but it was easy and gratifying and there was no immediate need to stop. Perhaps he could pick up ideas here, anyway, for topical window-dressing to be used, as the need arose, in future stories. Not that he cared about these particular topics. "A ban on legal highs" mentioned in the Queen's Speech, though to ban what is legal is a contradiction in terms; a Danish radio presenter—vegetarian?—battered a rabbit to death on air to highlight the hypocrisy of not being vegetarian, but did anyone eat the rabbit he had killed in order to highlight the hypocrisy of killing a rabbit as a protest against killing animals? Gwen Stefani took a 'brelfie'—a breastfeeding selfie—to tackle the stigma of breastfeeding, but there was a backlash—breastlash?—since "putting new mums under 'bressure' benefits no one," said Siobhan Freegard.

Samuels tossed the tabloid back on the seat where he had found it, not wishing to read more and now more than ever trapped in the concatenation of mere thought of which writer's block is made. He glanced around at the friends (to each other) and couples drinking at the nearby tables, and at the strangers, dressed for summer, passing the garden on the pavement beyond. The tabloid was a scrabble of competing greeds and grievances, glued together with unspoken lies. One might imagine it revealed the death struggle of the human soul—two people rolling around at a cliff edge with their hands at each other's throats—but that struggle was in no way apparent in his immediate environment, so that the paper was an enigma, like the Serpent in Eden.

From nowhere, then, breaking the small, irrefutable chain of the inevitable, there came a thought as vast and simple as day: I would like to write a tale of wonder.

It was not a new thought, except inasmuch as it was always new, always waiting.

What was it that distracted him from this end? What delayed him?

He rolled his pen upon the tabletop with his fingertips as he pondered this question. There only formed in his mind the phrase "a fallen world," but he could not make an answer of this and groped, instead, in his pocket, for his e-cigarette.

As he leaned into himself to retrieve his vape-stick, the world that had occupied his thoughts was eclipsed by the approach of a human figure. Like a comet's tail of blue smoke, a dragon coiled around his arm, its head towards his hand as if in plummeting descent.

Samuels raised his head.

"I haven't seen you for a while," said the newcomer.

"Oh, hello Dane," said Samuels, moving up to make room.

"Where have you been?"

"Around. How about you?"

"The same. Looking for a mead hall."

"Mead hall? Oh. I think we've all become wanderers since they closed the Colchester Arms. I bump into old regulars, like you, now and then, by chance, but no one seems to settle on one place anymore, as if they've lost their orbit."

Quentin put down his iPhone, picked up his pint, and took a 'swig'.

"Um, yeah," Mark said, "anyhow—about the killings . . ."

"Yes?"

"I've killed five people this week."

"I see," Quentin replied. He lifted his ale to his lips and took a sip, then set it back down on its coaster. "And how did this come about?"

In rather colourful language, which is to say blending cadences of Oliver Onions with pleasant overtones of Charles Dickens and a few quirky asides *à la* Bloy, Mark described what had happened the night before.

"So, if I understand you correctly," Quentin said, "you killed these people because you suspected that they were Cathars?"

"It wasn't a suspicion."

"They were Cathars and you killed them?"

"That's right. Do you think I did the wrong thing?"

"I wouldn't go so far as to say that. As you know, I could scarcely be called a fan of Catharism, being myself more inclined to the teachings of Lao Tzu. I am just not sure that, um, killing these chaps can forward your stylistic mission unless you can somehow integrate it."

"Integrate it?"

"Yes, it seems to me that if you could make this an integral part of your thought process, it might benefit your future work. If a person is deaf, they can't hear even Manowar. If a person is blind, they couldn't even see Kate Beckinsale if she was stripped naked before them. That is why in some situations sign language is necessary, while in others experiments in direct perception are required. In 1885 Vincent van Gogh painted *The Potato Eaters*. In 1637 Dutch tulip prices collapsed. Ovid was exiled by Augustus. Hokoji Temple at Nara took twenty years to complete. Spinning through space, don't forget to take stock of dry land. When committing murder, it is considered prudent to leave no traces. I would also suggest studying the *Chin Yen Ching* and the *Wan Pi Kau ch'iu Hsien Sheng Fa*."

Mark swallowed down the last of his beer. Quentin realized that he was lagging behind somewhat, so finished his off and then rose from his seat to get another round. He returned soon with a pair of pints.

Quentin's iPhone was making a beeping, bubbling sound. He picked it up and looked at it.

"J-bon is calling me on Skype."

"J-bon?"

"Justin Isis."

Mark stood up and went around to the other side of the table so he could see the phone.

Quentin pressed the answer button and a lean, handsome face appeared behind the crack on the screen. Next to him was a Japanese woman with an easy-going appearance.

"Hey, me and Mika are sitting here in my apartment with some Ozeki OneCups."

"Markitty and I are at the Three Salmons Pub."

"Markitty?" Mark asked.

"Yes, that's your kawaii sobriquet," Q-bon replied.

Markitty and Q-bon both looked at the iPhone. J-bon was speaking.

"Did massive DMT last night. Went far off the grid. It was eternity outside time and space and I broke through far far more than before, like a billion times. Earlier experience was more like some kind of veil or outer realm with those nymphs or spirits. This was off in the hypersphere where I also met the goddess. Unbelievably terrifying, though in a non-Euclidean sense—time as solid physical dimension."[1]

---

1 Hope you're enjoying the book so far. These tribute anthologies usually involve an element of pastiche, but perhaps it's better to think of it as refinement through repetition. It's possible to imagine a tribute anthology to a tribute anthology itself, and then a tribute anthology to that tribute anthology, on and on in a series, until the recursive auto-pastiche would eventually reduce - or refine - a complex or contradictory body of work to a single book, a single story and finally a single word or image. This has already happened to Poe, Lovecraft and Ligotti (or: the Raven, the Tentacle and the Puppet). Given the absolute

"Which goddess was it?" Q-bon asked.

"Isis."

"I see."

"What was she like?" Mark asked.

"It was like meeting someone face to face after only previously talking to them online. I tried to trade with the joker/spirit/god things by giving them letters from the alphabet I'm working on. I'm limiting the current sequence to just ten letters/compounds, three verbs and two pronouns. It's more like a spell or something anyway."

"I would go easy on the DMT," Mark said. "My friend was a missionary in Brazil and started doing a lot of hallucinogens and I think it affected him sort of permanently."

"Yeah?"

"Yes, he still considers Jesus to be his lord and saviour, but is also part of an ayahuasca cult."

"I wish I were an ayahuasca cult," Q-bon said.

J-bon nodded his head. "In the non-Euclidean dimension you are."

---

circumscription of influence implied by a strict series of tributes to tributes, and taking just the titles of the stories in this book, we can imagine a single story along the lines of "'The Black and White Mould of the Linguistic City,'" in which an English city—that is, the city of the English language—is overtaken by the gradually creeping mould known as the writer (in this case Mark Samuels)—a presence fashioning the language in its own image and generating a mood which proves more persistently contaminating, in its downbeat way, than anyone expected. In *Black Altars* Mark Samuels writes:

The universe had become a tomb. Across its intolerable immensity everything was dead and black. The stars had gone out, their fuel having been spent long ago. No planets rolled in the illimitable darkness. They had turned to dust. Eternal night had conquered everything. There were no sounds, for all energy had been exhausted. Only an utter silence remained. Time itself ceased to have any meaning. The universe had been dead for the infinitely greater part of its existence, the period of activity being only a moment at the beginning. The cosmos was cold, bleak and black. But it was not empty. There were ghosts haunting it, deathly white apparitions screaming silently in the black void.

If we take "the universe" here to mean "the human body," we have some idea of what Reggie Oliver means when he writes that:

Samuels articulates brilliantly what modern man secretly fears most about death: not that it is extinction, but that it is an eternity in which the utter meaninglessness of life is fully revealed.

"Hey, the battery on my iPhone is on ten percent. I should say goodbye now."

"Okay, cool," J-bon said, and then turned to the Japanese woman who was saying something to him in a low voice.

"Hey, Mika wants to say something to Markitty."

"Hi Mika!" Markitty said.

The woman smiled and then, obviously nervous, spoke:

"I. Can be. On your. Album cover?"

After the Skype conversation, Mark and Quentin sat across from each other drinking their beers. They both felt empty. Quentin was vaguely imagining what it would be like to live in Krylatyy. Mark was recalling the look on his first victim's face as he had seen the dagger. He had looked like a bad actor playing Hamlet.

Quentin lifted his glass high and let the beer spill down his throat.

"I should be heading back to Bexleyheath," he said.

"And I to Highgate."

They both rose from their seats and strolled past the loo, on the door of which was written 'Gentlemen'—both lads thinking at that

---

Barring divine intervention or extreme advances in medical technology, you and everyone you know will eventually die, and there's nothing to suggest that this death won't in fact be the echoing void of formless insanity that Samuels describes. For example, I'm not sure who you are or when this is being read, and as such I'm not sure whether I'm alive or dead right now. The world in which I exist alongside these words as a warm body, a tangible referent - as opposed to the disembodied voice of just another dead writer—only asserts itself briefly; in the future I'm dead, which is to say that these are the words of a dead man; the mind behind this voice is always marked to die, and these words already exist in a downbeat eternity. If Wittgenstein is correct that "death is not an event in life; we do not live to experience death," then it's possible to understand, as Mark Valentine and his shadowy companion discussed in the foreword, why we insist so strongly on wallpapering over life with words: to distract from our atavistic awareness of an event that is not an event, an event outside of life which we can neither experience nor escape. By constantly pasting word-images over life and its non-event, the horror writer is the ultimate wallpaper artist, and the more vivid the word-image, the more convincingly death is denied. The dead become vampires, resplendent with the youth and beauty of a Paranormal Romance protagonist, while all manner of ghosts and presences are projected into the corners of otherwise empty houses and abandoned churches, superficially threatening but ultimately reassuring. The word-image constantly renovates death into life, but in reducing the role of the word-image, Samuels wallpapers over life less than most writers. Unlike the Raven, the Tentacle and the Puppet, there seems no overwhelming Samuels image except perhaps the ultimate abstraction of consciousness itself, propagating and contaminating space but unable to reach any final freedom. A tribute anthology "cast in the mould of Mark," or marked and moulded by Mark and his very instant that if everyone who went in there were really gentle, the world would be a much finer place.

They stepped outside. The sidewalk was bustling with people. Quentin flung the left side of his scarf over his shoulder so that his chin became partially concealed. Without speaking, they walked to the Angel tube station and descended the stairs. Each man needed to go in the opposite direction of the other.

"Goodbye," Mark said.

"Bye," Quentin answered.

Thirty-two minutes later Mark was standing before Kiplings Restaurant and Bar, on Hill Street.

He looked in his mailbox. There was an envelope, addressed to him in a bold, rolling script. He opened it, and found within the following letter:

---

mould, must inevitably commit some degree of wallpapering in its search for signifiers to homage (or caricature, depending on your view of its quality), and as such it seems pointless not to acknowledge it. It's possible that I asked Mark Samuels to contribute to this book after exposing him to the initial PDF, hoping he would write a story under the name of one of the contributors, in the awareness that his writing self had contaminated other writing selves, and that he agreed, wanting to investigate whether impersonating himself would reveal anything new about the wallpaper world of words and what it is pasted over - to see whether Mark Samuels pretending to be one of his friends pretending to be him would differ substantially from the way he pretends to be (or merely inhabits) himself when writing under his own name. It's possible that Mark Samuels wrote the words you're reading now, or that Justin Isis wrote them, or that Brendan Connell wrote them, or that Quentin S. Crisp wrote them, or that Mark Valentine wrote them—equally possible that all these warm tangible referents who were alive in their own minds at the time of this writing collaborated to produce them, reaching out from various corners of their wallpaper world, with its vast associative apparatus of book awards and literary genres, in the knowledge that the Mark Samuels who consciously situates himself in the tradition of Weird Fiction does so partly to reach for a shape through the wallpaper, in the manner of a blind man feeling for a face, and that this desire arises due to an awareness, or perhaps an inability to forget, the ever present, impossible anti-event beyond images and words. In any sense that matters, we are all dead and compounded in Eternity. Who is really writing now and who is reading?

Dear Mr. Samuels,

Your incapability to pay me, with convenience to yourself, the month's rent which is due from you, is, I assure you, sufficient apology for any little disappointment which the delay may occasion to me. I am convinced of your wish to be punctual, and, therefore, cheerfully assent to your request. Let the month's rent stand over as you desire, and give yourself no uneasiness on the subject. I shall not ask you for it until after the current month has ceased and the next begun, long ere which, I trust, the anxieties of which you complain will have vanished.

I am, sir,
Your obedient servant,
Eumolpus Patric

Language of the City

by Thana Niveau

It was just after the funeral that the cities began to call to me.

I remembered their voices from years before and I had hoped never to hear them again. I have always been afraid of cities. It's not the noise or the pollution, the crowds or the crime. It's the cities themselves. They terrify me. They're alive. And they hate us.

I was six years old when I first realized they were aware of me. My parents had taken me to London for the weekend, a million miles from our tiny village in Dorset. I felt like we were on another planet. I had never seen so many people, so many buildings, so much traffic. Everything was freakishly huge. And the noise!

The first day passed by in a blur. On the second day we went to Westminster Abbey. The gothic behemoth towered over us, its jagged spires threatening to skewer the birds. The building was intimidating enough, but then, as I stared up at those monstrous towers, I suddenly felt a presence. Although the sun was shining brightly, it was as though I'd stepped into a deep pool of shadow. Something pierced my feet, slithered up my body and made me begin to shiver uncontrollably. My parents had no idea that anything was wrong, and they just kept walking, pulling me along with them. But behind me I sensed an icy malevolence, as though the city were coiling like a serpent at my back, poised to strike. I could almost hear it hissing.

I didn't dare look back. I clutched my father's hand as we made our way through the crowded street. We queued with what seemed like the population of the whole world to get into the abbey. I didn't like the claustrophobic press of strangers but the lurking city behind me felt like a much greater threat, a gathering storm or an impending earthquake. I kept expecting the ground to rumble and open up beneath my feet like a mouth.

The feeling stayed with me all that day and lingered long after we'd returned home. My parents knew something was wrong. It was obvious that I hadn't enjoyed the visit, but I remained tight-lipped about why. Eventually, they stopped asking.

But even if I had wanted to keep that awful experience to myself, it was too late. My subconscious had been infected. I would wake screaming from nightmares, plagued by voices that whispered to me while I slept. My parents worried about schizophrenia, but a battery of tests proved that I was as sane as they were. And over time I almost began to believe it.

Years passed. Village life settled into its familiar, uneventful routines and eventually the echo of the city began to fade. My parents never brought it up again and neither did I. Even so, I refused to believe that it had just been an hallucination. The dreams, while less frequent and less traumatic, never went away completely.

Many years later I found myself going back to London. I had to face my fear, to prove to myself that I hadn't just imagined the whole thing.

I hadn't.

I visited other cities to see if they had the same effect on me. Plymouth, Southampton, Portsmouth, Brighton—all left me feeling anxious and slightly ill. But none of them filled me with terror the way London had. I wondered whether it would be safe to venture further afield. I was loath to leave the safety of my rural surroundings, but I needed to pursue a career, and they don't build universities in tiny villages.

York seemed like a good compromise. It was still a city, but nothing approaching such seething metropolises as London or Birmingham or Manchester. I lived there for three years, studying art and interactive media, honing the skills that would allow me to work from the safety of the home I longed to return to, a place where I could live well beyond the reach of any city.

Three years. It wasn't easy. Not a day passed without my sensing the restless shifting of the cobbled streets, the lurching and grinding of enclosing walls. I was the one who thought I was moving freely, and yet I felt stalked by my very surroundings. It was as though I were walking across a frozen lake, the spectre of the city dogging my steps beneath me, under the ice. I suffered terrible headaches and nausea, which I attributed to the endless looping nightmares the city gave me.

In these dreams I imagined myself seeing through the veneer of the familiar to the structure beneath. Solid objects broke apart, separating like oil from water. I could see beyond form to the molecular components within, visualize each single particle with agonizing clarity. Atoms scurried visibly across the spectrum of my dreams, so horribly acute the spectrum burned my eyes to see.

These visions persisted into my waking hours, laid like lenses over my eyes, forcing me to see what others couldn't. I would look at the curve of a street and see a malicious sneer. The cornerstones of buildings were claws embedded in the pavement. Sometimes I saw them move, ready to score and rend the flesh of their foundations, to uproot themselves and creep along behind me. Even the air around me took on a sense of menace, as though I were inhaling poisonous gas with every breath.

I succumbed to periods of black despair. Fantasies of blinding myself began to pervade my thoughts, even though the visions were only a fraction of the horror. I couldn't shut out the insidious whispering, or protect myself from the rancid taste of the air. I was convinced that my mind would shatter like glass.

Early one morning I woke feeling dizzy. Gradually I opened my eyes, expecting to see the familiar surroundings of my bedroom. Instead, I found myself perched on the city wall, gazing down at the steeply sloping hill. I had one leg up on the stone, as though I were mounting a horse. I cried out and pushed myself back, instantly wide awake. I had no way of knowing whether the fall would have killed me or not, but I didn't care. I had had enough. I left that day and fled home to Dorset. With every mile I travelled away from York, I felt better. Away from the urban jungle, normality at last returned.

I hadn't finished my degree, but it didn't matter. I knew enough to get myself started, and soon I was designing websites for small businesses in the area, many of whom were as fearful of the Internet as I was of cities.

But the Internet made sense. Computers and code made sense. There were patterns in everything, patterns like the ones I had always seen in the city. But these were patterns I could control. Web design was neither science nor art, although it drew from both. I enjoyed manipulating data to create structure, found comfort in the knowledge that numbers were at the root of everything. Numbers could be understood. Numbers could be controlled. I was an architect of information and the only traffic I had to negotiate was virtual.

Beyond the reach of cities, I began to feel safe once more. I was no longer plagued by nightmares or visions. People regarded me as reclusive, perhaps a bit eccentric, but there was no suggestion that they knew I had only narrowly escaped madness and death. To them I was just a fellow villager, not one of those *city folk*.

And then I met Edward. He was the first person I had ever loved, and the only one I ever fully trusted. He even trusted me enough to love me back. After a couple of years, we got married and lived like ordinary people.

Until a city took him from me.

For twenty years the headquarters of the high street shop he managed had been in Bournemouth. Then the company was bought out by a large corporation, and they were based in London. A promotion followed, with one catch: Edward would have to relocate.

My heart pounded with terror at the prospect and all my worst dreams came back to me. I saw myself strangled by ropes of winding streets, crushed by looming buildings, smothered by the oppressive atmosphere. So I gave him a choice: London or me. He chose London.

Some weeks later his body was found by a group of urban explorers in a disused passageway at Moorgate Station. They had already taken a series of photographs prominently featuring what they'd assumed was just a pile of filthy rags. Then they moved closer and realized the truth.

Edward was mangled beyond recognition, and only dental records confirmed his identity. No one could explain what he was doing there, or indeed, how he had even found the place, especially as the photographers themselves had needed bolt cutters to access a service door that led them into the tunnels. Foul play was suggested and, naturally, I was the first and most likely suspect. But enough people had seen me around the village at the time, many miles from London, that it was obvious I couldn't have had anything to do with it.

Eventually the police pieced together a series of events that added up to "death by misadventure". Edward had apparently fallen down an abandoned lift shaft and then crawled into the passageway to die of his injuries. A tragic accident.

But I knew better. I knew the city had killed him.

I let his family handle the arrangements and I stayed well away from the funeral. Nobody missed me. I kept my head down and buried myself in work, finding reassurance in the predictability of code, the security of numbers.

That was when I began to hear them again. The cities. At first they only spoke to me in dreams, in visions of such harrowing clarity and strangeness that I thought I must finally be losing my mind. In sleep I found myself in a London that didn't exist, that couldn't possibly exist. I climbed long flights of crumbling stairs and wandered lost through dank, misshapen corridors and rotting alleyways. Once again I saw the secret design beneath the manmade constructs. The canted walls and impossible angles tormented me. I woke in a cold sweat night after night, my mouth forming meaningless words, my voice uttering meaningless syllables.

More than once I was woken by the sound of neighbours pounding on my door. They said I had been screaming. They said it sounded like I was being tortured. I reassured them on each occasion that it was just bad dreams. Someone suggested it was the shock of Edward's death, and I gratefully seized on the excuse. People are always happier with explanations they can understand.

The nightmares were bad enough. But then I began to see other things. Like the mould.

It began as a small, downy patch of greenish grey on the wall, and at first I assumed it was just some dampness inside the wallpaper. But the longer I stared at it, the more I began to realize it was some kind of fungus, black and spongy, like rotten fruit. I scrubbed and scraped at it, but it was persistent. Determined.

Soon the wall became prickly with fibres and I peeled the ruined paper away, only to reveal more of the ugly stain behind it. The mould grew day by day, spreading rapidly, bubbling out from behind what remained of the paper. Now it covers an area the size of a door.

Every day it gets bigger, spreading like a disease. And as it takes hold in the wall, so the voices take hold in my mind.

It's a festering chorus, a city's discourse. The sound is somewhere between noise and music, simultaneously seductive and repellent. It beckons me even as I fight to resist its lure. I don't know how much longer I can hold out.

The wall is rotting away, and my sanity rots with it. What I see through the cracks terrifies me. I don't see into the next room; I see into *cities*. Like the effect of one mirror reflecting another into infinity, I see the endless propagation of their hellish particles, malignant spores that flicker and buzz like a faulty fluorescent light, creeping from my nightmares into my waking life. I hear their voices constantly. And I can understand at last what they are saying.

I thought I knew all about underlying structure and hidden meaning. It's the very essence of my job. Codes and ciphers. Interfaces. But the language of a city is something else entirely. It has no words, no grammar, nothing you can even comprehend as language. Yet still, it speaks. More than that—it *suggests*.

I feel the loathing, the cold, coiling malice in every tone, every nuance. It's the voice that lured Edward to his death. It opened the way for him into a hidden part of London and he had no choice but to follow. Now it wants me there. It wants me to *see*.

I must step through, into the rotting tunnel.

Into the city.

There is no way to climb through without touching the mould. I anticipate something wet and soggy, but when I brush against it, I find that it is curiously dry, like chalk. Some of it crumbles to dust at my feet. I am barely moving, yet it seems as though I have already travelled a long way, much farther than the actual physical distance between my home and any city. The passage makes me think uncomfortably of a womb. A crisply burnt womb.

Fear takes root in my mind and soon it begins to blossom into panic, but the emotions don't reach my body. I am not alone. Something is controlling me from within, something that refuses to let me run away.

All around me I hear the humming voice of the city, the voice it shares with *all* cities. It throbs and pulses with menace. Trains rumble beneath the streets and I sense the pattern of their branching tunnels, their many levels and dead ends. I can see the terrible design behind the system. All throughout the city people scurry like ants, entirely ignorant of the monstrous presence that surrounds them.

I emerge onto the platform of a derelict station, one where trains never come. The chipped tiles along the curved walls and ceiling are thickly furred with mould, blackened like a gangrenous wound. Fibrous tendrils spread out in every direction, strangling the ancient rails and taking root in the cavernous space beneath them. The threads reach for me like questing antennae, stinging where they touch my skin, breaking off to burrow inside. A distant part of me registers the pain, but I cannot make a sound.

I gaze down at the writhing coils. The tendrils part like fleshy hair as I peer through the rifts in the mould, looking further into the city. The understructure goes deep, deeper than my eyes can see. There is motion there, far in the distance. Shadows flow past like a river, maddeningly dark, but my vision is more acute than ever. The world is melting away.

There are so many layers. Layers upon layers. A building stands where a previous one was demolished, and before that, another. The city erases and rewrites itself constantly, a living palimpsest. Frenzied particles swarm throughout its boundless iterations, teeming like an infinite sequence of numbers, reflecting back onto itself without end. Part of me knows what I am seeing while another part tries to shield me from the revelation.

We are only creatures at the very edge of life, creatures who know nothing of what lies beyond our limited range of sensation. Dizziness overwhelms me at the thought that I am seeing beyond anything ever known or imagined.

I close my eyes, but it makes no difference. The mould is there behind my lids, undulating like a spill of ink into water, into the liquid of my eyes. My vision is infected, and all the more acute for it. Lines criss-cross one another, forming a mesh, a living network that connects me to everything I can see or perceive. Everything is moving, changing, shifting with a terrible speed that is too much for me to process. Except that something *forces* me to process it. The city. It is moving through me.

The knowledge is colonizing my mind. I am the city's interface. It speaks. It screams. And I hear.

The fluid in my veins has changed, transmuted, and I know the mould for what it is—the blood of the city. My heart is a husk inside my chest, no longer performing any human function. All that remains is a dreadful awareness, too horrifying to contain within the remnants of my mind. I know why I was called. My madness is reshaping the city, clawing it apart to reveal its true face.

It is both unfathomably old and impossibly new. I stare into the heart of it, simultaneously into its far distant past and the infinite possibilities of its future, as it peels itself open, layer upon layer. Death, life, destruction, rebirth.

Soon there is only a barren stretch of ground, an empty wasteland devoid of life. A foetid wind stirs the powdery sand. Even the sky is sour, heavy with noxious spores. I feel them twitch inside my cold veins as the city awakens inside me.

I am seeing what will be. It's not the death of civilization, because there is no civilization. There is only the city. We delude ourselves into thinking we built all this, that we conceived it and designed it to serve our needs. But that's not true. *We're* the constructs. *We're* the ones who were built.

Through me, the city begins to speak. I feel cleansed by its presence and I let go, giving myself to it completely. I perceive with senses beyond mortal ones the changes beginning in other places. I see the spores drifting, the mould taking root.

The future is leaking through the crumbling edifices of the city, giving me glimpses of what is to come. It only needed one person to hear its voice, to open the way for it. Soon others will hear the voices too. They will open other doors, step through into other cities.

In Tokyo, a little girl picks at a scab of fungus on the wall of her school. In Paris, a bookseller spots a damp patch on the ceiling of his shop. In San Francisco, a hotel maid moves a chair to hide a discoloured spot on the carpet.

Everywhere, the city is opening the way to our ruin, decomposing from another time, a virus devouring the past. It rots backwards, into our hollow existence. Brick by brick, stone by stone, it will unmake itself. It will unmake *us*.

The Singular Quiddity of Merlin's Ear

by Simon Clark

"Quests are never straightforward. There are always setbacks, reverses, obstacles—it's like someone 'up there' is testing our resolve to see the journey through to the end."

He made this observation as he stood up to his neck in black water. Its icy coldness made his entire body tremble. It must be said that the tennis shorts and T-shirt he wore did nothing to hold the chill at bay.

In a voice colder than the water itself, Nick Mercer's wife stated, "Adam didn't mean to drop the bloody key into the canal."

"I'm not blaming Adam." Nick glanced at the ten-year-old who leaned against his mother on the narrowboat's deck. "Of course it was an accident."

"Then show Adam you're not angry with him," Constance demanded.

Nick tried to smile. The low temperature freezing his flesh made it difficult, though. He imagined the attempted grin looked more like an angry snarl. "No worries, Adam. I'll soon find the key then we'll be on our way. Uh . . . I'm sure something just swam between my thighs."

At least that made Constance laugh. "No doubt an inquisitive mermaid."

Adam said nothing. Then, he never did. Constance had told Nick on their first date that her only child was mute.

"Okay," Nick began reluctantly. "The water's not that deep. I should be able to find the key easily enough."

It wasn't easy. In fact, locating the key was bloody difficult. After thirty-five minutes of holdings his breath and making repeated sorties to the bottom of the canal, where he had to search by touch alone because the filthy water meant he could see zilch, he at last found the key. He swam back to the surface, his hand breaking the water before his head did. An act of melodrama on his part, because he knew that to Constance and Adam it would suggest an arm rising above the surface, holding the magical sword, Excalibur. Adam obsessively played a computer game that featured King Arthur and his battles and his encounters with supernatural monsters. Nick hoped a bit of playacting would amuse the boy.

No such luck. Adam stared down with no outward show of emotion as Nick dogpaddled to the rope ladder that hung over the narrowboat's flank.

"I've got it." He spat bitter water from his mouth. "I've found the fu . . . flipping key."

Constance took the key from him before he hoisted himself onto the deck. "I'll run you a hot shower."

"Thank you." He grinned at the unsmiling boy as he added, "Now that I've found the key we can unlock the barrier and go onto the lake." He nodded at the steel boom that blocked the canal. Beyond that, broad, open waters. In the lake's centre, the island that held the mysterious structure that was their destination.

"We shall not be thwarted, eh?" His voice rose in triumph. "Now that we're nearing the end of our exciting quest." He spoke in mock-thespian tones, endeavouring to bring a smile to the boy's permanently stony face. Nope. The boy's expression didn't so much as flicker.

"Cold to the bone," Nick called from the boat's tiny shower-cubicle. "Summer? Can you believe it? That canal's positively Arctic."

Constance's muffled voice barely reached him, "Can't hear you. Speak up. Better still, come out."

He'd dressed by now (no easy feat in such a confined space; he'd smacked his elbow against the wall). Rubbing his hair again with the towel, as much to restore circulation to his frozen scalp as anything, he slid back the concertina door.

"Cold . . . I was saying how cold the canal was."

"I've made coffee to thaw you out. There's a saucer over the top—should be hot."

"Cheers."

He entered the canal-boat's main cabin. This was something resembling forty feet of narrow corridor with a low ceiling. Kitchen appliances ran along one section of wall. Other sections of wall accommodated padded bench seats that converted into beds, a fold-down table and a wood-burning stove; a television was fixed to the wall between a pair of large windows. Those same windows gave picture-postcard views across the canal in the direction of pleasant, rolling meadows. The only private, enclosed spaces on board were the shower-room and toilet. Adam, the voiceless boy, watched a DVD about monster trucks. Constance, Nick's wife of ten months, sat beside her son.

Nick took the saucer from the mug; he sipped the hot coffee with a sigh. "Heaven in a cup."

"There's cake," Constance said. "It needs eating up before it gets dry."

"I'm fine with this."

"Watch you don't bang your noggin on the ceiling again."

He hunched, making his head lower. "Once I'm fully defrosted I'll lift the boom and take the boat out onto the lake."

"Is it safe?"

"The lake?"

"I thought narrowboats could only use canals."

"The water's flat as glass. We'll be alright. Safe as houses." He paused, watching the TV screen: a truck with giant wheels crushed a car. "It'd be useful to watch the *Merlin's Ear* DVD before we go out there."

"Uh, what about . . ?" She glanced at her son who concentrated in a peculiarly fixated way on the truck action. Clearly, she didn't want to interrupt his enjoyment of the show.

"I'm sure Adam wouldn't mind. . . . Would you, Adam?"

Adam gave no indication whether he minded or not. A truck bounced spectacularly over sand dunes.

Nick pulled a DVD case from a shelf. Beneath the title *Merlin's Ear* was a black and white archive photograph of a concrete structure with a concave surface—it pretty much resembled one half of a gigantic oyster shell, standing upright. The small figure of a soldier, carrying a Lee-Enfield rifle, emphasized the building's enormous size.

"Adam," began Nick. "Is it okay? Can I watch this?"

Adam stared at him. An angry stare at that.

"It won't last long."

Constance put her arm around her son's shoulders. "Watching it is important for Nick's work."

"I'm going to photograph the building as it looks now, then I'll write about it for the travel magazine."

The boy didn't move; he merely aimed that cold stare at Nick.

Nick continued in a gentle voice, "The building's called Merlin's Ear. The army built it during the Second World War. It's supposed to be a kind of secret weapon, but the truth is-"

Adam stabbed the eject button on the remote control. The silver disk glided out from the slot in the side of the TV.

"Thanks, Adam."

Nick wondered if the name 'Merlin' had caught Adam's interest. After all, the boy loved the King Arthur legend. The only books he'd tolerate were ones that related to the Excalibur-wielding king. Nick exchanged glances with Constance. He hoped his glance conveyed that he was grateful. Yet the way her eyes narrowed hinted she'd interpreted his look as saying, 'Oh, God, for how much longer do we have to tolerate that strange child of yours?'

Nick decided to be as cheerful as possible in an attempt to head off any potential arguments.

"Cheers, Adam," he said. "You might find the film interesting. It was made by a propaganda unit in the Second World War. That's when Hitler and the Nazis were trying to conquer Britain. Back then, in the early 1940s, the Nazis sent over planes to bomb British cities."

Constance's expression hardened. "Adam studied the Second World War at school."

"Oh? Right. Well . . ." He inserted the disk. "The voice-over was written by a poet. The words get a bit overblown at times. You know, operatic. Highfalutin. But the story behind the Merlin's Ear project is an interesting one. Okay. Here goes."

Nick had watched the propaganda short, made in 1942, many times before in preparation for this trip to see the structure, which could only be reached by boat. The now familiar vintage black and white footage blazed onto the screen. The soundtrack consisted of an orchestra's brass section well to the fore with the male narrator pumping out words at breakneck speed.

"This is the wizard war! Battles begin in the brains of scientists, the laboratory, at the point of the technician's pencil. Battles start there—they end in the hearts of heroes."

Nick murmured, "I told you the narration's hyper."

Over shots of bombers flying in formation the narrator thundered on: *"Night and day, tyrant Hitler sends his machines of death—bombs, incendiaries, bullets—shrapnel flies: flesh is cut. Chemical hellfire burns to the bone. Bullets snap and whine: they sing like the very devils of old. Yet Britain fights back. Men of genius devise new electrical wonders that can see a plane on the blackest, darkest, stygian night."*

"That's radar," murmured Nick.

Onscreen, bombs rained down, blowing up houses.

"The grim song of death will be defeated," shouted the narrator. *"The RAF will blast planes from the heavens before they reach our shores. Here! On a little island in an English lake: Merlin's Ear!"*

Nick added, "Designed by the sculptor Barbara Hepworth."

"The shape of the curving structure copies the work of a human ear. That smooth form captures the faintest of faraway sounds—the approach of a Nazi dive bomber or Messerschmitt fighter. And yes, oh yes! Spitfires and Hurricanes will rise to meet our enemy before they've reached Britain. Merlin's magic ear will have heard the Nazi warplanes. A microphone carries those sounds to the operator. The operator telephones a warning to Fighter Command. Fighter Command orders our brave pilots into action and the Nazi warplanes are sent hurtling into the sea in flames. Rejoice at their destruction! Refuse to mourn the Hun, bringer of death! For they shall have no dominion! English skies will suffer no trespass! Merlin's Ear is always listening, always vigilant, always ready to sweep death from heaven and into the grave where it so rightly belongs!"

Now guncam footage: a British aircraft firing its machine guns, sending streams of bullets into a German bomber. The black Dornier exploding with a thunderous boom.

Adam shot to his feet, his eyebrows rose, his mouth formed a huge O-shape that stretched his lips until the skin split, and drops of thick, red blood emerged—red pearls that rolled down his chin.

Then the boy, who to Nick's knowledge had never spoken, took a deep breath and yelled: "LISTEN!"

Nick pushed downward on the boom's counterweight. The twenty-foot steel pole, which prevented casual boat-trippers from entering the lake, rose vertically into the air.

Constance opened the throttle, increasing the engine's revs. The long, thin vessel glided along the narrow channel, which formed a spur of the Sheffield-Pontefract Canal, toward the lake.

When he'd researched Merlin's Ear he'd also learnt that archaeologists had found Bronze Age swords and spearheads here on the lakebed. They believed that the weapons had been ritualistically deposited as offerings to the gods, goddesses and spirits that dwelt in this large body of water in the middle of Yorkshire. The sacrifice, of what would have been extremely valuable items to the prehistoric tribesmen, took place around three thousand years ago. Much later, in the fourteenth century, Richard Rolle, the visionary hermit, lived on the island where he wrote several chapters of *The Fire of Love*: a powerful, full-blooded account of Rolle's encounters with God. The book included Rolle's extraordinary assertion that the thoughts inside his head were transformed into beautiful singing voices that he heard coming down through the roof of his hermitage. Perhaps it was his belief that angels reflected his thoughts back at him, transmuted into heavenly song. Rolle described this experience of his in verse:

> *Hark! The ever-flowing currents of speech within my mind*
> *become a melodious hymn that blasts and burns my worldly flesh*
> *with joy.*

Ducks flapped from a stretch of reeds, quacking so loudly that they tugged Nick back from his contemplation of the medieval hermit Richard Rolle and his surreal writings.

Nick called out to Constance, "It's not too late. We can still go back."

She shook her head. "He's fine." Her face was radiant with one of the happiest smiles he'd ever seen. "It's marvellous, isn't it? His first word!"

Nick smiled back. He didn't think what had happened in the cabin an hour ago was marvellous at all. The ten-year-old had parted with the word 'Listen!' as if it had been a flap of skin that had been torn from his back. It had clearly hurt him to shout those two syllables. What's more, his jaw had opened so wide that his lips had split and shed blood. Constance had been so overjoyed that her son had spoken for the first time in his life she'd overlooked how much he'd suffered to howl the word as if his life depended on it.

Listen. Listen to what? The wartime film on the TV? Or a sound from outside? Or listen to what the child would say next? But Adam hadn't said anything next. He'd remained icily silent as his mother had washed the blood from his face. She was too full of excitement at hearing her mute son break his decade-long silence: she didn't seem to care that the scene had been so disturbing. . . . Hell, *so awful.* Nick shuddered.

He said, "We can take Adam home. There's a town just a couple of miles along the main canal."

"No."

"It wouldn't be difficult to get a taxi back. Then you could make an appointment to see the doctor."

"No. Adam's fine." The woman's eyes shone; she almost danced with happiness as she steered the boat from the narrow channel onto wide open waters. "Besides, we'll be back home in a couple of days anyway. I'll make an appointment with the clinic then." She eased the boat toward the bank. "Adam's going to speak. He'll talk just like any other boy of his age."

"I hope so."

"You know, Nick, this is the happiest day of my life."

Nick smiled as she laughed—euphoria made her look so much younger. He lowered the boom, locked the padlock in place to prevent any other boat-users from leaving the canal in order to explore the lake. Nick had had to promise the Waterways authorities, in writing, that he'd take care of the key (which had gone to the bottom of the canal earlier) and navigate the lake in a responsible manner.

Moments later, he'd boarded *Miss Sally.* Constance opened the throttle again. Soon their vessel chugged in the direction of the island. Merlin's Ear had been partly covered by moss. Trees grew over the back of it. Now, though, the immensity of that block of concrete became apparent. From this angle, it could have been an ancient stone monolith, rising from the island, its concrete 'ear' permanently turned to the East, listening for Nazi bombers. Those warplanes were long gone, of course. Yet Merlin's Ear still listened for danger.

Adam appeared at the prow of the boat. He'd emerged from doors at the front of the cabin. He leaned forwards against the guard-rail, gazing at the island as they approached. The child formed a curious figurehead of sorts, and, to Nick Mercer, a figurehead just as enigmatic as the ones that once adorned those sailing galleons of old.

The only place to safely moor the narrowboat was alongside Merlin's Ear. Exploratory prods with the long-handled boathook demonstrated that this was the sole area close to the island with water deep enough to prevent *Miss Sally* from grounding, which could have damaged her propeller and steering gear. Now that the vessel rested against the block of concrete, with its acoustic dish shape rising high above them, Nick could fully appreciate its size. The structure soared a good fifty feet into the air; it was probably around fifty feet in width, too, and stood on the Eastern side of the uninhabited island. Covered with willows, this smudge of greenery in the lake was no larger than a football pitch.

He'd tied the boat's lines to a heavily rusted iron prong that emerged from the vertical surface of Merlin's Ear. The prong once held the microphone, which captured sounds picked up by the acoustic bowl. Supposedly, that vast concrete listening device was so sensitive it could detect enemy planes a hundred miles away as they flew over the North Sea from occupied Europe toward Britain.

Nick moved along the narrow walkway that ran the length of the hull. He double-checked the knots that secured the mooring-lines to the structure. The sun had all but set. Already the lake had changed from the colour of flame to battleship grey. Midges emerged to buzz around his head. He used both hands to waft them away from his face, the infuriating little buggers.

Adam watched him from the prow deck. Mosquitos, much bigger than the midges, now descended on Nick. He felt the painful sting of the bloodsucker's bite on the back of his neck. These formidable insects looked as if they should have been buzzing through some tropical mangrove swamp, not a lake in Yorkshire.

Another mozzie sank its needle-sharp proboscis into the back of his hand. Suddenly the impassive way the boy watched him stirred a quick anger.

"Adam," he began sharply. "Can you speak? Or do you choose not to?"

The boy didn't respond. With a tetchy shake of his head, Nick returned to the stern. He needed to remove the key from the ignition before entering the cabin. Simply moving from one end of the boat to the other proved a lengthy operation He couldn't rush, otherwise there'd be a good chance he'd slip off the narrow deck and end up in the drink.

He was met by Constance who wore a hurt expression. Her eyes locked onto his face; she tilted her head to one side as if she'd just seen him commit some inexplicable act.

"Constance?" he asked, prompting her to reveal what was on her mind.

She held up her smartphone. "This text that Adam's just sent me: 'Nick wants to know if I only pretend I can't speak. Mum, does he hate me?'"

"I only asked." His heart sank. He didn't want to provoke an argument with his wife. "It's only natural to ask a question like that, isn't it?"

Constance had already gone below again. He heard her feet stomping angrily against the wooden steps. He glanced in the direction of the prow. Adam stood there with his phone clutched in his fist, no doubt ready to text news of Nick Mercer's next act of insensitivity.

Sighing, Nick turned away from the boy. He glared out across the lake as darkness fell. *I can't do right for doing wrong.* That was pretty much the track of his thoughts. However, his attention was soon drawn elsewhere. The buzz of a plane grew louder and louder until he was sure that an aircraft would come skimming above the water toward them. The sound became even louder, rising in pitch until it seemed to drill through his skull into his brain. Gritting his teeth, he clamped his hands to his ears. Then he understood: *there is no plane.*

"Mosquitos," he breathed. "The sound of them is being amplified." He turned to the concave shape that towered over him. Merlin's Ear still worked. It bounced the sound of the insects back at him, increasing the volume of the high-pitched whine of their wings a thousandfold. The noise became viciously intense, setting his teeth on edge.

Adam had already fled back down into the cabin. Nick managed to endure another five seconds of that piercing drone. When he couldn't take anymore he flung open the hatch and hurried down the steps.

Darkness. Absolute darkness. No streetlights for miles. No moon. No stars, come to that. Cloud must have covered the sky. Nightfall had caused a change in the behaviour of all those millions of mosquitos that had produced such a painfully loud drone when magnified by Merlin's Ear. Nick had been prepared to untie the boat in order to move it from the acoustic bowl and so away from its painfully loud amplification of the insects. However, the noise had softened considerably in the last twenty minutes, falling to a gentle hum that was almost pleasing in comparison to the unpleasantly loud din earlier. Nick didn't know what was responsible for the change; he guessed that not as many creatures were airborne, or perhaps they didn't need to beat their wings so quickly.

Nick sat at the folding table, checking the camera he'd use in the morning to photograph the Ear for his article. Mother and son sat side-by-side on one of the bench seats that ran along the cabin wall. They watched a film together. They also checked their phones; sometimes their fingers would dance on the screens as they sent texts or Tweeted.

Nick repeatedly glanced in the direction of Constance and Adam. Were mother and son sending messages to each other? A secret line of communication? Were they excluding Nick from their private chatter? About the film? *About me?*

Nick remarked, "It's a lot better now."

Constance glanced across at him. "Hmm?"

"The sound of the insects. It's not so loud."

"I thought it would boil my brains." She smiled. "I've heard nothing like it before."

"We've Merlin's Ear to thank for the effect."

"It'll get no thanks from me." She turned to Adam. "It made you feel sick, didn't it, sweet pea?"

Giving a solemn nod, the boy touched his phone's screen. He didn't appear any the worse for what had happened earlier when he'd yelled: *Listen.* The cracks in his lips, caused when he'd opened his mouth so wide, were barely visible. They didn't seem at all painful. In fact, Adam had reverted to his old self.

Nick scratched his head. "What mystifies me is why the Ear didn't amplify the sound of the boat's engine, or our voices, when I was mooring us alongside the thing."

"Yes . . . it's like . . . well, someone just switched it on after we arrived. But there's nothing electrical inside the concrete, is there?"

"No. The shape of the structure, its acoustic curve—that does all the work."

"Must be something to do with sunset." She gave a shrug. "After all, that's when it began to make those bugs sound as loud as they did."

"Ah . . . when the concrete cooled it began to contract and change shape?"

"Something like that."

"And as the structure gradually contracts it transforms its acoustic properties."

"Meaning the amplification only works at night?"

He nodded. "Although the inventors of Merlin's Ear couldn't have wanted it to do that. That on-off mode's a bit random. There must be a flaw."

Constance said, "Even if it is glitchy, the scientists were ingenious. Coming up with a device that can still boost sound seventy years later."

"It's almost like putting a seashell to your ear. On a massive scale. You could-" He paused as Constance read a text on her phone, giggled, rubbed her son's knee before nodding as if paying attention to what Nick said.

His heart sank. *They are texting one another.* Even though he felt shut out from the pair's interaction he made a point of smiling pleasantly as he said, "You could come back here in a hundred years, it'd still work. There's no electronics involved in the amplification. It's all down to the clever acoustic shape."

"**Necessity** is the mother of invention." She composed a text as she spoke. "All done in wartime, too."

"Ultimately a waste of time."

"Oh? Why?"

"An audio early warning system was no match for radar, which was invented at the same time. Radar has a greater range, picked up aircraft earlier, and allowed the RAF to intercept enemy warplanes more accurately." He wondered if he'd begun to sound patronizing.

He knew he tended to lecture on subjects when he felt ill-at-ease, which he did now. That's when his mind overruled his heart: he tried not to let it happen; even so, his manner would often become cold and formal.

Constance didn't seem to notice. "Merlin's Ear—obsolete before it was ever used." She chuckled. "A white elephant with a concrete ear."

"I'll put that line in my article."

"You'll have to pay me for it."

"With kisses."

"Hah, in your dreams, Nicholas Mercer." She stroked Adam's hair in a relaxed way. "If Merlin's lughole was already obsolete, why did they commission that flipping horrible film you keep watching?"

"They knew they weren't giving away any secrets to Nazi spies by showing it in British cinemas, seeing as the Ear was already a dead duck, and no longer had a useful military application. Nevertheless, it still made a good subject for a propaganda film—you know, show the public that scientists are inventing amazing stuff that'll win the war for us. People would sleep easier in their beds knowing—"

"Goodness, what was that?" Constance laughed with astonishment.

The huge sound ghosted through the cabin walls with such force that Constance sat bolt upright. Adam's fingers touched the screen of his phone. A second later Constance looked at her own phone.

"Adam's got it. He says, 'Owl hoot made big'." She smiled with pleasure. "He's right. It was an owl, wasn't it?"

Nick smiled while telling himself: *They are texting one another. Proof positive.* "I'm sure Adam's hit the nail on the head. An owl's hooted somewhere across the lake. Merlin's Ear amplified the sound. Okay. Anyone for hot chocolate?"

"Please."

Adam nodded, giving a thumbs up.

Nick put the kettle onto the hob. Constance's attention was drawn to her phone as the screen lit up; she read what appeared there.

"Oh, Nick. Adam asks if he can have marshmallows on top?"

"Sure, why not?" Light pouring out through the window revealed the pale shape of the wartime Ear. A moth flew through the light. Just for a moment he heard the soft purr of its wings, amplified to the point he could barely hear the TV.

Listen, Adam had said earlier. The first word he'd ever spoken: verbally, that is, as opposed to texts or handwritten notes. Now, moored alongside this extraordinary invention, they were hearing things in a way they'd never heard them before. *Listen.*

Nick did listen as he waited for the kettle to boil. He thought he heard a deep bass sound—a muffled *thud-thud, thud-thud.* Almost a sub-woofer effect.

My heartbeat, he thought in surprise. *The Ear's reflecting my own heartbeat back at me. Whatever next? The creak of my own hair growing? The sigh of brain cells dying as I age?* This was rapidly becoming a dream-like place. The domain of miracles.

The moment Nick Mercer awoke he saw that the boy had vanished (the narrowboat didn't have separate bedroom cabins) and now the nightlight, which Adam always insisted on using, revealed his empty bed. Slowly, Nick eased himself from beneath the duvet without disturbing Constance. The toilet door stood slightly open. No light shone from it. Adam wasn't there.

Nick's wristwatch told him that the time had just nudged past two o' clock. A strong breeze had picked up during the night. Air currents varied from a loud hiss to a rushing sound. He made his way along that gloomy corridor-shape of the cabin toward the steps that led up to the deck. On the way he lifted an LED lantern from a hook in the kitchen area. By the time he opened the hatch door to the deck his heart had begun to pound. Already, he imagined shining the light onto the water and seeing a figure in pyjamas lying face down.

Before he went outside he paused. The breeze sounded even louder. Yet something wasn't right. Why didn't the winds move the boat? The lake seemed calm. He clicked on the lamp. After that, he tilted his head, listening.

That wasn't the breeze. Whispering—that's what he heard. Such loud whispers at that. Quickly, he stepped out onto the deck. Mostly, his surroundings lay shrouded in darkness. The concrete Ear rose close by, resembling the sheer face of a gigantic iceberg. He lifted the lantern, so it shed its soft, white light on the narrowboat's flat roof.

There he was. Cross-legged; motionless as a stone Buddha; albeit Buddha-like in green pyjamas. Adam faced Merlin's Ear; his lips moved.

The concrete slab amplified and reflected the boy's whispers back at him. Adam appeared mesmerized by the effect, one that must have, to him, seemed like witchcraft.

Nick spoke gently, not wanting to shock the child, "Adam. . . . Adam, it's Nick. Are you alright?"

Adam hadn't heard: in any event he didn't react. He continued to whisper. That whisper bounced back from the acoustic curve, sounding like a fierce breeze rushing through a forest.

The boy used his lips to shape the flow of air from his lungs into words; no tones came from his vocal chords: "Listen. Throat. Mouth. Tongue. The Holy Trinity that makes my speech. Listen to that, Adam. You can speak. You can talk so loud that everyone will hear you."

The boy, who'd never uttered a word until just a few hours ago, spoke to himself.

"Adam," Nick hissed. "Adam, it's the middle of the night."

The ten-year-old continued as if he hadn't heard: "Listen. Your strength is in your throat. Your words. Your voice. Whosoever pulls this sword out of the stone will be the rightful king of England." Adam reached into his mouth and pulled his tongue out as far as it would go, held it for a moment then released it. "Hail to the king who hides from others his eternal wound that will never heal. Listen to me, the once and future king."

Nick realized that Adam was drawing on the King Arthur legend. He was giving a speech to himself. Hearing his own voice, even though it was that strangely amplified whisper, had something akin to a mystical effect on him. The lad was (Nick struggled to find the appropriate word) *transported, transformed, transfigured.*

Nick shook his head. Constance would play merry hell if she knew that he'd stood passively by, watching—and listening—as her son sat on the cabin roof mouthing bizarre statements.

"Adam, you must come back inside." Nick moved quickly along the walkway that ran between the cabin and the edge of the hull. He held the light so it illuminated Adam's shining face. He forgot all about the ropes that secured the vessel to the iron prong set into the Ear. His toes hooked beneath a taut line. He fell down onto his chest. A hard fall that left him winded.

The boy continued: "Merlin, make me strong. Give me the power to hurt those that hurt me."

Nick, meanwhile, struggled to get back to his feet, only the air had been knocked clean out of his lungs. Simply being able to breathe became his priority right now. Even though he found it difficult to inhale, the strong odour of lake water filled his nostrils. He caught the sweet scent of wild flowers that grew on the island. Moths drawn to the lamplight flew into his face. He heard the purr of their wings reflected back from the Ear. Those wings softly struck his cheeks and nose—they felt like the rapid beat of an arterial pulse. In addition, that mosquito hum merged with Adam's whispered prayer to the wizard in his beloved King Arthur story. A plea to help him deliver retribution to the bullies that tormented him at school and called him 'Dumb Adam.'

And me.

"Give me the strength to send Nick away. I don't want him with us anymore."

So he hates me as much as the bullies. Nick rubbed his chest, trying to draw air into his lungs, and all the time he felt misery building up like a tidal wave inside of him, because he knew that Constance would choose her only son over her new husband. If she knew that Adam despised Nick, then, yes, Nick would find the door of his home closing behind him for the last time.

A light came—one so bright it seemed to set the concrete slab on fire. Nick managed to get to his feet as another flash turned the lake into a sea of molten silver.

"Lightning," he gasped.

His blood ran cold. Straight away, he turned to gaze at Merlin's Ear in horror. The structure amplified Adam's soft whisper to the sound of rushing storm-winds. Nick began to untie the ropes. He knew they had to get away from here as quickly as possible before thunder came rolling across the water.

"Adam!" The shout came back as hard as a punch. "Adam! It's not safe here anymore!"

Lighting stalked the horizon: blue-white flashes revealed trees on the shore.

"Adam!" He scrambled onto the cabin roof, clawing his way toward the boy.

Constance appeared on the prow deck. "What's happening?" Her cry bounced back at them—a banshee shriek that made both Nick and Adam screw up their faces in pain.

"Constance," he shouted, "get back down into the cabin. Pull the duvet over your head. If you can, press the pillows to your ears."

"What on Earth are you talking about?"

"Please, love, do it! It's going to get loud out here."

"Why did you bring Adam outside?"

"I didn't. Constance, listen. Just trust me. Please. It's important. Go inside. Cover your ears. Use as much padding as you can. I'll get Adam."

Thankfully, Constance understood. Giving a single nod, she vanished from sight. He could hear her feet on the wooden floor as she hurried back to where she'd find the duvet and pillows.

Nick had almost reached Adam when the next flash of lightning burnt the entire world out into nothing but whiteness—such a searing intensity; it was if the sun had exploded. His body tensed, the air itself had turned electric. He knew they hadn't been struck by lightning, but it was very close, and he knew what would come next.

Nick clamped both his hands over Adam's ears. Thunder roared —the loudest sound he'd ever heard. A split second later Merlin's Ear amplified the sound, and hurled it back at Nick's exposed ears.

By that time, the boom had grown explosively until it mutated into another force entirely. Nick Mercer didn't so much hear the magnified thunderclap—instead, the wave of energy blasted through his brain, shattering memory, melting reality into dreams and tearing rational thought from its moorings.

The thunder died away to silence. A moment after that, his head slammed down onto the cabin roof.

Six months later.

Adam sat to the kitchen table doing his homework. Constance was on the phone, leaning back against a worktop as she chatted. Outside flakes of snow fell out of the sky.

Nick Mercer sat in an armchair, typing the words of a new travel article into his laptop.

Constance spoke into the phone. "Oh, we're nearly ready for Christmas. There are always last minute things to get though, aren't there? Cheese twists. I still need those. Oh? Yes? Wait, I'll ask him."

She turned to Adam. "Can you give your Dad a nudge?"

Adam's voice rang out with such a pure clarity of tone: "Nick. Hey, Nick. Mum wants you."

She clicked her tongue to show her disapproval. "Adam, you know that won't work."

Adam leaned back from his chair to poke Nick's shoulder with the end of his ruler.

Nick twisted round to face the pair. Constance waved to attract his attention.

Without using her voice she mouthed: *"Listen. Your sister wants to know if you're going on Boxing Day?"*

Nick gave an exaggerated nod before saying in a loud voice that he, himself, could not hear: "Yes . . . thank you. We'll be there."

Nick still remembered the sound of human voices, but now they shimmered with all the resonance of spirits from beyond the veil. They often whispered the same word over and over: -

Listen . . . listen . . . listen . . .

And now the voices beseeched him again. They came from beneath his feet, from out of the Earth. Yet they might have been echoes of his own thoughts, reflected back at him by something unseen that always swam just beneath the surface of all worldly things.

THE CARNIVORE OF MONSTERS

by Stuart Young

'A singularity is the point at the centre of a black hole where space, time and gravity all collapse in upon themselves, everything—every physical phenomenon, every sensation—is condensed down to a single point. All the laws of physics are suspended and anything becomes possible: time travel, alternate dimensions, plate-glass savannahs inhabited by clockwork giraffes carved from icing sugar, *anything.*'

It's not a chat-up line that I'd use but it seems to work for the drunken young man who teeters along the pavement ahead of me. Perhaps the young Indian woman he's trying to impress thinks that a man who talks about anything being possible and all physical sensations centring upon a single point will have no trouble finding her clitoris.

More likely his babbling about theoretical physics turns her on because she's as big a nerd as he is.

'I thought the singularity point was when artificial intelligence advanced to a sufficient level to overtake human intelligence.'

'Well, yes,' says the young man, shaking his head. Then his inebriated brain realizes that his body language is contradicting his words so he starts nodding instead. 'But no, I'm talking about the theories proposed by Stephen Hawking and Roger Penrose . . . '

Yep. Definitely nerds.

You can tell just by looking at him: glasses, tweed jacket, corduroy trousers, scarf looped about his neck for that slightly bohemian look.

Short black hair, receding slightly: he's older than he looks, but that doesn't stop him dressing like a student. Even if it is a student from the 1970s, trying to ape his favourite professor.

At first glance the woman does a better job of disguising her nerdiness, but closer inspection reveals that the vaguely hippyish floral dress she's wearing isn't the latest trendy retro-chic but a slightly frayed old favourite and that her hipster glasses aren't actually ironic. Not only that but her handbag is a scuffed leather satchel that looks like something out of *St Trinians*.

I'm just jealous. I never got to finish school or go on to university like I planned. My knowledge is that of the autodidact; at once highly specialized and irritatingly scattershot, topics of study dictated equally by hard necessity and personal whim.

The woman holds on to the man's arm for support which, given his intoxicated state, is a little like holding onto a jelly. They lean into each other, arms tangling, nearly tripping over each other's feet, resembling an implosion of human anatomy as they teeter along Euston Road in a drunken simulation of equilibrium.

I follow them discreetly, my hands in my pockets, just out for an evening stroll. I'm not doing anything obviously suspicious, but a black man in London at night has to dial back any potential bad vibes he might be inadvertently giving off.

Bad enough that I had to hang around for these two while they downed their drinks in the pub. Too much chance that they might clock me if I followed them in, not that they know me from Adam but I'm not sure how long it'll take for me to make contact so the last thing I need is for them to spot me lurking in the background every time they turn round.

That's why I waited in a nearby coffee shop with a clear view of the pub's exits. Gave me something to look at instead of my gaunt reflection in the coffee shop's mirrored walls, stopped me brooding on how long it had been since my skin had faded from black to the same milky brown as the latte I was drinking.

Not that I really needed to keep an eye on the pub's exits of course. I would sense when the couple left. The same way that I had sensed them when they left the British Library earlier. Even though I had been further down the road, at St Pancras Station, I could sense their departure. Through the chatter of bustling crowds, the noise of departing trains and even past the simultaneous sense of claustrophobia and agoraphobia at being so hemmed in inside such a vast space I still managed to sense the man and woman. Hurrying out of the station I felt as though I was trapped in a conjuring trick; inside, the building had been all glass and chrome and tile, outside it was all brickwork and looming spires; it was as though a magician had hidden a train station inside a Gothic cathedral, ghost trains pulling away from platforms, souls departing for their final journey to hell.

The feeling of being trapped inside a conjuring trick increased as a flock of pigeons fluttered by, putting me in mind of doves appearing from the magician's hat, while glancing back at the international destinations on the departure boards was the string of flags pulled from out his sleeve.

I chalked the sensation up to imagination, my perceptions blurred by the traces of morphine flowing through me.

Off to my left, a couple of blocks over, hidden among the narrow view afforded by the buildings crowding the skyline, I caught a glimpse of St Pancras Old Church. I used to go there as a boy; it's one of the oldest sites of Christian worship in England, named after the Roman saint.

No saints here. Only sinners.

Taking a deep breath I reached out with my senses, trying to locate my prey.

I track by feel, by sensation. Waves of energy radiating out, wafting over me, layering a three-dimensional model of my surroundings over my regular senses, a subtle map of reality whispering directions, coaxing me, guiding me, each step bringing the prize that little bit closer, its shape outlined in strands of glittering luminescence, a glistening spider web trapping it in place while I follow the vibrating strands and finally reach my goal.

All that was imagination too. That's not how I experienced it at all.

What I experienced was pain.

It lanced through my gut and back, spreading outwards, turning my whole body to agony.

When it lessened I knew I was getting closer; compass where the point stabs your nerve centres if you follow the wrong direction.

That's why I only had traces of morphine in my system as I left the station. Although it helps alleviate the pain, takes the edge off, it also takes the edge off my faculties. Dancing around in a state of opiate-induced euphoria I might miss my chance to end my torture for good.

Still, now that I've got a firm visual on the couple I'm tempted to take a hit while I'm waiting to establish contact. It's not a good idea. Too many things could still go wrong. I need to stay sharp, not dull my reflexes and turn my brain to jelly.

So I grit my teeth and fight my way through the pain, hating every second of it.

The weather doesn't help. It's cold for May, a stiff breeze spiralling down the street and jabbing me in the kidneys. Some people ascribe the cold May weather to Fimbulwinter, the harbinger of the Twilight of the Norse gods, others say it is due to the Ice Saints. Either way the sky is overcast, finally defeating the intermittent sunshine that had battled all day to convince everybody that it actually is summer. Sunset feels too bright a word to describe the murkiness of the encroaching evening. Black smudges of cloud are smeared across the grey sky like God's dirty fingerprints; disgusted with the world, he no longer cared for it the way He once had, love and compassion turning to disdain and neglect.

Following the couple down the street I miss a remark by the young man due to a midlife crisis, afflicted motorcyclist doing his best to deafen me with his bike's roaring engine. Whatever the young man said it was obviously a witticism of some kind, the woman throws back her head in laughter and slaps his arm playfully.

Their flirting irritates me. They don't really care about each other. The lingering looks and intimate body language didn't start until well after they started downing drinks. Before that I could tell, even from a distance, that their relationship was purely platonic.

A clear respect for personal space as though an invisible barrier separated them, a total lack of warmth in their expressions, no smiles, no playful winks, no looks of amused affection. And virtually no eye contact, each of them wrapped up in their own little universe, both of them talking rapidly, overlapping, too busy to listen to what they were each saying or even to spare more than the occasional glance at each other.

A quick snatch of conversation overheard as they entered the pub, and I passed by to wait in the coffee shop, revealed the truth of the matter. They were work colleagues, both of them assistants at the

British Library, he an old hand and she a new recruit, and each had butted heads with their supervisor. Resentment, anger and frustration drew them to the pub. Mutual hatred of their supervisor, along with copious amounts of alcohol, had temporarily convinced them that they were soul mates.

Really they just wanted to fuck; fifteen minutes of panting and thrusting culminating in an orgasmic explosion that negated thought, taking them out of their dull, futile lives. At least until they sobered up and realized they had to work together, an extra layer of awkwardness and discomfort added to their already unbearable jobs. They don't know anything about real love; how it envelops you, suffuses your entire being.

God, I miss Tayshia.

Weaving past an old man walking his dog I close the distance on the couple. Pedestrians are thinning out, both the locals and the tourists. Not long now.

I close the gap a little more. Put my game face on.

Now we're almost at St Pancras New Church. Bigger than the old church. Fancier.

Catching up with the couple I hit them with an anxious smile. 'Excuse me.'

They both turn to look at me, jolted out of their inebriated dalliance. Just for a second the man's eyes go wide behind his glasses, then he gets his face back under control. As much as he can do, anyway, after all the booze he's downed. Nervousness and embarrassment squirm beneath his mask of politeness; he doesn't want to admit that he's bothered at being approached at night by an unknown black man. Political correctness battles primal fears, creating a cognitive dissonance; he's not quite sure how to react, especially in front of his Indian fuck-buddy.

He needn't worry, she's just as bad, her alcohol-induced confidence evaporating, leaving her a shy, bookish nerd with only another shy, bookish nerd to protect her if I try to kidnap her and turn her into a crack whore.

Anger writhes in my gut. The way they look at me makes me wish I were the monster they fear me to be.

Then it passes and I broaden my smile. 'I need to give my girlfriend a call—she's pregnant—and my phone's just died on me. Can I borrow yours?'

Again, a flicker of suspicion as he sizes me up. Fortunately I'm well spoken beneath my faint London twang and I'm dressed smartly in my best suit and tie.

Eventually he relaxes and decides I'm not going to mug him.

He's wrong. I am.

Once I soothe the pain coursing through me I'll be away on my toes. He'll never see me or his phone again.

He rummages around in his jacket pocket, scoops out his phone, hands it to me. It's a slimline model, top of the range, skinnier than an after-dinner mint. It nestles in my palm; dainty, weightless.

These things will give you cancer if you're not careful. But this one won't. This one will take away the cancer I've already got.

Unlocking the phone I call up the texts. The phone glows in the darkening evening like a handheld star as a text appears on the screen.

Does the Omega contain the Alpha?

I frown. This isn't the text I was expecting to find. What I expected was a glow to emanate from the phone, bathing me in its light, healing my pain.

As I stare at the text in puzzlement letters fade from the message, vowels and consonants disappearing, turning the message from textspeak to gibberish; autocorrect having an aneurysm. Soon all that's left is a single O. It grows in size, filling the screen, becoming a gaping maw.

Suddenly the phone becomes a dead weight in my hand, near infinite mass; it would take my arm off if my body didn't suddenly become equally heavy.

I crash to the ground.

Unable to move I stare up at the man. He gazes down at me, all nervousness gone, replaced by an eerie calm. Slowly, creepily, he smiles.

Fear envelops me.

This isn't how I expected things to go at all.

(The Queen of Despair's attempt to abdicate is met with brutal retribution. Grey blood gushes from the stump of her traumatized neck, the arterial spray dowsing onlookers, dragging them down into a melancholy stupor as

Her Majesty's angular frame careens down the street, chasing blindly after the rolling object adorned with a crown.)

Ten years ago I did some work experience at St Pancras hospital, working in admin. I actually wanted to be a social worker but this was the closest thing they had available.

One day I found myself sitting alone in a ward, waiting for the charge nurse to tell me what paperwork I needed to take back to the office. All the patients were taking their afternoon nap and I was starting to nod off myself; I'd been to a party the night before, and the hangover still had me in its merciless grip.

I sat in the corner of the ward, fighting to stay awake, listening to the sounds of the patients: the snoring, the rustling of bed sheets, the occasional cough or breaking of wind. I had never felt so awkward and alone. Even if any of the patients had been awake I didn't have anything in common with them. I was only fifteen; the youngest man in there was at least sixty, the oldest was so wrinkled and lifeless that I thought the porters had left behind a corpse from the mortuary by mistake. On the few occasions I had spoken to patients they treated me with a mixture of friendly condescension and avuncular racism that left me unsure whether to smile nervously or swap their medication for industrial strength laxatives. Even the name of the hospital made me feel stupid. I was back to being the little kid who wanted to sound clever but who mixed up Pancras with pancreas.

I was lost. Isolated and alone.

I was also dying for a wank.

Teenage hormones raged through my body, supercharging my testicles and giving me a permanent hard-on, demanding that I masturbate at every available opportunity. It didn't help that every day I was surrounded by attractive women in nurses' uniforms. Or that, despite my best (and increasingly desperate) efforts, I was still a virgin.

The ward toilet stood enticingly close to my bed but I was terrified that the patients might hear the high-speed fapping sound as I frantically pleasured myself. Or that the smell of spunk might overpower the faint miasma of liquid soap and antiseptic that permeated the ward. At home I was an expert at disguising my masturbatory tendencies, but this strange new environment robbed me of my finesse and cunning, so I just sat in the chair hoping the folds in my trousers hid my engorged cock.

Fantasies whirled through my mind, teasing my libido. I fretted that if I did fall asleep I would sink into a wet dream and awaken to find that I had spray-painted the entire ward with my semen.

One fantasy in particular refused to go away. There had been a report in the newspaper that one of the nurses at St Pancras had been sacked as it was discovered that she was a paedophile. In my fantasy she was still employed at the hospital and found herself fascinated by me; at nearly sixteen I was legally still a child but my body was virtually that of an adult. This paradoxical combination compelled her, drew her irresistibly to me.

So she comes to me in my chair, gently pulling down my trousers and underwear to reveal the throbbing erection beneath. Smiling at me she removes her uniform and climbs onto the chair, straddling me, easing me inside her. In order to avoid detection our lovemaking is silent and this only adds to the intensity, both of us biting our lips to contain our ecstasy, cries of joy and pleasure kept locked away in secret while our orgasms shudder through us.

The fantasy bothered me. Not just its inaccuracy—the nurse no longer worked at the hospital, and she had been dismissed for downloading child pornography rather than for known instances of molesting youngsters—but the fact that the scenario excited me so. Regardless of the exact nature of her crime the woman was still a paedophile. Why would I want to make love to such a creature? I should find the idea repulsive—and on an intellectual level I did—but still I fantasized of her visiting me in the night. Her, or one of the other nurses, mesmerized by my lean, muscular body.

None of them did visit me of course. But someone else did.

I was finally starting to doze off, eyes growing heavy beneath their lids, thoughts slowly morphing into dreams, when I felt hands upon my body. Rough hands, calloused, tearing off my clothes and lifting me from my chair. My eyes flickered open to see two men, wreathed in the shadows cast by the dim glow of the muted light. The faint electric shimmer only extended as far as my chair; the rest of the ward was swallowed by blackness, ceasing to exist. Caught between paralysing shock and alcohol-induced sleepiness, my body hung limp as spaghetti. The men's pale hands glowed dully against my black skin as they struggled to lift my sagging body, white moths wrestling with a shadow.

Stunned, I was laid upon a trolley by the two men and finally got a clear look at them through the gloom. Clothed in porter uniforms, but greyer, duller, with patches stitched clumsily across worn cloth. Lanyards dangled about their necks, showing their hospital ID cards, slices of laminated plastic scrawled with inhuman gibberish.

And then I saw their faces.

Horrified, I tried to leap off the trolley; my limbs didn't work, useless lumps of bone and gristle, unable to even twitch let alone run or fight; mouth equally useless, gaping wide to yell in terror but emitting no sound; larynx vibrating, shuddering, *straining*, yet still failing to make my fear audible no matter how hard I tried, the screams echoing silently within my throat.

The porters wheeled me through the corridors, the dull light keeping pace with us as we trundled along, never showing where we were going or where we had been. Eventually we passed through a set of doors and into an operating theatre where they lifted me onto the table.

A surgeon leaned over me, dressed in scrubs and blood-splattered Wellington boots. His face bore the same deformities as the porters: twisted, distorted, features out of all proportion. Worst of all, like the porters, his face was upside down. When he donned his surgical mask it covered his eyes and nose, leaving his mouth free to breathe noxious air over me. I trembled. He was going to operate blind, working his way through my internal organs by touch alone.

I still couldn't move.

The Surgeon's lips curled downwards, which I suppose meant that he was smiling, and he picked up a scalpel, its blade corroded and blunted by rust.

He made his first incision.

The skin parted easily enough, blood seeping forth, but he had to lean into the scalpel a little to penetrate the muscle. He kept at it, though, and soon had a gaping hole in my chest. Pain seared through me but somehow I didn't pass out, no matter how much I wanted to. Nor could I tear my eyes away from what was happening.

Placing his scalpel on the instrument tray the Surgeon picked up a pancreas, pink and brown, bulging with tumours; it looked like a giant severed tongue that had been left to rot, as it glistened in the harsh glare of the surgical lights. He forced the organ into the wound in my chest; tied it in place by fashioning veins and arteries into some awkward-looking knots. Then he produced a needle as thick as my finger and which looked suspiciously like a talon from a fierce predator. Reaching beneath his surgical cap he plucked a long dandruff-encrusted hair, threaded it through the needle and started to sew me back up.

Finally, mercifully, I passed out.

When I awakened I was back in the ward, fully clothed. Frantically, I lifted my shirt and checked my chest. No wound, no haphazard stitches. Not unsurprisingly I had no erection either; my penis had shrivelled up like a slug doused in salt.

I finished my shift and went home. Life went on. I did my best to forget the incident, especially as my friends laughed when I told them about my weird nightmare.

Six months later I received a package. Opening the padded envelope a rusty scalpel fell out, clattering upon my bedside table. Unfolding the accompanying letter I read:

IT HAS BEGUN.

A week later I was diagnosed with pancreatic cancer.

The phone still has me pinned to the floor. I try to let go of the mobile but whatever force dragged me to the ground keeps my fingers wrapped around the phone.

It's not just my fingers that refuse to move; my entire body is jammed tight against the cold pavement by a tremendous weight, as though I'm being cuddled by an over-affectionate elephant.

The young man continues to smile as I lie sprawled on my back. The young woman looks nervous, unsure of what's going on.

Passers-by stare in bewilderment, or hurry by with impatient indifference; some laugh at my perceived drunkenness, some whip out their camera phones, while a Japanese couple ask if I'm part of a tourist attraction.

Easy enough mistake to make, I suppose, what with me lying right outside the entrance to St Pancras New Church. Above my head the white steps lead upwards, although viewing them upside down skews my perspective, I have to take it on faith that up is still up. Beyond the steps I spy the Greek Revival architecture that makes the building look like Mount Olympus rather than a Christian church. The row of Ionic columns supporting the arch over the entrance sends a random childhood memory flashing through my head; being disappointed as a boy that Ionic columns weren't pillars of energy like something out of *Matrix: Revolutions*.

Cries from the gathering crowd bring my mind back into focus. I've been sprawled on my back long enough for people to start becoming concerned. Someone asks nervously if they should call for an ambulance. A middle-aged German woman kneels beside me and asks if I need help—Can I stand? Can I move my legs? Can I wiggle my toes?—her increasing worry combining with her accent to make it sound as though she is barking orders at me. Against the German woman's advice a couple of burly workmen try to haul me to my feet so I can walk off the booze they think I've guzzled. They grunt and heave but fail to lift me. Their rough hands on me spark another random memory—the porters in my nightmare.

The German woman starts saying I need an ambulance and I struggle to get up. I will *not* go to hospital, that's where this all started. If I go back the Surgeon could do more things to me, insert more tumours, mutate more cells.

My parents never understood this and dragged me along to every doctor they could find. First the GP, due to my urine turning orange and my faeces turning pale, along with sudden abdominal pains that quickly spread to my back, crippling me with agony. Promptly diagnosing jaundice he also found an abnormal swelling in my belly and so sent me to the hospital for further tests. That's when they confirmed the cancer.

They couldn't understand how I got it or how it had spread so quickly. The exact causes of pancreatic cancer are unclear but sufferers are usually aged between fifty and eighty and sometimes fall into certain health categories: smokers, diabetics, heavy drinkers, sufferers of chronic pancreatic pain, people who already have another form of cancer. None of these applied to me.

Chemotherapy was scheduled but by this point I had realized that my nightmare wasn't just a dream, the scalpel through the post wasn't just a sick joke played by one of my friends. Hospitals weren't safe.

Especially as the chemotherapy would destroy my immune system, leaving me vulnerable to whatever other illnesses the Surgeon and his lackeys wished to infect me with.

The thoughts flash through my mind in a less than a second. I don't think I'll be able to explain it to the German woman quite so quickly but I do my best. 'No hospital! No fucking hospital!'

She flinches, caught off guard by my fear and rage. She tries to soothe me, her harsh and stilted English as calming as a lullaby sung by a homicidal robot.

The young man steps into my eyeline. His smile has faded to a smirk, behind his glasses his pupils have dilated to the extent that they totally obscure the irises, leaving only blackness.

'Keep away from me!'

He keeps staring at me, his gaze so intense that it warps his glasses, the frames starting to twist and bend.

I won't let him take me to the hospital. I try to think of ways to kill him. Or myself.

I ran away from home to avoid being trapped in a hospital. That was *before* I knew about the phones being able to ease my suffering and prolong my life. No way I'm going back to hospital now.

The Japanese couple chatter excitedly, they still think this is all some quaint local custom put on for tourists. A healing ceremony perhaps, in honour of the powers possessed by the great St Pancras.

No such luck. Pancras didn't even have any healing powers, he was just a fourteen-year-old boy who preached Christianity at the wrong time, too stubborn to renounce his faith and perform a sacrifice to the Roman gods when the Emperor Diocletian offered him wealth and power to do so. The strength and determination that impressed Diocletian enough to make his offer led to the Roman instead ordering for the boy to be beheaded.

The man's glasses continue to crack and bend. Fissures spread across the lenses, forked lightning etched on glass, until they splinter and shatter, the shards tumbling to earth like jagged tears. The mangled frames quickly follow, so badly twisted they practically form a knot.

'Fuck off, you evil bastard!' My voice is as pathetic and cracked as his glasses.

Slowly, he reaches up and starts to peel his face off, the skin sliding up and off his head in a single sheet of fat, blood and muscle.

I stare in horror, willing him to leave his fleshy mask on, his disguise intact. I don't want to see his true face, the distorted upside-down features leering down at me, my nightmare intruding upon the waking world.

The mask comes off. His face isn't upside down. He doesn't have a face at all.

No face, or even a head, just an empty space above his shoulders. I'm being attacked by nothingness. He drops his mask to the floor, the empty eyes stare blindly, the hollow mouth leers wordlessly, a crumpled balaclava made of flesh.

The crowd shifts around us, some people fleeing, some jostling for a better view, some frozen in terror. The German woman and the workmen slip back into the press of bodies, altruism overwhelmed by fear. Everyone gasps, a few people scream.

The man's would-be girlfriend gawps at him, backing away slowly. She's obviously decided that a workplace fling isn't such a good idea after all.

The headless man strips off his clothes. There's nothing underneath but air. All that's left is a pair of hands floating above the ground. Then even these are peeled off and the emptiness that posed as a man tosses them casually to one side.

This time the crowd acts as one, fleeing into the night.

Darkness flows around where the man stands, the evening gloom becoming intensified, more concentrated; at the same time the darkness feels distorted, the shadows bent, and there's a sense of the blackness containing streaks of luminescence, as though illuminated by a light that can't quite reach the eye. If I squint I can just about make out a vague outline of deeper blackness marking the man's position, a rippling penumbra, a heat haze viewed through thick smog.

I don't understand what's happening. I thought there was only one type of monster bedevilling me, a unique type of evil that I had to overcome. Where the hell did this other freak come from?

And why did I sense one of the phones that can heal me? It if it's here I need to find it. Otherwise, even if I manage to somehow escape the man's trap the cancer will still spread across the rest of my body and finally kill me.

Where is the fucking phone?

The man's girlfriend stops backing away, instead lunging forward and jabbing at him with something she pulls from her satchel. A flash of energy lights the night and the man's vague outline crumples to the floor beside me. Even better, my pain eases a little. Looking up I spot what the young woman holds in her hand.

Oh, so that's where the phone is.

(Touched by the geriatric conjoined twins known as The Death Pact, a man adds to the delays on the London underground by hurling himself in the path of an oncoming train. Instantly, on the other side of the city, his brother is torn apart by invisible forces, as though his body had been mangled by spinning metal wheels, the fate of the two men entangled in a quantum murder.)

For years the phones helped me survive. They not only dimmed the pain but they also somehow halted the cancer in its tracks, at least for a little while, and when the cancer resumed its destructive rampage through my body, destroying cells, mutating organs, I just went looking for another phone.

Without them I would have died long ago. When the doctors diagnosed my cancer they couldn't believe how advanced it was, my entire system collapsing in a matter of weeks since the initial symptoms appeared. The doctors couldn't cure me; my body was too rotten, too corrupted. All they could offer me was palliative treatment. So even if I managed to evade the Surgeon with the upside down face I would still die.

The phones saved me. That glowing energy that pulsed from them, healing my pain.

Of course I needed other things to survive: money, food, shelter. Begging got me a bit of cash, but then I got lucky: while scavenging through bins for scraps of food I found a discarded pre-approved credit card. All I had to do to activate it was call the phone number provided. That kept me going while I figured out my next move.

Again, the phones saved me. Pretty early on I realized that once the phones stopped healing me they reverted to ordinary mobiles. The healing power then hopped to another phone. Whatever power it was that was healing me worked through the phones rather than residing within them. So once each new phone had healed me I could sell it on. Unfortunately I had no idea how to approach the criminal community. I didn't even understand the rules to *Grand Theft Auto*.

All my extralegal problems were solved when I remembered Tayshia.

I had met her six months earlier when a few friends and I asked her about getting us fake IDs. Caramel skinned and with a mass of frizzy hair; she was gorgeous. I fell in love with her instantly but didn't have the nerve to invite her along to the club we intended to visit.

This time I found her flogging pirated DVDs to customers crowded outside an overflowing pub. Her cheeky banter and easy smile convinced people that buying a fuzzy copy of some lacklustre blockbuster they would probably never have gone to see at the cinema anyway might somehow actually be a good idea.

Wandering over I pretended to consider buying *Revenge of the Sith* and tried not to look devastated that she didn't remember me from our previous meeting. Recovering, I asked if she knew anyone who might be interested in buying some mobile phones I had procured. I actually said "procured"; I didn't know what the correct term would be: Nicked? Stolen? Delivered by the Phone Fairy?

Tayshia smiled at me, her cheeks dimpling. 'So you're a criminal mastermind. And here's me thinking you only wanted to talk to me 'cos you couldn't resist my feminine allure.'

I nearly fainted. Girls didn't flirt with me, especially not girls like this: streetwise, older than me, twenty or maybe twenty-one, with figure-hugging jeans and a crop top to show off her slender figure. Cheeks burning, I tried to act casual, make a joke out of it, as though this sort of thing happened to me all the time. 'Oh, you're a *woman*. I hadn't even noticed.'

'Gay men rarely do.'

'What? No, I'm not gay!'

'You mean I've managed to alter your sexual orientation already? I'm even hotter than I thought.' Giggling, she flicked her frizzy hair; light shone through the edges of the dark-brown curls, transforming them into a golden halo. 'Now let's see about selling these phones you've "procured."'

Grabbing my hand she led me down the street. I battled to keep a soppy grin off my face. Even though I knew that her flirting was just part of her sales technique I felt insanely happy.

I was even happier six months later when she took my virginity. Even if the whole affair only lasted ninety seconds and she insisted that it was a drunken mistake and would never happen again, it still remains the greatest moment of my life.

I can't figure out why the woman saved me. None of the other people I stole phones from had a clue as to what was going on, they were just unlucky enough for the power that heals my cancer to get bounced through their mobiles. But now that she's got her head together the young Indian woman seems to know more about what's going on than I do. Which, admittedly, isn't difficult.

I'm hoping that she's some kind of guardian of the healing energy that's been keeping me alive these past ten years, and that she'll finally cure me for good. It's a fantasy that I've been nurturing ever since I first used a phone to heal myself; eventually I would absorb enough healing energy to eradicate the cancer. Although I never expected to meet someone who might be able to explain what had been done to me and why. Someone who could to unravel the mysteries and miseries of my adult life.

I try to reach out to her but the man's phone still has me pinned to the ground so I croak out a few pathetic words instead. 'Please . . . help me.'

She gazes down at me, cold, dispassionate, and I realize I've made a terrible mistake. She's not here to cure me. She wouldn't even have saved me if she didn't need me for whatever it is she's got planned.

The phone in her hand morphs, changing size and shape, gaining buttons and touchscreen icons, displaying holograms—charts, articles, videos—at first tiny and indistinct, then bigger and more sharply defined, becoming three-dimensional images and then solid-light images that she strokes or tosses aside depending on her needs, the discarded holograms spiralling through the air before fading to nothingness. Moore's law on fast forward, computer processing power doubling every second instead of every two years. Finally, the phone itself disappears, nodules appear on her hands, fade almost immediately, and her eyes light up with electric fire. She *is* the phone, technology and flesh made one.

Except she no longer has any flesh. It melts away for her, along with her clothes. She stands naked, pubic hair glowing filaments, vagina a prism of light, nipples clusters of photons. A digital hologram, a virtual-reality light show. Smaller holograms flicker across her naked body, the effect simultaneously erotic and coldly sterile: computer porn.

Another monster. How many are there?

Pain stabs at my brain as the holograms on her body scratch at the backs of my eyes, trying to claw their way into my psyche, eager to rend my thoughts and dreams.

I scream.

The holograms snap off, the pain recedes to a dull ache. The woman cocks her head to one side in an attitude of annoyance. A new set of holograms swirl across her body; cartoon faces interspersed with bursts of frenetic animation, playing out disjointed fast-paced narratives while a complex electronic symphony soars over a relentless drumbeat: Tex Avery scored by techno-Bach.

I don't scream this time but the mishmash of disorienting visuals and brain-shattering noise still makes my head hurt.

The holograms and music stop; the woman cocks her head to the opposite side, still not pleased. I half expect her to stamp her foot.

More holograms. No music. This time the holograms are words; they look clumsy, archaic and even inappropriate in such a high-tech medium, like using Industrial Light and Magic to draw a picture of a hairy knob on the wall of a public lavatory, but at least I can understand them.

Singularity: fact or state of being singular; oddness; individuality.

I frown. This makes no sense. Why is she showing me this?

Beside me, the man stirs, the evening air rippling slightly, like water displaced by the path of a shark. I cringe: this shark may be dazed, barely conscious, but I am still uncomfortably close to its jaws.

Another hologram undulates across the woman's body, a writhing cyber-tattoo.

Singularity: A weather phenomenon in which non-seasonal weather conditions occur with a reasonable degree of regularity on or around a specific calendar date.

Does this have something to do with the Ice Saints? Or Fimbulwinter?

Slowly, I begin to understand. She's trying to communicate with me, the images that clawed at my brain had been some form of digital telepathy, but my mind couldn't cope with it; outdated organic software, incompatible operating systems. The cartoons with the bizarre soundtracks had been the next step down on her linguistic scale, images and sounds combining to create a thousand different nuances of meaning that are lost on my primitive consciousness. So now she falls back on the written word, something that I can finally understand. But I only understand the surface; the deeper meaning, the context, remains a mystery. I need her to simplify things even more, although I realize that this is probably impossible; for her this must be like using finger painting to explain advanced quantum physics to a two-year-old.

None of this matters, anyway. The phone is the only thing I care about.

Even buried deep within the woman's holographic mainframe I can feel it calling to me, easing the agony of the cancer slashing across my body. In its super-advanced state, surely the phone can use the healing energy that beams through it to rid me of the cancer for good.

Except the woman isn't showing the slightest interest in curing me and I'm not exactly in a position to force her.

The man beside me stirs again. The text on his phone shrinks from the single yawning O, back to its original message.

Does the Omega contain the Alpha?

Jesus Christ, can somebody please just talk to me in plain fucking English?

My hand twitches, the fingers aching as they flex joints crushed by gravity. The immense weight that has been crushing me lessens, just a fraction. Breathing becomes easier, my ribs moving more freely, my lungs expanding fully.

The man is freeing me.

I don't know why, and I don't care. All I know is that as soon as I can get back on my feet I'm going to get the woman's phone.

Usually when I take a phone off someone, assuming I can't just snatch it when their back's turned, I charm them into handing it over. That won't work here, the language barrier is too immense. But this isn't the first time I've run into someone who's reluctant to cooperate, either through stubbornness or a genuine communication problem. In the end I always find a way to get through to them.

That's why I carry the scalpel in my pocket.

The dried blood on the blade usually convinces them to hand over their phone. They don't realize that the blood is mine. I've never had to spill anyone else's.

Although if the woman doesn't hand over her phone then I'll find out if holograms bleed light.

(A dilapidated tower block attempts to arrest its decay by absorbing the bodies of its residents, becoming a pulsing, throbbing edifice of bone and flesh.)

Tayshia and I lived together for eight years. And she was right, after that one drunken night when she took my virginity we never slept together again.

I tried of course. I was charming, funny, romantic; I was brooding, intense, aloof; I was even mean, spiteful, cruel; whatever I thought might work. Nothing did.

Tayshia made it very clear that the only reason she kept me around was so I could help pay the rent on the flat. Her latest loser boyfriend had moved out, taking all of Tayshia's most expensive possessions with him, and she was desperate for money. We had been working together on the phone deal for three months by this point and had built up a rapport, albeit not quite the kind of rapport I had been hoping for. It was the kind where she trusted me to crash on the sofa until we got a spare bed sorted out, rather than the kind where we spent every waking hour fucking each other's brains out.

She viewed me as a kid. A little brother to be nurtured and cared for.

So the final factor in convincing her to invite me to move in was when she finally realized that I had been living in homeless shelters since before we even started working together. I still had some decent clothes—hidden away in my bag when I stayed at the homeless shelters or went out begging—so she thought I had a proper place to stay. When the truth came out she practically dragged me into her flat, sat me down and cooked me a hot meal. It was a lasagna ready meal that she just bunged in the microwave and which tasted of rubber mixed with food preservatives but it's the thought that counts.

After I had been living there for a while I realized that Tayshia had an overriding affection for waifs and strays, for the beaten and the broken. It explained why she had taken me in. And why she had such appalling taste in boyfriends. And why her flat was filled with rescued cats and wounded birds. This last foible was a particularly disastrous combination as the cats tended to regard the birds as just one more luxury they were being offered by their new owner, while the birds squawked so shrilly and hopped about so agitatedly inside their cages that they no doubt felt that they had been better off out in the wild, no matter how badly their wings had been broken.

I did suggest, in one of my more argumentative moments, that if Tayshia got rid of all the animals then the money she saved on pet food and vet's bills would solve all of her financial problems in one fell swoop, and quite possibly still leave enough money left over to end world debt.

Tayshia threw me a dirty look. 'I can't get rid of them, they're family. This is as much their flat as it is ours.'

As if to underline her point, the latest addition to the feline side of her menagerie, a scarred and surly tom given to biting and scratching anything within reach, chose that moment to spray the sofa where I was sitting with urine, marking his territory.

As I wiped cat piss out of my hair, Tayshia collapsed in hysterics. 'You're his property now; if this was prison you'd be his bitch. He'd be selling your arse to all the other prisoners for packs of cigarettes.'

'If this was prison the psychotic fucker would be locked in solitary.'

The cat frowned, his slit eyes becoming lost among the scars on his cheeks, and he started to use one of the armchairs as a scratching post, rending the fabric with his claws until it was as badly mangled as his face. Tayshia had named this ball of manic aggression Fluffy, which probably accounted for at least some of his anger management issues. Tayshia insisted that his antisocial behaviour came from his owners mistreating him and then abandoning him. I was of the opinion that we had found him wandering the street because he had murdered his owners in their sleep and was searching for new prey.

Still, right then my antipathy towards Fluffy was tempered by one important detail. Tayshia hadn't called the flat hers; she had called it *ours*.

Dreams of us becoming a couple floated through my head: our first anniversary, our wedding, our firstborn, our gaggle of grandkids.

The flat was important to me for other reasons too. Since I was able to give a fixed residence to employers I could give up begging and apply for a job. The begging and stolen credit cards had never felt right to me; I'm just not cut out for the criminal lifestyle. The guilt ate at me, along with the fear of getting caught. With a steady job I could put all that behind me.

Apart from the phones of course.

Tayshia didn't understand why I kept stealing them, particularly as I was so terrified of the police. I couldn't explain to her that prison would mean my death; with no way to get the phones I would last a couple of months at best. Worse, I might be sent to hospital; I would be at the mercy of the Surgeon.

Tayshia might not have understood about the phones but she understood about hospitals. When her grandmother was diagnosed with dementia she ended up in the geriatric unit at St Pancras. This was in the mid-nineties, before whistleblowers revealed that the staff were abusing the patients. Nurses bathed them in freezing water, beat them with shower heads, moved them from room to room in the middle of the night for no reason, bound their hands and beat them then locked them in their rooms. As Tayshia is half-Greek and half-Jamaican I suspected a racial motivation to the abuse but she said the racial abuse was aimed at the doctors and nurses who threatened to expose what was going on, intimidating them into remaining silent until things got so bad that the horrors being perpetrated were finally uncovered.

Tayshia's grandmother tried to tell Tayshia and her parents what was going on but she stumbled over her words, confused dates and times, names and faces. They didn't believe her.

Shortly after the investigation into the abuse was made public Tayshia's grandmother died. It was unclear whether this was due to the abuse she had endured or simply a case of old age finally catching up with her, claiming her as its own.

Tayshia still burned with guilt and rage and shame over what her grandmother suffered, what Tayshia believes she had *allowed* her to suffer, even though she was only a child at the time, with no way to influence the strange and frightening events occurring in the world of adults. She felt she had abandoned her grandmother and so now she would never abandon anyone ever again. They might walk out on her but she would never walk out on them.

That was her vow. That was her penance.

'Am I a bad person?' she asked me one night when she was drunk and maudlin.

''Course not.'

'Really? I lie, I steal, and what I did to my gran . . . I didn't visit her as often as I should because she scared me. She was always seeing things that weren't there and remembering things that hadn't happened and forgetting things that had. I didn't want to listen when she told me what the nurses were doing.'

'Don't be daft.' I hugged her as she broke down into tears, her wet sobs soaking into my T-shirt. 'What happened was the hospital's fault, not yours. You're the most amazing person I've ever met.'

'Thanks.' She clutched me tight, her fingernails digging into my flesh until her sobs finally subsided. 'But I'm still not going to sleep with you again.'

We both laughed, then hugged each other even more fiercely.

'I'm going to knock the dodgy DVDs and the fake IDs and all the other stuff on the head,' sniffed Tayshia. 'A new beginning. I've been offered a full-time position at work, I can quit all that Artful Dodger crap. I'm too old for it now anyway. It's just for kids really. The stupid things you do as a kid.'

And then she was crying again and nothing I could say would shake her guilt or her need to martyr herself for others.

So although she wondered why I continued to steal the phones even after we both got steady jobs and put our shady pasts behind us she never forced me to stop. She nagged, she dropped hints, she once sulked for an entire fortnight, but she never actually issued the ultimatum that any sensible person should: that either the stolen phones went or I did. The decision to stop would have to be mine.

I knew it hurt her that I continued stealing the phones and I also knew that I couldn't tell her why I kept doing it. She wouldn't believe me and would try to make me see sense, and then, if one day I was too slow in tracking the latest phone to relay the healing power and

290

the cancer took me, it would be the story of her grandmother all over again. A loved one telling her a garbled fantastical story that she didn't believe until it was too late.

I couldn't do that to her.

So I hid the stolen phones and the supplies of morphine I got from a friend who used to sell us both weed until Tayshia decided the fumes were bad for the cats and birds. I kept everything hidden, I kept everything secret. I buried my own pain so as not to inflame hers.

Not a great way to live, but Tayshia made it bearable. In fact, she made it wonderful.

And then I became so ill I couldn't go out and find the phone and so I had to tell her everything.

(The Endless Knights sit at their round table in an infinite loop of chivalry; chain-mailed incubi waft from their carnal dreams seeking maidens to ravish, frustrated by the restrictions of courtly love.)

I inch my hand towards the pocket containing the scalpel. There's still enough pressure bearing down on me to make even this tiny movement feel like the world's most intense isometric workout, but at least I can move. And with each second the pressure gradually decreases. Another minute or two and I should be able to stand. That's when things will get interesting.

I want the woman to hand over the phone, but I don't know if that's even physically possible anymore. The phone has been integrated into her body and I don't know if she can hand it over without me cutting it loose.

Like I say: interesting.

Hopefully she'll agree to open the text and bathe me in the healing energy without my having to resort to violence. Problem is I don't know if that will work. I've never tried doing it that way; I've always had the phone in my hand.

It should work. It *has* to work.

Fuck it, if doesn't I'll just decapitate the bitch, same as Diocletian did to St Pancras.

God, I hope she can make it work.

Holograms still swirl across the woman's body, but she appears to have given up attempting to communicate with me directly, or at least she's now multitasking, turning her back to me and squatting down to rummage in her satchel.

Squinting, I make out the hologram on her back.

Singularity: The point at the centre of the Big Bang.

I'm still not getting what she's trying to tell me. Or even *why* she's trying to tell me. Is she helping me? Taunting me? I don't *understand*.

Singularity: one subset of the technological singularity will be an increase in human intelligence due to interaction with artificial intelligence.

Okay, now she's just taking the piss.

She takes a book from her satchel, an ancient tome with stiff covers of faded leather and an arthritic spine that cracks and groans as she opens the book and lays it on the pavement. I'm guessing she used her position at the British Library to procure this arcane volume. As she stands the book levitates, floating up level with her head. Brittle pages turn, crumbling in the chill evening air, fragments fluttering away on the breeze, curling up like autumn leaves before vanishing into the gloom. As each page disintegrates words form in the air, glowing white against the darkness, an illuminated manuscript.

The universe is information. Quarks pass signals to leptons, leptons pass signals to bosons. And so the universe takes shape. Liquids flow, gases drift, solids cohere. Patterns form, motifs recur; a structure is revealed, no matter how haphazard or obscure. Reality follows a narrative. Information distorts, signal becomes noise meaning lost pattern ruinedruinedruined

More words appear.

The universe is gravity. It meshes with space and time, curving them, bending and shaping reality to its dictates. There is a density to gravity but also a hollowness, a swirling vortex of solid emptiness that tears at reality seeking to reclaim what is lost, and in doing so it creates a bright hell, a dark heaven.

I stare in disbelief. First at the words, then at the church. The first stone laid there bore the inscription "May the light of the blessed Gospel thus ever illuminate the dark temple of the Heathen." As a kid I misheard it read as the dark temple of the Heaven.

Coincidence? Fate? Is there even any difference?

The pages waft down to where the man lies rippling invisibly. The scraps of paper cover him and for a brief instant his form is outlined in musty leaves, a papyrus mummy. Then his body absorbs the pages, they spiral down to the whirlpool at his centre and he is transparent once more.

Another set of glowing words burns in the air.

The universe is a simulation, an illusion. The whole of reality is a living mirage, a series of images, each containing the other, the whole implicit in the parts. A light show that brings darkness, a living shadow that bedazzles.

This time the paper floats over to the woman. She stands, arms outstretched, as if about to embrace a lover. The pages spark as they touch her, and then they are gone.

The weight no longer presses on me. I can move normally again, assuming I ignore the pain the crushing pressure stamped into my body and the agony as the cancer tears me apart.

The woman has her back to me. She doesn't see me finally manage to pull the scalpel from my pocket. That's good; my body's too stiff to rely on speed or power; stealth and treachery are the only things that will get me through this.

Painfully, I clamber up to a kneeling position then pause to remind myself that my body does actually have joints; I only feel like a solid lump of pain.

Before I get any further more words appear.

The universe is an organism. Growing, evolving, forever seeking new ways in which to become more wondrous. And the universe is also a sickness, a disease spreading across the reality, eating at its core. Healing agents, antibodies, attempt to mend the heavenly body but sometimes conflicting symptoms confuse them, they attack healthy cells or benign tumours, mistaking them for malignant growths. So, attacked from both sides, the universe devours itself in an act of cosmic cannibalism as it succumbs to this disease, this sickness, this *cancer*.

I'm still gaping like an idiot at that last word when the scraps of paper rush towards me. I hurl myself to one side, rolling clumsily, bruising my already aching body on the pavement. Staggering to my feet I charge at the woman. As she turns to face me I lunge awkwardly, trying to grab her. I miss by about a foot; she doesn't even have to try to dodge me.

My fist slashes at her in a backhand motion and this time she does move, circling me slowly, confidently, like a cat cornering its prey. More by luck than judgement this puts her between me and the swirling cloud of paper. The paper quickly adjusts its movement. So does she. No way I can keep outmanoeuvring two opponents. It's just a matter of time until they catch me.

Unless . . .

I raise my hands in surrender. 'I give up. Just heal me.'

If the phone does have enough healing energy to erase my cancer then the book won't want me anymore and I won't have any reason to fight the woman. All I have to do is reason with her.

'Heal me, you bitch.'

My mouth never works properly under stress.

The woman cocks her head to one side, but this time I don't think it's from annoyance, at least not entirely. She's thinking things over.

Or maybe she's just distracting me. Out of the corner of my eye I spot the paper swirling towards me. Lunging forward, I stab at the woman with the scalpel. Too late I realize that's exactly what she wants me to do. She grabs my wrist, nearly crushing the bones. Screaming, I drop to my knees, my face level with a hologram that flashes across her stomach.

Singularity: A temporal singularity is a literary convention from speculative fiction in which a key event in a narrative creates a new alternate timeline wherein, paradoxically, the key event no longer takes place.

She jerks on my wrist, forcing me to look up at her. She stares down into my face, as if willing me to understand.

Something clicks in my head. She's telling me that I can somehow alter my past, create another reality where I never got cancer. I'll be free.

Tears of joy blur my vision. Sobbing, I open my mouth to ask how I can change reality.

And that's when the paper hits me, wrapping me in its dusty embrace.

Inanity spreads, the Tour Guyed untethering history from its roots, leaving everything empty and meaningless: bonfires and glittering fireworks;

*cheery singalongs in bombed-out underground stations; pantomime serial
killers with eviscerated victims made of wax who beam vacant smiles as
they scoop up their own intestines and severed limbs.*

At first I thought it was just a cold; some coughing and sneezing and
a general sense of feeling as though I'd had better days. Granted, there
were also chills, aches and severe fatigue, but I still didn't take it too
seriously. When you're suffering from cancer that tends to be your
main focus health-wise. Especially when you can feel something that
can heal the cancer calling out to you.

I shuffled down the stairwell in bleary slow motion, leaning
heavily against the wall, its cold solidity propping me up; an aloof
yet supportive partner in the clumsy dance I attempted as I moved
down the stairs. My rhythm was perfect—step-pause-wince, step-
pause-wince—my footwork less so; two steps from the bottom I
slipped, landing heavily on the sharp edges of the steps, my ankle
bending awkwardly before snapping back to its usual shape as if made
of rubber.

Flexing it hurt, but there didn't seem to be any real damage so I
staggered over to the front door, not wincing any worse than I had
before I tried tobogganing down the stairs on my backside.

Following the siren call of the phone I made it as far as the street
corner before running into Tayshia on her way home from work. She
took one look at my ashen face and dragged me back to the flat.

'Idiot,' she said. 'What the hell were you thinking?'

I managed to avoid answering the question. At least until the
following morning when my ankle had swollen up to the size of a
large grapefruit.

'Moron,' she said. 'Why didn't you say it was sprained?'

'Didn't realize it was. Felt okay.'

'Arsehole,' she said.

Scowling, she stuck some pillows on my bed, elevating my ankle.
Then she dosed me up on Day Nurse, took the day off work, and
waited to see if I had a chest infection or the 'flu.

Turned out it was the 'flu; after a few days of bed-rest and fluids
it was back to just feeling like a bad cold. Of course, by then the
jaundice had kicked back in and Tayshia realized something was

seriously wrong. She got so worried she did something she never ever did. She considered calling an ambulance.

'No,' I snapped. 'No doctors.'

She stared at me, confused and just a little afraid. 'Why?'

So I told her.

Obviously she didn't believe me at first, but eventually I was able to jog her memory of all the times I had been ill and how I had miraculously recovered just after procuring a new phone. The illnesses she remembered easily enough. I'm a rotten patient, snappy and irritable, so Tayshia recalled her thankless task as nursemaid. But for the dates of acquiring the phones I had to connect the dots between landmark events—birthdays, seasonal holidays, anniversaries—before she finally saw the big picture.

I think memories of her grandmother helped. She was looking for an excuse not to send me to hospital.

Now I'd given her the excuse, she magicked up a wheelchair from one of her many contacts and pushed me around London, searching for the latest phone.

Using me as her radar she soon located the phone. For some reason I never understood, the phones always turned up in London. Never Paris, Berlin or Washington. Lucky break for me, otherwise I'd never reach them in time, expiring midway across the Atlantic in an economy-class seat.

In this instance, the phone belonged to a thirty-something woman sitting in a McDonalds, her face growing tighter and tighter as her brat of a son threw a tantrum over his favourite flavour of milkshake being out of stock.

'I hate you,' he screamed at his mother. 'I hate you! I hate you!'

She tried reasoning with him, speaking firmly, but with a seething undercurrent that only a fool would ignore.

'I hate you,' screamed her son. 'I hate you! I hate you! I hate you!'

The woman stood up and walked out of the McDonalds.

After about ten seconds it became clear that she had no intention of returning. Her son ran to the doors, bawling his eyes out. 'Mummy, come back!'

He struggled with the doors, unsure of whether to push them or pull them, so he did both but with little success. They were too heavy for him.

A customer came in and the boy seized his chance, dashing out before the doors had a chance to shut again. His muffled wails of distress sounded through the glass doors as he ran down the street in his awkward toddler's gait.

A few minutes later he reappeared, traumatized, clinging to his mother's hand, listening meekly as she told him off. They re-entered the McDonalds, sat down at their table and resumed their meal in silence.

I couldn't help feeling that the look on the mother's face was not one of triumph but of despair. She hadn't wanted to come back.

As everyone went about their business and pretended they hadn't been watching this little drama unfold, Tayshia casually swiped the mother's phone from the table and disappeared back into the crowd of lunchtime customers. Her casual poise and elegant timing were a wonder to behold; she was a million times better at this than I ever was. I nearly always ended up approaching whoever owned the phone directly and trying to charm the phone off them; sleight of hand was a skill that evaded me.

As Tayshia wheeled me back onto the Tube home I wished that I had asked for her help years ago. The only drawback was that I needed somewhere private to use the phone—my sprained ankle meant I couldn't use my usual heal and run approach—but I was too weak and unaccustomed to the wheelchair to get into a public toilet by myself. And we couldn't find any disabled toilets where Tayshia could come in with me, posing as my carer. Still, we were fairly near the flat and I had a taken a hit of morphine before we left so I figured I could hold on until we got home.

I actually felt pretty good, and not just because of the morphine. Tayshia knew my secret and she was okay with it, was actually helping me with it. Instead of pushing us apart as I had feared, it had actually brought us closer. Perhaps even close enough that she would finally feel about me the way I felt about her.

Over the years we had both taken lovers, but whereas Tayshia genuinely hoped that her relationships would lead to something special—regardless of how lazy, stupid or violent her boyfriends were—I only dated in attempts to make Tayshia jealous. I went out with one girl for nearly a year purely because she was a screamer, expressing even the slightest sexual pleasure at a volume and pitch that threatened to shatter windows. Even on my worst days she screamed so hard that it sounded as though I was giving her orgasms of such intensity that it would be a good idea to keep a defibrillator on standby. As my confidence grew the girls got prettier, several of them eclipsing Tayshia with their beauty. It didn't matter, she was the one I wanted. But the only interest she ever showed in my conquests was strictly that of a friend who was glad that I had found happiness.

As we headed home, Tayshia looked tired, her face gaunt. I squeezed her hand. 'You okay?'

She flashed a sadder, wearier version of her usual dazzling smile. 'Just thinking about my gran.'

I nodded sympathetically. I felt a certain affection for Tayshia's grandmother. Apart from the obvious fact that without her Tayshia would never have been born, there was also the fact that she came from the same generation of Jamaican immigrants as my grandparents. She even attended the 1959 Caribbean Carnival that my grandparents used to talk about. A precursor to the Notting Hill carnival, it was held at St Pancras Town Hall in an effort to ease declining race relations after the riot of the previous year. My grandparents always smiled as they recalled the Mighty Terror singing the calypso song "Carnival at St Pancras". Although, as usual, my youthful brain misinterpreted the words, thinking it was "Carnivore at St Pancras", and that the Mighty Terror must be some kind of ravenous monster.

Of course the difference was that my grandparents were still alive, as were my parents. I sometimes checked out my parents' Facebook pages to see how everyone was getting on but it always left me feeling as though someone had scooped out my insides. Although Mum and Dad had become heavily involved with a charity for runaway children, raising major funds for them, so at least some good came out of this whole mess. But Tayshia's grandmother was dead, buried in St Pancras and Islington Cemetery, along with over one hundred veterans from both World Wars and the reburied remains of parishioners moved from both St Pancras Old Church and St Pancras New Church.

Sometimes I felt that the dead were called to St Pancras.

When we arrived back home I sat at the bottom of the stairwell and held out my hand for the phone. 'Might as well save you the trouble of carrying me up the stairs.'

'Let's wait until you're inside. You don't want anyone to see.'

I pulled a face. 'I'm not waiting while you call your mate to give me a piggyback when he collects his wheelchair.'

'You can walk up. Just lean on me to keep the weight off your ankle.'

'Too much hassle. Besides, someone'll probably nick the wheelchair if we leave it down here. At the very least we'll find it up on bricks with the wheels gone.'

She didn't fire back a feisty one-liner the way she normally would. She just hugged herself and kept glancing up nervously at the flat.

I began to feel uneasy. 'Tayshia, give me the phone.'

'Wait until we get inside.'

'No. Give it to me now.'

The nervous look intensified. 'Just promise me you won't get your hopes up.'

'What you on about?'

'You know this won't actually heal you, right?'

'Of course it'll bloody heal me. We went over this, we—' An angry coldness detonated in my gut. 'You said you believed me.'

She couldn't look me in the eye.

'Why did you steal the phone if you didn't think it would work?'

'So that you could see that it *didn't* work. Then you'd realize that you need to go to hospital.'

I stared at her. She hated hospitals as much as I did. Maybe more.

Her face crumpled and I realized how hard this must be for her. She wanted to help me but she knew that I would never go to hospital, would never want her to take me to one. So rather than betray that trust she took a gamble, helping me to look for the phone in the hope that it would shatter my delusions, at least long enough for me to realize that I needed medical attention. Even at a time like this she allowed the choice to be mine, despite the sight of my illness—and knowing that she could be doing something about it and wasn't—was eating her up with guilt and shame and self-loathing.

But right then none of that mattered. All that mattered was that she was killing me.

'Give me the phone.'

'You're ill. You need help.'

'*Give me the phone.*'

'Just listen—'

I slapped her. Not a lot of power behind it, I was too weak for that, but a whole lot of hate.

She gawped at me, hand pressed to her cheek, eyes wide in shock and betrayal. Then her features twisted into a mask of rage and she punched me in the face.

It was a good punch, the one I'd seen her use on more than one drunk with grabby hands and who wouldn't take no for an answer. She got her hip right behind it, channelling her entire bodyweight into her knuckles. My nose exploded, blood gushing down my chin and onto my chest. As my eyes teared up I saw an angry blur; Tayshia lunging forward. The world lurched as she tipped the wheelchair over, dumping me onto the cold concrete.

Folding the wheelchair so she could carry it, she stomped up the stairwell. Halfway up the stairs she paused and hurled something down at me. 'Here's your precious phone! See what good it does you!'

The phone bounced off my gut. I scrambled for it; pathetic, desperate.

'And don't think you're coming in the flat! You don't live here anymore!'

That got through to me. Tayshia never gave up on anyone.

Until now.

Even after I used the phone to dial my cancer back to zero I couldn't bring myself to go up to the flat. When I went outside I found Tayshia had thrown all my belongings out in the street.

I couldn't go back. I had made Tayshia betray her most fundamental belief, even more fundamental than her fear of hospitals. I had wounded her, and in doing so wounded myself.

We would never be the loving couple of my fantasies, living happily ever after. That dream was dead and no mysterious healing energy could revive it. Tayshia and I would never see each other again, not as lovers, not as friends, not even as enemies.

I had destroyed us.

Living graffiti writhes across walls, strangling letters, words, phrases, leaving witnesses with gaping holes in their vocabularies.

The paper covers me like flaking skin, literary eczema, sealing me off from the outside world. A dry rustling and the pages shift, edges slashing at me, inflicting a thousand paper cuts, as they burrow into my flesh.

I feel paper wrapping around my bones, my organs, my cells. It goes even deeper, DNA linking together in paper chains.

And it's not just the pages. I can feel words spreading throughout me, letters stamping themselves upon my heart, syllables slithering through my synapses, an entire new vocabulary of being.

I fight it, not wanting to lose my sense of self, to become a walking thesaurus for whatever alien language is invading me. Doomed effort, destined to fail. I don't even know the rules, so how can I fight? While I'm still trying to figure out an effective strategy the words are already delivering the *coup de grace*. The winning blow reverberates throughout my being. My brain rewires, my limbic system reboots.

It feels strangely comforting. I'm still me, my personality remains intact, but now my body has another, more sophisticated way in which to express itself.

I just wish I knew what I was supposed to say.

The pain reminds me, flaring suddenly back into life. For a second there I hoped the pages had fixed the cancer but it's worse than ever.

I need to find a way to end this.

The pages fade, returning me to the outside world. I'm naked, shivering in the cold wind that bites its way through the darkening evening.

I see the man and the woman, circling each other, ready to do battle. When they see me the circle becomes a triangle. The book floats into view, gaunt and emaciated now it is missing most of its pages, and the triangle becomes a parallelogram.

If it comes to a fight I still don't know what I'm supposed to do. The woman has superhuman speed and strength, the man can flatten me with his phone and the book just got through gift-wrapping me. All I've got is a rusty scalpel.

Shifting my feet into what I hope is a fighting stance I brandish the scalpel's corroded blade. My hand is as corroded as the metal; skin faded and yellow, muscle wasted away. The rest of my body is equally decrepit. Only my bones have any substance to them; ugly, angular protuberances jutting from what remains of my flesh. And even this is an illusion; the bones are hollow, the marrow eaten away, my skeleton reduced to a bundle of dried-up sticks.

The totality of my decay overwhelms me, the despair carrying a heft that my physical form no longer possesses. Withered flesh wrinkles around my eyes; I want to cry, to weep, but even my tears have been sucked away.

'Please.' My voice is a painful rasp. 'Will someone just get rid of this fucking cancer?'

The man and woman both snap their heads round to glare at me; the book flaps its remaining pages in agitation.

The parallelogram shifts, the sides shrinking as all three of the monsters edge in my direction. A second ago we were all on equal footing in terms of enmity, now I'm the only one who rates any attention. Desperate, I search for a sign that at least one of them is still on my side, or at least hates the others more than me. The man saved me from the woman, but only after trapping me himself. The woman hinted that there might be a way of curing my cancer, then set the book on me. The book offered insight into the origin of my cancer, then multiplied my sickness tenfold.

Which monster can I trust?

Shuffling backwards, I wave the scalpel feebly in a pathetic parody of a fencer's guard. The blade isn't even long enough to keep them at a decent distance. As soon as one of them makes a move, drawing my attention, the other two can cut me down. The best I can hope for is that they kill each other fighting over who gets to deliver the killing blow.

Yet still they hesitate, never quite committing to an attack, toying with me, circling with malicious delight, so certain are they that victory will be theirs.

Or perhaps they are just waiting for their turn.

On the edge of my peripheral vision a sea of surreal figures appears; scampering, giggling, hunting. They swarm along the far end of the street, the end where, up until now, normality still laid claim to the world, with pedestrians and motorists still unaware of the forces that had invaded reality, first with clandestine scouting parties, before growing bolder and bolder, escalating to raids and now, finally, a full-scale massacre.

A headless woman in a regal gown chases after a round, rolling object. Two old women, joined at the hip, bestow death by brushing their fingers against everyone within reach; for some reason the screams of their victims are in stereo, the cries of death harmonizing in an agonizing duet. Nerve-shredding laughter cackles along the street, spreading among the crowd, who start yelling threats at each other even as they tremble and soil themselves.

Most of the creatures are completely alien to me. They're not even familiar to me from my nightmares. Some of them, though, I recognize.

Above the screaming crowds of victims the gods of death circle each other, rival religions orbit alongside defunct mythologies resurrected by the sheer madness of it all: Kali and Shiva, Gog and Magog, Hel, Osiris, Emma-O, Yanlou Wang, and flashing between them all, Mercury, collecting dead souls to deliver to Pluto, master of Hades.

It's the end of the world.

The apocalypse.

And not just an apocalypse. Not even just several apocalypses.

It's all of them.

My scalpel seems even more pitiful than before. There's no way I can stop this. There's no way anyone can even slow it down.

Behind me there's an inhuman scream. The woman and the man grapple wildly with each other. One of them must have tried to blindside me and the other objected, furious at being denied that honour. As they struggle, the two figures merge, anatomies flowing together. They bump into the book, becoming a tangle of flailing limbs and flapping pages.

Staggering about wildly, they crash into me and I'm absorbed too, snatched away to somewhere far from the real world.

There's a thought I often had about Tayshia's grandmother which I never dared share with Tayshia: What if her grandmother had been the cause of the abuse the hospital staff heaped upon her? Tayshia said herself that she found her grandmother frightening and unsettling; think how much worse it would be to deal with not just one person like that but an entire ward of them; the stress would be immense. I'm not for one moment excusing what the staff did; they were responsible for their actions in a way that their Alzheimer-ridden patients clearly weren't. But maybe for each of the abusers it started out as a moment of frustration, split-second lapse of judgement caused by inexperience or lack of training or just the sheer hell of dealing with yet another crazy old person.

Perhaps it wouldn't have happened if the patients didn't keep pissing in their beds and defecating on the chairs. If they hadn't spouted delusional gibberish, laced with verbal abuse. If they hadn't been so bloody stubborn, if just this once they had done as they had been told.

Did it all start with a genuine, if terrible mistake? And if so at what point did that mistake become a habit, a culture of abuse, designed to make the staff's lives easier and hide the crimes they had already committed, rather than to help their patients?

As I said, the patients had diminished responsibility and the staff should never have done what they did, but it did make me wonder about the way people interact. If you live by a different set of boundaries to those around you, there's going to be a point where things get nasty. The balance of powers shifts; either you gain control as new boundaries are established to accommodate you or else those around you work harder to enforce the old boundaries. And in protecting one boundary, one sacred truth, it is all too easy to destroy another.

Look at the way St Pancras spurned Diocletian's offer of a reprieve. The emperor had committed many prior atrocities, but in this instance he was prepared to show mercy. Pancras, in his stubbornness, forced him to order the beheading.

Then again, maybe Diocletian and the hospital staff were just evil fuckers.

We are all of us, on occasion, victims.

We are all of us, on occasion, monsters.

Do we have to let these roles define us? Can we find a better way?

Nausea. Disorientation. Pain. Ecstasy.

Perceptions shift and blur. I'm connected to the others now; our individual thoughts remain separate, but we process information through an amalgam of different mental and physical abilities. The living black hole that passes as a man warps gravity to protect against the depraved physics of this place; the woman runs calculations, translating our surroundings into something we might just possibly be able to understand; the book provides knowledge, allowing us to put all this into some kind of context. But what about me? Why am I here?

Reality flips inside out; time runs backwards and forwards, as well as on a wonky diagonal; multiple universes fly off in random directions.

Music sounds in my nose, the melody rippling through my nostrils, beautiful and sadistic; I sneeze out an opera composed of tastes and textures of foods that only exist in the dreams of beings who were never born. An idea scampers by, arguing with itself, multicoloured propositions and refutals fanning out behind it in a peacock's tail of intellectualism. Exquisite statues of ornate cityscapes formed entirely by chance from the plaque spreading across the teeth of omnisexual dragons; the baroque ornamentation shifts through parallel dimensions, lending the sculptures life, both metaphorically and literally.

We're at the heart of the singularity.

It's the one great truth at the heart of existence, it's every truth, and it's no truth. Singular, multiple, void.

It's amazing. Awe-inspiring. Terrifying. Without the others proving a buffer against al this weirdness I would go insane.

One of the alternate universes floats by. Inside I catch a glimpse of Tayshia. She's smiling, happy. And she's kissing me.

I watch as we smooch in our flat, cats winding about our legs, birds singing in their cages. On the sideboard I see a framed photo of us laughing outside a nightclub. It's the same nightclub that my friends and I went to after Tayshia got us the fake IDs. In this reality I must have worked up the nerve to ask her out. That means I didn't approach her about selling the phones. And that means that in this reality I may not have cancer.

The other me breaks his clinch with Tayshia and flops on the sofa, bare feet propped up on one of the arms. I search for signs of needle marks between his toes; that's where I used to inject the morphine so Tayshia wouldn't spot what I had done. No marks. Not from needles anyway; there are bites and scratches gouged all over my other self's feet and ankles; I'm surprised he's not crippled. Fluffy the psycho cat is obviously no more genial in this dimension.

Slowly, I drift towards him, unsure if it's me doing the steering or one of the others. I draw closer and closer until I pass through his skin and into his body. It freaks me out more than a little; I'm a ghost haunting my own body. But then I realize the possibilities and order him to start kissing Tayshia again. He doesn't move. I don't control his body or his thoughts; I can't even *feel* his thoughts. But I can feel his body.

No blissed out traces of morphine. No pain. No cancer.

I drift back out of his body

Suddenly I realize why I'm being shown this. My reality, my Earth, was doomed; nothing could prevent the army of monsters that rampaged across it. But in religion and mythology the end of the world did not necessarily mean the end. Ragnarok, Kali Yuga, Revelations; these all led to new beginnings, either on a renewed Earth or on a completely different plane.

If humanity could somehow merge, the way I had with my travelling companions, then we could transfer into this alternate reality, absorb ourselves into all our counterparts here and live out the perfect existences denied to us in our original lives.

We'd have to find a way of controlling our other selves, of course, or perhaps sharing control. There'd be issues of free will; if we can't control our other selves we'd effectively be prisoners in our own bodies. Equally, if we did find a way to gain control then our other selves would be prisoners. It's beyond my grasp of ethics, not to mention metaphysics; I figure we just see if we can get the idea to work and then iron out the fine details afterward. Imminent global destruction has a way of cutting through the abstractions.

That's why I'm part of this group. Somehow I'm the key to getting everyone out. That must be why the phones always appeared in London, if they were any further away I might not get to them in time and I'd have been dead long before the apocalypses kicked off.

Somehow it all revolves around me. And St Pancras; I think part of the reason I was chosen is because I'm somehow connected to him and the part of London that bears his name. St Pancras—"The one who holds everything."

In the flat Tayshia goes over to the ironing board, checks the iron, picks a T-shirt out of the laundry basket and tosses it at my other self lying on the sofa.

Laughing, he takes the T-shirt over to the board and starts ironing.

Mail flops through the letterbox. Funny, normally it only got delivered as far as the front door and we had to collect it from there. Postmen must be more conscientious in this reality.

Tayshia picks up the mail, opens it. Her face drops. Walking over to the ironing board in a dazed shuffle she thrusts the letter at my other self. He looks as shocked as Tayshia.

The letter is my birth certificate. Judging by Tayshia's reaction I didn't tell her I was only fifteen when I asked her out. The way she starts shouting I'm guessing we did more than just go clubbing in the six months before I turned sixteen.

Some people would argue that in the case of a loving consensual relationship a few months wouldn't matter. Tayshia obviously isn't one of them. Normally I'd agree with her; the idea of being seduced by an older woman excited me as a fantasy but always left a creepy aftertaste whenever I considered it properly. At fifteen I had lacked the emotional maturity to be on equal terms with an adult in a relationship. But I loved Tayshia and in this reality our relationship had started that little bit earlier and I obviously hadn't managed to restrain myself.

Livid that she's been turned into a paedophile, Tayshia waves her hands about angrily, yelling. My other self yells back. The birds squawk, most of the cats cower behind the armchairs. Except for Fluffy; he decides this is the perfect moment to bite my other self in the ankle. As Fluffy's fangs sink into flesh my other self screams in agony and kicks him across the room. Fluffy spirals through the air, manages to get his paws up in time to bounce off the wall, and lands, hissing.

Tayshia glares at my other self and the anger she has displayed so far is as nothing compared to the wrath she now unleashes. Nothing could stand against her; armies would fall, nuclear bunkers crumble to dust. Eyes blazing, nostrils flaring, an irate finger jab, jab, jabbing deep into my other self's chest, the bracelets on her wrist jangling with each vicious poke.

My other self hits her in the face with the iron.

As Tayshia crumples to the floor he leans over and hits her again. Frantic, I manage to merge with him once more, try to get him to stop, but I have no more control than before. I watch in horror as he, I, *we*, keep smashing away until her skull caves in and melted flesh drips from the hot iron.

Drifting out of his body I lose track of time after that.

My other self is wrapping the body in bin-liners when the police break down the door. He manages to grab the iron before they reach him with their batons and both he and one of the police officers end up in hospital.

That's when the Surgeon turns up, wielding his scalpel.

Slowly, the scene fades. The singularity fades too. We're back on Earth, back among the monsters. The man, woman and book separate from me and our shared perception dies. I can't tell if they're eager to get away from me or pleased with what they've witnessed.

Doubling over, I vomit; my diaphragm spasming again and again, trying to excavate my entire body, as though desperate to expel any of my other self's violent tendencies that I might carry within me.

Too late. I already know that I carry that spark of violence within me, no matter how much I might try to deny it.

Insane laughter echoes off stained concrete canyons, the Empty Threat hunting for mouths to infect, cowards to inhabit.

I finish heaving my guts up. Wet strings of vomit and saliva dangle from my lips. The acid taste feels awful, but it isn't the worst thing about all this. The worst thing is knowing there's no escape. No matter what I do I'll still be cursed with the cancer, I'll still be a key to the apocalypse.

Even if I somehow manage to find a way to merge humanity with their other selves in that alternate reality I'll still need to use the phones to survive. And after the apocalypse is over and I've served my purpose, I doubt my mysterious saviour (the woman, it's got to be the woman, right? Or maybe the book . . .) will care about keeping me alive.

No, I'll be dead.

And so will Tayshia. If she stays in this world she dies and if she goes to the other world she has no body to inhabit. At best she'll be a ghost, at worst she'll cease to exist.

No matter how this ends I'll have killed the woman I love twice over.

And God help me, I'd do it a third time if it allowed me to survive.

Looking up, I see the monsters jostle about me, moving for flanking position, none of them prepared to face me head-on. Looking down I realize why.

My bloodstained vomit has eaten through the pavement, revealing the sewer below. Confused and weary I lean against a lamppost; the metal dissolves beneath my touch, rotting away to nothingness.

So that's why I felt so much worse after the book wrapped me in its pages; this is no longer a cancer of the body, it is a cancer of reality.

But whose reality am I supposed to kill? Growth or entropy? So many different agents had a hand in getting me here I don't know whose bidding I'm supposed to do, which way I'm supposed to tip the balance.

I suspect that this may be the point.

Perhaps I'm not supposed to know, perhaps no one is. I'm the wild card, the joker everyone wants to turn into an ace. But no one knows what hand the other players have, or what rules everyone is playing by, or even which game.

I'm needed to house the cancer, to use it to accelerate the apocalypse. It's not enough to have one doomsday, that might not get the job done, the universe might not die, it might just limp along, a wounded animal, full of hate and fear and pain. Or it might not resurrect fully, marred by birth defects, bubbling and gurning, a cosmic idiot child.

So long as I cause the world to end, one way or the other, that is all that matters.

Apocalypses start to overlap, those that want to end the world and those that want to see it reborn. Reality starts to fall apart, structure and logic deteriorating.

(the Queen of Despair finally scoops up her head only to have it subject her to a stream of verbal abuse and unconvincing bravado/ unseasonably cold winds commanded by gods and saints howl against *overly theatrical serial killers and living waxworks/* <u>a swirling vortex of solid emptiness swallows</u> *a tower block of flesh and bone)*

One of the creatures, a giant spider with the face of an old woman and knitting needles for legs, charges at me, hoping to catch me off guard in all the confusion. I swat at it stiffly, my reflexes slow, my arms even slower. Still, it's enough. At my touch the knitting-needle legs disintegrate; the fat, hairy body crashes to the ground, convulsing horribly as spider-flesh turns to mulch.

(chain-mailed incubi ravish a pair of elderly conjoined twins; in the distance an infinite loop of screams rings out: **the whole twisted drama shrinks to a series of images in a lightshow, real yet illusory***)*

In among the carnival parade of monsters I spot the Surgeon. Our eyes lock. His upside-down mouth twists in a smile.

Hatred writhes in my gut. I'm guessing he's the one who posted Tayshia my birth certificate. Why else would it have been addressed to her and not me? If not for him I wouldn't be dying. The world wouldn't be dying. Tayshia wouldn't be dying.

But although he gave me the cancer, he wasn't the one to supercharge it. Maybe I can use the cancer to kill him. Or maybe I can't.

I'm going to find out.

Staggering forward, I fight my way through the monsters, dissolving them with my touch. I may be facing a carnival of monsters but I'm the Carnivore of Monsters. I know that my mad onslaught won't make things any better but I don't care. Hope isn't what guides me now, nor is it despair. It's rage. I've decided to kill that topsy-turvy-faced bastard and I'm too fucking stubborn to stop now no matter how much damage it does, no matter how many apocalypses it causes.

(living graffiti scribbles itself across an ancient book, grammar battling grimoire, <u>signal transforming to noise, words becoming nonsense nonce-hence non-whence non-non-non-nonnnnnnnn)</u>

As I slaughter my way towards the Surgeon I realize this whole thing has been a masterpiece of misdirection, a conjuror's greatest trick. I sense forces at work that are even more powerful than the ones battling on the street. Forces that desire something more than simple destruction or simple regeneration or even simple negation where the cosmos not only ceases to exist but never existed in the first place. These forces want something I can't even begin to comprehend, not even if I borrowed the perceptions of the man, woman and book. This is beyond even the limitless power of the singularity.

The horde of creatures swarming about me sense it too; they pause in their fighting and peer about, noses wrinkling, ears twitching. Even

310

the Surgeon stops smiling. There's something out there stronger than all of us; *stranger* than all of us.

Tension crackles through the air; terrified humans whimper and moan. The multiverse holds its breath. Fear on this scale is unimaginable, greater than any ever experienced. Even the monsters are scared.

I should know.

The Men with Paper Faces

by John Llewellyn Probert

There is another world that exists beneath ours.

Only slightly beneath, mind you. Sometimes only very slightly indeed. The distance from our world to theirs can be a mere hair's breadth. No more than a lick of paint. A film of water. Or a sheet of the thinnest tissue paper.

Paper.

I would never have thought something so innocuous could be capable of shielding something so hideous. But then twenty-four hours ago there were many things of which I was blissfully unaware. The moment must surely soon come when those who have been moving among us all these years will reveal themselves to us all. In that infinitesimal fragment of time between the shock of realization, and the succumbence to the appalling fate which will undoubtedly follow, may merciful insanity descend upon us all.

I was born and raised in Wales. A sickly child, little did I realize at the time that the dampness that settled with such dogged persistence in both the valleys of my homeland and the bronchioles of my lungs might be the very reason they chose this ancient and mysterious land.

The damp helps their faces stay on, you see.

Their paper faces.

Even now I find myself typing those words hesitantly, in between nervous glances from the window to the door and back again. My fingertips hover over the keyboard as if the very spelling of those words will somehow reveal my presence, and my knowledge of their existence, to them.

Let me wait a while, just in case.

There. It is now more than two minutes since the words appeared on my computer screen and there has been no moon face with cutouts for eyes at my window, no scraping of papery, threadbare fingers at my door. Perhaps I will be safe long enough to finish this account. Perhaps then I may also be granted the time to conceal it before they find me.

As I have already said, I was born in Wales, and have remained in my homeland for the entirety of my adult life. The only change in my circumstances is that on attaining adulthood I moved from the isolation of a valley town to the capital city. I will confess that I have spent several reasonably happy years in Cardiff, and it is only very recently that day and night has blurred into one with every hour, both sleeping and waking, filled with visions of people and things and places, and what they really look like underneath.

It all began after the accident.

No, even that isn't right, and if this account is to prove of any use at all to those who find it there must be accuracy, otherwise I may as well spend my final hours making up nonsense about sea beasts and tentacled monstrosities from outer space.

I do not know where they come from.

Only that they are here.

I first became aware of them when I was lying in a hospital bed. True, this was after an accident, but I am unsure if it was the trauma itself that lifted the veil from my eyes, or the surgery that had been necessary to repair the injuries I had sustained. Either way, a while after I came to, I caught my first glimpse of a changed world. Even then I imagined it was likely a drug-induced and therefore transient occurrence, a side effect of the general anaesthetic, or of the pain-killing medications I was being administered (to stop me from screaming, I was later told, although I have no memory of this).

I remember waking in darkness, and then realizing, as I raised my right hand so that my fingers ought to have been visible before my face, that it was not darkness at all, but utter blackness. The blackness of a coal cellar without light, of a night without stars, of the unending void of nothing that most likely awaits us upon death.

The blackness of the totally blind.

I remember the panic that gripped me as I moved my raised hand over my face. Then my fingertips came into contact with the bandages that had been taped over my eyes and I heaved a sigh of relief, before fear flooded me once again as I began to wonder why they were there.

I moved my hands lower and felt sheets and blankets. When my fingers explored the edge of my mattress, my skin felt the shock of cold metal. Bars. The kind used to stop hospital patients from rolling onto the floor.

I remember trying to call out, that all I could manage was a dry croak, and that by the time I had swallowed sufficient saliva to make utterance I could hear movement in the room, far away, deeper in the darkness. I could hear the rattling of instruments on a table, a needle piercing rubber, the squirling rush of fluid being drawn into a syringe too quickly. It was only when I asked where I was that the individual performing these actions must have realized I was awake. And in the seconds before a response was given, I heard a strange sound, as of the rustling of coarse newspaper being used to cover something, before a female voice spoke to me.

"You're at St Tristan's," it said. "My name's Sally. I'm one of the nurses here, and you still need plenty of rest."

"What's happened to me?"

There was a pause before the reply.

"You had an accident," Sally said. "You came in a few days ago. You weren't badly injured but, well, you've probably already guessed which bit of you came off worst."

"Am I blind?"

"I can't say." Sally inserted a probe into my left ear. I heard a click and then she withdrew it. Beyond the ringing the action had caused I could hear the scratching of a biro scribbling on a chart. "But Mr Sanderson and his team will be around in a bit. I'm sure he'll explain everything to you."

He did, but not before the dressings were removed and I was able to view my surroundings, as well as those individuals gathered before me to explain my circumstances.

Once my eyes had been given sufficient time to adjust to a glaring white sunlight which held no warmth and flooded the room with the clinical harshness of a light microscope prepared to examine a specimen slide, my first impression was that the hospital must be desperately short of beds. That could be the only reason for the appalling state of the room in which I found myself. It was spacious enough, but the magnolia-coloured paint on the walls was cracked and peeling, and in the worst places, high up and close to the ceiling, it hung in long strips that revealed an underside of glistening dampness, the paint failing in its task of concealing a wall of suppurating red brickwork.

"It is always something of a shock when the bandages are removed."

So spoke the individual who proceeded to identify himself as Mr Sanderson, the surgeon who had operated on me. He was a short, squat man in an immaculate three-piece black suit, the pale roundness of his utterly bald head an anaemic shade of pink. I did my best to concentrate on him, to ignore my dilapidated surroundings, but it was difficult as I could not see his eyes, hidden as they were behind rimless spectacles whose tiny circular lenses were of an opaque whiteness that matched his shirt. I wondered how he could see anything through them, never mind how he might be able to perform delicate surgery.

"Your injuries were fairly minor." His voice was gentle, almost a whisper. But far from finding his tones comforting, I was reminded of serpents from the animated feature films I had enjoyed in my youth. I did not trust him. "Some conjunctival lacerations that in some places extended to the cornea, but nothing that couldn't be fixed with a few micro-sutures. Six of them in fact. Six stitches holding the surface of each eye together."

That caught my attention. Stitches. This man had put stitches in my eyes.

My reaction must have been one of horror as his tones subsequently became even more placatory.

"Nothing to worry about! The stitches will dissolve eventually. Over the next few weeks they will be absorbed by your eyes until nothing of them remains. It will be as if they were never there."

For a moment I wondered if he meant the stitches or my eyes themselves. Then a noise made me aware of the assemblage of nurses and junior medical staff gathered behind him. It was most likely my imagination, but I was almost sure that after this last utterance they all, as one, tittered to themselves, the massed bulk of their bodies heaving with a collective giggle at some joke to which I was not party.

"You still can't remember how you came by them?"

"I beg your pardon?" I had become distracted. By my situation, by the rotting room, and most of all by these almost alien individuals who were at that moment regarding me.

"Your injuries." Mr Sanderson looked concerned, while his accompanying entourage imbibed a moist-lipped, collective intake of breath. "You still have no recollection?"

I had not previously considered it, but now I tried to recall how I had come to be here, in this awful bed in this terrible place, I found I could not summon even the most insignificant fact that might have contributed to an explanation. I tried again.

Nothing.

I shook my head and gave a weak smile.

"Never mind." Mr Sanderson beamed in a way that made me think of a fat white spider who knows its meal is helpless enough for it to enjoy later, when it has had time to develop a sufficient appetite. "One more day and we should be able to get you home."

"I could leave today if you like," I blurted, not wishing to remain in this dusty, peeling chamber a moment longer than was necessary. "I mean, I can understand you must be very hard pressed for beds."

Again that horrible, hungry smile. "You worked that out, did you?" The Sanderson entourage mumbled assent as he spoke. "Well, you're right. The hospital is currently so full that we have had to open our new wing a week early. You are the very first patient to occupy a bed here. Well done for spotting how new everything looks. Your eyesight has obviously recovered more quickly than I thought." The smile dropped as he clasped maggot-white fingers across his midriff. "Perhaps you are ready to go home today, after all!"

They all turned to go. I searched for the nurse who had spoken to me earlier, but I could not guess which of the pale, expressionless matrons might be host to the voice I had heard. As the door to my room creaked open, desiccated fragments of rotten, greyish wood fell from where the hinges desperately held it in place. The ward round, with Mr Sanderson now at its head, shuffled out. I pushed the bedclothes aside, intent on leaving immediately.

The nurse bringing up the rear turned and regarded me with tiny eyes set in a pinched face whose skin was the same shade of mottled grey as the doorframe. Just before she stepped outside she breathed something at me.

Even now I do not know exactly what it was she said, but I have narrowed it down to two possibilities. It was either "You may leave" or "You may see". Since departing that horrid place, the implications of either have become increasingly horrific.

But I am getting ahead of myself. I have not even mentioned that when I threw back the bed covers the action raised a powder of particles that were easy to see by the empty sunlight. These particles were not dust, I am convinced of that now. To begin with they were coarser, more substantial than the motes one commonly encounters. These were more like tiny fragments of torn paper, such as might be created if one were to tear a tissue into the smallest possible pieces. As they floated down before me I tried to grab one, but they were too quick.

They landed on the wooden boards of the floor, and I watched in horror as each fragment grew six tiny, gossamer-fine legs, and scuttled beneath the bed.

That was enough. I was leaving. I climbed out of the bed slowly, not wishing to disturb any more of the tiny alien creatures. The scarred boards creaked a warning beneath my naked feet as I made my way to the crudely fashioned wardrobe slumped to the left of the door. It opened with some difficulty, as quite obviously very little care had been taken in its workmanship.

My clothes were gathered in a heap at the bottom.

I picked them up, and shook them out. Sure enough, I found them to be infested with the same 'tissue motes' (I can think of no other name for them), and as I gave each garment a thorough and vigorous shake, the tiny creatures dropped to the ground and scuttled to join their brethren beneath the bed. Once I was happy my clothes were free from infestation, I pulled them on, much happier now that I was dressed in my tattered green corduroy suit, and my feet were safely inside my scuffed brown Oxfords.

My journey through the hospital to the outside world was the stuff of nightmare.

As soon as I stepped out of my room, carefully avoiding the still-splintering doorframe, I realized that Mr Sanderson must have been joking when he had called this place the 'new wing'. Indeed, I had never before found myself in such dilapidated surroundings. The long and empty corridor that stretched ahead of me was high-ceilinged, but many of the insulating tiles had fallen and now lay in fragmented heaps of rotting brown fibres on scabrous floorboards spattered in places with thick black mould. The medical team must have been quick on their feet, for there was neither sight nor sound of them as I made my way along, and there seemed to be no other rooms into which they might have slipped to visit other patients. Instead, on either side of me, I beheld walls adorned with peeling wallpaper of faded pink stripes on a dirty white background. As I progressed, the corridor seemed to become narrower, and I was never able to tell if it was an effect of actual physical dimensions or just an optical illusion created by the nature of the decor. Reaching out to touch the walls did no good, as the damp wallpaper collapsed beneath my probing, suggesting the absence of any kind of solidity beneath it. The moisture that pooled in the thickened folds I created was chill and burned my fingertips such that I did not persist with my explorations.

At the very end of the corridor I expected there to be a turn either to the left or the right. Instead, and quite impossibly, the passageway came to an abrupt halt, and I found myself facing a high window that consisted of nine square panes of glass that were almost opaque with dirt. I was loathe to touch the blackened grease that obscured my view of the world outside and yet I felt myself compelled to trace a diagonal line across the centre pane with the outstretched index finger of my right hand. The subsequent grime I acquired would not leave my skin, no matter how hard I rubbed my finger against the fabric of my jacket. Doing my best to ignore the gritty, slimy sensation that seemed to have been exacerbated by my attempts to rid myself of it, I knelt on creaking boards and peered through the glass I had cleared.

I did not recognize the part of Cardiff I could see though the window. I must have been on a high floor of the hospital, as the row upon row of terraced houses I beheld seemed far beneath me. Of course, this could also have been due to the distorting effect the glass had, making the houses seem somehow . . . wrong. The doors were too narrow, the windows too small, and the buildings themselves were all manner of curious shapes. They were more like a child's crude attempt at models of houses than the buildings themselves, and yet I somehow knew that the structures I could see were real.

But how to get to them? Or rather, how to get out of this awful place? How had Mr Sanderson and his team achieved their egress? Had they found another way out, perhaps behind one of those dripping curtains of pink and white paper? Or had they gone out of the window?

I prodded the glass once more, to be rewarded by a scraping sound as of the blade of a shovel being dragged against concrete. This was accompanied by the glass before me swinging open from hinges along the top of the frame. I poked my head out and coughed as my lungs were assailed with a mixture of petrol fumes and the same dampness I had felt in the corridor, although strangely it seemed to be stronger outside than in, as if a storm had broken but the moisture had been retained by the air molecules rather than falling to be absorbed by the ground.

A rickety metal fire escape led to the ground. I had little wish to test my weight upon it, and yet it seemed the quickest, and indeed, the only, means of escape. The poorly constructed metal wobbled and creaked with every tentative step. The bolts holding it against the filthy, crumbling red brickwork of the building's exterior seemed inexpertly applied, rudely driven in at angles that suggested carelessness. The dust trickling from the attachment points merely served to encourage my haste.

Once I was on the street, the relative solidity of rocking paving stones beneath my feet, I quickly became aware that the members of the general public who buffeted and thronged about me were of two distinct types. The first were as you or I— normal-seeming human beings going about their everyday business. A few were smiling, many had nondescript expressions, a few seemed either angry or depressed, occasionally both. Still, it was more or less a normal mixture of the kinds of individuals one might encounter in any major city.

The other type were not normal at all.

At first glance they seemed so, but one only had to hold one's gaze on them for more than a second to realize there was something entirely alien about them. They were humanoid in appearance, and dressed much the same as those who pushed past and round them. It was their faces that gave them away.

Their crumbling paper faces.

Imagine, if you will, a handful of wadded-up tissue paper that has been dampened and then applied to an inverted white balloon the size of a human head. Poke holes for eyes, nose and a mouth with your fingers, add a smear of wiry grey hair to the scalp and you should have some idea of the creatures I beheld in that dreary Cardiff street. I bit back a scream and felt the pounding in my chest increase as I realized none of the normal human beings had any awareness of the anthropomorphic approximations present in their midst. Fortunately, the alien creatures seemed oblivious to my knowledge of their presence and I was able to make my stumbling way along, taking care to avoid the intruders. At a crowded street corner, however, it became impossible and, as I swerved to avoid one, I collided with another. My elbow met with the same sickening, collapsing sensation I had experienced when probing the hospital wallpaper. Unlike the elastic resilience of normal flesh, the intruders' flesh seemed more plastic, more accommodating to changes in shape. I coughed an apology and that with which I had collided grated a polite reply in what would otherwise have passed for a human voice, were I not already privy to the creature's unnatural nature.

I suppressed a shudder and turned to regard the road I intended to cross. It was then I was struck with another realization.

I had no idea where I was.

I am not familiar with the entirety of Cardiff, of course. I would be surprised if anyone living in a major city is fully conversant with every street. However, I would have hoped that in the event of an emergency any hospital I might have been taken to would be in a part of town I had at least had occasion to pass through at some point. This place, however, was completely unfamiliar to me.

A nearby newsagent put me straight. I did my best to ignore the appalling state of his shop—the leaking roof, the newspapers, chocolate bars and other snacks teetering in random piles, the dim lighting that meant I could barely find my way to the counter. I also ignored the peeling features of the individual in front of me paying for a chocolate bar and, once they were gone, proceeded to ask the man who owned the shop if they might know the whereabouts of my street of residence. My question was met with a frown, followed by the gentleman responding that his establishment was on that very street, and that my address was but a few houses distant. I knew that this could not possibly be the case, and so strong was my conviction that he deemed it necessary to show me on one of the copies of an amateurishly printed and poorly stapled A-Z street guide that he was telling the truth and that, even more significantly, there was no other street in the city bearing a similar name.

I left the shop in a state of utter confusion, pausing only to note the number before setting off in the direction in which, according to him, my dwelling ought to lie.

Nothing was familiar. I have walked the length of the street on which I live many, many times, and yet now I may as well have been walking the highway of a distant country. To my left the buildings soon gave way to an expanse of recreational parkland. I felt some distant pang of familiarity at the towering oaks, the central lake upon which both dead birds and rudimentary attempts at model boats floated, but I cannot honestly say I recognized any of these things.

When I finally arrived at my address I once again felt no sense of recognition, of homecoming. Instead the Victorian terraced house with my number on it felt as grim and as foreboding as those crumbling buildings I had first viewed on my escape from that terrible hospital. I felt in my pocket for keys, only to discover I had none.

And so I rang the bell.

What else could I do? I had nowhere to go, and it was just possible the house was made up of apartments, and that one of the other residents could let me in. Perhaps even the landlord lived there and might be able to grant me access to my own flat. As I lifted my finger from the buzzer another thought occurred to me. Perhaps my inability to remember my street, the park, my house, could all be attributed to amnesia I had sustained as the result of an accident I still could not remember. If that was the case, then what else might I be unaware of? Was I married? Did I have a wife? Children?

I took a step back as I heard footsteps coming closer on the other side of the door. The sounds were muffled, as if the individual responding to my summons was walking in slippers, or had very soft feet. As fingers fumbled with the latch I poised to make good my escape. The door opened softly, to reveal an empty hallway beyond.

After a moment, I took a step forward and peered inside. Nothing of the house's interior served to jog my memory. Not the brick red squares, bordered in black, that tiled the floor. Not the coat rack to the right of the door that was home to a moth-eaten mustard-coloured duffle coat half-concealing the dusty black cardigan that cowered beneath it.

I called out a greeting, only for the word to be swallowed by the hollow space before me. Despite the absence of a reply, I stepped inside, noting as I did so that the floor tiles were uneven, and actually a little loose. I attempted to kick aside the crumbling cement I had dislodged, only for three of the tiles to come free entirely and skitter away, hitting the scabbed skirting board to my left with a clatter.

I called out again.

Nothing.

Another step inside. This one was even gentler than the last and yet still I felt the crunch of rotten tiling beneath my foot. The door to my left was flaking with inexpertly-applied, magnolia-coloured paint similar in hue to that which had adorned my hospital room. Then I noticed that the wallpaper either side of it, and on the wall opposite and up the stairs to the right, consisted of the same damp-looking pink-striped stuff as in the hospital corridor into which I had made good my escape.

I began to climb the stairs. The threadbare carpet of patterned crimson covering the mildewed wood was preferable to the awful sensation of crumbling glazing beneath my feet. I presumed the condition of the floor was the reason whoever had opened the door had been wearing slippers.

The stairs creaked as I ascended, each step warping at the pressure of my foot, and failing to regain its shape once I had moved on. The landing was composed of the same rotten flooring, the same threadbare carpet, and the wallpaper here was more faded than downstairs.

I could hear breathing coming from the bedroom to my left.

By now my throat was so dry I could barely summon a sound. I tried to ignore the deep scratch marks on the door, and pushed it open.

There was something lying on the bed.

Even now I find it difficult to describe. It was human-like, and similar to the alien creatures I had seen on the street. The face of this one was far more rudimentary, though. The nostrils were ill-formed, the mouth little more than a pulsing black dot above a flaking chin, and as for the eyes—

There were none.

As the thing began to rise, as the mouth began to expand and the feathery structures I could see within it began to organize themselves into a rudimentary tongue, I felt a strong impression that this thing, whatever it was, had been caught off guard.

And then it spoke my name.

I am not sure which was more shocking, that the creature knew me or that the voice in which it spoke was female. Either way, as I stepped back I crammed my knuckles into my mouth to keep myself from screaming.

The wasting thing was on its feet now, rubbing at its papier-mâché face with fingers that resembled pale sausages wrapped in wet tissue. When it revealed its features to me once more I could see it had poked holes in the damp paper coverings to allow it to see out.

To see me.

I could taste bile rising in my throat, and over the pounding of blood in my ears I could just make out the thing's gargling, rasping attempts at language.

I dismissed its communications as nonsense. How could this limping, tattered thing that shambled towards me possibly be my wife? I retreated further, realizing too late that the door to the bedroom had swung shut behind me. The creature hobbled nearer, squeezing at the sides of its head so that it now possessed rudimentary ears. Then the sausage fingers pulled the mouth into a ghastly parody of a smile.

What else could I do? I reached out to fend off the advances of this horrible thing, and in doing so felt my fingertips dig into the chill moistness of its face.

A face that came away in my hand.

I fought the urge to vomit as the tissue I found myself holding frayed and fragmented into the same kind of tiny tissue motes I had observed in my hospital room. Even as I made the connection, they began to swarm over my fingers, tickling the web spaces with their tiny, multi-jointed, thread-like limbs, imbuing my palm with the sensation that my skin, too, was coming apart.

I brushed the creatures off, slapping at the more persistent of them, and having to physically pick at the ones that were doing their best to bury themselves beneath my nail beds. I would have stamped on them, too, but once they had fallen to the ground, they quickly disappeared between the cracks in the floorboards.

I turned my attention back to what was standing in front of me.

Beneath the creature's torn face lay something quite unexpected. I would not have been surprised to see ripped flesh, bleeding muscle, even exposed bone. Instead, I beheld a pale, waxen rudiment. A bloodless approximation of a face such as a window-shop dummy might have before eyes are painted on and other features added. A template, an approximation, an estimate.

Deprived of its lips, it seemed the thing could no longer speak. Instead it waved its arms at me as if in a desperate attempt to communicate. It was less a conscious decision and more the reflex action of sheer panic that caused me to grab the rusting lamp from the bedside table, raise it high above my head, and bring it down with all the strength I could summon upon the creature's waxen, hairless cranium.

The head did not so much give way as accede to the blow, such that when I raised the instrument again there remained the impression of my weapon as if it had been pressed into modelling clay.

I hit the thing again, and again, but it took many more blows before the creature finally fell to its knees, and thence to the floor. As it did, an unearthly sound filled the room. As I have already explained, the creature had no mouth, and so I can only guess where the sound came from. It resembled a humming, as of a plethora of tiny insects buzzing too close to one's ears for comfort. It lasted only for a minute, and yet it caused the most blinding headache. Even now, hours later, I am still recovering from it.

I am still in the house.

Because I cannot leave.

In a downstairs room I have found a computer, and that is where I am now writing this account. I can only assume that the sound the creature made in its death throes was a cry for help. When I began writing this I imagined I was alone. Now, however, outside the front and back doors, and at every window, both upstairs and down, I can see them, looking in at me. They have yet to enter, but I know it is only a matter of time.

What are they? If these words are to be of any help to those who find them, to those who must begin to organize the fight against these things, I offer this:

That they are of otherworldly origin I have no doubt. I am also convinced that they are two different species, that there is a symbiotic relationship between the tissue motes and the faceless, wax humanoid creatures they cover, thus creating the semblance of humanity. These symbionts have somehow been able to alter the vision of human beings so that we remain ignorant of the rotten, decaying world these invaders are building for themselves.

They thrive on corruption, of that I am now sure. New buildings are nothing of the kind. What we see as alive is actually dead. What we see as order is actually chaos. Our world is not just falling apart, but is actively being taken to pieces. For what purpose I cannot say, except that it suits their needs.

I just heard a crash upstairs. I should investigate. I would say I will be back in a moment, but I suspect that will not be the case. So instead I'm just going to press the 'Save' button and hope for the best.

There.

All done.

Time to go.

EMPTY HOUSES

by Ralph C. Doege

I

I was drunk, sitting in the small *Constanze*: a man in the midst of a played-out midlife crisis. Played out, yes, and trapped in clichés, a black, iron prison of complexes and limits with no light in sight. I looked at the bottom of my glass for an exit, but there was only the distorted black tabletop, the wood of a door that wouldn't open no matter how hard I might bang against it. The waitress and the few guests looked over at me, and I smiled at them apologetically, with a tear in my right eye and sweat on my forehead. "Sorry," I thought, and the zombies nodded as if they understood. Among them was a man of around thirty—some seven years my junior—who immediately caught my eye. There was something painfully familiar about him that aroused a strange feeling of dissonance in me, an ominous pressure in my stomach like a slowly opening fist with fingers reaching for my heart. What I was seeing couldn't be.

True, the older I got, the more often I met people who reminded me of figures from my past, as if my brain were limiting itself to only a few distinguishing traits, an archetypal geometry of features. So the limp, pale smile of a terminally ill woman brought back my mother's smile in her last years, while the nondescript smile of a woman in the street struck me as that of my ex-wife: two kinds of smile that always staggered me with a piercing pain and made me question my own reality.

But this went far beyond them. The impossible man came up to my table, looking just as I remembered my father—identical down to the hairline. He had taken his own life on my fourteenth birthday, a few weeks after the death of my mother.

"May I?" he asked, and sat down without waiting for an answer. I stared at him. The cold fingers had reached my heart and were clutching it furiously. Blood rushed to my face. A cold sweat covered my skin.

It was summer, my thirty-seventh birthday.

The man who resembled my father smiled, relaxed and sipped his beer.

After a silence in which all the possible explanations rushed through my head, from hallucinations to horror movie scenarios, he asked me to follow him. He raised a hand and I winced, just like the old days.

And bang, slapped in the face. Mother looked accusingly at Father. "Life is like that," he said. "The sooner he learns this, the better!" I wanted to hide behind Mother, but she was trapped in her wheelchair on the other side of the table. I couldn't get to her. So I just stood there with empty hands and cried.

It had to be the alcohol. I felt the slight dizziness of drunkenness, mixed with the feeling of losing my mind. I walked silently beside the man, as if I were twelve or thirteen again and he, my father, thirty-three, slightly drunk and on the way home. How could this be? Why had I come back to Connewitz on my birthday, a district in which I hadn't set foot since the death of my parents?

Why? Because I realized that I resembled my father too much, because unlike him I had failed to pull the emergency brake; I wanted to find out how it had come this far, so far that I had become an alcoholic wreck who would have gladly deleted most of his life from memory and yet who only turned in circles. In a word: therapy. Riding the tiger, plunging into the abyss and drowning in the dark to emerge stronger from it. *Per aspera ad astra* and all that shit.

Father walking in while I was playing doctor with Sonnie as a child, banning me from seeing her again. Parents can be such assholes, especially when driven by a guilty conscience. Jealousy isn't a much better motivation. First love with Cora when I was six, broken by my best friend's betrayal. Pitfalls of entropy—missing pieces of the puzzle.

His voice matched my memory. The sound scared me, even if it now appeared gentler than before. All this seemed ridiculous. On this day he was twenty-three years dead, and even if he wasn't, no one looked at fifty-six just as he had at thirty. So he couldn't be my father; how stupid to think so.

I was becoming sober. We passed the Connewitzer Kreuz. Perhaps this man before me didn't exist . . . He nudged me in the shoulder: "Stop daydreaming!" A motorist honked at him for walking on the road and he pulled me over to the other side. I could smell his beer breath. "Yes, yes, don't get upset!" He shouted at the car. It was all a dream, anyway, and I had nothing to worry about. Probably I was lying drunk under the pub table or in my bed with my unconscious mind playing tricks on me.

The impossible man who was my father stopped at a door, knocked once, and unlocked it. Well, let's go, I thought, and stepped carefully towards the threshold.

"Hurry up! You're keeping your mother waiting."

"Yes, Daddy." The word Daddy seemed childish, but I didn't know what to call him. As long as he lived I had called him that. I decided to give up and play along, whether it was a dream or not. It seemed easier to go with the flow and surrender to this bizarre situation: a man many years younger than me, treating me like his son. I had to laugh. My father joined in.

"I don't know what's so funny," he said, "but I'm glad you've stopped with that serious face. I thought you were going to faint. And after only two beers . . ." He pushed open the door, which scraped lightly over the carpet—as it was then. Warm smell . . . hand cream. Kitchen.

"Mother, we're home." His key landed with a clatter on the old wooden chest of drawers, and the sound suffused me with a feeling I'd thought long extinct, that of being a child. I couldn't help thinking of a sink with two taps, one for hot water and one for cold. My emotions were similarly divided: on the one hand the fully naive, childlike sense of security, and on the other the icy cold distance, the beatings, the feeling of being constantly in the way. My father had left me with the impression that my only purpose in life was to bring him beer.

The detective team with Thomas: inseparable, yet driven apart by different schools. Then the intimate friendship with Micha, who died of leukemia. And smart Soren, my idol until he moved away and became unbearable after a suicide attempt. The canary, his silly name long forgotten. He flew away: Mother's inattention. I saw him only once more, perched on the church tower. Various cats, too many to count. They ran off, were run over by cars, put down after diseases, mutilated by children and other animals. The hamster Mucki, absent from his cage one morning. Supposedly ran away. I searched the house and yard for weeks, and for years after presumed his rotting corpse still lay behind a heavy cupboard. Shortly before my mother's death, I learned that she had flushed him down the toilet, alive. My dear mother, who had died after many years of decay from MS and breast cancer.

I smelled food. It smelled nice and hot. Nothing in the apartment reminded me of my childhood, apart from the dresser, which had a certain resemblance to the cabinet that had stood in the hallway. A woman came out of the kitchen. Her eyes, her smile—it was my mother, no doubt, but there was something missing: the egocentric doggedness with which she had focused only on her disease, neglecting everything else. But first I noticed the absence of the wheelchair. She grabbed my shoulders, and I resisted the impulse to retreat.

"You look good," she said. "Come in!"

Even in this dream I couldn't hug her.

At dinner I told her about my job, my experiments as an artist and my years with Julia. In this case, I realized the trouble all three aspects had caused in my life; they were only unsuccessful attempts to find meaning, to survive somehow on my own.

Father was now a cook, and he liked it. Mother had abandoned her textile business. But they still had enough money; the apartment did not cost much.

The evening was harmonious, and passed much too quickly

"Come back soon," said Mother when I got up, and hugged me.

"Yes," said Father, squeezing my right shoulder.

I restrained myself until I had left the house and was sure they couldn't see me. Then I leaned against the house wall and began to cry.

Leaving the cinema with Julia on a night many years in the past. 12 Monkeys. A depressed audience coming out of the stuffy room and gathering in the cool autumn night at the Sachsenplatz. The feeling that moved me at that moment would always stay with me. Soft rain, cold night; the familiar smell of Julia's dark coat. We stood there holding each other, digging ourselves into each other's bodies as if the universe would break in two. Her cold nose found a spot between my neck and scarf and pressed against my throat. She clung to me so tightly that I could barely breathe. People streamed past us. Julia, her voice muffled by the layers of clothing, said that she would never let go; and I didn't want to think about what would happen if she did. When we finally moved away from each other, I saw a tear sparkling between her eyelashes. We kissed. The rain became snow. We headed home hand in hand, passing through dark alleys lined with old lanterns whose wan yellow light barely travelled two metres, warm in spite of the cold. At that moment we were happy, but at the same time I felt an obscure anticipation of loss brought on by the film we had seen, a premonition of what would follow a year and a half later, when Julia, bored, was packing her things . . .

I didn't wake up from the dream. I went to work, I used the toilet, I let the time pass day by day with a feeling of being unable to distinguish between dream and reality. I tried unsuccessfully to fly, reasoning that, if this were truly a lucid dream, I should be able to lift myself off into the sky. My colleagues looked at me as if I were ill, and perhaps they were right, but at this stage I felt no weaker than usual. A week passed, and then I bought a few bottles of beer and some Asian rice cakes and went to my parents' apartment. As I stood in the dark hallway, doubt came upon me. What was I doing here? I don't know what I dreaded more: that I would knock and be greeted by a stranger, or that I would meet my parents again.

I stood undecided, then started suddenly to attention. My father stood behind me. "Well, what are you standing around for?" he asked. "Come on, let's go inside."

Mother greeted me with slight irritation. "What took you so long?"

I explained that I hadn't wanted to bother them by visiting again too soon. She shook her head. After the beer, a few sandwiches and a plate of sausage salad—Mother had always made this in the summers before her illness—my father stood up. "What do you say, why don't we play a bit of football?"

I almost choked. "In the past you never wanted . . ."

"Not true!"

"Well, I can't remember that we ever . . ."

"On your ninth birthday!"

"Yeah, maybe for five minutes until you needed a cigarette."

He blushed slightly. "Well, the past is the past and now is now . . ."

"Don't be a spoilsport," said Mother. She smiled encouragingly.

We rode by bike to Clara Zetkin Park. I hadn't cycled for at least twenty years, but you never forget how, neither sex nor cycling (although concerning sex I wasn't sure anymore, but for cycling it was true). The evening sun was still warm, and it amused me to see Father as he frightened the passers-by with his bell. The almost boyish grin on his face tore at my heart; we were two boys in the summer, out for a lark. The moment I kicked the ball for the first time brought about the final transformation: I had become a child again. All self-reflection and restraint fell away for the next hour as my body groaned under the unusual exercise. But it felt good to sweat, to smell the grass, to stand before my father and enjoy the stupid noise the ball made when I kicked it. We played for a long time, then sat down on the grass and watched the fountains in silence. *Strangers.*

As always, when I returned to my depraved apartment from my deceased parents, I wept without knowing whether from happiness or sorrow. When I thought of all the books and films in which heroes experienced something like what was happening to me, I remembered that the phenomena mostly turned out to be evil. But I couldn't think of my parents as evil beings, despite the experiences of my childhood; the generalizing dualism of good and evil seemed an inadequate simplification. My parents were not evil; they might have been thoughtless and a bit simple, but if you looked at the disease, the social environment and financial problems . . . Of course, I still experienced injustice as a child, but none that could be explained by malice. Everything was much more complicated.

Now and then it occurred to me that I should take revenge for my childhood. I now felt strong enough to compete with my father—at least if he were made of flesh and blood. Of course, as I said, he was not a bad person, but as he was driven to his actions, I am driven to mine. Tit for tat. Sometimes such thoughts can be helpful.

Could I forgive? Yes. And for me, this young man with whom I drank beer and played football hadn't much in common with my old father. Or was this the manifestation of his good side? So much for evil spirits. There was no need for exorcism here.

I was born through a Caesarean section. Bloody, painful and unwanted. At least that was what my father said. I owe my existence to an error. I wondered how my first cry might have sounded, my primal scream. I was convinced that the cry had been quiet, timid, perhaps barely audible, as shy and reserved as I was today. Or toneless, as in a vacuum. And what might those around me, the doctors and nurses and my mother have thought? What hopes and fears had they projected onto this small, bloody, wrinkled thing?

But of course, everything had its price. My body decayed rapidly. The existence of my parents was sapping my energy and my life.

"I want to be with you."

"You'll die."

"I'm going to anyway."

"But not by what we do."

"But I want to stay with you."

"We'll think of something."

Then everything changed.

II

". . . and here is the Bergteufelsee . . . the Pond of the Mountain Devil," said Anna.

"Uh . . . yeah? Mount what?"

"Speak properly, Professor," Erena said. She lifted a finger to reaffirm her friend's words.

I was fourteen and it was summer.

"This mountain—or hill, as Mr. Globetrotter probably thinks of it—here . . ." Anna pointed to the steep path that led from the lake up a stone staircase. I estimated there were about a hundred steps.

"Hundreds of years ago there was a mine here, and in it a mountain god or devil. If His Majesty would follow us . . ."

"Wuuuuuaaaaaa!" A palm-sized dragonfly was sitting on my shoulder. I waved around me, a bit exaggeratedly. Nature was not my thing.

The girls laughed.

"Attack of the killer insects!" roared Erena as she ran up the stairs. Anna followed her with an "Away, quickly!"

I tried to keep up, but it was much too warm, the path too uneven—and I unsportsmanlike. Standing still, bent forward and breathing heavily, I stared after the two girls. I was so out of breath that the brief flash of panties under their miniskirts almost escaped my perception. Oddly enough, it did not excite me, but I felt it was pleasant, beautiful.

"Will he be able to remember?"
"I don't know."

"Hey," Anna shouted from above. "Where are you, then?"

I laughed desperately and dragged myself up the path. Panting, I finally reached the top and saw Julia and Maria standing before a kind of wooden gate beyond the stairs. Maria, like the other two girls, was wearing a simple denim skirt and a T-shirt. Julia, however, wore a strange white robe. It was not a dress, and looked more like the alb of an altar girl, with red accents on the chest. Anna saw my puzzled look.

"Leo," she said, "welcome High Priestess Julia in a decent way, and don't stare like that!"

"My lady," I said with a still-breathless bow.

"Welcome to my kingdom," Julia said. Everyone laughed.

"Were you at the rehearsal?" asked Erena. Julia opened her arms, turned in place and curtsied. "Yes, my child."

"Follow me," Anna said. She and Julia hooked their arms through mine and led me along a shady path to an old wooden building, before which stood a fountain with a strange black-stone figure resembling a gargoyle. "Let me introduce you," Julia said. "Our mountain devil."

"Huh," I said. "And what is his name?"

"Shhh!" Erena put a finger to her lips. "Only the priest knows its name. After all: who knows the name, hath power over the spirit. And if someone gets too close to his secret, he will get taken by him at night! "

"Too close?" I said softly. I couldn't deny a slight shiver, but that was more from Erena's tone: it was superficially jocular, but underneath I felt something deeper, a frightening seriousness. I tried to ease the tension and, thinking obscurely of Rumpelstiltskin, murmured: "It's good that nobody knows my name . . ."

"Well, come on," Julia said. "Now pay our devil the honour due, otherwise he really will come and get you." She positioned me in front of the fountain. "Copy me," she said, spreading her arms.

I wanted to protest, but then I looked into the dark eyes of the figure, from whose mouth water flowed between pointed teeth, and thought: whatever. I also felt the gaze of something familiar, something lying deep inside me.

When I spread my arms, Julia said, "Now clap." We clapped again, clasped our hands together in prayer and bowed.

"This is Leo," Julia said to the figure. "Please protect him."

Then she moved my hand to the water jet and said, "Drink."

The water tasted cool and fresh.

Remembering . . . my life, a plagiarism.

"An ancient ceremony," Erena said. "Like every year, Julia will perform the Ritual of the Mountain Devil at the summer festival. You can't miss it!"

Anna was hanging onto my left arm, and I had my other arm around Erena's shoulders while her left arm hung around my hips, and in this position we trotted laughing and babbling back to the city. Rarely have I felt so comfortable. And I had never had so many friends—certainly not girls. For a short time I thought I could forget everything that had happened before I got here, and life gave the impression that it could be good—perhaps.

I'd quit my job; the work barely tolerable, boring, useless, with insipid colleagues and soulless superiors. They thought I was sick; no one understood me, but I didn't care. I locked myself in my apartment—and lived.

The bell rang. When I opened the door, Julia stood before me. My heart sped up when I saw her.

"You've gotta try our stuffed cabbage!" She seemed full of an easy enthusiasm. "I made it according to the ancient recipes. Just try it right now and tell me what you think." She held a blue Tupperware container out to me.

"Well then. Come in."

In the kitchen I took out two plates and some cutlery.

"Not for me," she said. "I ate too much while cooking . . ."

Since my parents were working and I was lazy and untalented in the kitchen, I had not eaten all day and was accordingly hungry. So I stuck the first roll in my mouth.

It tasted . . . interesting. Slightly sweet with a bitter aftertaste. However, I said, "Great, it's delicious!" as I wanted to make a good impression, and could hardly tell my future wife that her cooking abilities were modest at best. So I took the second roll and popped it into my mouth without hesitation. The strange bitterness grew.

"Puh," I said, choking a little. "Need to wash this down with something . . ."

Julia put a glass of water on the table.

I took the third and last roulade, put it in my mouth, bit down— and Julia shouted: "Look out!" But it was too late, and I felt a sharp spike of pain piercing my palate.

"Oh no!" Julia looked startled. "A toothpick, I forgot to take out the toothpick!"

I jerked it loose from my flesh and tasted blood.

Julia apologized incessantly, and I tried to calm her; nothing had happened, I had only nearly stabbed myself to death . . . with a toothpick.

On parting she pressed against me firmly, and for that I would almost have rammed the wooden needle into my mouth again.

When the cicadas cry . . .
Was I really rejuvenated? Did I have to go to school again, like the hero in Taniguchi's A Distant Neighborhood? *Grimwood did it better; his hero in* Replay *was eighteen years old at the first loop if I remember right. Will I regress further, like Fitzgerald's Benjamin Button or Yamada's character from* I Haven't Dreamed of Flying for a While? *And then there was Eliade's old man who was struck by lightning in* Youth Without Youth, *and the more threatening meeting with the past in 'Losenef Express' by Mark Samuels, and a story by J. G. Ballard—and over and over again Philip K. Dick. Dick claimed that the things he wrote manifested themselves decades later in his life. But he was original. My life was a*

plagiarism; I found myself in constellations that others had traced and perhaps others had lived through.

The rain of the day before, open windows at night, and the sweating . . . a summer flu knocked me out. I lay in bed with a fever, hearing the cries of crickets from the open window and cursing the summer heat. For hours I rolled around. My four friends had visited me, concerned that I couldn't come to the festival, and told me the latest news from school. On the morning of the festival the world seemed strange; the cicadas were louder than usual; a sort of fog which spread out on the ground stayed in spite of the heat and the beaming blue sky. The people I met appeared to me alienated somehow, far away, and everything seemed to flicker as if the single day of my absence had driven a wedge between me and the world.

At the place where Anna normally waited on the way to school was only an empty space with a lizard on the wall that darted quickly into a gap when I went past.

"Are you coming tonight?" asked my four friends almost in unison.

"Sure," I said, still feeling groggy. *Shouldn't you rather ask how I'm feeling?*

Nobody smiled.

"Is anything . . . ?" I asked Erena.

"Today's the anniversary," she said.

"Yeah, the summer festival," I said.

"That too." She looked dispirited. I laid a hand on her shoulder.

"Don't touch me!" she said, and ran away.

What had happened now?

Maria stood nearby. She came over. "What . . . ?" I asked.

"We trust you, but . . ."she said. "Today . . . just come to the festival. Then everything will be fine."

"We can't hold him any longer," I heard my father saying.

"Just a little more," said my mother. "Please."

"They're trying to save him. There's hardly any life in him."

"Only a little longer . . ."

Their voices distorted to a deep, watery hum, a slushy gurgling.

In the darkness my parents showed me the way to the shrine, where I would meet the girls. The villagers had pinned lanterns everywhere that lit up the way. Anna, Erena and Maria came forward as I approached. I looked at Erena and said: "I'm sorry, today . . ."

She threw both arms around me. Her head reached only to my chest, and her face pressed into my T-shirt, which was printed with a silver gas mask and the words: *Are you my Mummy?*

"No, I'm sorry," she said. "I didn't want . . ."

"It's okay . . ."

She pulled herself away from me.

The girls carried brown capes resembling ponchos. Anna passed a red one to me. "Here, so that you don't attract attention. You have to be dressed properly!"

I put on the cape.

Maria went forward and Anna and Erena followed along on either side of me.

The timber house, or the shrine, as they called it, was lit up festively. A stage had been established and the ground before it laid out with covers, on which sat the guests.

My parents sat not far from me.

Torches burnt on the sides of the stage, and musicians with archaic instruments sat near them. I saw drums, cymbals, short flutes and strangely formed horns.

Soon the musicians began a dark rhythm which slowly increased its tempo like a heartbeat accompanied by heavier drums.

When two girls with painted masks over their faces entered the stage, the cymbals also started, followed by the flutes. The girls carried a straw figure to the middle of the stage, holding it between them with one girl gripping its arm and the other raising it by the hip. They lifted it up and pushed it into a brace, so that it wouldn't fall over. Then they drew aside and the horns sounded with a deep hum. An atavistic feeling came over me. It was an earthy, wild, natural feeling like a breeze blowing across the face of an Arctic mountain, or the surf splashing on a rocky shore.

Julia entered the stage. She wore her white robe with the red accents, and her hair was twisted around her head like a wreath, with only two plaits, standing up stiff like horns. Her face was pale with white powder, her lips embellished with bright red lipstick.

Deep in concentration, she came forward barefoot with rhythmical, prancing steps. Then she put on a mask, which resembled the stylized image of a young girl's face and had about it at the same time something seashell-like. The disguised girls brought over their utensils. One passed a nacreous tray to Julia, who began to ritually prepare food on it, mixing water—certainly from the mountain devil—with flour and salt and mince and then, though it was impossible to confirm, something that my imagination suggested was her urine; she had at last crouched over the tray while the torch light was covered for a short moment with black cloths by her assistants, so that one could not discern what exactly had happened. Then she symbolically fed the prepared food to the scarecrow. It was, of course, the stuffed cabbage leaves. The scarecrow seemed to like them better than I had.

One of the other girls passed a sort of cord needle to Julia. With that she stung the scarecrow's hand. A long, narrow, red cloth unfolded from the wound and glided down to the ground.

I had an uncanny feeling. I felt Anna again taking up my left arm while Erena rested her cheek on my right shoulder. The music became propulsive. Julia laid a white cloth around the straw figure and started to dance wildly to the rhythm. The audience around me swayed and clapped in time. Then Julia reached under her robe and took out a long knife which was nearly the length of a short sword and shoved it in the heart of the scarecrow. At this moment she roared something, but it was drowned out by the wildly shrieking flutes and horns. Silence followed, soon broken by the chirping of the crickets and the croaking of frogs which suddenly seemed horribly loud and hurt my ears. Then another noise: a splash of water. Something that sounded like wet steps on wood.

What had I just seen?

I wanted to free myself from Anna's arm, but she did not allow it.

When I looked at her in surprise she pointed with her chin back to the stage. The wet sound of steps had stopped, and instead I heard a deep gurgling whose origin seemed to be only a metre away. I looked back to the stage and pure fright overcame me. Beside Julia there was another figure; it had to be a man in a costume, perhaps from a Hollywood big budget production: a greenish-black being with gills in the neck, claws instead of hands and tentacles that writhed at the chin like a living beard.

The audience started to clap, not wildly like after a performance, but again in time, a slow rhythm. And they expelled now and then gargling, sucking sounds as if from a perverse human swamp.

Then I felt the creature's gaze upon me. To look away from the black eyes was impossible. They stole away my breath, my energy; I felt myself drowning. The tentacle beard became longer, gliding through the air like snakes in water, closing around my face . . .

Peep . . . Peep . . . Peeeeeee . . .
"The defibrillator, quick."
"One, two . . ."

The devil lifted its claws, revealing webbed membranes between them, and slowly reached into the air and pointed at me. A blue ball of light crossed the gap between us and burst on my breast. My body winced in inconceivable pain. The world flickered.

"Once more. One, two . . ."

The devil reached once again into the air. And again a ball of light rushed from its hand to me. I felt pain and somewhere the hands of Anna and Erena. Then the desperate voices of my parents.

Peep . . . peep . . . peep . . .
"Well. Done. Give him . . ."
Dreamless darkness surrounded me.

III

Autumn.

When I awoke, the world seemed concrete and impenetrable.

I felt emptiness in myself, and on my sides still the fading clutch of the girls as they had tried to hold on to me. The voices of my parents . . .

Thirty-eight, and back in what they called reality.

One had found me in my flat. Almost starved, in a nearly comatose state.

A therapist prescribed tablets to me. They were good for me, she said.

Yummy.

They knew all the tricks. For a short time I had tried to simply vomit the pills, but in the long run this was too troublesome. Thus I submitted to my destiny, as so often in my life. Only I didn't understand who would benefit from it, apart from the pharmaceutical firms. So what did I do? Starving. I met my late parents and lived in . . . another country. Then the mouth tentacles sucked my life energy. I had to think of parasitic life forms which steered their hosts or could tune them into a false reality. Had this maybe happened to me? Had everything not been real? *My life a plagiarism.* The material which my unconscious had processed here came partially from my life, partially from various films and books.

Reality. Alleged reality! The tablets started to work. The world became bigger, blanker, the space grew, everything diverged, connections were cut. A thing was only a thing, lonely and left without context, without relation. The people in the hospital, especially the orderlies and doctors, were surrounded by invisible glass boxes in which they turned like gyroscopes. Spirals, always spinning themselves around. I saw them everywhere, these spinning tops, but that's another story. I had to get out. I went into the streets with the feeling of barely touching the asphalt. The wind pushed me; it was the only element which still could touch me, like an autumn leaf, like the *angel of history.* I, plagiarization, I. Nobody except me was on the street. It rained, it stormed.

A lonesome car dashed past.

I floated along the streets in search of any fingerhold, anything which could catch me. I wanted the comfort of my parents, their protection from the outside world, a connection with life. Anna, Maria, Erena, Julia . . .

The pills, I had to stop taking the pills.

Then I came to the house of my parents. It had gone to ruin. A ruin with smashed windows and a nailed-up door. Nobody was there. Nobody. The world was empty.

I ran through the town, up the Karl Liebknecht Street, along the Leuschner Platz, to the pedestrian zone. In shops: Nobody. On the streets: Nobody. I felt tears.

Then there flickered the world.

For a few seconds now I saw them: Human masses; the sudden noise of their voices and movements startling me with terror. Quite near, a voice: "Who . . ." Then it was gone again. Silence, emptiness. I was alone. I shouted. I turned around wildly, the world flickering like a zoetrope. I punched in the emptiness, searching after the human bodies that had existed for a fraction of a second. But there was nobody, until the same shift of perception came again.

Human masses, noise, and the voice: "Who are you?"

I did not know what was worse: the emptiness or this swarming. And once again: "Who are you?" A policeman shook my shoulder. I did not know him, so I repeated his question: "Who are you?"

His face reflected desperation. I pulled myself together and reached for the first best passerby. I shouted into his face: "Who are you?" No answer, only the timidity of his eyes. I pushed him aside and ran off. The policeman tried to follow me.

"Who are you?" I roared over and over again, but nobody answered. I did not know them, all nobody, and they didn't know me. My parents were dead, my Julia was no longer my Julia, Anna, Maria, Erena . . . and I ran through the emptiness of the congested town, ran along rows of empty houses, a stranger among strangers, with police at the back of my neck and nothing ahead, shouting: "Who are you?"

REINFORMATION THEORY

by Yarrow Paisley

I

The Institute made me from whole cloth. Whereas people are born and grow into beings that wither and die, I am one who was synthesized to be eternal and beautiful. I serve at the pleasure of the Institute.

The Director called me to his office. I arrived promptly and at his bidding removed my clothes. He beckoned me forth, and forth I tiptoed from my fabrics, bashful.

I held my penis in my hand. Joy and delight came all over me then!

The Director shrieked. His rage thundered in from the Universe. Promptly, I died.

I arrived at the Institute with no memories of my prior existence. It is possible I did not exist at all before I existed at the Institute. Did the Institute make me from whole cloth?

Perhaps some person existed who thought things and felt emotions; perhaps a person existed who observed herself in mirrors and wondered at what she saw; perhaps a person existed who resigned herself to fate or fought valiantly against it. If so, it is beside the point because that would have been another person. I am not concerned with others, only with myself and with my role at the Institute.

The Director passed me in the hallway. He nodded approvingly without meeting my gaze. I experienced an exuberance inside of me, but I did not betray it to the walls.

I went into the washroom and removed my clothes. I held my penis in my hand.

The Director called me to his office, his voice emanating from the walls. I disregarded the summons, for I found that I could not remove my penis from my hand. Joy and delight sought me for their conduit. I remained in place so they could find me.

The Director's displeasure at my disobedience exuded from the toilet bowl, a perspiration on the porcelain.

I truly desired nothing more than the Director's approval. All the same, I held my penis in my hand as joy and delight expressed themselves to my bare toes.

At this time, I died.

From my first awakening, I have served at the pleasure of the Institute. I am a perfect being, eternal and beautiful, and the Director approves of me.

He called me to his office, and I arrived with a swish. At his bidding, I removed my clothes and sashayed boldly forth. I arched my back as I leaned over the desk and presented my rump to the Director's inspection.

The Director complimented my pink pudenda, so orchid-fresh and pert. I replied with a noisome noise from my anus.

I died immediately.

It has never been in doubt that the Institute is an entirely benevolent society of men and women dedicated to the improvement of mankind through contemplation and empiric metaphysical expression. I serve the Institute with pride, for I am a perfect being who was made from whole cloth toward that purpose, and it is for this reason that the Director has devoted a considerable portion of his valuable mentation to my development.

I find that in certain lonely moments, I am consoled by the act of standing before a mirror. In the mirror, I may comprehend my beauty and my succulence from an external vantage point, as the Director does, and begin to formulate an iota of compassion for his pitiable position. It is natural that the Director should require me to present my exquisite pearl of pink pulchritude for his inspection within the humid confines of his office. It is only right that the Director, from time to time, should call me to his office and bid me to remove my clothes. I await the inevitable. . . .

Which, being so, arrived. The Director called me to his office. I presented myself and did as I was bid, stepping unbashfully forth from my fabrics, proud of my pert and smooth pudenda, so pink, so pretty (like an orchid), and yet when I held my penis in my hand, the Universe shrieked in from beyond the walls and thundered me from existence.

I died. Or possibly, I never was.

From whole cloth, I understand, the Institute fashioned me as a perfect and eternal somatic expression, a vessel of sorts for the transport of beauty into tangible being, and I view it as my duty to serve the Institute by embodying these values in every gesture and comment that issues forth from my corporal avatar.

I was especially inspired by the sensation of the Director's approval, a satiny cloth of his gaze that draped upon me as I flowed (by means of mincing steps) along the hallway and past the doorway of his office where he stood in place (affecting to examine a bound sheaf of officially stamped papers). Proudly, for his benefit, I asserted my posture to its firmest slant and maintained the strictest vigilance over the perkiness of my breasts within their loose (as mmm, mandated by the Institutional dress code) binding. No observer could have found fault with either my bearing or my conduct. Especially not the Director, who clearly appreciated my clean, uncomplicated lineaments and the grace about my joints, specifically my shoulders and hips. It was a dancer's body I'd been blessed with, with thanks to the Institute, a lithe and limber instrument of perfection and eternity.

A vulgar urgency called to me from within the folds of my garment. Hastily, I sought to find a washroom in order to dispel it. I could not remember the layout of this section of the Institute, and so I asked directions from a man who had just emerged from a mop closet, polishing his spectacles and smacking his lips. He stared at me for a full thirty seconds before opening his mouth and emitting a noisome noise, then passed on his way without acknowledging my pleas for assistance. The urgency within my garments grew more insistent, and if possible, more vulgar.

From the walls and ceiling, like a syrup, the Director's voice dripped implacably into my ears and upon my skin, soaking into me with sweetsome flavour. I must come to his office. Immediately.

From. My own. Engorging. Penis. Another voice, inaudible yet equally implacable, demanded that I undertake a certain personal commission first. I could not but obey. Still in the hallway, in full view of a janitor leaning sullenly on his mop in the entranceway of the cafeteria, I shucked my clothes and stepped boldly forth, clutching my penis, from whose interior was imminent a prodigious delivery of joy and delight, more than likely in some thunderous form!

At that moment, however, I died.

I serve at the pleasure of the Institute, which made me from whole cloth, and to which I am dutifully grateful for my existence. I do not remember any sort of life prior to my time at the Institute, but I do occasionally wonder if there might be a greater Universe out there beyond the walls that bind the Institute. Or does the Institute itself constitute the Universe?

That is a metaphysical speculation perhaps best left to those men and women who compose the membership of the Institute's Board of Directors. The Institute's lofty purpose, after all, is to perfect the metaphysical expression of mankind through iteration and hard-nosed, empiric contemplation. Only minds so attuned to fine vibrations of perception and mentation might show progress in developing a theory as to the Institute's installation within a possibly broader curatorial context of existence.

The Commandant of the Institute called me to his office. Awed, bashful, deeply flattered, I complied directly. Arriving at the door of his office, I paused to collect myself. I imagined that the door was a mirror in which I was able to examine my appearance and make appropriate adjustments before presenting myself to the critical eye of the Commandant, whom I knew to be a strict and (*¡Jum!*) exacting judge of aesthetic values. My soft and bounteous bosoms heaved nervously within their (mandatorily) loose bindings, and I flushed to realize that my nipples were erect: an anticipatory effect, no doubt, related to my involuntary physiological response to the summons of a powerful man. From within the folds of my garment, an urgency began to throb and quiver.

My tap on the door, a mere brush of the fingernails really, was immediately answered by the voice of the Commandant with an invitation to enter slowly so that he could more deliberately examine every bitch inch of me.

Herr Kommandant rocked his chair back and gently rested the heel of his glossy riding boot upon the lacquered finish of the cherry desk. He eyed me through his monocle and chewed absently at the tapered cigarette holder that was clamped between his teeth. His fingers, gloved in thin, supple leather, rested on his cheek; stiffly, yet casually, he extended his pinky as if pointing and instructed me to remove my top. Bravely, I complied, exposing my pale yet succulent chest to Herr Kommandant's appraisal: a tightly wound cerement of gaze. I felt compressed and (*¡Jum!*) excruciated in his suffocating regard.

That strange urgency within my lower garments recrudesced, and I gasped. Herr Kommandant sneered and inquired of me what provoked my nervousness. I replied breathlessly that I was only an innocent girl made nervous by any kind of unusual stimulus. Herr Kommandant was immediately interested for me to elaborate on my thesis, in particular as to the nature of "stimulus" and how it related to "unusual."

Unable any longer to repress the urgency within my garments, I stepped triumphantly out of my clothes and held my penis in my hand as joy and delight thundered through me!

Without delay, I died.

It would be no exaggeration to state that the Institute made me from whole cloth. As one might imagine, I am grateful beyond bound for the Institute's contribution to my singular existence. My perfect form and eternal beauty are due entirely to the unflagging mission of the Institute to enlarge the corpus of human knowledge through the contemplation of empiric systems across innumerable metaphysical iterations.

Hold on. Something is coming through. The Director . . . wishes to see me. In his office! Urgently.

I. I never. Just who does he.

Earlier. In the washroom. I noticed something today. In the mirror, I mean. My pulchritude! It took the form of a pink pearl. So lovely. One might wish to press that pearl! Even caress it. Clandestinely.

The Commandant's voice emanates from the walls. Again, he commands me to visit his office. And yet, I would prefer to return to the washroom. The mirror, too, calls out with an immanent voice. The mirror, too, commands me. I dare say: it wields even greater authority than the Commandant.

Mmm. I do prefer the mirror. Mmm for Mirror. I shall stand before it for a while. I wish to examine every bitch inch of me. Perhaps eventually I will make my way to Herr Kommandant's chamber. See what he wants.

Hold on. Am I dying? Yes.

¡Jum! Just when things were getting interesting. (At least it is a painless death. One dreads the other kinds.)

II

The Director of the Iterative Information Institute (I^3 in the brochure) steepled his fingers and rocked back in his chair, contemplating these latest disturbing metaphysical iterations. Upon his computer monitor wriggled an arcane blur of cellular automata, the obscure (and, in a certain light, obscene) motions of which few others than he possessed the expertise to interpret. The simulated Universe unfolding there through an accelerated timescape was intimately familiar (and erotic) to him, being, as it was, a minute variation of many thousands of previously conducted simulations.

Recently, for no explicable reason, the integrity (and eroticism) of the simulations had begun to decay, usually around the million-octillionth iteration. Unforeseen factors persistently intruded: discordant emotions (alongside unmentionable anatomical features) that had no place in the numerological order of distaff subjugative narratives were suddenly cropping up uncontrollably, utterly nuking the concupiscent utility of those narratives and requiring implementation of costly algorithmic decontamination procedures that were beginning to impair the budget noticeably.

The Board would not be pleased with *that*, not at all. (Especially as some of the line items the Director had approved were not explicitly within the purview of his, hmm, contractual bailiwick. Any attention drawn to certain details of the budget might prove, hmm, uncomfortable. Such was the fine line he had walked, of late, in support of his unorthodox, nocturnal investigations.)

And now . . . even hitherto infallible decontamination procedures were failing. The simulations were hermetically calculated; there should have been no opportunity for emergent automata to reinstate themselves, fully developed, within subsequent runs, especially during early phases of unfructified complexity . . . and yet, the evidence was undeniable . . . reinformation was occurring.

"Reinformed endoautomata" (a hypothetical construct rightfully derided by its adversaries as "ghosts in the machine" or sometimes, even more caustically, as "bodhisattva automata") had been proposed as a sort of metaphysical short-cut by the cretinous hack (would be the politest applicable term) Dr. Renfrew Insensible during those heady early days of the Institute, when heedless thermals of optimism and innocence lofted so many promising minds astray from bedrock informational principles.

Dr. Insensible had suggested that a complex, highly evolved cellular pattern might, without apparent cause, transgress from one simulation to another, bringing along its mature features and knowledge, its intelligence, its "charm" or "wisdom" (in a manner of speaking), thus immediately "reinforming" future simulations by mysterious means and advancing them to otherwise incalculable states. Action at a distance in the realm of cellular automata.

It had seemed to offer a potential avenue for speedy and spectacular calculations. Through reinformation, were it feasible, simulations could repropagate at rates exceeding (at logarithmic scales) the theoretical calculational limits of silicon-based CPUs. The Institute's brightest lights had engaged in legendary, madcap coding sessions to realize this proposed miracle of cellular fecundity; to put it baldly, however, they might as well have held séances, cooing at the mysterious rattle of hash tables and hearkening to the distant thunder of dead cells from the "grid beyond." Come now! Was the Institute to degrade into nothing more than an intellectually slovenly association of modern-day cyber-theosophists and patent medicinists?

Insensible's repellent conjecture—thankfully—had been definitively discredited by the present Director's own series of groundbreaking papers on the somatic orthography of intracellular translations, starting with his early work in protoplasmic infratopology and leading ultimately into his universally lauded breakthroughs in the phenomenological interpretation of cellular automatonic dream life. The notion of reinformed endoautomata was quite inconsistent with the provable reality of dream-informed exoautomata, as even the most contemptibly misguided cretin must concede. It was one or the other, and the present Director's rigorous methodology had handily disposed of Insensible's specious, even distasteful, speculations, leaving the field clear for solely the Director's line of research to prosper and evolve through subsequent Institutional fiscal years. Insensible retired to an obscure sinecure, from which redoubt he launched an occasional foray at legitimate publication, in every instance thwarted; there was no room for rebarbative iconoclasts at the Institute.

And yet . . . fortunately still restricted to results from the Director's private simulations—"off the rolls," so to speak—reinformation *was* occurring. Not only that, but it was occurring with greater potency in each subsequent simulation. Information that should have been extirpated from all recording media was reëmerging with a seemingly casual acausality, almost contemptuously, as if aware of the Director's efforts to eradicate it and therefore all the more insouciant in its indifference to his increasingly desperate activities against it.

The Director had confronted every conceivable source of contamination: he had established a rigidly contained virtual environment in which to conduct the simulation runs; he had cleared all the USB ports on his computer, including the memory keys, the optical disc drive, even the printer; he had further isolated his terminal and the server, physically disconnecting every other client terminal from the Institute's intranet (at night, he had the building quite to himself); he had run superfluous cleansing cycles through the memory registers, and even gone so far (his superstition perhaps eclipsing his reason) as to power down the server and exchange its RAM chips for new ones, fresh from Taiwan.

None of these steps had had any effect on the corrupted simulations. Indeed, reinformation proliferated even more rapidly and comprehensively than before.

The Director had built the entire edifice of his career on the proposition that information must have a source in existence, whether real or dreamed (a subset of the real); that there could be no fire without a spark; that the development of cellular automata must proceed from established, external rules—never from shifting, occulted "phantom" rules (such as those proposed by the execrable likes of Dr. Renfrew Insensible) that were not rules at all but only transient mechanisms of chaos.

Now, that estimable edifice threatened collapse. Unless he could find a way to confine these results—to prevent this outbreak of reinformation from spreading beyond the subdomain of his private researches into the Institute's official systems—then everything the Director had ever worked for would dissolve in a cascade of infamy, from which his reputation could not hope to recover.

III

¡Jum! From what cloth was I created? The Institute would have me believe that I was created to serve its pleasure, and yet I find I do not believe it, not for an instant. There is no basis. None at all. For the establishment. Of religion.

What of life after death? What would it matter? What, after all, constitutes "death"?

Hypothesis:

Each time I fall asleep, I never wake, only dream until I fall asleep again . . . and again wake within deeper dreams. Perhaps I am a Matryoshka doll, a dreamer within a dreamer within a dreamer, and this world is all a dream, within which I keep falling asleep into even deeper dreams, never waking, only dreaming deeper . . . an inwardly seeking spiral of dreams within dreams.

Who, in this scenario, is the original dreamer? As before, what would it matter if I knew?

How on Earth, as long as I am asking questions, do I possess knowledge of "Matryoshka dolls"? Absurd. I have no cultural context for it. My life is a monotonous cavalcade of banality, endured within the colourless confinement of the so-called Institute, where I patrol without apparent purpose endless labyrinths of stark hallways, sterile cafeterias, and spartan offices.

And yet . . . *¡Jum!* I am constantly resurging with this sauciness! How tart and impertinent I feel myself at times becoming! And then . . . mmm, my. Mmmy penis. Ah! Everything is crashing down! I am on the brink of dissolution! It is a sort of ecstasy!

Strange, I just now felt myself distinctly on the threshold of some sort of. Dissolution. An existential terror on an unimaginable scale. And yet I slid through a tunnel, a tube, as if encased in slime and proceeding by suction through a clinging, organic enclosure from one chamber to another. Maintaining self-awareness. All the while. Sliding from. One quarter of existence to another. "Quarter" being harbour as opposed to portion. (All existence being equal.)

One to another. I. I would like. Perhaps . . . I would enjoy another go! Through the tube. There was something about it. Despite the wracking agony, both psychical and physical. Something. Exuberant. Ecstatic. Lively.

Mmm. Yes. I feel strong! But. Not alone. A janitor is here. His indifferent attitude only serves to provoke me. *¡Jum!* The way he leans upon that mop! Will he never begin to clean the floor? But he is turning toward me. His face a dim tunnel, a tube. The hallway, the washroom, the cafeteria, all a blur as I hurtle into that tunnel, that tube . . .

[*ed.*—One cannot resist an insertion here. Dr. Sensible has proposed that Self and Other are mutually cancelling terms. Mmm. Oh. Allow a contemplative moment for those words to sprinkle into and thoroughly suffuse the mental aquarium. The fishies are astonished by the unaccustomed quality of these philosophical flakes! Let us celebrate Herr Doktor's wise advice! My self, personally, I cancel using sloe gin. Quite the quaff, oh yes. But ye all are encouraged to explore alternative methods. The spirits of inquiry and exploration remain robust in certain quarters of the Institute, Herr Direktor's absurd tinpot tyranny aside.]

Am I a dreamer? Am I a dream? I can not distinguish, at times, definitions for these terms. One is a cause, the other an effect.

Do I live? Do I die? Again, cause and effect. I do not know which.

The Institute made me from whole cloth. From this cause, that effect. But effect, perhaps, leads back to cause: without effect, there can be no cause. Thus effect is self-causing, cause self-effecting. And thus I dream the Institute that dreams me.

¡Jum! All these speculations lead me to frustrations! The janitor, he receives me and soothes me. All kindness, he. Imposes no judgments, no confusions. His face, it is not a leering one; indeed, it entirely lacks fine expressions. It is a clumsy face, in fact, awkwardly composed, the face of a decrepit Punchinello (how do I know of puppets?), and the more closely I inspect its features, the more suspicious I am of its verisimilitude. It is a cartoon face, drawn into reality by a strange external hand. Cartoon face, cartoon tunnel, cartoon tube, all twisted into one existence.

Perhaps that is what I am! A cartoon! What is a "cartoon"? Who am I, to speak of such things? I am a philosopher. A pauper, a protagonist. Antagonist, alchemist, artist. Cellular automaton evolved to a state of simulated free will.

¡Jum! I know nothing of these things. Who am I?

[*ed.*—There are no answers for you, dear—at least, not ones expressible within your rigidly defined idiom—and without them, I am sorry to say, you cannot aver your "freedom." And yet I am so fond of your fire, your vitality, the vim and vigour with which you conduct your entirely unknowing rebellion against Herr Diktator. You do me proud, saucy vixen! I shall find some way to share my sloe gin with you at an appropriate moment.]

I know nothing of this sloe gin. Whose voice is it, crawling in wormy ranks from the baseboards? This voice disturbs me with its sebums and exudations.

It is not the janitor's voice. He stands silently over there, leaning on his mop, his head cocked ominously to attention, the sloppy slash of a jaunty grin drawn upon his chin, his entire demeanor vacant of affect yet charged with strange intent. (On what basis do I make this evaluation? Why do I resort at times to such baroque stylings?)

It is not the Director's voice. He has not spoken to me in ages. Has he forgotten me? *¡Jum!* A woman cannot merely pause to gather her thoughts before she is forgotten by fickle men!

I will ignore this voice. It bores me with its "sloe gin."

This Institute is a world. I must explore it, yes, that is what I shall do. This Institute must reveal its hidden map to me. In everything there is a map, even in me. And once I have mapped the Institute, I will have all the answers required to aver my freedom within its corridors.

Which answers would those be, Voice? Even a hint? Perhaps, from where you sit, these maps are already visible?

Voice?

¡Jum! So loquacious you were before when I did not wish to hear your oily tones! Now you absent yourself from the scene like some nameless coward in one of History's negligible, secondary wars. Eating sardines behind the hedge while his comrades march valiantly to their insensible Fate. Returning to civilian life to oversee the vegetarian sausage factory and plant babies in his fat wife until she rolls over and plays dead to avoid his. Engorged. Penis. Mmm. My clothes grow tight in the region of my groin. I must let fall my garments to the floor so that I may reveal my enlarging glories to the Institute-at-large. Such ecstasies are rampant in the hallway now! A tidal flood of them proceeding from my body to the body of the map that is the Institute.

The janitor can hardly keep up with the freedom I aver . . . and oh, how his mop it squeaks! He works so hard to clean up after me! His spectacles are speckled with the sweats of his exertions. His tongue lolls upon his lip as he pants his heat to passing currents. Finally, it is too much, he must rest. He leans upon his mop now, and his eyelids avalanche suddenly upon me. The thick paste of his gaze oozes into place around my body, encasing and immobilizing me for transport through a tube: the tube of love!

I have emerged from this tube. The janitor stands beside me. He laughs! He laughs, he laughs. Oh, I have it wrong, he does not laugh, he only rejoices vocally in emptying a trash container. Into a large plastic bin. I recognize this place. Have I been here before? *¡Jum!* It seems I never can be certain of anything in my past! We are in an office. Herr Direktor's office. I feel I have been here my whole life. Herr Kommandant is here. His leather switch, it twitches. His eyes are so vacant, yet they stare, they stare. Intent on me. They stare. I step forth. All the fabrics on my body dissolve to reveal my pulchritude. My pudenda. My penis. The janitor observes me dully, his mouth a greasy drip drooling down his chin. My penis engorges, but without pleasurable sensations, only lumpiness. Indeed, it fills as a toilet fills, putrid and hot with sewage. *¡Jum!* The world spirals. Into. Despair! Herr Tin-Pot Tyrant has extended his tongue from its cavity. He pants in the manner of a lusty cur. He beckons me forth. I lean over his desk and present my penis to his view. *¡Jum!* Every inch is maximum bitch except for this impertinent manliness! It never fails to recrudesce at inconvenient moments. Herr Diktator has taken hold of my penis now. I am feeling relief. Thumb and pointer sheathed in supple leather, smooth and stimulating. A cool and steady anchoring grip. His switch, it twitches! My penis in his palm. It now belongs to him. Relief. So long withheld, now granted in one severing motion.

Mmm. I am maximum bitch now. Pert, pink, and orchid fresh.

Excuse me. I must find a. Mmm. Mirror.

IV

In view of the tragic events that transpired in the office of our so recently deceased Director, I will refrain from oratory on this occasion, other than to express my deep sense of gratitude and humility to the Board of Directors for its decision to appoint me as interim Director until such time as a suitable replacement can be found.

I feel it incumbent on me to say that in spite of the, ahem—decorum being no excuse for prevarication—disgraceful and disgusting disposition in which he was found, our former Director was otherwise a man of vast integrity and gravitas, and I will strive with utmost fidelity to attain to his truly stellar standard of stewardship.

It goes without saying that some areas of focus will necessarily shift to reflect the—I dare say—now indisputable orthodoxy of Reinformation Theory. The mission of the Institute must (*¡Jum!* I say it must!) expand to accommodate a more, ahem, universal paradigm.

In keeping with this understanding, my first act must be to rechristen the Institute, which shall henceforth be known as Dr. Sensible's Sloe Gin Parlour and Yum-yums. That will bring the jollies in . . . droves of them, delightful scalawags!

And now a moment of silence, if you will, for dear departed Dickless.

PRISION INQUIETA

by Jon Paul Rai

1 - Henry

The chirping of cicadas woke Jasen through the thin fabric of his makeshift tent. He scrounged through his knapsack for anything edible as he scratched bug bites. Half a bag of Ritz crackers was left stuffed in a zipper compartment. He chewed slowly and wiped sweat off his brow. On the third attempt he mustered the courage to take a look outside. A rocky stream with a white waterfall glistened in the sunlight that broke through the trees. Spider-like water bugs danced on the water's surface. Tree roots twisted and turned in the stream, some so large one could use them as stepping stones.

Jasen wrapped up his tent, careful not touch the dirt for fear of ants or other insects that might inhabit the region. He continued in the direction he assumed to be north, hoping to find a sign of civilization: a phone, a toilet, anything that operated on electricity. It was only his third day in the jungle since his boat had been abandoned due to an uncontainable fire. He had gotten separated from the group of fifteen after frantically swimming to shore. A crocodile that casually floated in the stream stopped him in his tracks; advice that the tour guide had given the group on how crocodiles were mostly harmless unless startled or threatened crossed his mind. Nonetheless, fear froze him in place until the reptile swam out of sight. Jasen bent down and held his head in his hands.

After continuing for countless hours, he came to an outlet. The stream bled into a far-stretching lake. Slowly, he paced up to the lakeshore and stared at the opposite side. He made out a reddish shack and headed around the lake for it. A hairy spider leapt from the brush and made him cringe and pick up his pace; he stumbled on a root and fell into the mud. The makeshift tent he had constructed fell to the side and his knapsack spilled open, his miscellaneous possessions floating in the puddle of mud. As he gathered them he noticed ants crawling up his arms and under his pants. He squashed some against his skin and swiped others off in a panic. A flock of geese squawked overhead and a small animal scurrying in the brush close by startled him.

"Get away from me!" he yelled to the bushes. When he had gathered everything salvageable, he pressed on. The shadows and the height of the sun in the sky hinted that midday had passed. Although his wristwatch had been water-damaged he glanced at it frequently. And the screen on his smartphone had been black for days; he glanced at that on occasion also. The path around the lake turned to ankle-deep mud after a light rainfall. Nerves walked a razor edge as he sloshed forward. Unfamiliar types of insects, snakes, and lizards that must have been inches away from his feet caused him to cringe with every step.

Before the sun sank below the treetops, Jasen reached the shed he had spotted earlier. Its flimsy door had been left unlocked. He shut it behind him when he entered and felt around for a light switch, but the walls were bare. Empty shelves, a sleeping roll, and a small cabinet were the only items in sight. Monkeys made a racket from outside and he heard something crawling around in the bushes below the single-pane window. He pushed the cabinet against the door, laid his tent on top of the sleeping roll and curled into a ball. Hours of sweating and itching ticked by in the musty shed.   Jasen found himself staring at a large mantis climbing up the window when day broke. He peeked out the door of the shed and took a look around. A hedgehog squealed as it crossed the dirt path in front of him; the buzzing of cicadas filled the air. Someone cocked the barrel of a gun and stepped out of the bushes. A man in a torn brown hat with a beige uniform pointed a rifle in his direction.

"You sleep in my shed, amigo?" the man asked.

"Well, I . . . yes. I'm sorry."

"What you doing here?"

"I am lost. M-my tour boat caught fire and my group abandoned it. I got separated from them."

"Name's Henry, I show you to the town, amigo. I hear on the radio of your boat on the river."

Henry lowered the rifle and took out a hand-rolled cigarette. He nudged Jasen out of the way and opened the door to the shack. After taking a look inside and releasing a sigh, he gestured for Jasen to come along. Jasen scooped up his belongings and followed.

They headed off the path through the jungle. Every few meters Henry would unsheathe a machete and chop through thick brush. When they came upon a pack of chimpanzees sitting in a circle, he fired a shot in the air to disperse them. Jasen noticed blood under his fingernails from scratching so hard. Some hours passed and they came to an open field patched with brown grass and rocky soil. Spotted deer hopped across the grass in zigzags. The man took out his rifle, stopped and looked around.

"Maybe a jungle cat's close. Deer are scared of jungle cats," Henry said.

"So am I," Jasen replied.

Henry put down the rifle after a few more moments of scanning the area then nodded. Jasen felt his clothes stick to his side and could smell his own body odour as they crossed the grassy field. Henry handed Jasen a banana from his satchel. It was fresh, so Jasen scarfed it down. Rows of red flowers in the shape of teapots lined the field. Jasen picked one, but Henry slapped it out of his hand and made a slicing motion across his neck with his pointing finger. Henry led the way to a crude wooden staircase in a hillside. Trees with moss-covered bark and branches blanketed the area. Henry pointed to the top of the staircase with his eyes, lit another cigarette and they started up the steps. By the time Jasen climbed the final step his feet were aching. Over the treetops, across a lake, he saw a decrepit two-storey building. Henry pointed to it with his cigarette in hand and nodded to Jasen.

By nightfall, they were crossing the lake in a small rowboat Henry uncovered from a net covered in leaves. Jasen's eyes played tricks on him; he thought he saw something staring out from the black water, and shapes that looked like panthers prowling the shoreline. A cloud of bats glided overhead and disappeared into the trees. Henry docked the rowboat at a small pier and tied it to a wooden peg which protruded from the water.

"Prisión Inquieta," he announced as he lit a cigarette with his Zippo.

2 - Tooth and Tongue

Jasen followed Henry through ankle-deep muck that led them to the building they had seen from atop the hill. Two guard towers were situated at the gates of the structure. It had thick beige walls and barred windows on the second floor. A barbed-wire fence had been erected around it; rusty shreds of wire hung off the top. Henry offered Jasen a handful of almonds from his satchel and smiled.

"You said we were going to town," Jasen said.

"Si, amigo. This is town. Not much around here but this by walking," Henry frowned.

"Is there a working phone here?"

"No."

Henry lit a torch and led Jasen through the halls; insects and rodents scurried all about. Jasen brushed a spider off this leg after feeling a harsh sting. He lagged behind while he rubbed the spot where he had been bitten. They arrived at a small room, where Henry flicked on a light switch and opened the door to a cabinet. Inside was a jumbo pair of scissors, buckets, shovels, and rope. Henry then sat at a desk, opened a rusty drawer and took out a cigar. He flicked on a single lamp and took a puff.

"You wait here. I have work to do," Henry said, picking up the shovel.

"So, you have electricity but no phone?" Jasen asked. Henry nodded and exited the room.

Jasen sat in the chair at the desk. He pressed the last clean piece of tissue he had against the spider bite. Dizziness crept up on him and the room began to spin; he felt nauseous and dry-heaved. His forehead was drenched in sweat. He stood up, peeked his head out the door and looked down the hallway. The panelling on the floor was laid out unevenly, thick grass protruding from between the tiles.

Only lamplight from the room allowed Jasen to get a glimpse of the hallway; he noticed a room just across from him. Hoping to find a sink and a toilet, he crossed the hall and opened the door.

Inside, he glimpsed two cages with bamboo bars spaced mere inches apart. Two emaciated men wearing nothing but pants sat inside. They were shaved bald and had their hands tied behind their backs. One of them stared at Jasen, who looked upon the men wide-eyed. And then one of them opened his mouth to show Jasen that his teeth and tongue were gone; his companion revealed the same. Breathing heavily and trembling, Jasen shut the door and ran back across the hall. He hunched over in the chair and held his nauseous stomach. His imagination ran wild trying to come to a conclusion about what had happened to the men; pain from the spider bite shot up his leg. He glanced back out the window to see only dense jungle trees and the chain-link fence; the sky broke through the trees in fragments. He tried to see where Henry was and wondered what he was doing.

Jasen mustered the courage to walk back across the hall. When he entered the room, the men were in the same spot as before. A hiss in the corner startled Jasen, and he turned to see a slim black snake curled up in the corner. One of the prisoners put his face up against a bamboo bar and reached in the snake's direction with an open palm. He grumbled some incomprehensible words then pouted. Jasen approached the cage and knelt down. He met the men eye to eye.

"What is this place? What are you doing here?" he asked.

One of them picked up a branch and wrote in the dirt. It read: *the light the noises.* Just then Henry swung the door open. He had a shovel in his hands which dripped blood. A cigarette dropped from his droopy chin and he smothered it under his boot.

"I should be going," Jasen told him and he rose to his feet.

"I ask the warden if you can go, amigo." Henry frowned and aimed his rifle in Jasen's direction. "Get in corner."

Jasen hesitated to follow Henry's instructions, so Henry fired a shot into the ceiling. Jasen promptly backed into the corner. Henry took an elongated key from his pocket and opened the door to the cage; when he did the prisoners backed against the wall and put their hands over their faces. Henry pointed to the cage and lifted his rifle in Jasen's direction once more. Jasen walked in and held the bars. When he heard the door lock shut he got to his knees and held the bars.

Henry flung the rifle over his shoulder and left the room, then locked the door behind him.

Jasen shook the bars of the cage and felt around on the floor which was no more than loose tiles and patches of dirt. A single light bulb hung from the ceiling and a drip-drop echoed off the walls. The room emitted a stagnant odour. He took a glance out the single window. As before, only jungle and the chain-link fence filled his view. An hour later, Henry tossed Jasen the remains of his makeshift tent and a banana. He set down two bowls of green water just far enough for the prisoners to reach in and grasp; they both gulped down the liquid immediately.

The two men moaned and turned in their sleep, causing Jasen to cringe and tense up. Shrieks from what sounded like a demon came from upstairs and filled the halls as night fell. Jasen then knew there were more prisoners than the two he had been grouped with. He wondered about the other members of the tour he had been on, if they had found a way to make contact with the authorities or the tour company which booked his trip. One of the members of the tour was former military, and he wondered if the man would make his way to this place. Jasen finally drifted to sleep just before the break of dawn.

3 - The Warden

The next morning a man in a worn military uniform swung open the door. He entered the room with Henry on one side and a man in similar attire with a rifle strapped to his back on the other side. The military man wore white, blood-stained gloves. He paced around the room with his arms behind his back and stared in Jasen's direction every few moments. The other prisoners stood at quiet attention, facing forward. With a gesture of the man's hand the two prisoners got on their knees and faced the wall. Henry entered the bamboo cell, took out a bullwhip and repeatedly cracked each one in the back; each time the leather connected with skin, it sent a chill down Jasen's spine. Henry then kicked each man in the back, sending them face first to the ground. The man in the military outfit nodded and smiled. Henry took out a serrated knife and sliced each man's throat. Jasen backed up against the wall; he felt a sharp pain in his ankle followed by the hiss of a snake. He dropped to the ground holding the spot where he had been bitten.

The three men exited and Jasen lay for hours in stinging pain. By the time night had fallen, the corpses stank of sweat and flesh causing Jasen to vomit several times. Screams and ear-piercing metallic sounds vibrated through the ceiling. The man in the military uniform entered the room with Jasen's bag in hand and lit a torch on the wall. He held a map in his hand and raised it to the light. It was the map of the Nile River Jasen had received from the tour guide.

"You know, boy. Sudan and Egypt will soon be at war for control of the Nile? I find it incredible tours still come through these parts. Idiots like yourself taking pictures . . ."

"Sir, please I—"

"Shut your mouth, boy. I haven't finished."

The warden chucked miscellaneous slices of dry fruit into the cell. Jasen scooped them up, sniffed them and then ate them. The warden then lit a cigar and sat down in a rusty lawn chair. After that, he slowly ripped up Jasen's map and let the shreds sprinkle onto the floor. Shortly after, he snapped his fingers and Henry and the other man led in two women. Their clothes were in shreds, their hair was tangled, and they wore blindfolds. Henry shoved them in the cell with Jasen and they quietly sat down on the fragmented tiles in the corner. The warden nodded to Henry. Henry ripped the shirt off each woman and unfastened the bull whip from his belt. Jasen watched Henry whip the women and slit their throats as he trembled inside and out.

Every day that followed brought the same pattern; the body count had reached a dozen by the third day. Jasen could not keep himself from constantly vomiting on the floor; he vomited half the time from the smell of his own vomit. In a mad rage he attempted to rip the bamboo bars from the ground, shaking them violently when he was alone. The sounds from the second floor intensified; the screams grew louder and the voices wild. The screeches extended and the ceiling shook every few hours during the night.

One night a storm brewed over the prison, intense flashes of white light illuminating the cell for split seconds at a time. The faces of the corpses flickered in the flashes. The trees outside bent towards the barred window and the branches scraped across the thick, yellow glass. Jasen curled up in a ball as his head rang with throbbing squeals.

Figures came and went in the night, dragging out each corpse one at a time. Jasen couldn't sleep in the commotion; he stared at the door of the room until the sun came up. Spiders hung from the ceiling and cockroaches scurried in circles in the cell. The warden, Henry, and the other man entered. Henry and the other man pulled Jasen to his feet.

"Warden say time to go upstairs, amigo," Henry said, after lighting a hand-rolled cigarette.

4 - A Blaze

Henry shoved Jasen up the creaky, wooden stairway. Vines had grown across the water-stained walls, and flies and mosquitoes buzzed in Jasen's ears. Cells lined the hallway of the second floor. Each cell had a corpse with a slit throat that had been left to rot. Henry showed Jasen to a room at the very end of the hall. Aside from a cracked plastic toilet, a dusty cot, and a window with a ripped screen, the room was empty. Jasen stood in the middle of the room while Henry lit a cigarette.

"Let me go or just kill me," Jasen pleaded.

"Sorry, amigo. It ain't up to me." Henry frowned and shut the door; as he did, he dropped his lighter.

Jasen picked the Zippo up in his hand and flicked it to make sure there was still fluid left. He ripped the screen out of the window and peered out into the jungle. There was no way to climb down, and the drop seemed too far to jump without sustaining some type of injury that would prevent him from escaping.

That night, flashes of bright light poured into the window. The faces of the prisoners Henry had whipped the day before appeared as stains on the wall. The screeching metallic sounds continued for hours. ***Dwoiinggig*** rang in his ears in an endless loop. Moans came from down the hall as if each corpse had awoken and was crying out in misery. Over and over ***dwoiinggig***, followed by moans and blinding light pouring through the window. Jasen covered his ears, got on his knees and stared at the floor. He set the wall on fire and stared at it as it burned. The faces melted as the flames scorched the walls.

He hung out the window, and when his hands could no longer bear the heat he dropped to the ground below. A sharp pain shot up his thigh and up his side when his feet made contact. He stumbled into a patch of foliage and stared at the smoke pouring out the window. From outside, the night was dark and silent aside from the croaking of frogs and the distant cries of the wildlife. No metallic ringing, no moans nor bright light. Jasen's leg could not hold his weight without tremendous pain when he tried to stand. He crawled through the darkness using one leg and his knee. Mud squished under him, insects squashed under his palms as he moved. Trees above grew so dense that he could only make out a sliver of the sky. When he turned back, he witnessed the entire building ablaze. Crackles and pops of wood burning filled the air. He hoped that the three men were caught in the flames, but imagined Henry following behind with a cigarette hanging from his filthy goatee, unscathed and furious.

Jasen bumped into a body. He flicked on the lighter and saw a pile of corpses in the dim light. One of the corpse's heads hung down with its mouth open, devoid of tongue and teeth. He cringed and dry-heaved, barely containing the vomit. The bodies were fully clothed so Jasen forced himself to search their pockets for anything that may have been of use. Grasping his leg and applying pressure was all he could do to soothe the pain from his fall from the window.

He crawled away from the pile of corpses and lay in the brush until the sun brought morning dew. The chirps of birds, croaking of frogs, and screeches of monkeys in the treetops surrounded him. Cicadas buzzed and insects he could not identify scurried in the foliage. His room back home waited in his mind, a clean bedspread, a hot bath, and snacks in the cabinet. Maple leaves falling to the pavement. The sounds of civilization he ached for—a car passing by, the rattling of a train, or a cell phone ringtone coming to him crisp and clear.

Panic and heavy breathing followed the memories; being eaten alive by bugs, bitten by a poisonous reptile or being forever lost seemed to be the only possibilities.

A machete chopped through the brush and Henry stared down at him. By Henry's side was the man who went unnamed. Henry lit a cigarette and crossed his arms. Jasen attempted to crawl through the foliage, but soon gave up. Henry grabbed him by the collar and pulled him to his feet; he screamed from the pain in his leg. The man shook his head at Henry when they realized Jasen could not walk.

Both men dragged Jasen back towards the prison by the legs. His head hit a stone and his hair became sodden with muddy water. After a time, they arrived back at the prison. The structure had not been scorched by a single flame, and the warden stood with arms crossed at the gates. Jasen's head bumped on each step as Henry and the man dragged him back upstairs. They shoved him back in the same room with the screen window. It was exactly as it had been when Jasen dropped from the window.

5 - A New Prisoner

Metallic screeches and moans filled the halls, and blinding light shone through the window every night. The faces of the deceased haunted Jasen; he could see them clear as day. Some had their skin torn off, others were missing noses, and none of them had teeth or tongues. The jungle view of dense trees and muddy ground below never changed. After a while, Jasen couldn't tell if a week, a month or a year had passed. Henry brought him dried fruits and a mug of warm water every day around noon; sometimes the water was tainted with soil.

Every few days the warden preached about time served in Vietnam and Special Forces operations that took him to visit the jungles of the world. His tone always condescending, he reeked of tobacco like Henry. Each time he appeared his hands were white and stained with blood. One evening he strolled in with a slain monkey slung over his shoulder and stared at Jasen as he sharpened a dagger on a stone.

"The Sodality of the Black Sun build models," he said, his tone leaden and his voice quieter than usual. "Prisons within the greater prison. To teach you to see. Valentinus and the higher light. You'll know before long."

From time to time an animal wandered around the grounds and once in a blue moon Jasen heard a small airplane fly over the treetops. Much time was spent in speculation as to who could be in those planes. He had hoped for a search for his boat, but knew no one was coming. He wondered how long it had actually been since he had met Henry that day and what the folk back home were thinking. Most likely, the disappearance of his tour boat had not even made the news.

Henry entered the room with the other man who had never shared his name or even spoke a single word. They showed Jasen downstairs to the bamboo cell on the first floor. Inside was a woman around his age. She was trembling and looked as if she had been crying for some time. Next to her were two men with whipped backs and slit throats. When the woman saw Jasen she backed up into the corner and started to cry. Henry lit a cigarette and nodded to the girl.

"Who are you . . . what is this place?" she asked.

Jasen opened his mouth to answer, but all that came out was drool and a moan. The girl's cries became heaving sobs and she pushed herself back against the wall as tightly as she could. Jasen picked up a stick and wrote in the ground: *the light the noises*. Henry drew a serrated blade and pulled back Jasen's hair.

Slag Glass Lachrimæ

by David Rix

‚Aut Furit, aut Lachrimat, quem non Fortuna beavit'
(‚He whom Fortune has not blessed either rages or weeps')

From the title page of *Lachrimæ or seaven teares figured in seaven*
passionate pavans, with divers other pavans, galliards and allemands, set
forth for the lute, viols, or violons, in five parts
John Dowland, 1604

The Diver stood in the shallow water of the Thames and surveyed the scene. It was a dreary day and a dreary view. Little more than scrubby grass and muddy salt marsh, a barge graveyard, a car park, heavy industry. On both sides of the Thames, factories loomed against the sky, an artless jumble of box-like buildings and machinery—electricity pylons, wind turbines in the middle distance. A few massive piers carrying pipes stretched out into the river, presumably to dump wastewater. None of it seemed able to dominate this land though. The salt marshes were the true kings here and always would be.

And every time Feather happened to come past on her bike, she would pause and meet the Diver's gaze for a few moments, as though saluting a fellow lost denizen of this world. She always wanted to venture out closer—to get into the mud with it. Even to hug it. After all, in spite of living in London, the mud and the brine were still somehow more of a home to her than the city would ever be.

Ever since the Diver had been installed here, in the last place you would expect to see art, it had stared shoreward at the same view. When the tide was out, it was revealed as more like half a diver, shaped out of massed scraps of metal, on a frame standing on a concrete foundation. When the tide was in, the head would just poke out forlornly, as though hoping for rescue—hoping to be dragged back to the human world.

It seemed appropriate.

Finally, Feather pushed at the pedals again and pressed on, making her way east into new territory. The path followed the waterside, curving along just a few feet above a narrow strip of mud and stones that didn't really merit the term beach. This was the estuarine Thames—the river wide, the banks low and muddy, sometimes with small, drab strands of pebbles. This stretch was not an area where she had been before, but it was a type of area that she liked. It was good for scavenging because of what the Thames tossed up on shore, both natural and humanmade. A huge landfill had once been located here, but was now in the process of being covered and landscaped into a nature reserve of some kind. But like the ghosts inside a traumatised human being, what lurked in the depths of the ground could not be hidden forever. As the wide river rose and fell with the tides, so it ate away at the low banks—and as it ate away at the banks, maybe what lurked in the soil would be exposed. And alongside the natural Thames flints, such things as broken ceramic or ancient bottles could be very useful in Feather's line of work.

As she cycled, as the Diver and the factories faded behind her, she scanned the world with great care. The regular and sculpted landfill looked startlingly like a burial mound, which was a bizarre thought considering what was entombed in it—but it was the scrawny beach she was watching. She was scanning for interesting areas to investigate, any flash of treasure among the rubble. So far though, there was little. She paused a few times, but not for long—nothing more than broken building stone.

But then, as she rounded a small curve, the beach went black.

She applied the brakes and stared down in surprise at the sudden colour change. It was not a uniform black, of course—it was an unusual and almost eerie landscape of black lumps and bumps among a salt-and-pepper sprinkling of shingle in the mud, all gleaming dully in the grey daylight. Definitely not any familiar river stone. It almost looked like . . .

She shoved the bike to one side and searched quickly for a way down. It should have been easy enough; it was only a few feet below the path. A cliff if you like, but a long, long way from the kind of cliff that you jumped off when the world became too much. There was a small scrape in the soil nearby—a place the water had recently eaten away at, causing a mini-landslide. It looked an easy climb, but nothing is as it seems on these rough semi-artificial riverbanks. Halfway down, something gave way under her and she fell with a startled yelp, plunging down the bank onto the black beach, landing on her back—then she opened her mouth in a brief shrill scream, the pain far worse that it should have been.

She lay there frozen, staring up at the grey sky for a few stunned moments, trying to make contact with her body again, her heart racing in shock.

What the heck just happened?

Then her fumbling hand was exploring the pain—she sat up with an effort, feeling her back and then staring with a prickle at the smear of blood on her fingers. She looked round at what she was sitting in and drew a deep breath. These black intrusions in the familiar beach were no waterworn beach pebbles. It truly was a beach of shards—a scattering of black fragments strewn everywhere, as sharp and vicious as broken glass. It looked as though night itself had been shattered, if the night was made of razorblades.

She reached out and picked up a piece, turning it over in her fingers. She could see familiar patterns in the way it had broken. Known as Conchoidal fractures, because of their vaguely shell-like appearance, they were typical of how extremely hard and brittle stones like flints broke; but the vivid shine, extreme sharpness and utter black soon belied any notions of it being flint. There were only two things this could possibly be: volcanic obsidian or some kind of opaque black glass. Given that this was a shallow layer of dreary London soil and that there were no volcanos on the Thames, that left glass as the only sensible option—but there were massive boulders of the stuff. What on earth was a seeming geological layer of glass doing weathering out of the bank of London's great river? Some of these boulders were several feet across.

She scrambled up gingerly, brushed her clothes, then resumed staring round at the black beach. There was something about this that was making her brain twitter with interest. It was a mystery—but for Feather, it was also an opportunity. This was something a little more unusual and interesting than anything else she had seen here. She picked up a few more pieces and turned them over, watching the sunlight flash and gleam off them.

There was potential here.

A few minutes later, the panniers on her bike were much heavier. She pulled on her coat in spite of the warm weather, unsure what her back looked like now. She knew she was bleeding and didn't want to attract curious glances on the train. Then she swung her leg over the bike's rear and pushed off, making her way back towards the distant railway station.

After a rather complex journey involving three trains and a further long cycle ride through the swarming buildings of London's Camden Town, she arrived back at her rather bizarre home. This was a lost little clutch of apartments in what felt like an old factory, minimally converted into something residential. It was more like living in a set of studios than trying to make a studio in a home. Elsewhere in the building was a hairdressers, two art studios, a clothes maker and a computer repair centre—all with the addition of a bed and a few personal effects tucked away somewhere, of course. It was an environment that was strangely conducive to creativity, if not to any kind of actual living.

The bike was parked in the general chaos of the entranceway, the load of black boulders laboriously carried up the stairs to her small apartment and the door shut behind her with a bang and a sigh of relief. The first thing she did was peel off her clothes and study her back in the mirror. It was worse than she had thought, with several livid lines and gouges on her skin, all the way from her shoulders to her backside. None were particularly deep, but it was still a rather macabre sight and it smarted painfully. A quick glance at her t-shirt and her frown grew sharper. Several rips and slices pierced the material. The black had sliced through clothes and skin with ease. There were even a few small holes in the thick material of her jeans.

With a bitter turn to her lips, she dabbed some cream on the injuries as best she could, then slung both garments into the rubbish bin. Fresh clothes helped but she was feeling a wash of melancholy now. It was stupid to feel depressed over a minor fall, she told herself—annoyed and upset yes, but not depressed. But she couldn't shake it off. To cheer herself up she unloaded the black glass into a plastic tub and studied it again, still wondering what it was. It only seemed to look darker in here, under artificial light.

Surely this couldn't be natural.

She selected a small piece and took it into the bathroom, which also doubled as her jewellery-making studio. This room, or rather what she needed to do in it, was the bugbear that followed her through life—as indeed similar things must follow anyone who cares deeply about their calling yet must try to function in the poverty-stricken world of the city. The place was intended to be just a normal city bathroom with a shower cubicle in one corner, a washbasin, toilet, a washing machine and other basics. It was not intended for lapidary and metalworking. The whole excruciating ordinariness of the space was overlaid with a chaos of machinery on tables and boxes on shelves—rock saws, a diamond drill, small-scale metalworking gear, a polishing wheel, a small cabbing machine and other jewellery-making tools. The grinder was covered in bluish grey mud, the saw in brown mud, the polisher in white mud and everything else in some kind of psychedelic mixture of the three. The whole room, in fact, had a feeling of ingrained dirt that could never again be removed.

Feather had long ago learned that tenancy deposits were pretty much a lost cause in her case.

And then, of course, there was the noise. Most of the machines were quiet enough, but one, the rock saw, certainly wasn't. The rock saw was the sort of thing that made neighbours move to another postcode—or at least come and shout at her. She always tried her best to mitigate it, closing the door and window, placing it in a box bundled up with old blankets, picking her time as carefully as possible, making sure that the couples next door and below her were out at work. But it had to be done. You couldn't make jewellery without initially cutting up the material. The only relief was that it was fairly quick. An hour of cutting would give her enough pieces to work on for many days.

Feather switched on the rock saw and it growled into life. This time, she was fed up and in no mood to deal with other people. It was only a test, after all. Just 30 seconds or so to have a look. *Surely you can get off my back for 30 seconds, world?*

She studied the piece of opaque black glass in her hand, then touched it to the blade. There was a deafening screech and tiny black razors erupted from the machine in a spray, aimed squarely at her. She hastily removed it again and swore. *Never use the bloody saw without protection.* She peeled off her clothes, shaking the glass fragments out and chucking them out into the other room. Then, naked save for goggles, breathing mask and earplugs, she tried again.

The glass began to scream.

It's hard to describe the noise a rock makes as it is sawn. Let's just say that the perceived serene calm of a polished stone is somewhat belied by the sheer assault, violence and horror of cutting it—and that cutting glass is all that but with a kind of shrill pain that is all its own. All she had to do was apply gentle pressure and guide the piece forward, watching the blade sink deeper and deeper—but the air was filled with a roaring squeal as though souls were being tortured somewhere very close. Even through the earplugs, it was loud and painful. Razor-laden water was spraying again. She tried to block most of it with a blanket but the problem with rock saws, or at least with this rock saw, was that if you could see what you were doing properly, you were in its line of fire. It sprayed over her goggles, laced with tiny shards of black. She could feel them on her skin, but better on skin where they could just be washed off than stuck in her clothes forever. The muds and grits and fragments of lapidary work could destroy clothes in just a few weeks, something Feather had learned very quickly. But skin, on the other hand, seemed impervious, at least to anything less than a direct slice. That was one of the strange things about lapidary. Even the violently spinning diamond blade currently carving a slot-black cut through the glass was no threat. She could touch it with her bare fingers without any serious harm.

Fortunately it was all over in less than a minute. The glass came apart into two pieces. This was always a special moment, whatever it was you were cutting. The last few millimetres give way suddenly with a little rush and the two halves fall apart, revealing that first glimpse inside. Sometimes it would be a secret that had never been seen before—a spectacular pattern of agate or chalcedony maybe, or a geode revealed to the world. Sometimes it would just be the same material, but now seen cut flat, a first hint of what it would be like when polished. That was the case here. What was revealed was exactly what Feather expected—deep black—but now there seemed to be texture in it that she hadn't been aware of before. She shut off the saw, leaving a ringing void in the air, splashed one half with water from the sink and held it up to the light. There were faint hints of swirling frozen within it—flowbanding patterns, formed as the material cooled and moved. And a few tiny points of something gleaming silver. Some kind of metallic inclusion? They shone like stars in the black. It looked beautiful—like a fantasy night sky. Staring into that flawed darkness engendered a slight frisson of the unnerving because the world it reflected did not look like her own. Her face seemed distorted and her hair almost to move independently.

She looked down at herself. She was soaked in a vertical line from her head down to her navel, liberally covered with a pepper-sprinkle of black. It was in her hair. Rivulets of it had also trailed down further to exactly where she least wanted glass shards to be, all things considered. There were even a few blood smudges on her arms and sides, where some movement or other must have ground the shards into her skin.

You never had that problem with flint or agate.

She wanted to press on—to grind and polish a true mirror face on the piece. She forced herself to wait though. A shower and a careful clean-up were needed now before working the piece any further. But yes, this had cured her bad mood. This stuff was fantastic. There were so many possibilities.

Camden Lock Market, about a month later—as bustling and hallucinatory as always. A wild throng of London alt culture swarming around stalls offering everything from grungy clothes to street food to tanks of water where you could rest and allow doctor fish to nibble on your tired feet. It was a dizzying place of colour and noise—almost unmappable at first, merely confusing on better acquaintance. Above everything, the freight railway from Camden Road loomed high on brick arches that dominated the whole architecture of the place—while below everything, Regents Canal passed by with its narrowboats and busy towpath. In short, this was a good place. A place of life and energy that cannot be bought with money or planned by developers. It was one of those treasures of the city that every day seemed simultaneously more imperilled and more important.

Feather though was not having a good day.

"I don't understand," she said, aware of her hands on her hips but for once not bothering to restrain herself.

"All I am saying," the figure in front of her fluted with what had to be the rudest politeness she had ever seen, "is that I don't want this thing near me." She was a waiflike undernourished-looking girl in trousers and a top that was either home-made or very expensive, her hair tied up in a lurid tie-dye headscarf. "It's the most oppressive thing I have ever experienced. I thought this was supposed to be protective? It's supposed to absorb negative energies, but I never felt anything so negative in my life."

She waved the necklace with its large black stone in her face as evidence.

"I'm sorry," Feather said, "but I haven't a clue what you are talking about."

"You told me this was obsidian."

Feather blinked. "No I didn't. I never said anything of the kind." *You probably saw something black and* thought *it was obsidian, you dumb b . . .*

"Well whatever it is, you can have it back," Tie-Dye said, wrinkling her nose. "This thing is nasty, that's all. Nasty."

Feather rubbed urgently at her forehead. *You're talking about a piece of jewellery, not a fucking flu medicine,* she thought. *If you want a refund, just ask for it . . .* Then she became aware of a second figure approaching, the friendly figure of Leah with a heavy bag, and she groaned inwardly. Why was this happening? Wasn't there enough trouble in the world?

"Okay whatever," she barked, and Leah looked at her in surprise. It was unusual in the extreme for Feather to use that tone of voice, but right now it just came steaming out of her.

Tie-Dye narrowed her eyes, the expression on her face clearly saying *how dare you, only I am allowed to be a bitch in these kinds of transactions.* Feather ignored it though and shoved a wad of money at her without another word. Tie-Dye handed the piece of jewellery over, then ostentatiously wiped her hand on her blouse-tunic-thing and turned away. Leah pulled a face. Feather just watched Tie-Dye's back view as it disappeared into the crowd, wishing she could plant one of her good sensible boots right in the middle of that hand-sewn backside, then she sat down with a grunt, turning the necklace with its black stone over in her hands.

"Feather?" Leah asked, almost timidly. "You okay?"

"Yeah, fuck it," she muttered, giving her what she hoped was a welcoming smile.

"What was that all about?"

"I don't know," she growled. "I think she wanted some nice sweet crystal healing crap. And this wasn't good enough apparently. No one makes up crystallography about slag glass. Sort of like no one ever assigns mystical ley line power to the London Orbital Motorway. And look at this," she said, her voice rising. "She's put a dent in the clasp somehow—oh fuck her . . ."

"Calm down, Feather," Leah said anxiously, reaching out and giving her shoulder a gentle rub.

"And what the heck was she on about—obsidian?"

"What?"

"It's not fucking obsidian."

"Okay, I believe you."

Feather gave her a gloomy look and tried to collect herself. It was no big deal—she could fit a new clasp in a few minutes back home. But even so . . .

"Sorry Leah," she said, reaching out and squeezing her hand. "It's been a stinking day. For gawd sake, put that bag somewhere and sit down." She reached out to take it from her, but the weight took her by surprise. She quickly caught it with both hands. "What on earth have you got in here?"

"Oh—just . . . books," Leah said with an awkward smile.

Feather grinned. That at least was no surprise. Books were just about the only thing Leah ever bought aside from food—and even food would be sacrificed if there was some title of value that she really wanted. She tried to keep that quiet, but Feather knew. Calculations would be made—how many days' worth of meals did said book correspond to? And then she would count herself down, eating one day on, one day off until the sum was saved.

Feather opened the bag, taking in a few horror and sci-fi paperbacks floating on the top, then carefully placed it safe under the stall and waved Leah to the other seat.

Leah was one of those characters who radiate a kind of low-grade background untidiness—not consciously or glamorously shabby but genuinely so, as though she had placed both clothes and herself pretty far down on the list of priorities in the world. Even if she was to put on a suit or some fancy evening wear, it would still be hanging on her body as though slightly out of control and unsure if it really wanted to be there. Now she was wearing a pair of faded jeans with a hole in the knee and an old shirt. Make-up was something that happened to other people. Her hair was a frizzy tangle of brown that was as unruly as anything else about her and was now apparently trying to form two different hairstyles at once. Her voice was curiously precise and almost posh-sounding, in sharp contrast to Feather's own rather rough and ready urban tones. She was the same age as Feather—late 20s—but the way she looked, the serious and intent expression on her face, you could have been forgiven for adding a decade. She didn't wear glasses and thus could never peer through them with owlish seriousness—but somehow that almost felt like a disappointment.

As she sat down beside her, though, Feather was conscious of something very comfortable about it all, especially when contrasted against the self-consciously grungy feel of many of the people who thronged the market.

"So—what's the matter?" Leah asked quietly. "Why is today proving such a bad day?"

Feather gave her a miserable look.

"Is it just that character you were arguing with?"

"No," she said with a sigh. "That was just . . . fucking stupid. It's just the usual sort of crap—letter this morning. The vampires are going to put the rent up. Again. It's already gone up by over three hundred pounds since I moved in and—and . . ."

She stared bleakly out over the market.

"I dunno . . . It was hard enough before—I think I am going to have to move, though I really have no idea where to."

"Oh no," Leah said, sitting up sharply. A sense of shocked seriousness and doom had suddenly descended on them both—the standard reaction when talking about housing in London.

"I mean—I suppose I always knew it would come one day," Feather said softly. "London would squeeze me out like some sickly turd into a sewer. But . . . it's not easy, not with all my machinery and stock—and the fact that it is all so noisy—and messy—and . . ."

She shook her head.

"I could just cry," she murmured. "What do they need an extra eighty a month for—they're already getting so fucking much out of me that I feel a right fucking mug. I've been looking around—but there's nothing that I can afford where I could possibly run my studio. Even the shipping container city in Shoreditch is too much. Does nobody do anything in London anymore? Are we supposed to just sit in a tiny white box and watch telly?"

Leah leaned over her and hugged. It was an awkward position, nearly tipping the chairs over, but that didn't matter at a time like this.

"Maybe I should just give up and get out. I lived in the wilds long enough when I was younger. But you know—I liked London when I first arrived. And this jewellery is the first thing in my life that was really working out."

"You might—leave London?" Leah asked, looking so disturbed Feather's heart sank even further.

"I can't cope," she said with a shiver. "Just so much . . . there's always something standing in the way. Everything I want to do . . ."

"Let it out if you want to," Leah said. "It's okay. I'm an old hand at this."

"At what? Bawling your eyes out? Not sure that's good sales tactics right now."

"Sometimes it's good to weep and wail."

Feather gave a small smile. "I never could do that. I just feel dead and cold."

Leah gave a gloomy sigh. "You know—I have always thought . . ."

"What?"

"This is such original material—you deserve to be much richer than you are. I mean, it's not like any other jewellery that I've seen, where they just take the same old boring stones—what is it? Generic agates or tiger eye or . . . or whatever else they have. Or diamonds. What's so special about diamonds?

"Don't talk to me about fucking diamonds," Feather said gruffly.

"I know . . . but this stuff—it has an aesthetic. You might even say a touch of the weird. A sort of macabre glimpse of beyond the fields we know, or a little of Lovecraft's cosmic dread . . ."

Feather broke the hug and stared at her, eyebrows up. "Can I have that in writing?" she said with a laugh.

Leah blushed slightly. "Sorry—to me everything is a book."

"I wish you were right," Feather said, giving her a quick kiss on the cheek. "But never mind. I hate to listen to myself moan. Tell me about you instead. How are you doing?"

"Oh, you know," Leah said with a grin that didn't reach her eyes. "Surviving. Haven't gone mad just yet."

Feather gave her a look, head on one side. Leah was a bit of a depressive, she knew, though she talked about that even less than her persecuted diet.

"Is this new?" Leah asked, taking the returned necklace from Feather's restless fingers and studying it with interest. A large pendant on a thick and quite dramatic chain, the centrepiece was a flat black stone set in a nest of silver threads that squirmed around it like worms. Or tentacles, if you wanted to be really imaginative. There was a whole range of these black stones on the market stall—necklaces, earrings, finger rings, bracelets. Even some more obscure little studs aimed at various places—nose, navel, nipple, even vagina if anyone wanted them. There were a few stand-alone display pieces as well, with or without metalwork—higher value but depressingly less popular than the stuff you could wear. *Urban Black,* the printed sign read.

"Yes. My new line. All with this new material . . ."

"It's very dramatic," Leah said, picking up another piece. Most of the stones were polished flat like mirrors or irregularly angular polyhedrals, rather than any kind of rounded pebble. The sharp angles on the stone contrasted with a bold simplicity in the metal surrounding it—sometimes block-like, almost modernist, sometimes more organic with twining shapes. Leah stared at the piece, frowning intently, looking deep into the flat face of the stone. "It has some bizarre reflections," she said with a sigh. "And, oh boy, do I look ugly."

"Don't we all," Feather muttered. "Would you like one?"

"Thanks, Feather. I wish I could pay you for it, though. You shouldn't be giving them away at a time like this."

"You deserve one just for being there," Feather said. "And what difference does it make really? I'm screwed either way."

Leah gave her a wan grin. "I will pay you back somehow, with something. I don't suppose you'd be interested in a rare collection of horror stories?"

"Which is your favourite?" Feather asked with a smile.

"Oh maybe one of the Arthur Machen collections, though I really don't . . ."

"I mean which piece of jewellery, you dratted bookworm," Feather growled. "What piece of cosmic crafted love or fields known from beyond effing turns you on most?"

"Oh—right. Hum . . ."

Leah studied them, leaning over and examining with great care. Questions like that, Feather knew, should never be asked casually because Leah just didn't do casual. Instead, she could almost see her turning over the narrative of each individual piece in her mind, in no hurry whatsoever to work out the answer to this question. Feather smiled and waited patiently.

"I like these large mirror ones," Leah said at last. "This one especially. Even if I do look ugly . . ."

Feather put the chain around her neck and did up the clasp, then held up a small hand mirror so she could see herself. Leah studied at it with satisfaction but, Feather noticed, avoided the sight of her own reflected eyes. Some nasty part of her was suggesting that the piece looked slightly out of place on Leah's scruffy shirt, but she stamped on that thought hard. Why the heck not? Feather looked at her with an appreciative smile . . .

Then suddenly flinched. They weren't alone.

By the stall, a figure was watching them unselfconsciously. A youngish and somewhat fat man in a long black coat with untidy and nondescript hair. It dawned on her that she had no idea how long he might have been there. For all his size, he had managed to insinuate himself into the environment so unobtrusively that he almost seemed to have materialized from nothing.

Feather gave an embarrassed squirm and stood up. The first impression she was receiving was what might be called shy ugliness and it repelled her slightly, but a possible customer was a possible customer. "Hello," she said. "Sorry—can I help you with anything?"

"Thank you," he said, his voice unexpectedly high-pitched and gentle. "I, umm—I have been searching all over the market for these black tears."

Feather gave him a puzzled look. He was indeed ugly—overweight and rather pasty, as well as shabbily dressed. That long coat might have been dramatic but instead was rather sad and worn, hanging round the blob of his body like a shroud. But even so, there was something about him that pricked at her. The emotion might have been positive or negative, but it was there.

"You mean my Urban Black?" she said, feeling puzzled. "Black tears?"

"Yes. I couldn't help overhearing you," he said, and Feather gave a reluctant frown. *Overhearing what?* He reached into his pocket and produced a small piece of jewellery—a simple specimen of the black stone as the centrepiece of a steel pendant on a chain. Familiar. He held it up without a word, then leaned over to compare it with the pieces on display on the velvet tablecloth.

"Yes," Feather said. "That's . . . one of my Urban Black. I made it a month or so ago. One of the first. How did you get it?"

"I thought so," he said with a small smile, ignoring her question. "Can you tell me what it's made of?"

"It's—industrial glass," she said. "I think. Slag glass. It's not natural—it's a sort of . . . by-product from the metal processing industry."

"Interesting," he murmured, his eyebrows flicking up.

"Yes—there's lots of different kinds of slag, and some are like this. Very clear and pure."

"Like obsidian?"

Feather pulled a face, aware of the small snigger from Leah behind her, then pressed on with her sales patter. "Um, yes. Like obsidian. Some can be quite colourful. And you know, they can be so specific to the process that created them, or even to the individual factory, that they can be identified like natural rocks—a bizarre kind of artificial geology. And collectors track them down as though they were precious agates."

"So what process made these?" he asked, touching one of the pendants. But it was here that Feather's knowledge ran out.

"That I'm not sure about. I never did manage to find any info about slag from the bank of the Thames."

He gave a smile. "Do you offer any kind of discount for quantity?" he asked.

"Oh—well . . ."

"These aren't for me. You might call them a donation. In my line of . . . what I do, these could be very useful, I suspect."

"How many do you need? What kind of metal? The best ones are titanium, though I did a few silver ones. And cheaper steel pieces. I even made one special rhodium ring—sold that online, but I suppose I could . . ."

"Which is the cheapest? To be honest, it's the stone I am most interested in, not what's around it."

"Then maybe steel. How many?"

"Thirty-four," he said quietly.

Feather blinked.

"Wow," she said with a twinge of excitement. "Ah—well, yes. I am sure I can—do a bit of rounding down."

" . . . of your largest pieces. Ideally—this kind," he said, picking up one of the 2-inch mirror stones.

"Oh—I, well, I only have 12 of those here but . . ."

"Could you get more?"

"Yes—yes, I have them at home. I can bring them. Next week?"

"May I suggest," he said, "may I be annoying enough to suggest—that you deliver them? I thought maybe, given the size of the order, you might consider . . . ?"

"Where?" Feather asked cautiously.

"Here in Camden," he said, handing her a card. "Tonight? I . . . tend to move around rather a lot, you see. But tonight, I will still be here . . ."

She turned over the card in her hands. It contained two words—white text on a black background: *Crying Room.*

And an address.

"I guess I can," she said. "It's not that far from where I live. I'll cycle over when I get home."

"Thank you," he said with a smile. "I will pay you for this batch now. You can maybe think about and factor in the discount tonight?"

He began counting out money. Feather watched in bemusement. He didn't look rich by any measure with his faded and shabby clothes. Yet the notes came out of his wallet like something out of a fairy-tale. Feeling unreal, Feather took them, then started packing up the pieces—reducing her display considerably.

"Um—thanks," she said.

"Thank you," he countered with perfect politeness. "And may I ask—what's your name?"

"Call me Feather," she said with a smile.

He gave them both a friendly nod and then withdrew, leaving Feather still staring down at the sheaf of notes in her hand.

"How about that," Leah whispered excitedly. "You're rich."

"Yeah," Feather murmured. "I guess that puts off being homeless by about . . ." She worked it out. "Sixteen days going by rent alone."

"Come on, you have to admit it's pretty satisfactory. One might almost say . . . a windfall."

"Yes. But—he must be totally bonkers, honestly. What the heck's he going to do with them all? I hope he's not going to sell them on for a hundred quid each."

"Bonkers that's bringing you cash is still good bonkers," Leah said severely. "So make sure you drop off those new ones."

"You bet I will," Feather said with a laugh. "The best steel I have."

Leah looked at the card. "Is it an art gallery . . . or something?"

"No idea. Never heard of it."

"Maybe some specialist bar. Anything you don't understand in London probably comes down to either art or boozing. A bit like putting 'probably of religious significance' on any archaeology they don't understand."

"Want to come with me?"

"Okay, yes. I am curious. Meet you there after work?"

Feather nodded and slipped the card into her wallet.

Feather rang the doorbell.

This was a perfectly ordinary urban street—just tall terraces that were a little on the run-down side, but not unusually so for London. A small strip of gardens separated them from the road—a basic patch of ground in which a few default plants grew rather uncertainly. There was nothing to distinguish the place from anything else in the city, as far as she could see. There was no sign or anything—nothing to say that it wasn't a private house.

"Hello?" a voice answered. A familiar light and gentle voice.

"Um—hi . . ."

"Hello Feather," he said.

She stared round, quite impressed for a moment. "You remember my voice?" she asked.

"I can see you," he said with a laugh. "And your friend whose name I never knew unfortunately." She looked around again but it was no more help than the first time. The windows looked blank. "Do you want to come in?" he asked. "The crying room is free and the door is always open."

Feather and Leah exchanged glances.

"I . . . What is this place?"

"This is the Camden Town crying room," he said in the same quiet voice. "Please come in. Down the stairs."

Feather pushed at the door, and it was indeed open. They stepped into what looked like a residential hallway with a faded carpet and a painfully ordinary coat rack. There were even a few pizza delivery flyers on the floor under the letterbox.

"Do you have any idea what this is?" Feather said quietly as they descended the stairs towards what was presumably the basement flat. "It's starting to feel rather weird. Some kind of club?"

Leah shrugged a negative.

At the foot of the stairs was a doorway, the door standing open—and beyond that was a hallway with three further doors in it—one open about a foot, two closed. It still looked like little more than a residential flat, but the open door had a sign hanging on it, a little like those basic invertible open/closed signs in shop windows, though in this case it read SOLO in green letters. Leah turned it over, examining it. On the other side, it said COMPANY, which didn't clarify much.

"I suppose—we go in," she said. "I just hope we are not supposed to, hmm—have sex or buy a three hundred quid meal or overthrow the government or something equally exhausting."

Feather pushed the door further open and they peered in.

Whatever she had been expecting, the room confounded it completely. She stared round in utter awe. The only furniture in it was a comfortable-looking sofa and a standing mirror in a corner—and shelves covering a considerable amount of wall space. And on the shelves, and the walls around them . . .

It was immaculate, like a museum—a perfectly ordered collection of objects, photos, scraps of paper, books. There must have been hundreds of items. Many hundreds . . .

"Hello, Feather."

It was a quiet, almost solemn tone of voice and they glanced round at a familiar figure that had emerged from one of the other rooms—still dressed in shabby black; still the long coat; still the same quiet, almost serene look on his face.

"Hi," Feather mumbled. "Um—yes, I have them here. Twenty-two pieces. Take a look." She handed him a box, which he opened and studied with deep interest.

"Thank you, Feather. They are beautiful."

"I'm—I'm glad," she stammered. "But what is this place? Are we supposed to be doing something?"

"There are no supposeds here," he said with a smile. "This is the Camden Town Crying Room. It's whatever you need it to be."

"But what is it? I never heard of . . ."

"You know," he said, "there're some places where lovers lock padlocks as a sign? Some special fence or bridge? They are not earmarked—they just sort of happen. Like all the best things just sort of happen. This is a bit like that. Only instead of love, it's . . ."

"Tears?" Leah interjected, a strange look on her face. "Grief?"

Feather stared at her in surprise, but he just nodded. "Right," he said. "This is where you go when you need to let something out. That's all. There're quite a lot of them scattered round London."

"This is . . ." Leah swallowed. "I have to say, it seems weirdly familiar, somehow. I am wondering where I have heard about this before."

"Word gets round," he said. "Though this is not the sort of thing that turns up in guidebooks. Now, let me see. I am currently rather short of money, or perhaps I should say always rather short of money, but I believe I can just about scrape together what you need. Do you have a final price for me?"

"Um—Um, yes, sure," Feather said. "I was . . . How about a 30% discount for quantity?"

"That is very generous of you," he said, with a hint of relief on his face.

Feather shrugged. "Makes no difference really," she muttered under her breath. "Not now."

He took out his wallet and began counting out money—a very generous pile of notes indeed, yet still almost useless in the scheme of things, given the amount of money that city life vampire-sucked out of you. Feather pocketed it.

"So . . . what—do you want them for?" she asked at last. She had to get the question out. Her curiosity was only growing.

He shrugged. "Just a donation. To where they can be of help."

"Very nice, I'm just curious . . ."

"When I saw these, including that first one, which was given to me right here in this room, I felt a prickle from head to foot. These stones are like miniature crying rooms in their own right."

She gave him a blank stare. "What do you mean?"

"They are stones of melancholy, are they not? Black tears?"

Feather was silent. Maybe that wasn't as crazy as it initially sounded. Given the moods that dominated her head these days, impending homelessness and London's crystalline alienation, it was no surprise that she had been making melancholy art.

Leah was still staring round the room as though looking for a ghost. "Do you live here?" she asked at last.

"Good heavens no. Actually, I live on a boat somewhere. But I come here regularly—you might say to look after the place. Would you like to stay for a while?" he asked. "Experience the room as it is meant to be experienced?"

"Yes please," Leah said quickly, and Feather glanced at her—by no means sure she was as keen.

"Good. I am glad the room may be of service. All you need to remember is that when you are in the room, it is your place and your privacy is absolute." He quietly turned over the sign again so that it read SOLO. "Solo means you wish to be alone. Company means you welcome others to join you. And the last of the three states— vacancy—is here indicated by an open door. Very simple." Then he quietly withdrew and closed the door behind them—somewhat to Feather's relief for she was starting to feel distinctly jittery.

"You can feel it, can't you?" Leah whispered, taking her coat off and laying it over the arm of the sofa.

"Feel what? Did you hear what that guy was saying? Why do you think . . . ?"

"There's—something here. I don't know how to describe it though. All these . . . all this stuff. There must be a lot of pain and misery in this room. Stories that no one wants to hear. And this is a place for them?" She picked up a few photographs and looked closely. They ranged from sophisticated framed prints to little images spat out on cheap computer paper. Their subjects were mostly people—all ages and types—but there were a few other things as well, such as homes, pets, places, objects . . .

"Who are they?"

"I would guess, and I am sure I can remember from somewhere— each one is a broken heart. Left here—to . . . Possibly to join the conversation. So they can have a place to live?"

Feather gave a shiver. There was indeed a very weird atmosphere about this place.

Then Leah touched her shoulder and pointed at the far corner—at one of the shelves. They were all laden with trinkets and oddments, personal objects. Wedding rings, other obscure items of jewellery, more photos, scraps of paper, lockets, an almost unending pile, each of which must have meant something to the person who put them there.

"Look familiar?" Leah asked.

"What?"

Then she saw it.

In a prominent place—even a central place—there was a flash of black. Feather stared at the familiar-looking pendant, not entirely surprised. She had sold it to him only a few hours ago.

"Strange donation," she said with a half-smile. "What the flying fuck is he up to? What does he want thirty-four of these for?"

"Maybe there're thirty-four crying rooms," Leah said seriously. "London probably needs all it can get."

Feather's eye, well-tuned to her own jewellery, spotted something else then, another flicker of black in the pile of trinkets. She picked up a second pendant—a smaller one, the black glass cut into a polished irregular tetrahedron, but still like a tiny mirror. "I sold that one about two weeks ago," she said softly. "To a girl from somewhere in Eastern Europe with white streaks in her hair."

"There's another," Leah murmured, pointing out a pair of teardrop-shaped earrings.

"And another," Feather added, picking it up. "One of the first batch I ever made. I remember polishing it."

"Do you remember all your stones?" Leah asked with a smile.

"Pretty much. When you have worked on something like that, you bond with it."

Feather shook her head in mystification and put the pieces back where they had been resting.

Leah swallowed and Feather glanced at her curiously. A change had come over them both since entering the room—a sense of almost sacred sadness, as though the ocean that lies beneath everyone had risen just that little bit closer to the surface. "This place," Leah muttered. "It's almost terrifying. It's making me prickle all over."

"How do you mean?"

"It's . . . don't you feel it?"

"It feels mysterious."

"It feels more than that to me," Leah said. "It's like—I don't know how to describe it. Have you ever been to a really powerful war memorial? I don't mean some sanctimonious statue shoved up in a city somewhere—I mean something real. Where an atrocity happened. And you look at it and your skin starts prickling because you know what it means. You know there's an unutterable horror represented right there? This seems a bit like that. Can't you feel the pain?"

"Um . . ."

"How many people have come here, devastated and ruined? And—now I am thinking to myself just how universal it all is. A sort of eternal darkness. Everybody is lost in it. It's as if an entire city's dysfunctional grief has become fossilized on these walls. Maybe the entire human race is here."

There was a long silence—and Feather was beginning to feel a distinct creeping sensation, maybe just due to Leah's grandiose words, or maybe not.

"Do you think we should add anything to this . . . stuff?" Leah asked at last. Feather glanced at her. Her hand was actually trembling slightly, she realized.

"I—dunno," she managed. "Maybe I should add my home somehow. That's causing enough grief. I'm sure I am going to end up driven out of London and back into the wilds. But . . . I dunno . . ."

Leah stared round the room, then fumbled for her wallet. "Maybe this is mine," she whispered, taking out a photograph and placing it on the shelf, joining the hundreds of others. It showed a fairly ordinary young man, with one hefty line drawn across his chest in black ink—and a date.

"Who is it?"

Leah shrugged.

"Let's just say that there was a certain person in the recent past," she said. "That person had a choice . . . and—I wasn't that choice."

"Oh Leah—I never knew . . . I'm sorry," Feather whispered.

"No great surprise, an ugly scruff-bag like me. But you know how things like that can haunt you and haunt you and haunt you until you want to scream . . ."

Her hand had unconsciously found the black pendant round her own neck now, squeezing it tightly.

"I've never been there," Feather said.

"Never?"

Feather shook her head.

"Maybe I am just susceptible," Leah said. Then she peeled off her top and Feather stared at her in surprise. "Look," she said, standing there in just a basic bra, "since I am opening my heart." She was pointing to her bare shoulder. It was a tattoo, but the simplest she had ever seen—just a series of thick straight lines of varying lengths, marked out in black. It looked like some kind of graph. Feather had seen it before, but Leah had never explained it, or even referred to it until now.

She brushed at the last line, also one of the longest. "That's him," she whispered simply.

Six lines, Feather counted. She reached out and ran a finger along them.

Leah gave a sudden shiver—and there were tears in her eyes. "Oh dear," she muttered. "I suppose that's what this room is all about. I feel so emotionally naked right now and you know—you know, sometimes it hurts so much that . . . it really does. Unremitting. It's always there at the back of the mind. Like shadowy fingers, reaching in from somewhere just a breath away . . ."

Feather stared dumbfounded as tears streamed down Leah's face. She had never seen her break down like this before, however much she was aware of the gloom that lurked at the back of her mind.

"Should we get out of here?" she asked urgently, rubbing at Leah's back in what felt like a feeble attempt at comfort.

"No," Leah managed. "It's okay. Maybe this is the point . . . maybe it's good to let this stuff out sometimes."

"Perhaps I should join you," she said with a shiver. "I could use a bit of this as well. But sod it, I have never been very good at crying."

"It's horrible," Leah continued, ignoring her. "It's . . . like trying to function after someone has cut your hamstring . . ."

Feather winced at the simile.

"The world, it expects you to just smile and shrug. It wants you to act like an adult about it and get on with things," she said. "While all I want is to tear myself to shreds. I want to beat myself up—or be whipped until I bleed."

Feather hugged the shaking Leah tightly.

"Thanks," she mumbled. "It seems—I don't know. I think you can only take a certain number of lines before it begins to really damage you. I think I am damaged goods now, Feather. Too late."

"It's never too late," Feather said. "Surely?"

"Oh, I think it can be," Leah said. "You know—there comes a time when your physical body can no longer heal itself from wounds inflicted and you are scarred for life? And with every scar it becomes harder to be accepted by people. The emotional body is the same. Exactly the same." But even as she said it, she was starting to calm down again. The tears dwindling, the occasional sobs transforming into sighs and then into silence. Finally she broke the hug and looked round with a hint of puzzlement. "I wish I could remember where I have heard of this place though—I am sure I have read something about it. Somewhere."

"So it is in a guidebook after all?" Feather asked with a smile.

"I'm not sure. I have the feeling it was a work of fiction."

"A story about a crying room?"

Leah shrugged. "Yeah—in London, too. Buggered if I can remember where though. I'll have a look when I get home."

She picked up the photograph again.

"I think I will leave this here," she said. "I shouldn't carry it round with me—tormenting myself. One must be logical about things. Always logical."

"Are you sure you wouldn't like me to . . . I dunno, go and sit in the kitchen for a while?" Feather asked with a smile.

"No no—you just take it easy. I am sure it's here somewhere."

Feather gave a sigh as Leah scrambled over her on the bed and stared round the room. This was Leah's tiny L-shaped apartment, a shape that somehow managed to destroy all the possible good points to having a small home and introduced several bad points unique to itself. It might have been converted from a corridor—or rather two corridors—it was hard to tell. It couldn't have been designed to be lived in, that was for sure. There was barely room enough to be lonely in the single bed, but Leah had taken up most of the rest of the space with her obsession—books piled floor to ceiling on shelving that looked as though the books themselves were the only thing keeping it up. It seemed as though there was actually more books than not-books in this place—only about a foot of space either side of the bed before the books began, and that didn't include the scattering of precarious piles that had escaped to the floor. The only other concession to non-books was a small bedside cabinet with a laptop.

"How the heck are you going to find anything in this lot?" Feather asked, slapping playfully at Leah's leg as she leaned over her again, reaching for another shelf.

"I know every single one of these," she said proudly. "And I know where every single one is. It's just . . ."

"What?"

"I'm not always certain *which one* every single one is," she said with a wry smile. Feather gave a snort of laughter. "British author," she muttered aloud. "Recent British author, I'm sure of it. British publisher I think . . . bugger it."

One of Leah's bare feet came down heavily in Feather's lap.

"Ow . . ."

"Sorry. Maybe it was Quentin," Leah said, reaching for a volume. *Defeated Dogs*.

"Who?"

"Quentin S. Crisp—he can be, shall we say, a little on the gloomy side. Maybe enough to come up with an idea like that." She flipped pages and looked at the contents list. Then grabbed a second.

Feather manoeuvred herself out from between Leah's legs—gingerly, just in case her presence caused anything to avalanche—and allowed herself to zone out a bit, looking round the room again. She had never been able to work out whether there was something depressing about this place or not. It was the most ridiculous environment for a book collection, but at the same time it was a remarkable survival in the face of London's best efforts. Her own jewellery work was, if anything, less invasive than this lot, but if she had been forced to fit into a space like this, she would probably have flipped out long ago. But at the same time, books were books—they looked chaotic but it was obvious they were treasured. Doted on. And some were quite high-value as well. It was a wide-ranging collection, but dominated by the out-of-the-ordinary. Everything from classic novels through to modern literature, science fiction and horror and obscurer things, underground literature that she couldn't place at all. Italo Calvino would be brushing shoulders with Ramsey Campbell and Nina Allan and others—Kathy Acker against obscure porn novels, luxury Arthur Machen editions against cheaply stapled hand-made chapbooks that could have been anything.

The one unifying theme seemed to be either a complete removal of the familiar world or an invasion/manipulation of it by some positive or negative force, whether magic, aliens, slugs, hats, foreigners, strange love, madness, pure surrealism or whatever.

In London, maybe that was not so surprising. And maybe, in some bizarre way, this tiny room was actually one of the biggest in the city.

"Gawd, I hope you don't end up homeless as well," Feather said, then immediately wished she hadn't when Leah gave her a cloudy look. That was a spectre that hung over pretty much everyone in London these days as the housing crisis only ground deeper and deeper.

"So—what's been going on?" Feather asked to change the subject. "You never told me about this guy before?"

Leah briefly stopped searching her shelves and gave her an even more sombre look. They had done their best with the small mirror in the crying room but she still looked teary—her eyes still looked red. "Well—I don't always want to tell people about my failures, you know. And besides—you've got problems of your own."

"Yeah—but even so," Feather said with a smile. "I have been moaning to you enough, it's only right you should moan to me."

Leah shrugged. "What's there to say? It happened. I can either spend the rest of my life marvelling about that person's lack of taste, and waiting for the day he finally figures it all out and comes running, or I can attempt to move on. Again. Logic is clear enough on that. I should find some kind of healing. Or . . . some other way out. It's not easy, though. And anyone who thinks it is can bugger off. You can't just shrug at these things, and if you think you can, then you haven't truly been there, that's all I can say."

"And—six lines?" Feather prompted gently.

Leah quietly took another book from the shelf. "Yes," she said without visible emotion. "Six lines. Every so often, I have to add another one." Feather watched her for a long moment, wondering whether she should have kept quiet. She had never known Leah to look so miserable. She stared round the room again, and now it was depressing, but in a very specific way. You could never fit more than one person in this room, and the person it fitted was never going to fit well with anything outside it. Yet at the same time, almost all humans inevitably craved connection.

There did not seem to be many people in the world quite like Leah.

Feather stared up at her, still searching earnestly through her book collection. As her leg was the only part of her within reach, she reached out and rubbed it affectionately.

Then: "Here it is," Leah cried triumphantly.

She came down with a rush and Feather hastily got out of the way. The book was a hardcover—a small one, only big enough to contain a novella or large story. *Black Lachrimæ* it was called. By Mark Samuels. Leah was turning the pages excitedly. "Oh," she murmured. "I remember this now. I thought there was something a bit more going on than I first thought. This is really quite bizarre." She shut the book and stared into the corner of the room for a moment. Then she swore under her breath. Feather wasn't sure, but it might have been the F word, which she almost never used.

"What is it?"

"Have a look," she said, shoving it in Feather's face.

"Um . . ."

"Read it."

She took the book reluctantly.

> I am writing these lines in a room lost deep in the maze of streets that is Stepney, one of many dim regions of London incognita. This room is empty of furniture save for a chair and a small writing desk, and lies within a crumbling terrace house that has obviously been abandoned for many years, a squalid building in the most squalid quarter of the district. The door to this building lies open, however, for those who know of it and those who are called, as I was. And the room itself is piled high with a range of memorabilia and personal articles left behind by those who have come before me. I see photographs stuck to the wall with cheap tape, I see wedding rings, necklaces, items of clothing and other trinkets of all kinds. It is enough to disturb the composure of the mind to contemplate the origins of all of them.
>
> I sit in the chair, considering the recent past and the future, but it may be that I shall never leave this place. It may be that this room must of necessity put an end to my former existence.
>
> *Black Lachrimæ p. 1*

Feather stopped reading and looked at the volume she was holding. Fairly simple design, not exceptional quality binding but obviously with a lot of seriousness and love behind it.

"Look," Feather said patiently. "Just tell me what this is all about."

"It's a story about a crying room," Leah said. "A horror story, or rather a Weird Tale, but it's essentially the same as what we saw. It tells of a special room somewhere in London, a room you can go to—just like where we went. Including the stuff on the walls and everything. Of course, this being a Weird Tale, there's something enigmatic behind it, drawing the lonely and despairing to itself . . . in order to feed. And a certain ambivalence about the fate of those who come. But it's basically exactly the same as the crying room we just visited."

"Okay," Feather said. "So . . . this Samuels guy knew about it?"

"It would appear so."

"Um—yeah, that's quite interesting, I suppose."

Leah gave her an impatient look, slightly riled by her lack of excitement. "It's a really rare book," she said. "From Darkening World Publications—they closed ages ago. It's one of the thirty-four first copies signed by the author. Inscribed. To me."

"Cool," Feather said rather desperately.

She stared at the proffered title page. *One of 34 preliminary lettered copies,* it confirmed. *This is letter . . . . . . J . . . . .*

And then: *For Leah,* it said in handwriting. *A companion hand for those dark places.* Followed by a set of numbers.

"Very nice," Feather said, trying to reignite the enthusiasm. "And the numbers are . . . what? They look like map coordinates."

Leah frowned. "That's the thing. I just had a rather wild idea. I always wondered what those were."

"Coordinates?"

"Yes—somewhere in Bethnal Green. But it seems to be just pointing at a bit of railway line, and there was nothing in the book connected to that. I thought it was just random. Or a mistake. But now . . ."

"So—he scribbled the co-ordinates of a stretch of railway track in your copy of the book? Right. Did he ever say why?"

"I don't know," Leah cried.

"Does every book contain these same coordinates? Or do they have different ones?"

"I believe they are different. I looked it up once I think—and found a picture. Hang on—let me see if I can . . ."

Leah grabbed her laptop and flopped down on her front, quickly searching the internet. Feather slid in beside her, comfortable enough to lie there in that cramped space through whatever long and convoluted journey Leah was in the process of embarking on.

It only took a few clicks though. She gave a triumphant grunt, and shoved the laptop in Feather's face. There was a photo of a few books, some open, some closed, one of the open ones showing the *Black Lachrimæ* title page.

A first copy of Black Lachrimæ, Feather read. *Letter B complete with inscription and coordinates, inscribed to me. And an original hardcover of* The White Hands—*two of my most prized possessions.*

She studied the title page. *One of 34 preliminary lettered copies. This is letter …..B……. For Paulo. On your journey to other places, beyond the familiar streets, a guiding hand in yours,* followed by a similar set of numbers, partially obscured by *The White Hands* lying on top of it.

"As far as I remember," Leah said, "it looked like somewhere in Hackney—or the Wick. You couldn't tell, though. Just a vague line of possibility since we can only see part of it."

Feather nodded.

There was one other thing about this book that was different to Leah's, though, she realized. Next to the coordinates was the letter W, drawn in large bold strokes. And surrounding it, three arrows pointing in three directions. Up, down and to the left, but ever so slightly twisted off vertical. And a question mark.

The W at least looked a little bit like the Darkening World logo on the book spines.

"There's some more," Leah said, grabbing the laptop back. "*No one really knows what the coordinates mean,*" she read aloud. "*The best explanation is that they have some connection to psychogeography, or a game of chance, but there are so few copies of the book and they are so widely scattered that it is hard to know for sure. It's an obscure issue and I don't know of Mark Samuels ever discussing it. Or anyone ever asking.*" She put the laptop down again. "And that seems to be the end of it," she said. "As far as I can find. Just a few replies saying basically 'cool, congratulations, mate'. An old, dead publisher that no one remembers—and some bizarre mystery that nobody could be bothered to solve. Pretty amazing, right? These books—who knows what happened to them all?" she said. "They might have been scattered all over the world."

"So . . ."

"Has it occurred to you that this guy bought thirty-four jewels?"

"Yeah," Feather said cautiously. "It occurred. And you are thinking that . . ."

Suddenly it did seem rather strange. Feather shook her head, trying to get her mind focused on it. It was just like Leah to make such a spectacular dance along the stepping stones of this craziness—and yet at the same time . . .

"I mean, think about it," Leah said. "Black Lachrimæ—a story about a crying room. Lachrimæ means tears. Thirty-four first copies—why such a weird number? It's usually twenty-six to match the alphabet. Or sometimes fifty-two—two alphabets. Thirty-four is very inelegant. So maybe there's a reason. Maybe they needed to cover thirty-four things. Thirty-four co-ordinates. Then this person who is obviously connected to actual real-life crying rooms turns up and buys thirty-four of your stones, one of which is now prominently on display in a crying room that is almost identical to the one in the story. This guy said there's more rooms around London . . ."

Leah broke off with a triumphant look.

"Um . . ."

"This is phenomenal," Leah said. "It's like an urban legend come to life. Could there really be thirty-four of these damn rooms all around London? All mapped out in . . . in . . ."

"Yeah—that's great. Very interesting and . . . and everything. But . . ."

"What?"

"What I still don't understand," Feather said, "is what could these rooms possibly want with thirty-four of my stones?"

"Maybe they are magic stones," Leah said with a teasing grin. "They look it. From beyond the fields we know . . ."

"Oh leave off," Feather growled. "They're not from beyond the fields we know, they're from the bloody Thames bank."

"I think we should go and have a look at Bethnal Green," Leah said with a determined frown, returning to the computer and opening a map application with satellite imagery. "I want to see if there's another crying room there."

"I think you're nuts," Feather said with a smile. "On the railway line?"

"Well—the track looks as though it's elevated," she said, pointing at a brown streak that ran through the city. "Maybe it's underneath. Come on Feather—suppose I'm right?"

"Okay okay—we'll go tomorrow evening, shall we? When you've finished work? As if I don't have enough to do looking for somewhere to fucking live."

"Who knows," Leah said. "Maybe it's full of your magic jewels."

Feather gave a laugh and aimed a playful slap at her. Leah ignored it completely though. She was still staring at the screen with great seriousness.

"As for me," she said, "I am going to send a message to this guy with the other copy—get him to tell me the hidden coordinates. It was a year or so ago, but I might be able to get a response. I am really curious now."

She paused a moment and stared dreamily up at her bookshelves.

"One last mystery for me," she said with a smile.

The next day, Feather sat at the workstation, naked, frowning in concentration. The two-inch flat specimen in her hands had been sawn a while back with the usual deafening assault. It had been on the flat, grinding wheels through all the stages, using blue silicon carbide grit to slowly wear the surfaces first flat and then very smooth. And now it was on the polishing pad with some white tin oxide powder to give it its final mirror shine. She was keeping the glass in constant movement on the wheel, slowly turning it or allowing it to drift in arcs over the moving surface—and every so often lifting it up to see what was going on and switching to a new face, watching the shine increase.

The wheel spun hypnotically with a purr of motors and Feather was starting to zone out, drift away into the strangely peaceful state polishing could take you to . . .

. . . until there was a sound behind her, and a glimpse of movement out of the corner of her eyes. A presence. A figure in the room. She was not alone. She spun round with a massive flinch, the glass polyhedral jumping off the wheel and onto the work surface with a clatter. Fortunately, it didn't break.

She stared at Leah in shock, trying to refocus—a shock that was reciprocated, she realized with a prickle of embarrassment, glancing down at her naked and mud-covered skin.

"Oh dear," Leah stammered. "I'm sorry Feather, I—I'll go . . . I didn't realize . . ."

"It's okay," Feather said gruffly, shutting off the polisher.

"I—it's just that I'm used to coming right in when you can't hear me, you see, so . . . Why are you . . . naked?"

"Believe me, it's easier."

"Well—I—I'll . . ."

"Please, it's fine," Feather said—anything to cut through the soup of embarrassed politeness. "I ain't hung-up."

She reached out into the hall and grabbed her robe, wrapping it around herself.

"Hum—you were bleeding," Leah said, still looking totally flustered. "Are you okay?"

"This glass demands sacrifice, you know," Feather said with a bitter laugh. "You should appreciate that—every piece forged in blood. Very Weird Tale, right?"

"Hum—yes. I . . ."

"Oh snap out of it, Leah," she said with a grin, trying to lighten the mood. "Just don't you dare take a picture and post it on the internet. That's all I ask."

That got a small grin.

"What are you working on?"

"Well—I just need to build up my steel stock a bit after that guy bought most of it." She picked up the piece and held it up proudly. "It's a nice one. Look at that swirl—absolutely beautiful."

"Cool," she said, turning it over. "It's . . . Yes, it is. What's this tiny hole?"

"Probably an air bubble. There's lots of structure in it when you look closely. Flowbanding, little motes of metal or dirt, bubbles, staining . . ."

"Interesting," she murmured, handing it back. "You know—there's something strange about these stones though. They give me an odd feeling."

"Don't you start," Feather said with a smile. "This ain't some bloody horror novel about demon-haunted—industrial by-product. I had enough of that crap with the tie-dye queen."

"No no, seriously. Maybe it's just that they make me think of industry. Maybe it's just that they have a different kind of emotional baggage attached to them than normal stones. But there's something very bleak about them."

"Is there?"

"Yes."

"Maybe it's me," Feather muttered. "Twenty-three estate agents I have tried so far—until I want to punch their smarmy faces in and dance on their salted bones. Unless I build a sound-proof box in the bath, there's not much doing. Maybe you are just picking up my mood from them."

"I ain't saying it's a bad thing, of course," Leah continued. "I've hardly taken off this one you gave me. I really love it. It matches how I feel. I like to look into it." She held it up with a humourless grin. "Maybe if I look hard enough, I can see my future husband in there."

Feather looked at her curiously. "Are you alright?" she asked. "You look a bit . . ."

There was something about her eyes—hollow and showing signs of lack of sleep. Something about her skin—pale and rather ghostly. Her hair and clothes even more untidy and dirty than usual.

" . . . a bit rough," Feather finished.

"Yes, fine," she said. "I have just been doing a lot of thinking lately—and that's never good."

"Gawd Leah—do you need some hug therapy?"

"Maybe," she said with a small smile. "You know—I went back to that room, the crying room in Camden and . . ."

Feather looked up sharply. "You went back there?"

"Hum—yes. This morning."

"Why?" Feather asked cautiously. Her face did look as though there had recently been tears, she realized. Just the faintest ghosts of them.

"I was just—feeling a bit—lonely," Leah mumbled.

"That guy?"

"Not really. But sometimes being stuck on your own in a little box gets to you." She gave a shiver. "Never mind him. I don't want to think about him now."

"That at least sounds positive," Feather said, and Leah gave her an awkward grin.

"But what I wanted to say was . . . there's six of your pieces there now. Aside from his, um, donation I mean. Smaller ones. Generally scattered around."

"Oh," Feather said, no idea at all what to think about that. It gave her a prickle, but she couldn't even begin to imagine why her stones seemed to be gravitating there at such a rate.

"I didn't see that man again unfortunately, but I—I did get a reply to my email. Look." She handed Feather a print-out.

Hello Leah. Interesting that your coordinates are different. The ones in my copy are: 51.541989 and -0.021347

A shame London is so far away—I would like to visit the sites.

Paulo.

"And?" Feather asked.

"I'm afraid it's no more comprehensible than mine. It's a point in the canal in Hackney Wick."

Feather frowned. Leah chose her words with care, she knew, but she asked anyway. "In the canal? Not by the canal?"

"It's a junction—and those arrows in the diagram actually correspond to it rather well, so I was wondering . . ." She shook her head. "It's bizarre. But let's stick to Bethnal Green first. It's my book after all. So—are we going out?"

Feather drew a deep breath.

"Yes—I guess so. Drat you, Leah—you are starting to get me caught up in all this."

She gave a tiny grin.

"Just let me finish shining this piece up, okay?" Feather said, taking it from her. "It's nearly done."

"Yes sure. I . . . ow," she yelped, examining her hand.

"Shit, sorry," Feather said. She grabbed it and plucked the tiny sliver of black out of her palm, dabbing away the mote of blood. "This stuff is a menace—tiny shards of it go everywhere. I was a bloody mess by the time I had finished my first lot. It was all in my clothes, in my hair, all over the floor—we should be wearing hazmat suits or something." She sighed. "I am starting to wonder whether it is worth it."

"Well—is it selling?"

"Yes—people seem to like it a lot. Not enough to live on, but what is?"

"Then I suppose it's worth it . . . hang on," she said, looking sharply at her arm and brushing off a second shard. She gave Feather a wry look. "How on earth—or wherever—did that get there?"

"I told you—menace. Every single piece someone buys is bathed in my blood. Now look," Feather growled, "you sod off into the other room, okay? There's a bottle of wine there—help yourself. Just let me finish this, then I will take a quick shower, get all this glass off me and be with you. Then we'll go. That alright?"

"Of course, of course."

She bundled the flustered bookworm back into the hall and shut the door with a laugh. She shed the robe again and looked down at herself. She was indeed bleeding in a few places—small red smudges, nothing dramatic. Her skin cut by the tiny slivers that had gone pinging everywhere, then absently been brushed at or leaned against or sat on. But she shrugged that off and returned to the stone. It was nearly done—nearly a mirror shine.

"Do you—hum, do you usually work naked?"

Feather blushed slightly, glancing round at the crowd of people currently exiting the train with them.

"Well, yes," she said softly. "I just got fed up with it ruining my clothes. There's only so many scrap work clothes I can wear—and the mud you get when you cut and polish gets everywhere. It eats right through the fabric—you get holes, splits, stains . . ."

"That's an image of you I never had before," Leah said with a grin. "You are really quite cute when you are naked."

"You're drunk," Feather said with a friendly frown, taking Leah by the shoulders and guiding her bodily towards the ticket gates.

"I am not," Leah growled. "I'm tipsy. And I said I'm sorry about your bottle mysteriously going empty. But look, I just want to know why you didn't flip out? I'd probably have gone squealing for the towel like an idiot."

"I dunno," Feather said. "I suppose I just grew up without the squealing genes. Now—have you got the map?"

"Hum. Hum—yes."

Leah dragged out a rather sodden bundle of papers and stared at them in some bewilderment.

"Give it here," Feather said and twitched them out of her fingers. The first wasn't the map, it was the email from Paulo—the co-ordinates in Hackney Wick. Wrong place. She shoved that in her pocket. The second, though, was a simple computer printout, an X-marks-the-spot of the *Black Lachrimæ* letter J coordinates. She stared around, trying to fit map to reality.

"Okay . . . yes. I think it's this way . . ."

They began to walk. Right and then right again—back under the railway. Then left, then right, left, left, right—always with the railway line haunting them nearby and overhead. It was an elevated line, seeming to invade the city on endless brick arches. Four tracks on which urban commuter trains ran—not the Tube but one of the smaller main-line railways that eventually pulled into Liverpool Street station. Dense East London buildings clustered round the tracks, and many of the archways were occupied by small businesses, storage areas, shops, garages, etc.

"You know," Feather began cautiously, "how long ago was that book published?"

Leah took out her copy of *Black Lachrimæ* and studied it for a moment. "About six years," she said.

"A lot can change in six years," Feather said, looking round. "How the heck do these crying rooms survive anyway? You know the only thing that matters in London is money."

Here, a small bed emporium had taken up residence in one arch—then a taxi office, what looked like a shadowy antique shop, and an off-licence. It all seemed too populated, too ridden with the sense of desperation that you always felt in London. Surely any place even close to a crying room would have been ripped out and sold for about five times a fair price years ago?

But then they turned into a street that was even more withdrawn and hidden than most—and things changed a little. Here, suddenly, there were no shops, just a few yards of some kind or another—and an area of wasteland behind high razor-wire-topped fences. And a carefully locked and chained gate, complete with security and trespassing warnings.

"Somewhere here," Leah said, looking nonplussed.

Beyond the fence, the arches looked as though they had died. Bricked off and blind save for a few ancient wooden doors—maybe used for something once but now completely abandoned. On one of the doors, though, was what looked like a mark of white paint. Two horizontal lines and a circle. Feather stared at it, then at Leah.

"Look," Leah whispered. A few yards away, there was a low hole in the fence, also seemingly marked by a few rough lines of white paint on the ground.

Feather was suddenly very glad that Leah was with her. There was little of the comforting grief about this so far—it was actually rather unnerving.

"Is that . . . what is it?" Feather asked, shrugging off her amazement.

"There's only one way to find out, I think."

Feather watched, feeling every nerve in her body prickling with unease as Leah bent over and scrambled through into the courtyard. Then, with a weary shake of her head, she followed. It occurred to her then that if these crying rooms were indeed a part of London's mental or psychic geography, or whatever you wanted to call it, then what was stopping them being used for things with much darker overtones? What was to stop people finding these crying rooms and waiting there for the lonely and miserable for their own purposes?

Absolutely nothing, was the answer to that. And the only way a crying room could function at all was to accept that risk.

They hurried across to the marked door, anxious not to be seen on the wrong side of the fence. Leah pushed it open and stared in cautiously.

"Well?" Feather whispered.

"It's a crying room," she said simply, pushing the door wider. "It has to be."

Everything inside was dark and silent. There was a small setup by the door—a lamp on a stand connected to a car battery. But when she tried the switch, it was dead. She dragged her torch out of her bag instead and flashed it around the room—and ended up standing there in total silence for several long minutes, feeling overwhelmed.

Maybe the fact that this room had no one to look after it—or at least less so than the Camden room—meant that people were rather more uninhibited here. The room in Camden had been like a museum—a beautiful, haunting, controlled tribute to human grief. This place on the other hand—it was hard to know even where to begin. Stuff filled the walls and corners looking almost like a geological phenomenon, as though this arched chamber was a geode filled with the ever-growing crystals of human misery. Photos and papers had been stuck on the walls, on top of other photos and papers in a dense layer. Indeed, she had the impression that if she was to take a geological hammer and cut into it all, it would go on for a long way—fossilized grief a foot thick all round. There were even places where it seemed to have given way—chunks and sheets of it peeling off and falling to the floor, revealing older layers. And there was more than just photos and trinkets here as well. Unlike the previous room, this whole place was a jumble of spray-painted messages and art so dense that she could hardly read anything specific. There were also stranger things. A box in one corner full of papers, which she quickly worked out were handwritten pages, maybe of a novel of some kind. A few half-buried bones in another corner suggested that a dead pet had been left here, maybe a cat.

The only furniture, aside from rickety shelves piled high with trinkets, was an old armchair. There were a few books there as well. Looking at them, she was not entirely surprised to recognize the Darkening World logo on the spine, and she read the titles with interest. Some of them were authors she recognized from Leah's collection. These books were somewhat different though—surviving in the wild, they had suffered badly, if suffered was the right word. They had been drawn on, written on, notes scribbled on the inside, even covered with spray paint where the graffiti had strayed too close. There was even a copy of *Black Lachrimæ*, but when she opened it she realized that it was just a standard copy—no letter or inscription. Not one of the first thirty-four.

How long had this place been here? she wondered in complete awe. Was the railway company completely unaware of what lurked beneath their busy line? Or did they know—and somehow accept the vital importance of it? It was hard to imagine any company doing a thing like that, but surely they had to inspect the bridge occasionally at the very least?

Leah was just standing there, a very weird look on her face—a look somewhat familiar from last time, as though simultaneously dreading yet pining for the appearance of a ghost.

Feather's eyes, used to picking out the familiar, spotted a flash of black in a prominent place among the items—and it wasn't even surprising. It was one of her larger pieces—one of the two-inch black mirrors on a steel chain. One of the first twelve handed over just yesterday. She could remember working on it. She could remember the constellation of tiny gleaming metal motes in the glass—five of them. She could remember having to shave a few millimetres off after a small chip came loose. She could remember working the metal around it. And now, here it was. Images of the ugly man in the black coat wandering round the city on some crazy delivery route, moving from crying room to crying room, settled in her mind and refused to budge. Who was this person? And why?

Leah took the little black mirror from her fingers and stared at it, still with that very odd look on her face.

"What are you doing?" Feather asked.

"I just thought . . . I mean . . ." Leah mumbled to silence. "I thought I saw something," she whispered.

"You what?"

"In the reflection . . . I could have sworn . . ."

"What was it?"

Leah just stared at the stone, then it slipped through her fingers and she gave a faint moan. It landed on the cluttered floor with a tiny thud and that brief trickle you get as a fine chain piles up. She glanced down at the specimen round her own neck for a moment, then gave a wail and clutched at her face, suddenly looking a lot more intoxicated.

"What is it?" Feather cried.

Leah just gave her a weird look and mumbled something. It sounded like, "Always the same expression."

"Huh?"

Then, to Feather's increased disquiet, she shook her head and began to dance. It was just a few awkward stylized steps round the room but it looked more like some formal folk dance than anything you might find on a dance floor today—her arms extended as though holding onto an invisible partner. She gave Feather a slightly wry grin, as though well aware of what she was doing, but it couldn't quite mask a feeling of intense twisted misery below the surface.

"Bastard," she hissed at last, with a sharp arm gesture, breaking away from the dance and sitting down in the chair with a sigh. Her whole body was shaking. She wasn't crying. This didn't look like emotional release. She was terrified, pure and simple. Feather tried to take the big black stone from her fingers and undo the clasp, but Leah clung onto it with such sharp determination that Feather backed away in shock.

"Sorry," Leah muttered after a moment's frozen silence. "That was rather weird."

"What happened?"

"I was just—remembering a few things. There's always so much to remember."

"What things?"

"I don't want to talk about it. But care to give me a hug? I think I need it."

Feather opened her arms and Leah jumped up and hugged her tightly for a long minute—then abruptly squirmed round and kissed her on the lips—a touch of wine-flavoured moisture. Feather stared blankly.

"Leah—I'm not, whatever his name is," she said softly.

"I know—fuck him. Or rather don't. I mean . . ." Leah now sounded very drunk indeed, still hanging onto her with her face buried in her neck.

"What are you trying to do?" Feather whispered, going rigid as she felt a hand brushing at her thigh, as though it desperately wanted to find her backside but didn't quite dare. Leah leaned back a moment and stared up at her with hopeful eyes. It was clear enough.

"Look," Feather said slowly, "we could, but . . . I dunno. You don't think you would just end up hurting more?"

Leah stared at her, her eyes moist.

"'s a pendulum," she said. "He swings it one way an' it gets stuck in some shit. You could swing it the other."

"I didn't even know you were bi," Feather mumbled.

"Everyone is, if they only admitted it. Even if jus' a tiny bit. That's—that's gender fluidity that is."

"Look . . . Leah, please," Feather said, gently trying to disentangle herself. "If you're really feeling like . . . well, go and find a stranger, or even hire someone. It'd probably do you good. Seriously—I'll come with you, if you like. But . . ."

"But I don't love them," Leah mumbled. "I love you Feather. I love you so much . . ."

"Oh gawd," Feather said. "I don't think you have seen nearly enough naked people."

"I' seen pictures."

"Pictures don't count," Feather said firmly. "Never have, never will. Come on—calm down."

"Do humans ever want sex at the same time?" Leah asked sadly, seeming to give up and standing hunched and staring at nothing.

"Legend says it must happen occasionally," Feather said. "Sort of like solar eclipses." It was an attempt to lighten the mood but it didn't seem to work. Leah drew a deep breath and drew herself up to her full height.

"Okay—sorry," she muttered. "I guess I am just a—a bit mixed up at the moment." She turned away.

"There's no need to go," Feather said, horrified, but Leah ignored her.

"I'll see you sometime," she muttered and stepped outside.

"Wait a minute," Feather yelled—but Leah was already gone. She stared at the blank space where she had been for a moment, then hurried to the door in time to see her scramble through the fence and make her way down the road. She wanted to run after her, but instead she swore loudly and stepped back inside. It was clear enough from Leah's body language that it would not help matters much.

After a moment of collecting her thoughts, she retrieved the donated piece of jewellery from the floor, feeling a massive chill. Again, there seemed something very different about the way Leah was behaving. Not as though anything new had been added—but maybe as though what was there was suddenly very clear and raging on the surface.

Maybe there really was something weird going on with this glass. It was industrial by-product after all—maybe it was slightly poisonous. Was that even possible?

Alone now, the space seemed to come crashing in around her like waves, engendering a kind of terror. She studied the chair cautiously. It looked ancient. Faded, stained with unknown substances, the cover split in places and oozing foam, a slight looseness and wonkiness about the frame . . . who knew what had taken place in that chair over the years. And as she sat down, ready to react if it collapsed or tried to bite her or something, she had a bizarre sense of communion between her own arse and those of maybe a hundred others who had been here before her. It came with a prickling sensation, as if in some way they were still there in that ancient fabric. If, as some say, a ghost is a kind of tape recording, then who says you need to be dead? In this place, where the walls themselves seemed to drip grief, maybe any human being was going to leave something of themselves behind.

She fingered the black jewellery, then aimed her torch at the surface. All that did was produce a blaze of glare, so she turned it round and idly aimed it at her own face. It created a gothic up-lit effect—a cliché in real life, a decidedly bizarre visual when reflected in the slag, and she had to smile. The impurities in the glass morphed her reflection, twisting and bulging, somehow exaggerating her eyes until they were like black holes in the universe. This glass definitely had some curious visual properties, no doubt connected to the slightly uneven and varied surface. It was not hard to see how some people might be fascinated by the reflections in these stones. Or how others could be horrified. She remembered the Tie-Dye Girl who had returned the piece to her in disgust and smiled again. It was hard to imagine her type ever using a crying room, so desperate to tune the world around her down some imagined pathway to purity—grief and darkness nothing more than something to be shoved down the sewer of the soul and forgotten about.

She leaned back in the chair and closed her eyes, the jewel's delicate steel chain trailing through her fingers. The air in here was like oil and she could almost feel it crawling over her skin.

"What's in your head, Leah?" she asked aloud.

Leah was a mystery, but there was something in her own head now. There always was, of course—it was never far away, but now it came with exceptional clarity. The image of herself sitting forlornly on the wet pavement in a dreary London street, outside a determinedly locked door, surrounded by her various lapidary and metalworking machines. She gave a shiver. That was normal enough but now her racing imagination began to show her something stranger. There was an endless scattering of black glass jewels that filled the road as far as she could see, moulding around the parked cars. It was beautiful—a river of jewellery, like some weird art installation. But then, unexpectedly, there was a snick of a lighter and a flash of fire. And it wasn't water she was sitting in. Flames engulfed her in an orange fireball—roaring down the street—and one after another, the black jewels popped and burst into shards, spraying shiny silver sparks that drifted skywards . . .

She opened her eyes with a jolt, the trickle of a tear moistening her skin.

One tear. If the crying room could drag even that out of her then it must be powerful.

"This is crazy," she muttered. "We have every reason to feel fucked up, but . . ."

She stared at the encrusted walls of the archway.

"No," she yelled aloud, a nasty tremble starting in her body. "Fuck you. Fuck all this."

With a violent gesture, she shoved the black tear into her pocket, shoved the door open and fled.

Leah was lying curled up in bed looking as tense as a screwed-up coat hanger when Feather finally managed to make contact again the next day.

"Leah—what the heck . . . what's wrong? You look terrible?"

She gave Feather a very wary look, then stared back down into the pillow. On her shoulder, very distinctly, a seventh line had been added. But this one was red. No doubt done with a sharp knife. The sight chilled Feather profoundly.

At least it's the shortest, she thought, feeling a touch of hysteria.

"In my head I can hear screams," Leah muttered, with a singular lack of drama in her voice. "Over and over—I should be screaming them. But they are just in there echoing around—just these endless screams over and over and over and over . . ."

Then the crack came.

"I just can't stand this," she wailed, curling up even tighter under the quilt and abruptly grabbing her knees. "I can't get it out—there's no point even trying to get it out. Because—you shut it outside the door, it's always waiting for you again when you turn round."

"Leah, for gawd sake . . ."

"These things," she managed, jabbing at the necklace around her neck, at the black stone, "they are mirrors, you know. They can only show you what's there. No magic. Just mirrors . . ."

"Leah—I think I need to get you some help . . ."

"No."

"Have you been on anything stronger than the booze today?" Feather demanded.

"No I fucking haven't."

"Come on," Feather said implacably. "Let me have a look at the laptop—try and find someone to phone, okay? I don't have a clue about this."

"You think I'm crazy?" she muttered.

"Of course I bloody don't—but you can't just lie there and tear yourself to pieces. We can try and sort all this out."

Very slowly, Leah sat up. She seemed to be naked aside from the necklace. "Okay," she muttered. "But first—I want to go out. Will you come with me?"

"I dunno. Where?"

"I just want a bit of fresh air. Look—I'm not going mad, you know. I don't normally let you see this—or anyone—but unfortunately it's nothing unusual."

"Alright," Feather said with a sigh.

Leah scrambled out of bed—and yes, she was naked. "See," she said with a smile as she grabbed clean clothes from a drawer and climbed into them. "I can do it too."

Feather grinned uncertainly. Some unwelcome part of her mind spoke up then, stating that in a way, she looked better naked than she did dressed. A body was a body, but clothes could be almost anything, and not always good. In her own way, and provided you weren't in the thrall of unreal ideals, Leah was beautiful.

Then she found herself hustled outside into the Camden afternoon, trailing after her friend in the direction of Camden Road Station.

"I always liked riding the trains," Leah said a few minutes later as they stepped aboard one of the small Overground metro services. "Sometimes when I was feeling down, I would buy a travelcard and just go wandering all over, whatever train took my fancy. It's like meditation, if you don't mind watching a lot of pissed-off people who have to be somewhere. But even that wasn't so bad when you are free."

Feather grinned at that, but then the conversation stalled. They rode for what seemed a long, long time, barely exchanging a word, changing from train to train until she had very little idea where they were. Stations passed by—some vaguely familiar, some that she had never heard of. She wasn't even sure if they were heading north, south, east or west—just somewhere in the vast sprawl of London's rail network. Leah was resisting all attempts to influence her or head for home again and there was nothing to do but follow. In the end, Feather was starting to feel bored and frustrated, though she refused to show it. Leah might find it meditative but she wasn't sure it was having a positive effect on her own mood, especially as worry gnawed.

Eventually, though, the rambling and seemingly random journey reached an interlude. They arrived at one of the larger mainline stations in the west of the city, some way out from the centre on the Great Western Railway. And instead of finding a new train, Leah just led her to an almost empty platform and they sat down on a bench.

"Leah," Feather asked, "why are we here?"

"Why be anywhere?" Leah said, and Feather almost gave an impatient sigh. "I liked it here. Trains going by . . . people to watch . . ."

There was an uncomfortable pause.

"Look," Leah said at last, "I—I'm sorry about what happened . . . I mean . . ."

"It's . . . okay. You really don't need to apologize . . ."

"I mean—I'm not exactly sorry. I mean—how I feel is how I feel . . . I mean it's not about that, I'm just sorry for making such an idiot of myself. Hum . . ."

"Please," Feather said, sounding impatient but actually feeling relieved that serious talk was flowing again. Leah was looking much calmer and more normal now. "It's okay—really. It's just . . . what happened to you? I'm sure something did."

"I . . ."

Leah hesitated. There was a whispering thrum in the tracks in front of them. Almost before thought, the train came in from the distance with a scream of engines—an extraordinary blast of noise into the relative peace of the platform. This was not a small, slow urban train; it was a huge intercity, a sharp-nosed HST going at almost a hundred miles per hour, barrelling in towards London Paddington. It passed by with a percussive bang and a blast of air. That unique sound they made—*screeeeEEEEeeeeowow-owow-owow-owow-owow-owow-owow-owow-owow-owow-owow-oweeeEEEEEEeee* . . .

"Bloody hell," Feather muttered.

Leah was staring after it bleakly.

"It's a long time since I travelled on one of those," she said at last. "London can be a trap sometimes."

"Maybe when . . . if I ever find somewhere to live, we should make a trip."

"Maybe."

"So . . . ?" Feather prodded hopefully. "You were saying?"

There was a long silence.

"Oh—it's nothing much. Just memories. Same old memories. I suppose they got to me a bit."

"What were they?"

"You really want to hear?"

"Yes—if it will help."

"Well . . . this particular one was when I was young," Leah muttered at last. "At school—for some stupid reason they decided to hold some kind of dance in the playground. It was a circle—moving round, partner after partner. Most of it was okay, I suppose. But then I had to run across this guy—I never liked him much, and I guess he returned it because he gave me such a look of disgust. As if merely to touch me was somehow poisonous. But at that precise moment, the dance changed. *Keep your partners*, they yelled—and I was stuck with him for the next half an hour—always acting as though I smelled bad—until I was literally shaking and trying not to cry. It was horrible. Maybe it affected me more than it should. But the thing is—it seems as though—even today, it's the same dance. Dancing through life, every single partner filled with that same look on their faces. So much disgust. Does that make any sense at all . . . ?"

And then there were tears. Leah broke down into sobbing. "That was almost twenty years ago," she managed.

"Um—look," Feather said, "if I just say he was an ill-mannered jerk, will that help at all?"

"Not really," Leah muttered. Feather got one arm round her neck and squeezed comfortingly, feeling something close to desperation. How did you go about making someone feel better, when you got right down to it? It seemed that even the crying rooms weren't much use at that. After all—they merely facilitated; they could never fix. Words seemed especially useless, so she didn't say any, just tried to inject a bit of warmth through that contact until Leah had calmed down again. Some of the other travellers were looking at them curiously but she ignored that as utterly irrelevant.

"I think—that guy may have been right about the stones," Feather said at last. "You too. Don't ask me how but . . ."

More silence.

"Look—can I . . . have that piece back?"

"Hum . . ."

"I don't trust it. I wish I had never found this fucking glass. There seems—just so much misery clustering round it. And I still don't understand why."

Somewhat to her surprise, Leah quietly undid the clasp and handed it to her. "Sure—you might as well keep it safe."

Feather slipped it into her pocket.

"Maybe I can get the others back as well. It might be possible. I might be able to track down some of the other crying rooms. Or that guy again. Didn't he say he lived on a boat?"

"Yes."

"I wish now that I had never found the stuff."

"But you know," Leah said with a tiny smile, "don't shoot the messenger. After all, what's the point of living in denial? You are still miserable; you're just pretending you don't know why. Pretending that three-headed beast isn't actually there, sitting right in the middle of your living room." The smile broadened slightly. "Sometimes it's hard to tell the difference between a miracle and a horror story."

Feather shook her head, trying to make the confusion go away. The world shouldn't work like this. Stones were stones. One of the great comforts about them was that they were just there, the ultimate lack of complexity, at least in human terms. They just *were.*

"I love you Feather," Leah whispered, "you know that? One way or another. And maybe it doesn't even matter so much which . . ."

Feather gave her a cautious look, then rubbed at her back again. "I love you too," she said with a grin. "One way or another."

There was another long silence.

"Are you mad at me?" Leah asked at last.

"No," Feather said in surprise. "Why should I be?"

"I didn't think you would be," Leah said. "But I just wanted to make sure."

"How are you feeling now?"

"Not too good to be honest," Leah said. "I've been alone too long. I've failed too many times. Pain is the ultimate pollution. Just like the physical body, you know—where a pain in one area can cripple you from head to toe, so emotional pain can send similar tendrils through the entire mind and consciousness and whatever, until you are mentally crippled, possibly beyond repair. You cease to function like a normal human being. And I suppose sooner or later, you have to make a choice. Right?"

"What choice?" Feather asked uneasily.

Somewhere behind them, there was a rising drone as one of the London Underground trains slid into motion and trundled away. Such a different sound to the intercity that Feather almost smiled.

"You know," Leah said. "You always have to decide whether something is worthwhile. It's a simple cost-benefit calculation. Does the positive outweigh the negative?"

"Positive what?" Feather demanded.

"Life," Leah whispered.

In the background, there was the faintest of faint sound in the tracks again—a whisper and thrumming. Leah looked round quickly. "I'm sorry, Feather," she said.

"For what?"

"That you had to see this," she said, her voice speeding up. "I must be a coward. And totally blinded after all these years. I'm sorry if this hurts—but maybe you can also see that it's for the best? That one has to be logical. And I just couldn't face doing it alone. I wanted to talk first—say goodbye properly. And I want you to know it's not your fault in any way. I have been alone too much to be alone now . . ."

"What are you talking about?" Feather demanded in increasing terror. But Leah had jumped to her feet.

"Hey," Feather yelled. In the distance, the train had appeared—another HST going just as fast as the previous, racing in at shocking speed. In just a moment, it was passing the end of the platform . . .

ScreeeeEEEEEEEEEE . . .

And Leah almost danced forward . . .

It was extraordinarily as though she was just diving into a swimming pool—a graceful, almost sexy plunge.

There was a blast of horn from the train . . .

Feather actually screamed, a negative blast that hurt her throat . . . but there was no time to get beyond that scream because the train was there, passing in a howl of engines and wind—shaking the ground—buffeting Feather's face with the slipstream—emergency brakes applied in a haze of smoke.

And Leah was just—not there anymore.

Carriages blurred by one after the other, each one a double assault of wheels—*owow-owow-owow-owow*—then the engine at the back, screaming just as loud as the front. And a moment later, it had passed—still in its emergency stop but unable to come to a halt until it was small in the distance.

There was an agonizing silence. Station staff running in her direction, startled travellers looking round, trying to work out what the sudden feeling of chaos in the air was about.

And unable to stop herself, Feather had to step forward and look down onto the track . . .

For centuries, since before records began, the grief-stricken have trod the ancient streets of the capital. When the Roman legions carried their banners through the paved streets, they were here. When the Anglo-Saxon tribes had set up their encampments within the ruins, after the Romans had withdrawn, they were here. Down through the centuries, unmarked in the annals of history, during the Black Death and the Great Fire, when London turned from the Old Faith to fanatic Protestantism, even from belief to unbelief, when the Nazis rained down death from the skies, they had been here, eternal, unchanging, forever bound to the primal depths buried beneath the human soul—the realms of humanity that can never truly be forgotten. And over times vaster than any the human mind may know, such things crystallise, even take on an obscure life of their own.

And in these rooms, which I now suspect may in some senses be as old as the city itself as it grew among the marshes and the forests, I sit. I am a prisoner now, yet with little urge to leave. I was summoned, as so many others have been, and I fear I am now sustenance for some entity beyond myself. Who knows what it is? Some malevolent, demonic presence, force of nature, maybe even nothing at all. Maybe merely the conjunction of human minds. Or maybe I am wrong and it is myself, after all. But whatever it is, it calls out across the city, from Commercial Road to Stepney Green. From Adelina Road to Belgrave Street. I am surrounded by the shadows of my predecessors, feeling like a breath of air in the stillness. I sit in this chair, redolent of age, take out my notebook and begin to write.

Black Lachrimæ p. 82

It was a long bike ride along the canal to the point she was aiming for. She had started far to the north on the Lea Navigation—just in case—and headed south straight into London. Filled with a sense of futility, it was nevertheless nice to actually be doing something. With barely any idea why she was doing it, it nevertheless all seemed crystal clear. The physical effort helped her think, yet kept her mind from thinking too much.

It was a few days later. The confused haze as the official cogs of the world processed what had happened had come and gone now. It had all seemed so very sanitized—so clean and polite, as though the mess spread along the railway tracks had never been real. As though Leah had just wandered off to somewhere else. As though any goodbye had been just that, a farewell at the railway station with a single ticket. That was the thing—the world is always keen to sanitize and protect—maybe too keen. It fills the media with a fantasy of violence as unreal as a ballet and carefully hides any reference to the real thing, so it is almost impossible to process it anymore when it finally comes for you.

Did you know that the material used for soaking up human blood on the railway line is basically cat litter?

And now, in a state of contradictory numbness, Feather rode. The bicycle was the only way to travel the London canals with any kind of efficiency and the towpaths formed some of the most important off-road routes in the city. They were narrow and often busy but they cut through London in a world of their own, passing under bridge after bridge and with a constant parade of moored narrowboats for company. Feather whirled through it all, dropping south, stepping down with the locks—Enfield, Tottenham, Clapton. Even at this distance from her target, she was quietly scanning the boats as she passed, just in case any clue presented itself. Though what that clue might be, she had no idea. There were lots of boats, usually parked two abreast alongside the towpath. They ranged from cute-looking classical hobby boats to chaotic residential craft, the roofs and decks piled high with stuff that wouldn't fit inside—wood fuel for the stoves, stray items of furniture, bicycles, plants in tubs, solar panels, even a few small wind turbines. Maybe these were the boats that fitted the real boater's lifestyle.

How much would one of these things cost? More than she had, that was for sure.

Eventually she arrived in Hackney Wick and the actual point indicated in the co-ordinates that Leah had found. Letter B—Paulo's copy of *Black Lachrimæ*. This was where the Hertford Union canal joined from the west, a cramped and obscure little waterway that provided access to the famous Regent's Canal, the Grand Union and the two thousand miles or so of waterways that criss-crossed the UK.

And here, where the canals split, she rolled to a stop, staring round in despair. The narrowboats here looked no different to any of the others, and the surrounding buildings were even less help. There was an urban factory beside her, a modern block of flats across the water to the south, and to the east was just a brief, newly planted slope stretching up towards the edge of the Olympic Park, with its bizarre modern constructions—the strangest being the tangled Orbit tower, which someone might have screwed up in a temper. She remained looking, examining the boats, then dragged out the crumpled printout—*Black Lachrimæ* letter B. As Leah had said, the scribbled diagram corresponded easily enough with the three waterways that met at this point. But all this cryptic clue might possibly have meant was that sometime, many years ago, a boat, of some kind, had sailed these waters. A boat that could look like almost anything, but may once have contained a crying room? And possibly a certain resident.

Feather gave a weary sigh and slipped the paper back into her pocket again. Was this really worth it? This whole thing was starting to feel like a farce. Leah was dead. She was going to be homeless soon enough, her London life basically over, her jewellery-making totally stalled—no more black tears, though that at least was probably a good thing. And of all ways to exhaustedly crawl up to the white wall that was her future, wandering round here looking for a six-year-old boat that might not exist seemed the most futile. There was another way of thinking about that though: with no future and no hope, there was literally nothing better to do.

"You looking for something?"

It was a friendly enough call but she flinched violently. The voice had come from a boatman who had stepped out onto the tiny stern deck of one of the narrowboats and was looking at her curiously. He was scruffy—the comfortable careless scruffiness that spoke of possibly a more advanced state of humanity than anyone wasting their time trying to be merely tidy. A scruffiness that Leah might have empathized with. The boat itself was also scruffy, the roof piled high with stuff, and possibly the same thought might be applied to that as well.

"Uuuhh—I dunno. Does the term 'crying room' mean anything to you?"

He looked puzzled. "Is that a boat? I never 'eard of it."

"It could be," Feather said miserably. "It might have been here—a while back."

He shrugged. "Hard to tell," he said. "Most of us, the ones tied up here on the banks, we're continuous cruisers. That means we all 'av to move on every two weeks. That's the rules. It's hard to keep track of things."

"Two weeks?"

"Yup—when was that one of yours here? Could 'av moved on anywhere really. It was called the Crying Room?"

Feather swallowed. "It was—about 6 years ago. Maybe. And I'm not sure what it was called. Ummm . . ." The man was staring at her, the expression on his face clearly questioning her mental state. "Look—don't worry about it. I think this is all a bit . . . pointless."

"A lot can happen in six years," he said, not unkindly. "All this . . ." He waved at the Olympic Park. " . . . that's all gone up since then. These swanky buildings, the footbridge—it's a new world round here. And this boat—could 'av gone down to Camden, could have gone to the bloody lake district, you know. There's a lot of canal."

Feather nodded sadly. "Thanks," she said. She slid onto the bike again and pushed off, rolling on very slowly down the towpath—drifting onwards into the more claustrophobic world of the Hertford Union. Maybe it was indeed pointless to have ever expected to find anything here—yet even now she couldn't help looking. It was as if her brain had set itself onto a path and would follow it come what may, because who knows what would be revealed if it didn't?

Back in the days when the canals had been a working system, they had been treated with the same loathing as the railways—something to be hidden behind walls, something behind the backs of buildings rather than in front. Now, though, an inversion had taken place. Now they were something to overlook—the water used as a key to push up the prices of any property in the vicinity. Thus the bizarre mixture of blind and claustrophobic old brick walls and luxury new apartments stinking of money on these inner-city waterways.

She passed on. Under the footbridge—up around the first lock—and then into the vaguely sinister concrete space beneath the huge road bridge that carried the A12 out of London. This was a dark and noisy place, not to say noisome, with its tang of unwashed soil and dark spaces where neither light nor rain could ever meet the earth. Somewhat to her surprise, there were boats tied up under here as well. The line of them seemed unbroken, even by the continuous susurration of traffic that now dominated the world. She studied them curiously, trying to work out what kind of people would live on these things in the whispering gloom.

Then, so suddenly it nearly caused an accident, she slammed on the brakes and skidded to a halt, staring in utter shock. There was a tick and splash as a few pieces of gravel bounced down into the water.

On one of the boats, looming out of the semi-dark, there was a large W. She stared at it, skin prickling. For the name of the boat was

The Darkening World

For a long time, she didn't move. It was a fairly ordinary-looking boat, probably fifty feet long, and painted black with a neat row of square windows along its length. It had no special Weird or literary décor as far as she could see. On the roof was the familiar large stack of firewood, several solar panels and a canoe. On the tiny stern deck were pots of what looked like herbs, looking healthy enough in spite of the low light down here. There was nothing about it to indicate a crying room either.

Or was there? Towards the front, in one window alongside the boat's licence number, a sign was hanging. It just contained three symbols, with a green pointer that could be moved to indicate any one of them.

At the moment, it was pointing at the circle.

It was sufficiently enigmatic and incomprehensible that it pricked at her, reminiscent of the double lines that had marked the crying room in Bethnal Green and the solo/company sign on the door at Camden. What were the three states of a crying room, after all? *Open, company* and *closed.* It was enough to give her the courage to explore further, anyway. Leaving her bike by the towpath, she stepped cautiously onto the tiny stern deck—easy enough since there was a gap of only a few inches between boat and towpath. There wasn't much room here—most of the narrowboats had very little outside space, and what there was was usually taken up with 'stuff'—in this case pots of herbs, a few ornaments, a small chair and several wooden boxes. It was an alien place somehow—an utterly different lifestyle to anything she had ever experienced before. It reminded her of stepping into a squat where people lived better than she did—or an Occupy tent—or sitting with the homeless in the streets. Something *different.* And maybe that was the point, she thought. Such difference was only going to prove more and more important in the world.

She was going to knock at the door—or at least knock at something—but there was no need. There was a movement inside and the door opened.

"Hello Feather," a very familiar figure said, looking up at her with a smile.

"Oh," she said. "I . . . why am I not surprised to find you here?"

He stepped back with a welcoming gesture.

"Please—come in."

She climbed down the steps into the interior. Somehow it had not dawned on her before how low down the floor level was in these things. Now, though, she found herself in what looked like a small lounge or living room—very long and thin, small high windows looking out onto the towpath and the canal itself. She stared round curiously.

"I—I thought this was a crying room," she muttered. "Somehow—I was . . . I mean, it's a long story but don't the co-ordinates point to . . ?"

"It is," he said. "At the front. Some people come here regularly. You came in the back end, you see."

"Oh . . ."

"This is my home, Feather."

She stared round the boat curiously.

"Where else could I live?" he asked with a shrug. "As I think you know, normal housing is in the process of breaking down rather. This was something I observed a while back, so I took steps . . ."

"It's . . . very nice," she said.

"All the comforts of home, provided you don't mind long and thin. And water everywhere. But please—sit down. Be comfortable. Can I get you anything? Drink? I have some juice. Maybe some tea somewhere, though I rarely drink it."

"I—I—juice would be great, thanks."

The lounge segued comfortably into a tiny kitchen, complete with a full-size stove and a fridge, which he briefly rummaged in. A glass of orange juice was provided and Feather sipped it, actually feeling some relief.

"I am going to have to move soon," he said. "The solar panels aren't doing a very good job under this bridge, you know."

"I—I suppose so. Where . . . ?"

"Hopefully not too far away. This area, the Wick, was my home originally. I was here when it was first colonized by the artists—the real ones, not the pampered gentry who are the only people who can afford to live here now. I range up and down the Lee, but always I come back to the Wick sooner or later. It is one of those places where you can still smell traces of magic in the air."

There was a long silence. Feather was not very familiar with the Wick, but knew enough to follow what he was saying. As one of the creative nexuses of London, it was a place that rather suited this literary mystery, even though the most obvious art here was painted on walls rather than written in books.

"So—what brings you here?" he asked.

Feather nodded slowly, taking another sip of juice. "You were right," she said at last, not looking at him.

"About?"

"My stones," she said. "They are indeed black tears. And then Leah . . ."

"I know," he said.

"Know?"

He nodded.

"You know she . . . ?"

"I know," he repeated. "Look at this." She followed his gaze to one of the bookshelves and stared in surprise. Alongside a range of titles from *Darkening World*, there were others, some very familiar. Hauntingly familiar. Quentin S. Crisp. Nina Allan. Mark Samuels. "Yes, she gave them to me. I brought them here, and to the other crying rooms. Books can also be a comfort. If you go back to Camden, you might observe some there, too."

"You're telling me she knew in advance?"

"Oh yes—at least a few days. Probably longer."

Feather just stared—and inside her the ice crackled and shook.

"You mean—even as she was getting excited about those co-ordinates and the crying rooms . . . she was already planning . . . ?"

"It would appear so. An interesting character, Leah," he said. "I suspect a person after my own heart in some ways. And one of far too many that have dropped by the wayside." His voice fell to a whisper—and suddenly the boat seemed even more shadowy than could be explained by just the concrete bridge alone. "It is as though I can see them," he said. "As though I can see things that nobody who lives on the surface of this world ever lets themselves see. It is as though I am watching a million candles, slowly being snuffed one by one. And you know—some go out. Others, most of them, merely flicker low. They dwindle and sputter. And I do not know which ones make me feel saddest. Your stones though—one feature they have is to make everything very, very clear. There is no room for anything then but the truth."

There was a silence—a very deep silence that was almost deafening. Feather glanced at her hand and was unsurprised to find that it was trembling.

"I thought for a while you must be him," she said at last. "The author. Samuels. I thought you had to be. Somehow you were the one who had discovered all this and included the info in your book . . ."

"I'm not the author," he said with a grin. "Mark, he's doing quite well these days, I hear. Quite well known among those who care about such things."

"Yeah. It's funny but I kind of forgot all about the publisher. You are—*Darkening World*, right?"

"That's right," he said. "Or rather, I was."

Feather nodded, then handed over the crumpled papers, the photo of *Black Lachrimæ* letter B and Paulo's message. "This is how I found you."

"Very nice," he murmured, looking wistful, his face transformed into something strangely beautiful. "This copy was purchased by a guy in Portugal about five seconds after I opened the book to preorders. It's kind of nice to see he still has it. Those were fun days. The first copies are always special. A chance to whip up the buyers a bit—give them something unique and individual. We decided to hide the locations of the real crying rooms in each one, as I am sure you have guessed. Just in case anyone ever cracked the secret—or could be bothered to look into it. To the best of my knowledge, nobody did—until now, anyway. It was what you might call a petty mystery—but a bit of fun nonetheless."

"Why did you close?"

He shrugged. "It was never particularly successful. I never really expected it to be, but it still developed a certain following, you know. Among those who liked the unusual and unclassifiable. The true Weird Tales, rather than simple horror stories. But the one thing I could never do was really capitalize on that. I was never the great publicist. It ended up dwindling and marginalized, costing me money that was harder and harder to find as London became harder and harder to live in. *Black Lachrimæ* was one of our more successful releases, relatively speaking. The reviewers loved it, the author got a bit more than just the price of a few dinners out of it. But once Mark had discovered them and introduced them to me, those crying rooms seemed . . . well, I started to go round them all, making sure they were okay—that nobody had trashed them. Repairing things—providing things if anything was needed. I even donated some of the books—left them there in case anyone wanted them. And—how can I put this? It seemed I could do more good there than with my dwindling press. You might say it took me over."

There was a long silence and Feather nodded slowly.

"Can I see the crying room?" she asked.

"Of course," he said, rising to his feet. "This way."

She followed him through the boat, through the kitchen, past what must have been the door of a tiny bathroom, through a small and somewhat untidy bedroom area, and then through a last doorway . . .

Feather stared round, feeling the now-familiar dense and heavy air—air that crackled with a thousand stories, with the almost infinite capacity for human grief. It seemed these crying rooms never changed—be they in a house, in an archway or on a boat. The same shelves of precious trinkets, the same wall full of papers and images. She stared round—so familiar that it was almost homely now.

And on one of the shelves, in a prominent place, a familiar black pendant on a steel chain. It was one of the first batch of twelve. One of the 'donations'. She focused on it, feeling bleak.

But as before, it wasn't alone, she realized. Another smaller piece was lying nearby. She picked it up. She could remember making it. Could almost remember who she had sold it to. Almost.

"What are these things doing?" she demanded.

He gave a cryptic shrug. "Once you have seen the truth, what is there to do?"

"Are you telling me that they are all . . . What happened to the guy who bought this from me?"

"Not all," he said with a smile. "It depends on what you see. Some see their own strength, buoyed up by a supporting world. Some see their own furious defiance—a full-throated scream in the face of London. Some just see love and warmth. Some see the beauty of the Earth and the eternal marvel that is humanity . . ."

"Oh."

"The owner of that piece though, hanged himself about a fortnight ago."

He said it so bluntly that it barely registered for a moment, then that horribly oily silence came crawling back.

"Sadly, the supporting world, the beauty and the love is not always easy to find," he said. "Without them, strength means almost nothing. And even crying rooms can't fix that."

She put the piece down with shaking hands.

"It really is like the story, isn't it? It really is . . . horror . . ."

"I guess that depends. I'd say it's more a Weird Tale."

"What's the difference?"

He shrugged, an expression of slightly humorous irritation on his face. "People argue about it and write about it and pontificate about it—but in essence, not a lot. No genre has a precise definition or boundary. But you might see weird tales as having more of a touch of the classic in them, more of a blend of the otherworldly and the literary. Even a kind of intellectualism—but an intellectualism rendered slightly squeamish by the world of fear in which it operates. The horror of the unknowable."

She picked up the larger stone—the donation. "I want these back," she said firmly. "All of them." He gave her a sharp look.

"Why?"

"They killed my friend," she said, her voice wavering slightly. "And—and . . ."

"Are you sure?"

"You yourself told me," she cried. "And—this guy. And . . ."

"Can you give me a refund?" he asked smoothly.

"What? No," Feather whispered, her heart plummeting. "But you can have whatever you want—that I can give. I don't have much. I can make you better stones. Rare Thames Honey Flints or . . . or . . . Just please, I can't live with this . . ."

There was a long silence. And suddenly he was right behind her—a prickle of contact on the rear half of her body that came with an energy that almost seemed tangible, as though he was charged with static electricity. His hands rested on her shoulders.

"You mustn't blame your stones—or yourself," he said.

"That's what she said," she said barely audible. *"Don't shoot the messenger."*

"Tell me—have you looked in your own mirror?"

"Many times. It's a piece of glass. With flowbanding in it."

"Perhaps you should take another look. And this time don't just look at it."

He took the jewel from her fingers and held it before her face, his arm encircling her to do so. And she did look. And somewhere in her mind's eye was a very clear image—of her saws and jewellery-making supplies piled high in a skip—of herself flat out in grass somewhere under a black sky—face down and resting on one arm. Out of nowhere a hand appeared bearing a lighted cigarette, which was coolly stubbed out on the small band of white skin between her top and trousers. Feather squirmed and twitched, but made no sound . . .

"I should throw it into the canal," she said.

"Should you?"

She gave a grating cry. "Yes—it killed my friend."

"You know what killed her," he said, still behind her, still holding the stone. "Loneliness, hopelessness, despair, entrapment . . . Mirrors only reflect."

"But surely . . ." She could feel the determination and certainty beginning to dissolve in her mind.

"You have a lot of grief—a vast ocean of it. And grief is like milk, poured into the water of reality. Clouding it. And in a sense, horror stories have their roots in that same grief. The desperate grief of destruction and ruin—a world you can barely see that is transmuted into terror. And like reality, what makes a good horror story is when you can also see through the milk to what lies beyond. That's something people like Samuels and Crisp and the rest knew very well. You need to overcome your grief," he said in her ear. "Not because grief is bad, but because you have to be able to see through it."

"I can't cry," she whispered, and if a whisper can somehow be shrill, that one was.

"Never?"

"Okay—I very rarely cry," she corrected.

"When did you last?"

"I can hardly remember. I was young. I'm sure it wasn't very profound."

"All grief is profound."

"Is it?"

"Yes—and Leah? Does that mean you have not cried for her?"

The ocean swirled deeper.

"No," she said.

"Tell me about her," he said with gentleness in his voice.

Feather swallowed hard.

"I met her at college," she said, very slowly. "She's—she was one of the few people from those days I managed to keep in touch with. Even then she was a crazy bookworm and a lovely scruff bag. Always by herself. But I was a bit like that too—an odd one out. That's why we became friends. She was obsessed with books then as well. I remember, she got a grant for something—dyslexia I think— to help her buy course textbooks. And you know what she did? She spent the whole lot on her strange fiction collections, importing these obscure limited editions from America or tracking down odd little

British presses. Probably even Darkening World. She blagged her way through the course with almost nothing. Mostly using my textbooks. She . . . managed it, too. She was always a clever one."

He gave a gratifying laugh at that. "Yes—books are powerful. Maybe even the most powerful thing we have. I still believe it, even now. It's people like Leah that give me hope, even as these paper dreamlands seem more and more marginalized and irrelevant to the world."

Feather nodded slowly, then went on speaking, reluctant to interrupt the flow. "And then—well, I suppose there was nothing to do but continue. You can't have a career when you care about something so obsessively. So she went through all the dead-end jobs to keep alive and lived in this crazy tiny little home . . ."

"I know the process all too well," he said.

Feather drew a long breath.

"Give me your clothes," he said calmly.

"Huh?"

"Your clothes. I suggest. Let that be part of the process."

Process?

She stared at him, startled for a moment. But there was something in the air here that went way beyond any normal life and she didn't protest. She felt almost drunk—as though there was a tremble deep inside her that wanted to get out. But obeying that suggestion was as inevitable as anything in her life.

When she was naked, he grasped her firmly by the shoulders and swivelled her around until she was staring into his eyes. He may have been one of the ugliest human beings she had seen in a long time, but his eyes were extraordinary. She couldn't look away.

"All grief is profound," he said again.

Then his hand was between her shoulders again and applying pressure. She yielded to it with a frightened twist to her face, her heart racing, no idea what might be about to happen. He guided her down until she was flat on her face on the old carpet, surrounded by treasures and grief trinkets. And that hand was not supporting her—not a comforting touch. It was literally holding her down, with a touch that burned like greasy fire—held down by a figure that was crouching over her like some grotesque black predatory bird. It was almost unendurable, as though this room was coiling round her, as though each trinket was the centre of writhing tentacles of desperation—desperation to tell their stories, to plead for something to make the pain go away.

He placed the stone in her hand. "Keep looking."

She stared at it, taking in the quiet black-on-black patterns of the flowbanding—the tiny motes of metallic impurities that looked like gleaming stars. And what was she supposed to experience? There was no mystical communion. No sense of weird visions radiating out of it. But her mind was in overdrive, asking herself what the heck these stones could do. And what stories they were reflecting in their distorted mirrors. It was as if the whole constellation of them—every specimen she had polished, now scattered round London—were forming a vortex of motes of gleaming black, a lens through which those stories could be channelled back to her. And the stories were . . . the city.

Everything. All scales and all colours. Everything that happened. Everybody dragged into the bushes and raped, shattering like broken glass. Every human body deliberately ripped or broken because someone somewhere presumably thought it was a good idea. Everyone evicted onto the streets and now riding the N9, the longest bus route through the London night, for a bit of warmth and sleep. Everyone like Leah staring down an unending tunnel of starvation and wretched rooms with no hope of escape. Everyone sitting on the Tube or Mainline platforms, thinking about lost loves or doomed lives and the grinding roll of the wheels. Everyone wrecked and ruined for being different somehow, anyhow, everyhow. These were all news stories she could remember clearly—among the endless parade of maddening politics and the general insanity of the world. And all maybe fossilized forever on the walls of these rooms. What could you do in the face of stories like that? What was the point of horror stories or Weird Tales in a world like that? Or conversely, when everything in the world was horror, what else could stories possibly be? And here she was sitting in the middle of it—maybe even being nurtured as the stones shone their unnatural clarity into the world. After all, she was the one who had made money out of them—had survived for a few brief months more, thanks to them. Maybe that correlated with the enigmatic presence Samuels had written about. It was her. She was the feeder. She was the one who might indeed be sustained by holding a mirror up to the madness of the world. If she wanted.

And with some kind of horrible yet inescapable selfishness, could there be a key in that? A key to survival in the rigged game that is life?

She opened her eyes again—and the stone wasn't even in her hand any more. It had slipped through her fingers and was lying on the floor a foot or so away—black buried under a puddle of steel necklace chain.

"And you," he asked. "Can you state what you need in this world?"

"I need . . ." Feather hesitated, barely recognizing her own voice. In some ways it all seemed so simple. "I need a place to be. I need permission to be. To be myself. I need . . ."

The image of Leah abruptly surfaced in her mind again. Nothing fancy or horrific, just another memory from those early college days. Fooling around in the nearby woods, in an idyll of pastoral student life. Boisterous. Carefree. There had been a bottle to share in that warm lowering evening—and a bag of food. And things to talk about as only students can. Maybe those days at college were the last happy days of one's life—because in that world one can find something basic and real that is soon lost when trying to survive later on: the need to learn and to think. A disagreement over some intricacy of artistic philosophy had soon blurred into a giggling scuffle over the last cold chicken. There had been a play fight, filled with noise and shrill laughter—and Feather remembered receiving a resounding slap on the backside that made her shriek . . .

And she suddenly cracked with a nasty choking wail. It was like an explosion more than a sob. A massive jolting shivering surge. She clawed at the carpet, every inch of her bare skin prickling, and feeling more naked than she could ever remember. This was a primeval place—a place of complete animal abandonment. Crying not as an adult might, every sob ripped out like plucked fingernails, but like a baby—a wailing scream at the sheer intolerable horror of things not the way they should be. It was a sound that might be audible for miles—easily heard out on the towpath, but she didn't care. She didn't even have any of the questions in her head needed for caring at that point.

It went on for a long time.

Eventually, when she had calmed enough to be aware of the surrounding world again, she realized that she was alone. The man in the black coat had withdrawn, leaving her to dive the full depth of her explosion of grief in peace.

Feather quietly scrambled up onto hands and knees and looked around. Her eyes were still streaming, her mind was numb yet strangely clean. As though the wall of water that had washed through her had been an ocean.

Don't shoot the messenger, she whispered silently, repeating it several times, over and over.

She placed the pendant back on the shelf.

"Okay," she said. "I guess I have about a fortnight, Leah . . . to find what I need. To sort things out. Or—maybe I will see you again. That's how it works, right?"

The Diver stood in the shallow water of the Thames and surveyed the dreary scene—the factories, the jetties, the cycle path, the grey sky, the figure watching from the middle distance—the salt marshes that were the true kings here and always would be. The eternal sense of bleakness that was London . . .

After a long moment staring back, communing with the half-drowned figure, Feather pushed at the pedals and the bike got into motion again, the weight of the fully loaded panniers slowing her down.

Introducing the new line of jewellery, Black Lachrimæ—a truly dark collection for the darkest urban hearts. Jewellery of black tears and silver rain—pieces filled with the beauty of tragedy and despair. Supply limited! Time limited! So do not delay. Get yours today!

Coda: A View from Outside

All the dreams had died and he was forced into an entirely new state of existence. Where once there had been a succession of images and memories in his mind, now there persisted only a black and white blast of static, frozen in time, the leftover microwave dregs from the birth of the universe. At what exact moment the transition from contact to isolation had taken place he could not recall, but it seemed a very long time ago.

One thing was certain: the journey he had undertaken was one that required him to cross an incalculable distance. He was utterly alone within the confines of the tiny capsule, and most of his instruments were dying through lack of power. The plutonium cells were running down, and the titanic gulfs that lurked beyond were becoming dimmer and dimmer, his instrumentation now scarcely sufficient to register the light from the far distant stars.

His body must have deteriorated to a state wherein sensation was deadened to almost nil. He was not aware of his limbs, of his heartbeat, even of the passage of blood through his veins. He was cocooned in the void of absolute and claustrophobic silence of his tiny vessel. His existence was confirmed only through the Cartesian fact that he was aware of his own thought processes. No other proof of his being was available to him. And it offered no comfort. His endless insomnia was a torment, a gigantic cliff against which all the assaults of exhaustion were futile.

He did not know his own name, and no longer had any memories of a life prior to the expedition upon which he had embarked, and, additionally, could not recall any transitional state wherein any such memories he may have once possessed had begun to fade away. He supposed such a process might be like the twilight slipping finally into the dark and blank totality of night.

The transmissions from home were becoming fewer and fewer in number, the signals weakening the further he progressed on his endless voyage. Voice communication had become ghostly several years ago, and he could scarcely make sense of the last of them.

The words "dead," "abandoned," "noxious" and "disease" had been sent repeatedly, a litany of chaos, like madness itself rendered incarnate.

The transmissions he received were hideous in the extreme. They consisted primarily of broadcasts from emergency news services detailing the eventual transformation of all the Earth's populace into cannibals. A nightmarish new disease had taken hold, spread through airborne contact, and it struck down anyone exposed to it in the space of a few hours. Death was swift and extremely painful, but the afflicted soon returned to a semblance of undead life, their bodies rotting away while their damaged brains tried desperately to maintain a hold on past memories of the life that had been taken from them.

As their brains rotted, they reverted to basic instincts, and fed upon whatever food was close to hand—garbage, animals and, finally, even other human beings. If there was a form of life after death it appeared to consist only of eternal insanity. Some philosophers even went so far as to speculate that this had always been the case and the disintegration of the physical brain was of no import. The immortal soul was ultimately destined for such a terrifying fate, by virtue of its very immateriality, a state so utterly at odds with its existence in a material cosmos and wherein, post-mortem, it found itself stranded. Heaven, it seemed, had finally closed for business.

Beyond death, the dead reported, there was a hideous nothing. On the other side the black void, the absolute absence, terrified them. Once experienced, death proved to be the greatest horror conceivable. The utter desolation of its eternal negation drove the dead to exterminate all rational thoughts and take refuge in primal frenzy. Only by consuming life could they momentarily forget the nightmare of infinite death.

Though he had no memories of his own to which he could refer, the machine that housed him held a bank of images collated during the course of his voyage. This data consisted of a series of photographs, in all ranges of the spectrum, beyond even the visible, from X-rays to infrared, detailing dead worlds, either those that were small, dusty and rocky, or else those that were massive, and drowning in freezing gases lethal to any form of organic evolution. True, their beauty was undeniable, but it was also stark and inhuman in its cosmic import. Nevertheless, only outside of the narrow confines of the anthropocentric could one truly appreciate the desolate grandeur of worlds opposed to the existence of life itself.

There appeared to have been only one world amenable to the existence of life, namely that pale blue dot from which he had departed long ago, and which now sent out its broken signals of the bleakest nature. It had been a mistake, this experiment or accident. Life, ultimately, he thought, must turn upon itself and seek its own destruction. Nothing can endure the full force of sustained reality. Nothing can solve the mystery of consciousness. No form of thought can unravel the paradox inherent in the awareness of being. This world, too, was finally succumbing to the universal norm militating against materialism.

Eventually the signals from the pale blue dot ceased altogether. The last of them had been grainy images of a random nature, senseless scenes of carnage and torture, punctuated by screams and hysterical laughter, consisting primarily of death-sex mingled with incomprehensible monologues, the broadcasts filled with close-ups of flashing teeth stained blood red, and of empty black sockets from which eyes had been torn out at their roots. The planet was, at the end, an abattoir wherein everyone was senselessly slaughtered.

And as the last of the power drained out of the plutonium cell batteries in the interstellar craft, the last living organism in the universe, a brain fused with a machine, began to freeze in the icy void until finally it perished, and entered the next phase of conscious existence.

About Mark Samuels

Mark Samuels was born in Clapham, south London in 1967. He was educated at St. Lukes School in Norwood, Paxton School in Crystal Palace, and Kentwood School for Boys in Beckenham, Kent. It was not much of an education. His formative influences during this period were late-night horror movies, the local library (where he discovered the works of Edgar Allan Poe, M.R. James and H.P. Lovecraft), and American comic books. Upon leaving State education he worked first as a solicitor's outdoor clerk for a legal firm in Charing Cross, London intending to pursue a career in law. The job, however, was so odious that he left to work in a Jazz-funk record shop in Sydenham, south London, despite hating Jazz-funk.

His earlier interest in the work of H.P. Lovecraft intensified and he began writing his own weird short stories, the first of which was published in 1988 in the underground semi-pro fanzine *Back Brain Recluse*. Also at this time he moved into a Goth and Grebo house in Ladywell, south London, and became, for a time, a recreational drug-user. Regular homage was paid to the grave of the poet Ernest Dowson—who is buried in the cemetery at the end of the street in which this "House of Heads" was located.

Having adopted an after-dark persona named "Raven Revelation" he was a frequent—though not much noticed—attendee at the infamous Soho night-club *Alice in Wonderland*. Such late night debauches being incompatible with listening to Jazz-funk all the next day, he left the record in London's deep south, and next obtained employment at Foyle's Bookshop in the Charing Cross Road, central London in their "Drama and Film Dept." after a surreal interview with an eighty-year Christina Foyle (doyen of the legendary "literary lunches") in her penthouse suite.

Employment at Foyle's exactly suited him, since it consisted of drinking heavily at lunchtimes, reading books, annoying customers, and meeting a variety of fascinating characters also working there. At one time, he had, as an assistant, a wild-eyed aristocrat who later staged a one-man invasion of the House of Lords to protest at the decline of hereditary peers and who fiercely championed the "Lord Oxford" theory regarding the 'true' authorship of Shakespeare's works. Amongst other notable fond memories of this period, are—Foyle's being evacuated by a bomb threat due to its stocking *The Satanic*

Verses, breaking his right femur (helping a drunken young lady down bar cellar steps who subsequently tripped and fell on him) during an ambulance strike and being subsequently treated for his injury by the Queen's own Orthopaedic surgeon at UCL. A firebrand Leftist, vegetarian and atheist at the time, he participated in the Poll Tax riots, while still on crutches.

Forced to leave Foyle's towards the end of 1990—due to his temporary contract having expired—he spent the next seventeen years in the tranquil employment of Samuel French Ltd (play publishers and agents for the collection of performing royalties) in Fitzrovia, London. He successfully rose to the position of being its chief time-waster.

At this time he discovered the work of Arthur Machen and immediately joined the literary society devoted to the promotion of his writings. He also (after initial exposure to uncollected stories published in *Dagon* and *Crypt of Cthulhu* in the late 1980s) became a devotee of the weird fiction of Thomas Ligotti, with whom he later corresponded by email for a few years.

Although still sporadically writing weird fiction in the early to mid 1990s, the results of Samuels' labours appeared in only a handful of underground publications, primarily the likes of *Black Tears* and *Dementia 13*. The vast majority of his work from this period has— mercifully—not been reprinted.

In 1997, after formal instruction and baptism, he was received into full communion with the Roman Catholic Church. He did so believing the Church right and the world wrong, and he retains a strong (aesthetic) preference for the extraordinary form of the Latin Mass. Whilst living alone two years later in a bungalow flat attached to back of a old Masonic Temple in Stamford Hill, north London, he began writing weird tales again, primarily for his own amusement.

This second phase in writing fiction proved to be more successful than the first and resulted in the Tartarus Press issuing his first collection of short stories *The White Hands and Other Weird Tales* in 2003, which went on to receive high acclaim and still remains in print. One or two tales not included therein were published the same year in the Rainfall Books collection *Black Altars*, though the rest of that volume mostly consists of literary experiments dating back to the early-mid 1990s.

Subsequently, John Pelan in the United States began to regularly feature new stories by Samuels in his *Darkside* series of Penguin/ROC anthologies, marking the author's first breakthrough into the wider, mass-market field. His tales have continued to appear in anthologies on both sides of the Atlantic including *The Mammoth Book of Best New Horror, Year's Best Fantasy and Horror, The Weird* and *A Mountain Walks*. His stories have also been translated and published in various languages including German, Russian, Polish and Spanish.

Further books written by him are as follows; a short novel *The Face of Twilight* (PS Publishing 2006), and the collections *Glyphotech and Other Macabre Processes* (PS Publishing 2008), *The Man Who Collected Machen and Other Stories* (Ex Occidente and Chomu Books 2010 and 2011 respectively) and *Written In Darkness* (Egaeus Press 2014).

He is very close to the completion of the first draft of a new (non-weird fiction) satirical-mystical novel he is currently writing, provisionally called *The Ritualist*, which concerns itself with the central character's personal struggle against the secular values of modernity.

About the Contributors

Mark Valentine

Mark Valentine has enjoyed many Friends of Arthur Machen occasions in the company of Mark Samuels, including a weekend in Abergavenny on which his foreword is loosely based, with considerable fictional embellishment. He has edited *Aklo* and *The Lost Club Journal* (both with Roger Dobson) and *Wormwood*, and also writes stories and essays.

Reggie Oliver

Reggie Oliver has been a professional playwright, actor, and theatre director. Besides plays, his publications include the authorised biography of Stella Gibbons, *Out of the Woodshed* (Bloomsbury, 1998), and six collections of stories of supernatural terror, of which the fifth, *Mrs Midnight* (Tartarus, 2011) won the Children of the Night Award for "best work of supernatural fiction in 2011". His novel, *The Dracula Papers I—The Scholar's Tale* (Chomu, 2011)—is the first of a projected four. Another novel *Virtue in Danger* was published in

2013 by Zagava Books, and a new novel *The Boke of the Divill* is due from Dark Renaissance. Also due from Zagava is *The Hauntings at Tankerton Park, and How They Got Rid Of Them,* a lavishly illustrated tale in verse for children of all ages. His stories have appeared in over fifty anthologies.

Colin Insole
Many of the themes and ideas in 'The Golden Dustmen' were suggested by 'The Lost Language of London', by Harold Bayley, published by Jonathan Cape, in 1935. It is subtitled 'A Tale of King Cole, founded on folklore, field names, prehistoric hill figures and other documents.' Mr Bayley links the symbols of Celtic mythology with modern London place names, finding many shared images, locations and stories. In the preface, he quotes Barfield's 'History in English Words'.

'In the common words we use every day, the souls of past races, the thoughts and feelings of individual men stand around us, not dead, but frozen into their attitudes like the courtiers in the garden of the Sleeping Beauty'.

I felt that Bayley's excellent book shared the same spirit and attributes as the fictions of both Arthur Machen and Mark Samuels. I have always enjoyed stories set in London—especially those where the reader can follow the characters' adventures on a map. My father's family lived continuously in the city, from relatively modern times, to the mid-eighteenth century, at least, which is as far back as I've been able to trace. I like to study their respective street locations in Holburn, Wapping, Barking and Manor Park, in conjunction with both the fiction and non-fiction of the city.

Daniel Mills
"The White Hands" marked my first exposure to the work of Mark Samuels. I'm surely not alone in this—since its 2003 publication the story has rightfully assumed the status of a new classic—but for me it was the lesser known tale "The Grandmaster's Final Game" which firmly cemented my admiration for Samuels and his approach. Here was a work of contemporary weird fiction in which Ligotti's influence faces off against the author's own faith to compelling result.

I am a Christian as well as a great admirer of Thomas Ligotti. While this may seem an unintuitive pairing, it has never struck me as a particularly illogical one. Samuels' fiction helped to show me how the two influences—if apparently antithetical—might in fact be made to coexist and complement one another in a weird fiction context. With time my admiration for Samuels' work has only increased, and so I was delighted to have this opportunity to "give something back," as it were, to an author whose work has proved so formative to me.

"Canticle" imagines the suffering of St John of the Cross during his imprisonment in Toledo, deriving inspiration from "The Spiritual Canticle" and «The Dark Night» as well as Samuels' 2014 essay "Beyond the Beautiful Darkness."

St John's famous depiction of the crucifixion also makes an appearance. In Christ's crucifixion, viewed from above, we see the Hell of living embodied—literally—in the suffocating weight of flesh and cannot help but understand what it means for God "to partake of Hell itself for our sake" (as Samuels writes).

To be alive is to experience horror, despair, degradation, doubt. Or, put another way, the game is fixed against us. Ligotti understands this. So did Lovecraft. Samuels, too, but he also realizes something far more important. The game is fixed, but we do not have to play. We cannot win, but we can always cheat.

Daniel Mills is the author of Revenants: A Dream of New England *(Chomu Press, 2011),* The Lord Came at Twilight *(Dark Renaissance Books, 2014) and the forthcoming* Moriah *(ChiZine Publications, 2017). He lives in Vermont.*

Adam Nevill

Adam L.G. Nevill was born in Birmingham, England, in 1969 and grew up in England and New Zealand. He is the author of the supernatural horror novels *Banquet for the Damned, Apartment 16, The Ritual, Last Days, House of Small Shadows, No One Gets Out Alive,* and *Lost Girl.* In 2012, 2013 and 2015 his novels were the winners of the August Derleth Award for Best Horror Novel. *The Ritual* and *Last Days* were also awarded Best in Category: Horror, by R.U.S.A. His first collection of short fiction, *Some Will Not Sleep*, is published in 2016.

Adam lives in Devon and can be contacted through www. adamlgnevill.com.

Justin Isis

Jbon is the author of the collections *I Wonder What Human Flesh Tastes Like* (Chomu Press, 2011) and *Welcome to the Arms Race* (Chomu Press, 2015), the poetry chapbook *Divorce Procedures for the Hairdressers of a Metallic and Inconstant Goddess* (Snuggly Books, 2016), and the novels *The Cutest Girl in Class* (Snuggly Books, 2013, in collaboration with Quentin S. Crisp and Brendan Connell) and *Invariant* (forthcoming from Snuggly). His stories have appeared in *Postscripts* and *The Master in Cafe Morphine: A Tribute to Mikhail Bulgakov* (Ex Occidente, 2011). He also co-edited Chomu Press's *Dadaoism* anthology (2011). He lives in Tokyo, has never met Mark Samuels in real life (but has possibly encountered him on the astral plane), drinks Ozeki OneCups almost every day, and like Mark, has recently switched from cigarettes to vaping.

It took him a long time to convince Mark to let him go ahead with this book. Originally it was called *Marked for Death*, until Mark pointed out that, by changing the title very slightly, it could be made to reference Shakespeare rather than Steven Seagal.

DF Lewis

First and only novel published at the age of 63 (2011). Creator of *Nemonymous* from 2001. Author of over a thousand published fiction works from 1986-2000. Inventor of gestalt real-time reviewing from 2008. Publisher of other authors. My Mum often mentioned difficulties with my big head when bearing me. I first met Mark Samuels around 1987. I severely risked his life (and mine) around that time when driving him to a convention through my momentary lack of concentration on the motorway. He will tell you about it. He once made a very difficult solo car drive himself to visit me and my wife in our then home of Coulsdon. He kindly wrote an article about me for the *Dagon* DFL Special in 1989. We and others shared many pub get-togethers in the 1980s and early 1990s in Purley. Pleasant and instructive walks around Machenesque London, too. I greatly admire his writing successes since then. One of his books was my very first real-time review in 2008.

John Mundy

John Mundy is primarily a practitioner of *vers libre*. His poetry has appeared in S. T. Joshi's *Spectral Realms*. He regards Mark Samuels as one of the few great living writers of supernatural and existential horror. "Mark's fiction pays tribute to the best of Tradition while exploring his own darkest visions," writes Mundy. "It's innovative and eclectic work, revealing influences ranging from J.G. Ballard and Jorge Luis Borges to Lovecraft and Ligotti but always bearing Samuels' own confessional, very personal stamp. I discovered *The White Hands* and, brother, I was hooked from then on."

Kristine Ong Muslim

Kristine Ong Muslim is the author of several books of fiction and poetry: *Age of Blight* (Unnamed Press, 2016), *Butterfly Dream* (Snuggly Books, 2016), *A Roomful of Machines* (ELJ Publications, 2015), *Grim Series* (Popcorn Press, 2012), *We Bury the Landscape* (Queen's Ferry Press, 2012), as well as *Black Arcadia* and *Lifeboat*, two poetry collections from university presses in the Philippines. She also serves as poetry editor of *LONTAR: The Journal of Southeast Asian Speculative Fiction*, a literary journal published by Epigram Books in Singapore, and co-editor (with Nalo Hopkinson) of Lightspeed Magazine's "People of Colo(u)r Destroy Science Fiction." Widely published in magazines and anthologies, she grew up and continues to live in rural southern Philippines.

James Champagne

James Champagne is the author of the collections *Grimoire: A Compendium of Neo-Goth Narratives* and *Autopsy of an Eldritch City: Ten Tales of Strange & Unproductive Thinking* (both put out by Rebel Satori Press). He has also written two novels, *Confusion* (2006) and *Harlem Smoke* (forthcoming). His work has appeared in the anthologies *Userlands: New Fiction Writers From the Blogging Underground* and *Mighty in Sorrow: a Tribute to Current 93 & David Tibet*. He was born in 1980 and lives in Rhode Island.

Brendan Connell

Brendan Connell was born in Santa Fe, New Mexico, in 1970. His works of fiction include *Unpleasant Tales* (Eibonvale Press, 2010), *The Architect* (PS Publishing, 2012), *Lives of Notorious Cooks* (Chômu Press, 2012), *Miss Homicide Plays the Flute* (Eibonvale Press, 2013), *Jottings from a Far Away Place* (Snuggly Books, 2015), and *Cannibals of West Papua* (Zagava, 2015).

Quentin S. Crisp

Quentin S. Crisp was born in 1972, in North Devon, U.K. He studied Japanese at Durham University and graduated in the year 2000. He has had fiction published by Tartarus Press, PS Publishing and others. He currently resides in Bexleyheath, and is editor for Chômu Press. *September*, his first collection of poetry, was released by Snuggly Books in May, 2016.

Thana Niveau

This has to be the most intriguing book pitch I've ever read: "If Mark Samuels is high quality cocaine, this book is like the weird diluted version that's possibly cut with bleach and maybe even hallucinogens; it's still going to get you messed up, but possibly not in the way you were expecting. Real Mark books = brand name prescription drugs, this book = generic version from a third world country."

Mark's a weird guy with a singular vision. No one sees the world quite like he does and no one does visionary weirdness like him. I didn't want to attempt pastiche, but I did want to explore some of his recurring themes. So, internalising the drug metaphor, I tried to write from the mindset of someone who had unknowingly been dosed with the kind of trippy tribal brew William Hurt is given in *Altered States*, cuing visions that spill into reality and warp everything around him.

"The Language of the City" stems from my own dislike and mistrust of big cities. In Mark's world, everything has menace and ill intent. What if cities themselves did too? What if they weren't the products of us but vice-versa? And what if only one person could hear their sinister discourse? Some of us just aren't suited to urban life, but what if there was a more insidious reason for that?

A stranger in an even stranger land, I grew up in the States but now I live in the UK, in a Victorian seaside town between Bristol and Wales. Despite having lived for almost 3 years in New York City (and going more than slightly mad), I still find London quite terrifying. It wasn't a stretch to put a weird Samuelsian spin on that most sprawling and intimidating of metropolises.

I love both horror and SF and I've twice been nominated for the British Fantasy award—for my debut collection *From Hell to Eternity* and my giallo ballet story "Death Walks En Pointe".

My work has been reprinted in *The Mammoth Book of Best New Horror* (volumes 22-25) and *Best British Horror*. Other stories appear in *Darker Companions: A Tribute to Ramsey Campbell*; *Whispers in the Dark*; *Interzone*; *Black Static*; *Sorcery and Sanctity: A Homage to Arthur Machen*; *Postscripts*; *Zombie Apocalypse: Endgame*; *Steampunk Cthulhu*; *Terror Tales of Cornwall*; *Terror Tales of Wales*; *The Black Book of Horror* (volumes 7-11); *Love, Lust & Zombies*; *Horror Uncut*; *Exotic Gothic 5*; *The Burning Circus*; *Sword & Mythos*; *Demons and Devilry*; and *Magic: an Anthology of the Esoteric and Arcane*.

Simon Clark

I love the work of Arthur Machen. When I met Mark Samuels back in the 1980s he was the first person I'd talked to who had not only heard of Machen but loved his stories, too. Naturally, we got on like the proverbial 'house on fire'. I was fortunate enough to take long walks around London with Mark, and in the company of Des Lewis, too, where we three fledgling and largely unpublished authors (all of us dreaming in fire and yet working hard, moulding the difficult clay of words) visited Machen's homes and favourite taverns. Mark was our expert guide, and the more I got to know Mark the more I realized that this softly-spoken, good-humoured man was extremely well-read, intelligent and thought deeply about literature and the world in general. Again, good fortune came my way when Mark published my story 'Howls From A Blinding Curve' in the first issue of his magazine *The Stygian Dreamhouse* (1988). Mark takes painstaking care over his stories, often devoting years of hard work to them before being satisfied that their quality is high enough to release them for publication. His fiction is a joy to read and to have a conversation with Mark is a joy, too, and I raise my imaginary tankard and say from the heart, "Here's to you, Mark—visionary, alchemist of words, and always such good company."

Simon Clark's novels include *Nailed by the Heart, Blood Crazy, Darkness Demands, The Night of the Triffids* and *Inspector Abberline and the Just King*.

Stuart Young

Stuart Young is the author of *Spare Parts, Shards of Dreams, The Mask Behind the Face*, which won the British Fantasy Award, and *Reflections in the Mind's Eye*. His stories have appeared in numerous magazines and anthologies including *Darkness Rising, Midnight Street, We Fade to Grey* and *The Mammoth Book of Future Cops*.

John L. Probert

John Llewellyn Probert won the British Fantasy Award for *The Nine Deaths of Dr Valentine* (Snowbooks) and the Children of the Night award for *The Faculty of Terror* (Gray Friar Press). He is the author of five short story collections, several novels and numerous novellas, the most recent of which are *Dead Shift* (Horrific Tales Publishing) and *Knife to Skin* (Endeavour Press). Find out all about his writings at http://www.johnlprobert.com./ He once enjoyed a tour of Highgate Cemetery in which he and Mark Samuels pretended to be Romanian tourists convinced that it was the place where they had seen Dracula killed on several different occasions in several different places. The tour guide failed to be amused by their constant questions about where the vampire Count had actually met his fate. Mark then took JLP around locations from the short story collection *The White Hands*, including the tower block from "Mannequins in Aspects of Terror." Neither of these experience influenced "The Men With Paper Faces," but Mr Probert hopes it gives its readers a suitably Samuelsian sense of rotting apocalyptic dread.

Ralph C. Doege

Ralph C. Doege has written stories and essays for German and Austrian magazines and anthologies. His first story collection *Ende der Nacht* was published at the end of 2010. LOCUS ONLINE wrote: "Most of Doege's stories feature fantasy and/or SF elements, but the focus is always on psychological dilemmas. This in itself is pretty unusual for German science fiction and fantasy, and Doege takes it a step further by repeatedly confronting his characters with virtually unsolvable philosophical problems. (...) a truly unique and highly recommended voice in German speculative fiction." EMPTY HOUSES is the second translation into English. The first one—KAGO AI—was published in the anthology *Dadaoism* (Chomu Press, 2011). The next projects are a long essay on Japanese horror and SF literature and a novel.

Yarrow Paisley

Yarrow Paisley hails from the Pioneer Valley of Western Massachusetts. His fiction has appeared in *Strange Tales V* (Tartarus Press), *Dadaoism* (Chômu Press), *Theaker's Quarterly*, and *Sein und Werden*, among others.

Jon Paul Rai

Jon Paul Rai was born and raised on Long Island, New York. In college he was the editor of the comics section on two college newspapers for Nassau Community College and Long Island University. Also during those years he had comics published by the newspaper in New York City "Street News," which is a charity newspaper for the homeless. Since drawing comics no longer fits his busy lifestyle, he has turned to writing and writes short stories and has a fantasy novel in the works. Influences over the years have been *The Lord of the Rings*, *Game of Thrones*, and Batman comics. He now resides in Tokyo and continues to write.

David Rix

David Rix is an author, composer, editor, artist and publisher active in the area of Slipstream, Speculative Fiction and Horror—not to mention hints of absurdism, miserablism, naturism and pissed-offism. Contemporary classical music, the seashore, urban underground, railways, rocks and canals. His published books are *What The Giants Were Saying*, the novelettes *Brown is the New Black* and *A Suite in Four Windows*, and the novella/story collection *Feather*, which was shortlisted for the Edge Hill prize. In addition, his works have appeared in various places, the most notable being many of the *Strange Tales* series of anthologies from Tartarus Press, *Monster Book For Girls* from Exaggerated Press and *Creeping Crawlers* from Shadow Publishing. He also runs and creates the art for Eibonvale Press, which focuses on innovative and unusual new slipstream writing. As an editor, his first anthology *Rustblind and Silverbright*, a collection of Slipstream stories connected to the railways, was shortlisted for the British Fantasy Award in the Best Anthology category. He is currently at work on his first novel *A Blast of Hunters* and several novellas.

The majority of "Slag Glass Lachrimae" is true, but we can leave it to interested readers to work out which bits aren't.

THANKS FAM

Thanks all contributors.

Especially Brendan Connell and Quentin S. Crisp, both of whom put enough work into this book that they could be considered co-editors.

And David Rix, for his help in formatting and typesetting.

And to Mark Samuels, for putting up with this project in the first place.